Prai... W9-DJC-547

The Lipstick Chronicles

"Plenty of camaraderie and romance lighting up the DC skies . . . a delight for romance readers . . . a warm tale of friendship and love."
—*Midwest Book Review*

And more praise for the *Lipstick* women and their novels:

Emily Carmichael

"A fresh, funny charmer of a romance. I howled with laughter."
—*The New York Times*

"You are guaranteed the unexpected from Emily Carmichael."
—*Romantic Times*

"Carmichael has created yet another wonderfully written romance."
—*Booklist*

Vivian Leiber

"Touching romance."
—*Affaire de Coeur*

"Great fun to read, high humor at its finest."
—*The Romance Reader*

Kathryn Shay

"Kathryn Shay is a master at her craft."
—*New York Times* bestselling author Catherine Anderson

"Kathryn Shay never disappoints."
—*New York Times* bestselling author Lisa Gardner

"Refreshing contemporary romance." —*Midwest Book Review*

more Lipstick chronicles

Book Two

Emily Carmichael

Vivian Leiber

Kathryn Shay

BERKLEY SENSATION, NEW YORK

THE BERKLEY PUBLISHING GROUP
Published by the Penguin Group
Penguin Group (USA) Inc.
375 Hudson Street, New York, New York 10014, USA

Penguin Group (Canada), 90 Eglinton Avenue East, Suite 700, Toronto, Ontario M4P 2Y3, Canada
(a division of Pearson Penguin Canada Inc.)
Penguin Books Ltd., 80 Strand, London WC2R 0RL, England
Penguin Group Ireland, 25 St. Stephen's Green, Dublin 2, Ireland (a division of Penguin Books Ltd.)
Penguin Group (Australia), 250 Camberwell Road, Camberwell, Victoria 3124, Australia
(a division of Pearson Australia Group Pty. Ltd.)
Penguin Books India Pvt. Ltd., 11 Community Centre, Panchsheel Park, New Delhi—110 017, India
Penguin Group (NZ), 67 Apollo Drive, Mairangi Bay, Albany, Auckland 1311, New Zealand
(a division of Pearson New Zealand Ltd.)
Penguin Books (South Africa) (Pty.) Ltd., 24 Sturdee Avenue, Rosebank, Johannesburg 2196,
South Africa

Penguin Books Ltd., Registered Offices: 80 Strand, London WC2R 0RL, England

This is a work of fiction. Names, characters, places, and incidents either are the product of the authors' imaginations or are used fictitiously, and any resemblance to actual persons, living or dead, business establishments, events, or locales is entirely coincidental. The publisher does not have any control over and does not assume responsibility for author or third-party websites.

MORE LIPSTICK CHRONICLES

A Berkley Sensation Book / published by arrangement with Lark Productions, LLC

PRINTING HISTORY
Berkley trade paperback edition / May 2004
Berkley Sensation mass-market edition / March 2007

Copyright © 2004 by Lark Productions, LLC.
Cover and design illustration by Rita Frangie.
Interior text design by Kristin del Rosario.

All rights reserved.
No part of this book may be reproduced, scanned, or distributed in any printed or electronic form without permission. Please do not participate in or encourage piracy of copyrighted materials in violation of the authors' rights. Purchase only authorized editions.
For information, address: The Berkley Publishing Group,
a division of Penguin Group (USA) Inc.,
375 Hudson Street, New York, New York 10014.

ISBN: 978-0-425-21498-5

BERKLEY SENSATION®
Berkley Sensation Books are published by The Berkley Publishing Group,
a division of Penguin Group (USA) Inc.,
375 Hudson Street, New York, New York 10014.
BERKLEY SENSATION is a registered trademark of Penguin Group (USA) Inc.
The "B" design is a trademark belonging to Penguin Group (USA) Inc.

PRINTED IN THE UNITED STATES OF AMERICA

10   9   8   7   6   5   4   3   2   1

If you purchased this book without a cover, you should be aware that this book is stolen property. It was reported as "unsold and destroyed" to the publisher, and neither the authors nor the publisher have received any payment for this "stripped book."

Contents

Touched for the Very First Time

EMILY CARMICHAEL

Chapter 1

For the past few weeks, days at the Allheart offices in Georgetown were more peaceful and productive if writer Dana Boyle worked from home, and since Dana had been nursing an on-and-off flu for the last month, that happy situation occurred more often than not. On the other hand, things were definitely more interesting if she did show up at the office, as was the case on this dank December day. Interesting as in eventful, tumultuous and distracting. Interesting was never as productive as peaceful, but it did keep the Allheart staff from a case of the winter blahs.

On this morning, after a two-day absence trying to drown the flu bug in Tylenol and DayQuil, Dana had stormed through the reception area with barely a nod, thundered down the hallway to her office and shut the door firmly behind her. The closed door was no impediment to her coworkers, however. The executive staff at Allheart, all creative, on-the-go women with their feet firmly set on life's fast track, were more like family than mere professional colleagues. They cared, worried, nagged, supported, argued and meddled like sisters. They were interested in each other's lives. They were concerned. In short, they were snoopy.

So when normally amiable Dana Boyle (no slouch in the meddling snoop department herself) had started her Jekyll and Hyde act, her coworkers were naturally curious. When her signature sunny smile had turned into a curled lip, her creative juices turned to vinegar and her enthusiastic energy wilted to weary plodding, her friends worried. But so far, no amount of friendly prying had inspired Dana to confide in anyone. She scarcely talked at all, in fact, as if all her words were bottled up inside. Downright scary, that was, for Dana, the queen of words. Allheart's maven of greeting card copy, she wrote the snappy greetings, the clever rejoinders and the heartfelt romance that made Allheart.com's online greeting cards so special. But she had no words to confide in her friends. And naturally, her reluctance to spill her guts made them even more curious.

The Allheart trio that gathered in the vicinity of Dana's firmly closed door puckered their brows, gave each other knowing glances and shook their heads.

"I remember when Dana used to walk into this office like a ray of sunshine," graphic designer Alix Harris said with a sigh. Of all the women, Alix worked the most closely with Dana.

"I wouldn't exactly say she was ever a ray of sunshine," Carole Titus commented.

"Well, at least she wasn't an ugly storm cloud." This from Robyn Barrett, young assistant to Elyssa Wentworth, Allheart's CEO. "Scary, you know? Spitting lightning and all that. That's what I meant."

A loud *thump* from inside the office sounded like something might have been thrown against the wall. A second *thump* made the snoopers flinch.

"Ouch!" Robyn said.

Alix speculated, "Snow boots."

"Transformed into missiles," Robyn added.

A nasal epithet carried though the barrier of the door.

Carole turned motherly. "She still has the flu, poor thing."

"She has more than the flu," Alix drawled. "I wish we knew what's been turning her into Miss Cranky of the Millennium. We might be able to help."

"Why don't you try talking to her, Alix?" Carole suggested.

"Right. I'd just as soon try to pull a thorn from a lion's paw."

Robyn grinned. "Maybe it would turn the lion into a pussycat."

"Or turn the thorn-puller into raw meat. Why don't you give it a try, Carole? You're the one with the housemother gene."

Carole raised her hands in denial. "Me? No. You're closest to Dana, Alix. You're the one it's gotta be."

Unintelligible words from inside made them perk up their ears. Robyn, younger and somewhat less inhibited by good manners, went so far as to glue her ear to the door.

"Oooooh. Very bad words. I think the lion has its tail in a knot. I can just imagine the card copy she's going to come up with today."

"Excuse me?" said a voice that brought the trio of busybodies to attention. Elyssa Wentworth stepped out of her office and regarded them with meaningfully narrowed eyes. "Good morning, ladies. Did someone declare today a holiday?"

Elyssa was the dynamo founder and fearless leader of Allheart.com. She was a good-hearted slave driver, but a slave driver just the same. At least according to her staff.

"Dana's in there," Alix told Elyssa.

"Bravo," she replied, just the hint of an edge to her voice. "It's nice to have her in the office for a change."

Robyn rolled her eyes. "That's a matter of opinion!" Elyssa gave her a sharp look, but Robyn ignored it. Robyn had a talent for ignoring such things. "We need an intervention," she said with all the wisdom of her twenty-four years.

"I'll admit that being in one's office working seems to be deviant behavior around here," Elyssa commented sharply. "Perhaps we should have the intervention for those who loiter in the halls listening at doors where people are presumably trying to start on the day's work. Robyn, please call the building management and tell them the temperature in my office is still hovering around zero, and Carole, I would like to talk to you about the chocolate account."

"Fannie May?"

"That's the one. Who came up with the idea for their Valentine's Day ads, anyway?"

"They're lame, but we have plenty of time to work on it."

"Not if we don't get on it we don't. It may only be December, but February is rather close to December, in case you hadn't noticed."

The little crowd dispersed, but not before Carole tossed Alix a look and jerked her head toward Dana's door. *Someone has to do it,* was the silent message. Alix grimaced, heaved a martyred sigh and raised her fist to knock. The "Come in" that answered her hesitant knock was just a grumble.

"Hiya, Dana," Alix ventured as she walked in.

"Mmmmmmph!" Dana's head was on her desk, facedown.

Red hair tumbled over a disorganized jumble of files, computer disks, notepads, and an old issue of *Glamour* magazine. One silky red strand narrowly missed a dunking in an unpleasantly crusted coffee cup.

"Dana!"

"What!" The head came up, the face puckered in a frown. A yellow Post-it note was improbably stuck to red bangs.

"I wish I had a camera," Alix said. "You look like a poster girl for Monday mornings."

"It's not Monday. Is it? God! What day is it?"

"Wednesday."

"Unnhhhh." The head dropped back to the desk.

"Girl, what is wrong with you?"

"Nothing."

"Yeah, right, nothing." Alix raised a perfectly arched mahogany brow. "The office staff has a pool going about when you're going to go into complete meltdown, and another pool on how long before Elyssa fires your butt."

The head came up again. This time the green eyes snapped with indignation. "That's ridiculous."

"You don't believe me? Ask Malcolm. He's running the pools."

"That goofy intern?" Dana half rose from her chair. "I'll show him whose butt's on the line."

"Slow down, girl. I didn't mean to set a match to the fuse. But you know, we'd all like to know what's going on."

"I don't know what you mean."

"Don't bullshit a master bullshitter, girl. You've been out of the office as much as you're here, and when you're here, you're like a troll lurking in your lair. As a matter of fact, this office looks kind of like a troll's lair." Alix glanced around the office with a grimace. Size eight snow boots lay by the wall against which Dana had thrown them. The crumpled heaps of fur and leather looked like dead creatures of some sort. The windowsill had become a storage shelf for dirty plastic cups. The smell bore witness to at least two weeks' worth of petrified coffee. Dana's winter coat, a vintage Chanel creation that she had once dearly treasured, lay heaped in a chair. The desk was the true disgrace, however. It looked as though a waste bin had been emptied on top of it. Alix suspected the mess was a reflection of the current state of Dana's mind.

"Girl, we need to have lunch together and you can spill your guts to your good friend Alix. It'll make you feel way better."

Dana groaned. "Alix, no offense, but butt out."

"I can't. I'm your friend."

"Just leave me alone."

Just then the door cracked open and Carole's head poked in. "Alix, E wants to talk to you about the graphics on the Easter cards."

Alix grimaced. "The boss calls. I'll be back, though."

Carole poked the rest of her body through the door. She stood looking around Dana's office with the air of a mother viewing a teenage daughter's bedroom. "Did a tornado come through?"

"Can it, please," Dana warned.

"You'd better pray that Mother Superior doesn't cruise through here."

"Why are you guys ganging up on me? I'm in no mood to be ganged-up on."

"What's that on your monitor?" Carole's instincts unerringly homed in on the trouble spots on her colleagues' horizons, no matter how subtle or well hidden. This trouble spot was neither. "Are you developing a new line here?"

Both of Dana's uninvited visitors descended upon the

computer monitor, which pulsed brightly with the text Dana had neglected to delete. Carole read the copy out loud, her voice catching somewhere between laughter and horror.

" 'Life sucks through a straw; get over it.' 'Love bites; learn to bite back.' 'The ideal companion on the road of life comes with a leash and flea powder.' "

Alix nearly choked. "Dana! What is this?"

"Reality cards," Dana replied with a flip smile. "It's a line we ought to develop."

Carole and Alix exchanged a meaningful look, and Alix fixed Dana with a steely eye. "Lunch, girl! We are definitely going to have a heart-to-heart over lunch."

Because she was too weary to protest, Dana allowed Alix to drag her to Cafemyth.com, a cyber café that was one of the Allheart gang's favorite Georgetown lunch hangouts. Over baba ghanoush and a good white zinfandel, she mollified Alix by spilling, if not all her guts, at least some of them. Her colleagues were going to hound her until she gave them some morsel to chew on, and a good whine was always a mood lifter—something she sorely needed. Paul, her man of the month, had dumped her with the complaint that there just wasn't anything between them but sex—probably the first time in history a man had complained of that! And then she had suffered the ultimate humiliation: During Thanksgiving dinner, her younger sister smugly announced her engagement to a resident in orthopedics at Georgetown University Medical Center. Her mother was ecstatic, of course. Doctors were still very high on most mothers' list of whom they wanted their daughters to marry. The fact that Dana was a major player in an up-and-coming dot-com company didn't count for nearly as many brownie points as marrying a doctor.

Not that Dana wanted to get married. Did she? Or maybe she just didn't know what she wanted, Dana admitted. At twenty-seven, shouldn't she know exactly what she wanted and how she was going to get it?

Alix was as sympathetic as any whiner could wish, nodding, murmuring and sighing in all the right places. She even offered Dana her place at a meditation and stress management seminar that she'd signed up for then decided not to attend. Dana was halfway interested until she learned she'd have to go halfway across the world, almost. The seminar was at a resort in Arizona, of all places. Cowboy boots weren't her style, she laughed, and told Alix not to worry so. She could manage her life without some yogi chanting over her. New Age crystal gazers and redneck cowboys—what a combination. And people said DC was bad! Sweet offer, but no thank you.

Dana went back to the Allheart offices in an improved frame of mind. She hoped whining to Alix might serve as a catharsis and lighten her mood, but within a couple of hours, the cheering effect of a good whine had worn off. Her mother called with the news that her sister Lara had chosen lavender and cream to be her wedding colors. Dana wondered if Lara had chosen lavender specifically because it somehow made her older and unmarried sister look jaundiced and sunburned at the same time. That alone was enough to blacken the rest of the day, but her mother also reported seeing a news story about the many dot-coms that were going under in the tumultuous technology industry. Couldn't Dana get a job with a real company, or get married like her little sister?

That managed to send Dana over the top. The Valentine's

Day copy she was writing turned into verse that could have been written by Freddy Kruger.

The next morning she tried hard to be cheerful. She really did. But midmorning Paul e-mailed her. Hunky "we never talk" and "there's got to be something more" Paul. He didn't want her to take what he'd said on their last date the wrong way. No hard feelings, he explained. She was a great gal, and there was no reason they couldn't see each other every once in a while. (When he was horny, Dana interpreted.) In fact that very night he happened to be free. (Couldn't get a date, Dana thought.) And he remembered that great club where Dana knew the manager. (Another guy she'd dated three or four times before they'd given each other the mutual heave-ho.) Maybe Dana would like to go there this very night? (Paul knew he couldn't get into the club without her connections, even on a dreary Wednesday night.)

Great, Dana thought. This was what she was reduced to, being a pass into a club for a barely interested guy. Robyn chose that unfortunate moment to stick her head into the office and tell her that Elyssa wanted to see some of her ideas for the Valentine's Day line.

Dana let off a bit of steam. "Aaaargh! Doesn't anyone in this frigging company ever knock? How am I supposed to concentrate on work if everyone feels free to just walk in?"

Robyn drew back as if Dana had hit her. "But Elyssa—"

"Just go! Tell Elyssa she'll be the first person to hear about my ideas, when I have some."

"Fine!" Robyn snapped in a hurt voice.

"Fine!" Dana repeated, guilt at her behavior making her feel even worse.

It took less than ten minutes for Dana to receive a summons to Elyssa's office. It was definitely a summons, not an invitation. Robyn delivered it by phone in a flat, business-like voice.

Elyssa would have her drawers in a knot, Dana was sure of it. She didn't like prima donna behavior, she didn't sit still for staff tantrums and Dana had once overheard her tell Alix that if she wanted to suffer from PMS, she'd better do it on her own time, not Allheart's. As she crossed the hall to Elyssa's office, Dana wondered just how much trouble she'd gotten herself into. What would she do if Elyssa fired her? Maybe get a real job and please her parents. Maybe live in a garret and try to write the Great American Novel. Maybe just shoot herself.

She knocked on the executive's door.

"Come," Elyssa invited from the seat of power. She looked up from reading a brochure when Dana walked in. The rest of the staff was also there, Dana noticed. Carole and Alix sat on the cushy leather couch. Robyn perched on the corner of Elyssa's desk, a somewhat sulky look on her face. All her comrades, her friends, the people she had used as her emotional punching bags, regarded her grimly.

I've been summoned to my own lynching, Dana thought with a wince.

"Dana," Elyssa greeted her in a deceptively soft voice.

"Elyssa." Dana wondered if she should just cry mea culpa and invite them to stretch her on the rack. "So, okay. I've been a bitch." She grimaced. "I'm sorry."

The boss tapped a pen on her desk blotter as if she was considering her options. "You *have* been a bitch."

Ouch. It was one thing to admit it, quite another to hear it on a friend's lips—especially when that friend was your boss.

"You know I don't tolerate such foolishness in this office."

Here it came.

"If you were a clerk or an intern, your butt would have been out of here—days ago."

Dana held her breath.

"But since you're the best writer in the greeting card business—and a friend—I'm not going to show you the door."

Dana released her breath. "Thank you."

"Yet."

Oops.

"This is an intervention," Carole said cheerfully.

"Kind of like Alcoholics Anonymous," Robyn chimed in with relish.

"We want to help you return to normal," Alix said.

"And stop yelling at perfectly innocent people." This from Robyn, with a pout.

"And quit thundering through the office, spitting bullets." Carole was really getting into it now.

"And show your happy, creative, productive face around here much more often," Elyssa said. She handed Dana a manila envelope. "This has a plane ticket to Phoenix, Arizona, along with a confirmation number for a stress and meditation workshop from December 27 through December 30. Also directions how to find the Gardens of Oak Creek Conference Center and Resort, where this thing is going to be held."

Dana looked at Alix and silently mouthed, "You didn't!" Alix confessed with a lifted brow and wicked smile.

"If you need more time there, you can take a few days of vacation. The office is going to be closed from Christmas through New Year's Day, anyway."

"Elyssa . . ."

"Yes?" Dana's boss regarded her as a high school principal might eye a troublesome teenager.

Dana had never been quite so humiliated or embarrassed. An intervention, indeed, as if crankiness was an addiction like cocaine or booze. She felt as though she were being hustled off to the Betty Ford Center.

"Elyssa, Alix already offered me her place at the workshop, and—"

"This isn't an offer, Dana."

Dana flinched at the tone. The boss really was torqued. The soul of courtesy and good business manners, Elyssa never interrupted someone unless steam was about to explode from her ears. "Okay, it isn't an offer," Dana continued cautiously. Very cautiously. After all, she did really like her job. And her stock options weren't yet vested. "Then it's a . . . a . . ."

"Consider it a job requirement," Elyssa told her with a tight smile. "We are all very concerned for you, Dana. We want you to take this time to do some thinking, relax, enjoy a different environment and then come back to work a new woman. Or rather, the old woman. The old Dana that we all know and love."

Dana knew when she was beat. She might as well go out and start trying on cowboy boots. Arizona, indeed! She took the envelope from Elyssa's hand. "I could have bought my own plane ticket," she said with a sullen pout.

Elyssa raised a brow. "Not if I fired you, you couldn't."

Dana grimaced.

"You have ten days before you leave to come up with some sparkling Valentine's Day copy. Alix has some cute ideas on the graphics. Get together with her and turn out something wonderful, will you?" As if nothing unusual had occurred, Elyssa was right back to business.

"Okay, then." Dana backed toward the door. Everyone was still looking at her as though she might at any moment release a toxic gas. She exited the office without another word.

As Dana left, Robyn chortled. "Okay! She's gone. Let's look at the brochure again."

The others gathered around Elyssa's desk as she once again spread out the glossy four-color brochure. There in front of them was a photo of the Gardens of Oak Creek, the majestic red rocks of Sedona and an articulate summary of the goals and benefits of the seminar. Best of all, on the back was a picture of Kieran, the guru himself, along with an impressive résumé.

"Now that is hot stuff," Robyn declared.

"Very hot," Alix agreed. "Almost makes me wish I were still going."

"Maybe we should have told Dana this guy isn't exactly an ancient graybeard on a mountaintop."

Robyn giggled. "Nah! Let her be surprised."

Eleven days later, Dana wound along a narrow road in her rented VW Beetle. One hand held the steering wheel. Her other hand wrestled with the map of Sedona that she'd picked up at the visitor center in town. There was no such thing as a straight road in this whole benighted state, even in town. And where she was now was definitely not in town. She had hoped this resort would at least have easy access to the boutiques, art galleries and Native American craft shops that made up the bulk of Sedona's businesses, but she had left the shops behind and now was headed toward the wide open spaces. She expected the Good, the Bad, and the Ugly to ride from behind one of the rocky bluffs any minute.

Finally she found her turn-off. A small sign announced the entrance to the Gardens of Oak Creek. The driveway was a narrow gravel road. On either side was the most lush vegetation she'd seen since boarding her flight at Ronald Reagan National Airport. Vine-covered fences sheltered a profusion of late-blooming flowers and neatly tilled fallow vegetable gardens. Through the greenery she spotted red-wood benches shaded by trees, some still bearing leaves. Fishponds, a little fountain and a picturesque little wooden bridge spanning a trickle of a creek completed the bucolic scene. On the right, a broad path led down to Oak Creek— or at least Dana assumed it was Oak Creek, given that every business she'd passed in Sedona seemed to be Oak Creek this or Oak Creek that. Sun glinted off quiet water, beckoning the wanderer to rest and meditate by its cool green pools.

And aren't I just the philosophical one? Dana interrupted her own observations cynically. She'd better watch out or she'd board the flight back to Washington wearing hippie beads and flowers in her hair.

A quarter-mile down the driveway the conference center appeared. There were three buildings, all similar in their pueblo-style architecture. Earth-tone stucco walls matched the reddish color of the bluffs that towered above the valley. Well-tended flower gardens, still in bloom, softened their unadorned lines. A sign pointed the way to the registration area, so Dana parked there. Several other cars were parked in front, including a Mercedes sport convertible and a Jag. Dana parked next to the Jag. The contrast between the sleek sports model and her homey little Beetle made her smile.

But the smile lasted only a moment. What the hell was she doing here? She felt entirely out of her element, a fish out of water. The two-hour drive from Phoenix had taken her through a spectacular kaleidoscope of desert and moun-tain landscapes, beautiful but harsh. For a girl who loved the soft greens of the east coast, the cry of gulls, the cool, moist caress of salty sea air against her skin and hair, coming to Arizona was like traveling to another planet.

Not to mention that she had four whole days of New Age mumbo jumbo to endure. What a way to waste precious time off!

Opening the car door, she unfolded herself from the driver's seat, climbed out and smoothed the creases from her Diesel jeans and matching denim jacket. Jeans and denim weren't exactly her day-to-day style, but if she had to spend a week in cowboy land, she might as well dress the part. She refused to stoop to cowboy boots, though. Her Jimmy Choo boots with the kicky three-inch heels were as close to cowboy as she was ever going to get.

As she stretched stiff muscles and looked around, Dana's spirits began to lift ever so slightly, boosted by the magnificent setting. The air was beautifully mild. Her cashmere sweater and the denim jacket were plenty warm enough. Mixed scents of roses and evergreens perfumed the air. Her sinuses had miraculously cleared and the headache that had plagued her for a month no longer throbbed at her temples. No snow. No ice. No slush. All around the valley of Oak Creek, natural towers, cathedrals and castles of vermilion rock rose from the greenery in truly majestic splendor. One couldn't fault the scenery or the climate.

And speaking of scenery—a resort employee had spotted her arrival and was on his way to assist her. Dana allowed herself a moment's wicked enjoyment, because this fellow could set any female heart to beating. Tall, broad-shouldered, all-around big without being a bit overdone, he moved with an athlete's unconscious grace. His jaw was chiseled, his mouth something a woman could dream about. Worn blue jeans, hemp sandals and a homespun-looking tunic seemed to be the uniform of the day. Thick black hair fell in artlessly tousled waves to just past his shoulders and the white of his tunic set off very bronze skin. This guy fit right into the Sedona atmosphere—a New Age hippie. Many of the shops she had driven past hawked personal pendulums, crystals, vortex tours, spiritual healing, even maps to find the nearest alien landing points.

He smiled when he noticed her looking at him. The smile was open and uncomplicated, a country smile having none of the subtleties and nuances of a big-city smile. Big-city smiles could be wary, flirty, contemptuous, probing, leering, dangerous, cold, dismissing or degrees of all the above. This smile was an honest welcome. It crinkled his eyes and warmed his face. And it was very, very sexy.

Actually, the whole package was very, very sexy.

"Hello," the hunk said. "Welcome to the Gardens of Oak Creek."

"Thank you."

"Cute car."

"Rental," she admitted, but she was proud of her choice. A Chevy Corsica would have been much too plain, a Lincoln or Cadillac ostentatious, not to mention beyond her budget, but a sunshine-yellow bug was both cute and stylish, more like a fashion accessory than a car. It made a statement about her, and Dana was feeling just insecure enough to need positive statements.

"How's it do on hills?"

"Perks right along." She handed him the keys. "My luggage is in the trunk. I don't know my room number. I still have to register."

He hesitated a moment before taking the keys, then gave her a lopsided smile that made her bones turn to water. "Okay."

"Is registration through here?"

"Right through those doors over there. You here for the workshop?"

"I am, sort of." She let cynicism color her voice. She wouldn't want anyone to believe that she swallowed this hocus-pocus, even someone who worked at the resort.

"That's good." He lifted her huge suitcase and duffel bag out of the trunk as if they were packed with feathers. "I hope you enjoy it."

"I don't normally go in for this kind of thing, but a few friends got together and gave this to me as a gift." More like the office staff hog-tied her and dragged her to the airport. "What is that odor?" she asked.

"Odor?" He stacked her luggage curbside—enough to last her at least three weeks, probably, but what was a girl to do when she didn't know exactly what she was walking into? Pack everything, that's what.

"Yes, that very . . . uh . . . pungent odor."

"Probably the goats."

Dana had a sinking feeling. "Goats?"

With the hint of a smile, he took her arm and guided her toward the other side of the parking area. From there she could see a complex of sheds and pens farther up the valley, but not far enough, apparently. There were also two more stuccoed, pueblo-style buildings a bit smaller than the hotel.

"Those are the livestock pens up there. We have beautiful Nubian goats, rabbits of all kinds, peacocks, geese, ducks, chickens and pigs."

Ee-ii-ee-ii-oh, Dana commented silently. "The animals live in buildings?"

He laughed. It was a hearty, from-the-chest sort of laugh, and he had the breadth of chest to make it boom. "No. The buildings are dormitories."

Vegetable gardens, livestock, dormitories and guys wandering about in long hair and hemp sandals. She had a bad feeling about this.

"Is this some kind of a commune?" She pictured brainwashing and drugs, sordid rituals, suicide pacts and innocents like herself sucked into the community and forced to stay. "Tell me this isn't a commune."

His expression was oddly gentle. "Do you think communes are bad?"

"Well . . . no, not really, I suppose." As usual, when she should have been articulate or clever, she was stumbling over her own tongue. "But there have been some, uh, cases . . . and, well, I thought this was a resort."

"The Gardens of Oak Creek is many things, depending on what you need."

She definitely didn't want a commune.

"We have a resident school here for people who feel the need to immerse themselves in philosophical study or simply retreat from the hectic world for a while. The gardens and livestock provide food for the student community and for the conference and teaching center. In turn, the students care for the gardens and the animals. Many find that communion with the animals brings an inner peace that the outside world can take from us."

His smile was still gentle. Not condescending. Not contemptuous. And his eyes—well, a woman could get lost in those eyes. So dark brown they were almost black, deep wells that drew you in, promised warmth, rest, joy.

Dana caught herself before she fell into those eyes. Next time she needed to work up a soft, cozy, sexy mood to put into Allheart card copy, she would conjure up a memory of this guy. She wondered what he did around here besides carry luggage and charm the female students.

"Are you a student at the . . . uh . . . up there?" She gestured to the dormitories.

"Sometimes I stay there awhile."

"They let people come and go?"

He chuckled. "Of course."

"Ah." He had perfect white teeth, she noticed. "This Kieran fellow, the one who teaches the workshop, does he own this place?"

"He is the founder."

"So he owns it."

"Ownership is more"—he flashed those perfect teeth in a brash grin—"I hesitate to use the word *communal,* considering. Let's just say it's a nonprofit foundation."

"He isn't the type who would stir up a vat of hemlock tea and tell all his . . . uh . . . students to drink up in order to protest the evil of the world, or maybe to liberate everyone to join with some mother ship in outer space, is he?"

His eyes positively laughed aloud. "Knowing Kieran, I doubt he could cook up anything. Even hemlock tea."

She flashed her own set of perfect teeth in a smile. "Good answer. You should be a lawyer, not cleaning up after livestock."

"I was a lawyer."

"Oops."

"No offense taken. I assure you that the goats are much more pleasant to work with than most of my former clients."

Oh cripes, Dana thought. The hunk had been a lawyer. Now he carried luggage, talked to goats and wore hemp sandals. Is this my future? she mused facetiously. She could almost hear the Allheart staff moaning: *Poor Dana. She was once a genius at the clever quips, but since being brainwashed at that workshop she's reduced to milking goats and weeding flower beds, and her nails are an absolute mess!* It could happen, Dana mused with a private smile. She'd already sunk to wearing jeans and denim jackets. What next? Peasant skirts and Birkenstocks?

"You're smiling now," her lovely bellman said. "That's good."

"I was trying to picture me milking a goat and finding inner peace."

A heavy masculine brow arched upward. "It might work. Maybe you should try it while you're here."

She laughed again. "I'd better check in."

"I'll take your luggage in."

"Thanks so much." She handed him a generous tip. A lawyer who schlepped suitcases and cleaned goat pens needed it, Dana figured. "You've been really nice. I hope I see you around during the workshop."

"You will," he assured her, the smile still alive.

Chapter 2

The reception area looked pretty much like a standard hotel. Though certainly not as upscale as the nicer hotels in the Washington area, it was pleasant enough. The clerk at the registration desk was a young man with close-cropped hair and a friendly face who introduced himself as Jerund. His welcome was as pleasant as the bellman's, though not backed up by the stellar good looks and a smile that alternated between gently compelling and boldly brash.

"The meeting rooms are in the south wing," the clerk explained. "Through there is the pool, Jacuzzi and spa."

"Goodness!" Dana said with a smile. "The place comes equipped with everything, doesn't it?"

"Yes ma'am! The restaurant and coffee shop are in the north wing. And your room is down that hallway over there. Your roommate has already checked in."

"Roommate?" Dana's brows shot upward.

"Yes ma'am. The workshop Saver Plan provides for

workshop tuition, breakfast in the coffee shop and double-occupancy rooms. That's the plan you signed up for."

"I did, did I?"

He looked puzzled by her tone, and Dana had to remind herself that the clerk had nothing to do with Alix reserving steerage-class accommodations. Reminding herself that she had come here to exorcise her crankiness, not exercise it, she forced herself to smile. "That'll be fine. Absolutely lovely."

That bit of gushiness seemed to win him over. His smile once again radiated the light of inner peace, or whatever the denizens of this place were seeking. "Do you have luggage I can help you with?"

"If you don't mind. It's piled over there. Your bellman brought it in for me."

"Bellman?" Jerund frowned. "Oh, you mean . . ." His eyes widened slightly and a grin spread across his face. "Yes, of course. Here's your key. I'll be right behind you with your luggage."

As Dana walked down the hall, she heard the clerk laugh out loud. That funny, was she?

In consideration of her unwanted roommate, Dana knocked on the door before swiping the key card through the reader.

"Enter," came a quiet reply.

"Hi," Dana said as she opened the door. "I'm your room-mate, Dana Boyle." *And I've been committed here for terminal bitchiness,* she added silently. *So watch out.*

A somewhat pudgy middle-aged lady unfolded herself from an improbable cross-legged position on one of the queen-size beds and gave Dana a bright smile. "I'm Tamara." She pronounced the name Ta*mar*a. "Just getting a jump start on getting my head together."

"It looks pretty together to me."

Tamara chuckled politely. "I have a long way to go. This is my second workshop with Kieran. You?"

"First."

The woman drew in a delighted breath. "What a wonderful experience you have in store. Kieran is just the deepest, wisest, most enlightened teacher I've ever had. And I've tried others. It's so important in this day and age to find a spiritual center, don't you agree? Everything else in life becomes so trivial when you come face to face with the truth of how little we know about ourselves and our place in the universe."

"Uh . . ."

"I'm thinking about joining the school here full time," she continued happily. "I believe intense study is what I'm called to do. But I wanted to attend one more workshop, just to be sure of my commitment. Kieran is such a wonderful guide to my inner self." Her eyes glowed, her lips were moist, her nostrils flared with pleasure.

Dana wondered just how this Kieran fellow went about probing this woman's "inner self," and if she should call the department of public morals.

Then, an almost childlike smile lit up Tamara's face. "But you'll see for yourself. Those who seek after truth always are led to the right path. It's just that sometimes the journey is long and there are detours along the way."

"Well, right now, I think I'm going to take a detour to the restaurant," Dana said. "Care to join me?"

"Oh no! I need lots more quiet time before I'm ready to face the workshop tomorrow. Those who are prepared are those who best learn the secrets of the universe!"

Dana tried not to let relief show in her expression. Tossing her denim jacket onto the empty bed, she smiled to herself. The universe would never catch *her* doing homework before she'd even been to class.

The next morning came too early, as mornings were apt to do lately. There had been a time not too long ago when Dana had regularly awakened before her alarm jerked her from sleep, when she had faced each new day as a challenge, looked forward to work and the give-and-take between the staffers at Allheart, and slept soundly each night knowing her life was on the right track. Not lately, though. Lately she'd dragged herself from bed each morning after a night of uneasy, on-and-off sleep.

Her first morning at the Gardens of Oak Creek was no different. Though her roommate bounded from her bed with a smile on her face and threw open the drapes with an ecstatic sigh, Dana regarded the bedside clock with a groan and dove more deeply beneath her covers.

"What a sunrise!" Tamara declared. "What a beautiful new day. The universe is good!"

"If the universe were truly good it would let me go back to sleep," Dana grumbled, hoping to discourage further warblings of joy.

"Come, Dana! You must see the sunrise. This is the first day of the rest of your life!"

Even greeting card copy didn't get that schmaltzy. Not at Allheart, at least.

"Come! Come! Enjoy the morning. Besides, Kieran frowns upon tardiness, and class begins in an hour."

Kieran could go jump off a cliff, Dana growled to herself. Actually, that was the polite version of what she was thinking.

The sunrise was spectacular, Dana discovered when she managed to drag herself from bed ten minutes later. High, wispy clouds streaked the sky with feathery fire, and the ruddy light of morning turned the cliffs surrounding the valley a deep, glowing crimson. Such a spectacular show from Mother Nature made it difficult for even Dana to keep the proper edge on her grumpy mood.

She scarcely had time to finish her morning routine of hair and makeup before Tamara announced that it was time to leave for class. Tamara had brought her a bowl of fruit and a cup of herbal tea from the coffee shop, then had patiently watched her roll hot curlers into her just-past-shoulder-length red hair and apply the Bare Essentials daily regimen of makeup designed to beautify her with a completely "natural" look. She agonized over the choice of wearing her sleek Calvin Klein pants and matching jacket or simply clean jeans and the cotton flannel shirt her mother had given her last Christmas. She'd never worn it, for obvious reasons. Flannel just wasn't her style. The fact that she'd even packed it said much about her state of mind.

"Casual," Tamara suggested, obviously fidgeting to leave but too polite to leave the workshop freshman on her own the first day of class. Dressed in a peasant skirt, sweatshirt and clogs, the lady practiced what she preached. Her beauty routine had included running a brush through short salt-and-pepper hair wet from the shower and treating her complexion to a dose of hand lotion.

But she was good-hearted, Dana reflected. Maybe she should put more stock in good-hearted.

"Ready!" she declared after tucking her shirttails into designer jeans and sucking her navel to her backbone so she could close the zipper. "I'm ready to be enlightened."

The meeting room was like no classroom Dana had ever seen. The floor was cushy carpet. A big corner unit sofa, plush and comfortable, made an L along two cream-colored walls. Cushions of various sizes and shapes were strewn about the floor. Students sat on the sofas or relaxed on a floor cushion as they chose. Some chatted. Others sat silent, eyes closed, probably focusing on that elusive inner self, Dana thought. The group was small—six counting Dana and Tamara. But it was surprisingly varied. Four women and two men. Young, middle-aged and old. One woman looked to be at least in her seventies.

Dana chose a comfy-looking cushion and sat. Tamara settled in beside her. "Don't be so tense," her roommate advised. "Just wait. You'll be glad you came."

"I'm not tense," Dana lied. *And I will not be glad I came,* she thought. That would give her bullying friends at All-heart entirely too much satisfaction. Then the door opened and in walked the revered Mr. Enlightenment himself. He smiled expansively at the group, and Dana only just managed to stifle an audible gasp. Heat flooded her face and neck, and she tried to discreetly hide behind Tamara as the much-vaunted Kieran introduced himself. He was tall, broad-shouldered, with black hair that made her hands itch to touch it and a killer smile that made her hot and cold at the same time. Her bellman wasn't the bellman; he was the teacher, founder and guru of this place. *Lame-brain Dana strikes again,* Dana moaned to herself. Why oh why hadn't she asked the guy's name before making a fool of herself? Why hadn't she just kept her smart-ass mouth shut? What a moron she was!

Their esteemed teacher went slowly through the roster of his students, greeting each of them with a personal word of welcome.

"Dana Boyle," he said with a slow smile. His eyes left the roster and met hers. They glinted with mischief, with knowing what a smart-mouth, moronic jackass she was. Dana wanted the floor beneath her to open in a yawning cavern and swallow her whole. "From Washington, DC. You've come a long way, Dana."

And she wanted to go back, right now.

"We're very glad you came."

Dana clenched her jaw. Words failed her completely, refusing to form in her lame excuse for a brain. It wasn't fair. Kieran was supposed to be a gray-bearded hermit type, an ancient wise man one would expect to find on top of some holy mountain spouting the mysteries of life and all that garbage. Gurus weren't hunks. They didn't have athlete's bodies, drop-dead gorgeous eyes and killer smiles. They didn't pose as bellmen or make jokes about goats. They most certainly didn't make a woman's blood rush through her veins in a steaming hot river and make her break a sweat just contemplating the sculpted curves of his mouth.

Unfair, unfair, unfair!

Kieran moved on in the list, but now and again his eyes strayed back to Dana, his mouth quirking into a little smile that Dana knew was a private "gotcha." She wondered if she should just leave now or endure the next four days as punishment for being such an idiot.

Tamara leaned toward her and whispered, "Isn't he something?"

Kieran was something indeed. Yes, he was. Dana hunkered down on her cushion and prepared to be mortified and miserable.

The inevitable first order of the morning was introductions. Dana hated such public exposures, telling a group of strangers facts about herself that no one was interested in anyway. When her time came she was very brief, almost curt compared to the other students' loquacious ramblings about background, aspirations, philosophies and personal lives.

"Dana Boyle. Washington, DC. I'm a writer for an Internet greeting card company." She started to sit down, but Kieran didn't let her off the hook.

"What are the most important things in your life, Dana?"

"What do you mean?"

"Family? Husband? Children? Work?"

"I have a mother, father and sister." *Upstart, gloating, engaged little sister.* "They're important." *They are, even though they're genuine pains in the butt.* "I have close friends at work." *Who shanghaied me into this workshop. But annoying as they are, they mean well.* "They're important." She shrugged. "I like my work. I guess it's important to me."

"What do you think is the most important thing in your life?"

Getting out of this workshop and going home to my own familiar screwed-up life. "I don't know."

Kieran smiled in a way that made Dana suspect he could read her mind. Later, when all the introductions were over, he latched onto her statement of philosophical ignorance to launch the morning's harangue. At least Dana thought it was going to be a harangue. That was what these "teachers" did, wasn't it? But what followed was more of a discussion than a pedantic lecture, and this teacher treated his students as if their contributions to the discussion were as valuable as his own. Dana started listening more to what he said and less to her own thought balloons of resentful cynicism.

"Too many people don't know what the most important thing is in their lives," he told them. "The pace of modern life doesn't give you time to find out. Out of every day, most of us could probably schedule about thirty hours, even though the day has only twenty-four, last time I checked."

The students nodded and smiled their agreement.

"Your bosses want a big chunk of your time."

That's for sure.

"Your spouses, children, lovers and even your pets want a big chunk of your time."

Don't forget parents. They can want your whole life to go according to their agenda.

"Then there are chores, errands. Even relaxing the way society says you should relax—that can be work in itself. Club hopping. Dating. Softball leagues. Workouts at the gym to get that buff look that fashion says you must have in order to be a worthwhile human being."

Dana had to smile to herself. Kieran didn't look like he missed many workouts, unless he was just naturally muscled like an Olympic gymnast.

"We get too little time to sleep," he went on. "Too little time to just crash in a chair and relax, without the TV blaring, the kids whining, the spouse bugging you about this or that. In short, we get too little time to think. Just think. Think about the universe and our place in it. Think about our own personal need to grow as a spiritual being. Think about what is really going on beneath all the bustle of the oh-so-busy, oh-so-important world.

"Have you ever listened to the Earth breathing?"

Dana wondered if she could use that line on a card.

"Have you ever lay outside on a clear night to watch the stars?"

His voice was spellbinding. It was impossible not to listen. Deep, melodic, it was friendly rather than intense, but even with the friendliness he conveyed a deep conviction. *This is important,* the voice said, not in words as much as in tone. *This is what life is about. Listen. Learn. Believe.*

"Have you ever taken the time to look inside yourself and explore who you really are, what you want, what you need?"

What Dana was beginning to want and need had nothing to do with philosophy. There was something devastatingly compelling about a man who crawled inside your head and demanded your attention, whether or not you wanted him there. And that something had nothing to do with the man's physical attractions. Of course, the fact that Kieran was a hunk didn't hurt matters any.

Kieran went on to explain that the rapid, demanding pace of modern life robbed people of their ties with their inner selves and separated them from everything but a shallow, hurly-burly world. The result was stress that resulted in depression, violence, failed relationships, broken families and spiritual derelicts unable to find purpose in a universe rich with purpose.

Dana found herself hanging on Kieran's every word. His voice resonated inside her, in her very soul—though she hadn't ever really considered whether she *had* a soul. It was a question she had never taken the time to contemplate. When he explained that the solution to society's lack of spiritual depth was a return to meditation, she nodded and smiled along with the rest of the class, every bit as sucked in as any of them. When he instructed them in the basics of meditation—solitude, inner silence, focus—she focused upon the mouth that spoke the words, the eyes that seemed so warm with compassion for the students' needs, for her needs.

When the morning session drew to an end, Dana was scarcely aware that three whole hours had passed. Even the rumbling of her empty stomach hadn't distracted her.

"Your first reading assignment is the first three chapters in the book you've been given." Kieran held up a copy of the hardcover text, *Finding Strength in Meditation.* He grinned. "A shameless plug for my book, but of course, if I hadn't thought that it was worthwhile, I wouldn't have written the thing, would I have? Anyone who wants to buy a copy can talk to the clerk at the registration desk, but during the workshop, the books are provided."

Dana opened the copy she had picked up at the beginning of class. The last page was a photo of Kieran flashing that killer smile. She immediately decided she would buy a copy.

"And as an exercise," he concluded, "I want you all to try some meditation this afternoon. Try to find your center. Look inside yourself, not balking at what you see. Not stumbling on pride or self-doubt, but simply approaching yourself as a work of art, the artist being the Universe, or God, however you choose. Throughout the afternoon and evening, I will have the opportunity to talk personally with each of you in individual appointments. Times are posted outside the door, and there is also a schedule at the registration desk. Tomorrow morning, we will meet again as a group."

Dana sat still as the class began to leave. Her roommate seemed equally reluctant to move. Kieran smiled at them. "Tamara, it's so good to see you again."

"You have no idea how good it is to be back, Master."

Dana was running the odd title of "Master" around her mind when Kieran turned the full impact of his attention on her.

"Dana, I hope you weren't offended by my not introducing myself when we first met. I didn't intend it as a joke. But sometimes it's easier to become acquainted with people without the baggage of being the teacher."

"Offended? Me?"

"I'm very glad you're here. I look forward to discussing some of your needs this afternoon."

Some of her needs she'd damned well better keep to herself, Dana warned herself. Lusting after the teacher was probably grounds for expulsion.

"Come on, Dana." Tamara touched her arm, breaking her

thrall. She had been staring wordlessly at Kieran with her mouth agape. "The coffee shop has great mushroom and avocado sandwiches. Grown right here in the gardens."

"The goat's milk cheese is very good also," Kieran said with a grin.

He was laughing at her, Dana knew. But somehow it didn't matter. Lunch didn't sound nearly as tasty as simply staying to bask in Kieran's smile. And if Tamara hadn't pulled her out of the room, she might have been foolish enough to try to do just that.

Dana left Tamara enjoying lunch in the coffee shop and chatting with fellow students. She had eaten her sandwich fast, scarcely noticing how it tasted. Everything offered was health food, so how good could it have tasted? Dana's greatest hunger at that moment was to resume connection to the real world.

Alix answered the phone on the second ring.

"Good!" Dana said. "You're home."

"I was about to meet Marc."

"Marc can wait," Dana declared with a pang of envy for her friend's suddenly successful love life. Lately all the All-heart women had been scoring romantic home runs—Elyssa with Joe Monteigne, Carole Titus with the country's youngest new senator, Alix with her Marc. Even young Robyn had her on-again, off-again with heartthrob Steve. Was Dana the only one whose love life was a minefield? "Alix!" Her voice cut through the phone lines with a definite edge. "Do you know what you've gotten me into?"

"Something good, I hope."

"Alix! This is a frigging cult! They have organic gardens and goats!"

"Goats?"

"Goats!"

"I don't think having goats makes them a cult, Dana."

"How about pigs, chickens, bunnies, turkeys, geese and so-called committed students that live in communal housing and sit around listening for the universe to say something to them personally?"

"Well . . . what about Kieran?"

"Kieran." Dana huffed indignantly. "Kieran is . . ." *A hunk. A hunk with a smile that could have her wizened maiden aunt climbing out of her drawers.* ". . . is a sideshow." *Star material.* "Oh, he's dynamic. I'll give him that. He even sucked me into his speech this morning. Everyone in the room was practically throwing flowers at him." *Or bras and panties. Except that most of the women there weren't wearing bras.* "He could talk a cat into kissing a dog, I swear. The man is dangerous."

"Sounds interesting. Is he . . . good looking?"

Dana heard something in her tone. She held the phone handset away from her ear and narrowed her eyes at it as if Alix could see. She put it back to her ear without losing her suspicious frown. "You knew, you little—"

"Mind your temper, honey. You're supposed to be there to chill out, remember."

"You guys thought I was going to get the hots for this guy and suddenly mellow out to become Miss Congeniality."

"That good, is he?"

"Don't you know?"

"Just from his picture on the website."

"If you were here, you treacherous bitch, you'd be melted into a hot, steaming puddle of lust."

"Mmmmm. I should have kept him for myself. See, I've done you a favor."

"Alix, in my current mood, I don't need to have my hormones doing jumping jacks while I try to calm the rest of me down."

"Don't fight it, girl. Mother Nature always wins."

"I don't need a man! I especially don't need to be lusting after this man. He's a nut. A twenty-first-century hippie. Today he tells us to listen to the universe. Listen to our inner selves. Tomorrow he'll probably say we shouldn't shave our armpits, use deodorant or eat meat."

Alix laughed. "No way anyone could get me to have hairy armpits. Listen, sweetie. You just relax. Enjoy looking at the guy. Listen to what he has to say. Take the part you can use and throw out the rest. No one expects you to come back to Washington a hairy vegetarian."

"Alix! Don't hang up."

"Gotta go now. Take care of yourself. Enjoy."

A gentle click broke Dana's connection to civilization and the sane world. She was catapulted back to the Gardens of Oak Creek. Organic food, goats, meditation and a man called Kieran. Never-neverland.

Dana escaped the room before Tamara returned to start gushing once again about "the Master." This time, Dana was in no mood to be tolerant. On her way down the hall she passed her elderly classmate talking with two male students—one middle aged, one still looking for his first shave. They discussed the merits of yoga versus the benefits of Tai Chi as methods to ease stress. In the lobby Jerund and another student engaged in a lively debate over the difference between reincarnation and repersonalization. Dana felt rather like Alice falling down the rabbit hole. She found refuge in a nook of the garden. A shaded bench sat beside a man-made brooklet where ornamental fish swam among lush water plants. An evergreen vine climbed the tree trunks, the legs of the bench, the wooden handrails of the little bridge that crossed the water, and peeking through the vines here and there, marigolds and wild roses added a touch of color. Dana was amazed that such things could grow here even in December.

A city girl, born and bred, Dana felt more comfortable with concrete than such luxurious growth, but at the least the bench offered privacy from the fruitcakes that seemed to inhabit every corner. The schedule at the registration desk had her listed for a three P.M. meeting with the Great One himself, and she wasn't about to spend the next two hours debating philosophy with her roommate.

So she sat. The bench was comfy. The plants and trees, she reluctantly admitted, lent the little nook an air of soothing quietude. The brooklet rippled happily. No traffic sounds. No horns blaring, tires squealing, sirens wailing. No television, radio, or Muzak. No voices in conversation or bosses wanting clever, creative one- and two-liners from a writer who was just about clevered-out. Here in the garden was blessed silence, broken musically by occasional birdsong and the laughter of water.

Dana closed her eyes, deciding that it wouldn't kill her to try a little of that inward thinking that Kieran talked about. She was quiet. She was alone. And she did have stuff to ponder. Family. Work. The whole parade of men that had come briefly into her life and hastily departed, either because she had found fault with them or they had found fault with her. The very annoying knot that so often tied her tongue when she had to communicate with her mouth rather than with her fingers flying on a keyboard.

Was the answer to all her problems somewhere inside her, as Kieran seemed to think? Find her center, he had said. Listen to the earth breathe. Tune in to the universe.

The only thing she saw at her center right then was Kieran. He was smiling that gentle, mysterious smile that made her heart somersault. His eyes drew her in, dark pools that made her feel warm and safe. She could almost see the black waves of his hair move in the breeze. The nostrils of that classic nose flared suddenly. The gentle smile turned bold, teeth flashing in a brash, challenging grin.

Dana's eyes flew open. What was the man doing to her? Was he going to be waiting for her every time she closed her eyes and relaxed?

She tried again, closed her eyes, soaked up the peace of her surroundings—the gentle sound of the brook, the whisper of breeze through the trees, the call of a bird in the distance. She was not going to see him there inside her mind, Dana vowed. He had no right to be there. He was not a part of her world. A New Age swami with long hair and sandals was not a candidate for man of her dreams, and he would not get in the way of her concentration on serious stuff like life, family, work, love, sex—oops! Sex? There he was again, smiling that smile, inviting her closer with those deep, dark eyes.

Dana muttered a soft curse. This silly stuff was harder than it looked, especially when your teacher was a world-class distraction. She looked at her watch, noting that she was only five minutes away from her appointed time with the master. Time had passed much faster than it had seemed. A whole hour one-on-one with Kieran—this was going to be interesting. Interesting and a little bit scary.

She made her way down the path to the bank of Oak Creek, where on a flat rock shelf that jutted over the water, denizens of The Gardens had built a medicine wheel. It wasn't very impressive, really, just a circle of water-worn stones set in a big circle. Four spokes of similar stones indicated the cardinal points of the compass.

Kieran sat cross-legged not far from the circle. He looked utterly relaxed as he gazed at the lively waters of Oak Creek. A drifting piece of wood bobbed along the ripples, and all the man's attention seemed centered on it. Dana saw nothing special there. The wood got tossed about, swept against rocks, pulled under by the current, then shooting upward again, until it finally found refuge in a quiet pool close to the shore. Kieran seemed so focused on the little scene that Dana hesitated to interrupt. In fact, she was about to use his preoccupation as an excuse to slip away when he demonstrated that he was very aware of her presence.

"Dana Boyle." His deep voice, though quiet, was more effective than Surround Sound. "Welcome, Dana."

"Uh . . . hi." Dana Boyle, Queen of Words, tongue-tied once again.

Still looking at the piece of wood, he asked, "What do you think of Sedona?"

"Very pretty." *Right. That's going on a greeting card. Not!*

"Is that all?"

"Well . . ."

"Many people who come here think that Sedona is special, that it holds something significant for them."

"Uh . . ."

Finally he looked at her. The impact of his eyes was a fifty-megaton soul-shaker. If he could bottle his own personal magnetism and put it on the market, people would be clamoring for the stuff. Just like the snake-oil salesmen of old. "What does Sedona have for you, Dana?"

The image that came instantly to mind was something

she didn't dare express. No doubt the swami of Sedona would take a dim view of lust in the Sedona dirt.

"Why did you come here, Dana?"

"Uh . . . I guess to get some of the stress out. Life has been . . . has been pretty hairy lately."

"Life always is. Sit down, please. No, not there. Over here, across from me."

Dana lowered herself gingerly to the bare, hard rock in the spot he indicated. They were so close that their knees nearly touched. "Couldn't spring for a bench or two, huh?"

He smiled only slightly. "I find it's easier to be in touch with oneself if one is close to the earth."

If the earth were just a little softer Dana might concede the point. But more than a moment this close to the earth was going to make her butt bones poke right through the seat of her jeans. And speaking of jeans, hers weren't designed with sitting Indian-style in mind. They were cutting off all circulation to her legs.

Kieran regarded her with amusement that he didn't attempt to hide. "Dana, you must breathe while you meditate."

She gave him a weak smile, which won her a chuckle and a shake of his head.

"It's important to be comfortable during meditation, because discomfort is a distraction we don't want. Right?"

Fashion wasn't made for comfort, but men never understood that.

"Here. This will help." Before Dana realized what he was doing, Kieran reached over and deftly flipped open the waist fastening of her jeans.

"Oh my!" She took a deep breath, relieved as she was embarrassed.

"Better?"

Dana regarded him suspiciously, but both his tone and expression were totally innocent.

"Loose clothing is best," he advised. "Now, straighten your back and breathe." He shook his head at her attempt. "Breathe into your stomach. Deep, deep. Now hold it—one, two, three, four—and slowly release, all the way from your toes." He laughed. "Dana, Dana, you put so much effort into it. Relax."

Gracefully, effortlessly Kieran unfolded himself and moved to kneel behind her.

"Close your eyes. Relax."

Dana felt his big hands on her, one at the small of her back, the other just below her diaphragm. A shiver of delicious pleasure traveled through her body, and it had nothing to do with meditation.

"Now breathe. Deeply. In. Hold. Hold. Hold. Hold it down in your belly. Now release. Slowly." He pressed gently on her middle. His breath was a warm breeze threading through the back of her hair. No part of him touched her except those wonderful hands, but Dana could feel electricity arc between them, across the inches that separated her back from his chest.

"Again, Dana. Breathe. Now concentrate on something wonderful."

No problem there.

"Feel it flow through you, starting at your head" . . . where his words tickled the back of her neck . . . "and traveling through your chest, your thighs, your legs, and out your toes. Make the relaxation complete, and when it is, then you can begin to search inside yourself for the answers you need."

What Dana needed right then was quite basic and not very spiritual. And she didn't think Kieran wanted to hear it.

"That's good. Very good." His hands moved to her shoulders and kneaded gently. "Do you feel the inward flow of energy? That is the state you seek to achieve while you meditate. Block out the world, look inside. And to do it, you must be relaxed, comfortable, at peace. Now, come back to the world, Dana, and we will talk about you. Hm?"

Dana didn't think she wanted to talk, but somehow she found herself talking. They walked in the gardens, where neatly tilled rows of fertile soil patiently awaited the coming of spring. For a change the words flowed from Dana's mouth. Usually words flowed only at her computer keyboard, and those words were impersonal drivel meant for people she didn't know. Always the words from her heart had been bottled up, but it seemed Kieran had popped the cork on the bottle.

She told him about her temper, her depression, her downright bitchiness. She told him about being shanghaied to Arizona. She even told him things she'd never realized before. Loneliness. Isolation. The weeds of dissatisfaction that threatened to choke her creative abilities. All of it came out. Dana expected to be embarrassed once she was away from Kieran's reassuring presence, but she wasn't embarrassed there in the gardens, with Kieran's gentle smile upholding her.

"You have done the correct thing," Kieran finally said to her. "And your friends have, too." He chuckled softly. "Sometimes when we can't see the right path, those who love us must nudge us in the way we should go."

A boot in the backside was more like what Dana had gotten.

Their circle of the gardens led them back to the medicine wheel, which Kieran promised to explain another day. Kieran gently touched her cheek, and somehow his touching her seemed as natural as his smile. "Our time is over for now, Dana, but I want you to go somewhere peaceful and comfortable and think about all you've shared with me. You are a tumultuous spirit, my friend, but your potential shines like the sun on a summer day. You can learn to discipline your thoughts and emotions. Examine your spirit, and remind yourself to keep your focus on what is important in life. Tomorrow we will be together again."

Tomorrow we will be together again. The words seemed to echo in Dana's mind.

Dana left Kieran by the medicine wheel and walked up the garden path toward the hotel, dizzy with a world that seemed to have shifted its axis. Or was she the one who had changed? She was not the same person who had walked this same path earlier. The new Dana had a heart that felt light. She had lips that wanted to smile, and feet that longed to skip along like a child.

Most of all, she wanted to get to her laptop computer and write—not reality cards. That was a product of her dark days. Today she burst with love songs, declarations of friendship, heartfelt sympathy, flirty come-ons, hearty congratulations and still more love songs—all the kinds of wonderful words that made Allheart.com the best there was.

Dana Boyle was back, better than ever.

Tomorrow we will be together again. Yes, indeed. Life was good.

Chapter 3

The next two days followed the same schedule as the first. All six students spent the morning as a group. Kieran tossed out subjects for their examination and comment, answered questions and provoked debates. And he kept referring back to the meditation techniques that would, he assured them, help them toward inner knowledge and pursuit of their own personal truth.

Afternoons were reserved for private meditation and individual consultations with the Master. In her own mind, Dana stopped putting quotes around the honorific. Kieran was a master at what he did. Only a master could have calmed her restless spirit and started the healing process that lightened her step.

Dana's second consultation with Kieran was once again in the garden. He tailored the meeting places, he explained, to where each individual student felt most comfortable, and he believed she could open up best among the growing things of the earth.

"That shouldn't be," Dana told him with a laugh. "I'm a city girl, born and bred. The land of concrete and smog is my native habitat."

"Perhaps in this life that is true."

"Oh, right!"

He endured her skepticism with a good-natured grin, never trying to persuade her to his way of thinking and never scoffing at her traditionalist mind-set. But his eyes frequently twinkled as if he knew a great and wonderful secret that she would someday learn.

While they dabbled their bare toes in the cool water of Oak Creek Kieran explained the symbolism of the medicine wheel and how Dana could relate it to the progression of her own life.

"It all seems rather simplistic," Dana complained to him as she looked at the primitive circle of stones. "East, west, north, south. East is the sunrise, beginning, the springtime planting. South is summer, growing and fulfillment. West is autumn harvesting, and north is the winter, when everything rests."

"The simple truths are the most profound," he told her.

"And this relates to God and the Universe how?"

"There is symbolism here, Dana. You must think on it and relate it to your own life."

What she really wanted to think about was how the sunlight gleamed in Kieran's hair and how the muscles flexed in the strong column of his neck when he turned his face to the sky.

During their next session Kieran led her up the hill toward the dormitories and livestock area.

She objected. "Aren't we going to talk in the gardens?"

"I thought you might like to apologize to the goats for the derogatory remarks you made about them," he said with a wicked smile.

"Wait a minute! I told you I was a city girl. And besides, I meant no insult to your precious goats."

"This might be a revelation to you."

"I don't need a goat revelation! Let's go back to the garden. I have tons more questions about the medicine wheel."

"You nearly fell asleep when we talked about the medicine wheel."

She hadn't been sleeping so much as fantasizing, but Dana wasn't about to confess. "I was meditating."

"Uh-huh."

The ploy wasn't working.

"You might find that you like animals. They can be very soothing to the spirit. As a human being, you can't isolate yourself from your brothers and sisters on this planet and expect to be a fulfilled and complete being."

"I am not sister to a goat!"

His smile was broad. "Maybe a cousin."

"Not even ten times removed. You are so full of what they clean out of these pens."

It was a friendly, laughing exchange that moved them along the road from master and student to friends. Friends that just happened to be a man and a woman, something Dana never forgot when she was with him. No matter how platonic and circumspect he was, a certain sexual tension emanated from Kieran that set Dana's hormones on full alert. She suspected he was aware of it, even though he ignored it. Did the tension exist with all his female students, or just her? She wished that she had the time to find out.

Never would Dana have believed when she boarded a jet a few short days ago that she would end up wishing for more time away. Without Kieran to steady her, her life would return to chaos, her days to depression, her nights to alternately wishing she were on a date or wishing that she wasn't.

Since she had come to this place, Kieran had invaded her night dreams and occupied most of her waking thoughts. Her reaction to him was unlike her relationship with any other man in her life. Most hunky guys made her worry—first about how to get close to them, then how to get rid of them or why they had gotten rid of her. But Kieran didn't make her worry. He made her smile, calmed her spirit, made waking a joy and retiring a pleasant anticipation of dreams to come. Dana's state of mind had become so downright positive that her roommate couldn't send her into a fit, even though Tamara talked of nothing but reincarnation, crystals, aliens and which flavor of incense was best to aid meditation. If Dana had been forced to spend a day with Tamara before she met Kieran, the lady would have been mincemeat.

Yes indeed, Tamara probably owed Kieran her life. Dana owed him her present happiness, and she wasn't yet ready to leave that behind.

Nevertheless, she wasn't sure even Kieran could get her to apologize to a goat.

As they went through the gate to the livestock pens, Kieran greeted two middle-aged but fit-looking men. "Hello, Caymon, Ya-teh-mah. Meet Dana, a workshop student."

The men smiled an open, friendly welcome. "Have you come to admire Yasmin?" one said. "Caymon thinks she will deliver today. I think it will be tomorrow."

Beside the men was a very fat brown goat with long droopy ears and a woebegone face.

"She looks like she'll give us twins this time."

"Or maybe triplets," Caymon said.

On Kieran's urging, Dana gingerly made Yasmin's acquaintance. The goat nibbled on her jeans in a friendly hello.

"She likes you," Kieran said with a grin.

Ya-teh-mah laughed. "Yasmin likes anything she can put in her mouth. But here is Sheila."

"Sheila?" Dana eyed the next goat uncertainly.

"She's our character barometer," Kieran confided. "Butted Caymon clear out of the pen when he first came to stay here."

Caymon smiled. "She was just having a bad day is all."

Dana reached out a tentative hand to Sheila, who lipped her fingers gently.

By the time they made the rounds of the pens, Dana felt like Farmer Jane. The goats were actually quite clean, and so were the pigs. They were tame as well. A litter of piglets napped beneath an empty hay rack, and Mother Pig was quite content to let Dana approach her brood and stroke a little piglet. Obviously these animals had never known anything but kindness from their keepers, and Dana did find a special kind of joy in such trusting acceptance from the beasts. She was delighted to find two warm, just-laid eggs in a hen's nest, and marveled at the velvety feel of the old draft horse's nose. At the last she let Kieran show her how to milk a goat. Sheila patiently stood on the milk stand and tolerated Dana's amateurish attempts to coax milk from the silken-soft udders. Only drops appeared, and she finally leaned her head against the goat's warm flank and sighed. "I'm acquiring a real respect for milkmaids."

Yet she felt strangely content with warm, soft goat against her cheek and the thrum of animal heartbeat in her ear.

"You have to do it like this." Kieran sat down at her

back, crowding close on the stool, and put his hands over hers to demonstrate the proper technique. Two streams of warm, sweet-smelling milk jetted into the bucket. Sheila the goat gave them both a look that plainly said "About time!"

What would her Allheart friends think if they could see her cozied up to a goat, Kieran's hands wrapped about hers, his chest plastered against her back, all in front of an audience of pigs, geese, turkeys, two cult members with very strange names and a retired plow horse? Knowing the Allheart gang, they would probably laugh and say "Go for it!"

Go for what? Dana wondered. What could she possibly go for with this man? The next day was the last day of the workshop. After the morning discussion group, the students would be packing their things and heading back to the real world. Except for Tamara, of course, who had decided once and for all to join the "school" at the Gardens of Oak Creek. From now on she would be the one milking Sheila and playing with baby porkers. For one Twilight Zone sort of moment, Dana actually envied her.

"All right," Dana conceded as she and Kieran walked back toward the hotel. "I admit it. Being with the goats and piggies and other beasties does put a person in a more peaceful frame of mind."

"Animals react to people on a very basic level," Kieran told her. "Therefore when we're with them, we regard ourselves and the world on a more basic level. Sometimes such a viewpoint can help us remember what is important in this life."

"You keep talking around that question," Dana said irritably. "What *is* important in life, according to Kieran?"

"What is important in life according to Kieran is not

really relevant to Dana Boyle. She must discover what is important in life according to Dana."

She pouted. "It would be easier if someone like you would just tell me."

He chuckled warmly. "I know."

That evening, in celebration of their last night together, the workshop left the cloistered peace of the Gardens of Oak Creek and celebrated at the Cowboy Club in Sedona. For the occasion, Dana slipped into sleek Gucci pants and a ruffled jacket in eye-catching red. She loved to wear colors that the fashion mavens put off-limits for a redhead. Ralph Lauren Romance cologne, Charles David slingbacks with three-inch heels and a touch-up to her Maybelline Reckless Red nails completed the ensemble.

Sedona might lean toward cowboy boots and chaps, but four days in jeans was quite enough for Dana. She was accustomed to looking like a woman.

"Wow!" was all Tamara had to say when they were ready to leave. "Very uptown!"

Tamara, with her crystals and incense, probably didn't know uptown from out to lunch, but Dana smiled and thanked her anyway. She really was feeling like the Dana of old.

They filled a table for ten—the workshop students, the Master himself and three of the Gardens' full-time devotees who had decided to indulge in a night on the town. They cleaned up rather well, Dana noted. Not a whiff of goat among them.

Kieran cleaned up well also. Not that he needed cleaning up. He was a head-turner in worn jeans and his guru tunic. But tonight, in tan Dockers and white polo shirt, he could have passed for business casual. The white of his shirt set off the deep bronze of his skin and gleaming jet of his hair, which for this occasion was neatly tamed and tied into a ponytail at his nape.

The civilized look suited him, Dana decided. She could almost see him working at a real job in a real place—a place like New York City or Washington, DC. Of course, the guru look suited him as well. In fact, she couldn't imagine a look that wouldn't suit him.

Dinner was the equal of anything that one could order in the "big city," though Dana was the only one who ordered the thick steak that the place was famous for. As she watched the others nibble their rabbit food—salads, bean dishes, tofu, eggplant, spinach lasagna pretending to be the real thing, she decided not to be embarrassed about it. Now if she could just find something wonderful and chocolate for dessert. All that health food at the Gardens had her longing to binge.

The celebration didn't end with dessert. The Club had a band—of sorts. They played classics from the fifties and sixties, mostly slow, but that suited Dana just fine when her turn came to dance with Kieran. He was a good dancer, much to her surprise, and they moved together as if they had been made for each other—as dance partners, Dana reminded herself. Only as dance partners. Tomorrow the workshop was over. Goodbye, Kieran. Hello, real world.

"You look . . ." He paused, then gave her a somewhat crooked smile. "I'm trying to find a word that doesn't reduce you to a sex object."

Make me a sex object—pleeeease! Dana laughed at her own reaction. Aloud, she assured him, "There are times a woman enjoys being reduced to a sex object."

Did she see a sudden flare in his eyes? But he moved the conversation toward safer ground.

"Have you enjoyed your stay in Sedona?" he asked.

The question was more than polite conversation, Dana sensed. He really did want to know.

"I did," she admitted. "I didn't expect to, you know."

"I know."

"But now the time has come to leave, I find that I'm not all that eager for the gray skies and dreary cold of the East Coast in January."

"Sedona spoils people for the rest of the world."

As they moved around the dance floor, Kieran's eyes measured her. For what? Dana wondered. Still, she didn't feel at all intimidated. Instead, on this last night in Sedona, she felt a bit daring, even provocative.

"So . . . Kieran." She drawled his name in a manner that inspired one black brow to arch upward. "Here we are at the end of our time together, all friends, and the parting of the ways has come . . ." Her green eyes shot out a challenge. "I think you should tell me your real name."

His grin lobbed the challenge right back at her. "You do, do you?"

"I do. I'll bet it's not Kieran any more than the goat minder is really named Ya-teh-mah."

"What is more real, Dana? An arbitrary name given to us when we first pop into the world, an unformed lump of human potential, or a name we assume once we learn who we truly are?"

"That's guru double-talk, and you know it. You at least have to have a last name. Why don't you want me to know? Is it so lame that you're embarrassed?"

He chuckled. "My name is Kieran."

"That's your whole legal name?"

"Do I need a court to tell me who I am?" He tightened his arm around her waist and executed a few dance steps that claimed her full attention.

Dana laughed. "Nice try, but I'm not distracted. Are you sure your name isn't Fred Astaire?"

"I think that name's already taken."

"Well then, let's see. Maybe it's Walter. Walter Bovnik."

"Nope."

"Sherman?"

He grinned. "Wrong."

"Claude."

"Way off."

"Joe, John, Trevor, Alfred, Caleb, Michael, Kiefer. Jones, Smith, Ford, MacDougal, O'Halloran, McGinty—"

"McGinty?"

"You look Irish. Black Irish."

He laughed. Cripes, but she loved the way the muscles of his throat worked when he laughed.

"You're being stubborn. Stubbornness is a very unenlightened trait. Maybe you should meditate on it."

"You're very nosy, you know that?"

"It comes with being female." She grinned up at him. "And don't tell me I should meditate on it. It's an integral part of who I am."

"Joshua," he said unexpectedly. "Joshua Gellis."

For some reason, Dana felt as if she'd been afforded a peek into his private soul, "Joshua. For real?"

"That's it."

"Joshua is a wonderful name. Where did you come up with Kieran?"

"Kieran is my grandfather's name. Kieran Tolleson. During World War II he lived in Norway and helped many people to escape the Nazis. In my eyes, he was a great hero against something very evil. I took his name as a baptismal name, to honor him, to try to give myself something to live up to."

"So Kieran is your real name after all."

"Any name you take for yourself, because it is a part of you, that is a real name. I have always been Kieran more than I have been Joshua Gellis."

In spite of the fact that Kieran danced with all the women students, Dana felt somehow that she had gotten special attention. The thought gave her a warm feeling as well as a tingly case of the nerves. A peculiar excitement suffused her. Something was about to happen. She told herself sternly that this was an end, not a beginning, but her instincts denied it.

So when Kieran took her arm as they piled out of the van back at the Gardens, Dana was almost expecting it. He guided her toward the garden, where the sound of rippling water made the night seem very peaceful. The few buildings around them were mostly dark, but the sky was alight with stars. The dry, clear air made them gleam like a million shards of crystal strewn across a black velvet sky.

"Dana," Kieran asked her, "do you feel that you've fulfilled your time here? That you've done everything you were meant to do in this place?"

If that wasn't a loaded question then she'd never heard one. "What do you mean?"

"I mean . . . uh . . ."

Dana didn't think she'd ever heard the articulate Kieran at a loss for words. His tongue wasn't tied for long, however. He seemed to straighten his spine just a bit.

"What I mean is this. If you have time to stay for another couple of days, I could show you some places in this area that might have some meaning for you."

For a moment Dana forgot to breathe, so hard was she trying to read the thoughts behind Kieran's invitation. Then she decided to simply be honest. Kieran wasn't a man who played games.

"You want me to stay?"

A pause, then, "Yes. I do."

"Who wants me to stay? Master guru Kieran, or Joshua Gellis?"

"Both," he replied without hesitation.

The Allheart offices opened for business again January 2, and today was December 30, but Dana remembered Elyssa's invitation to take all the time she needed. And she needed this, Dana decided. Maybe she needed what more Kieran could show her, or maybe she just needed the man himself. She wanted to find out.

"I'll stay," she said simply.

The smile that curved those sculpted lips was not Kieran's guru smile, Dana realized. It was a smile just for her. A frisson of anticipation ruffled her nerves clear down to her toes.

Dana didn't feel quite so cocky the next morning at seven o'clock when the rude ring of the phone jerked her from sleep. Tamara had moved into the school dormitories and was no longer there to wake her with gushings about the sunrise. Dana fumbled for the phone with a grunt.

"Are you ready?" Kieran's voice queried.

"Wha—? Whatimeizit?"

"Seven. We have a full day planned. Get up, Grasshopper."

She groaned.

His chuckle was rich and deep, and suddenly Dana did want to get up and meet the day.

"Unnnnh! All right, all right, Jiminy Cricket. I'll be down."

Kieran met her in the lobby with a cup of hot coffee and a granola bar, which he didn't give her time to eat. She did

manage to gulp it down in the little green four-wheel-drive
Jeep that he claimed could go anywhere and do anything.

"Are we going driving in the Outback?" Dana asked du-
biously.

"No. But this thing is fun to drive. The places we're going today are spiritual places, not tourist traps. I want you
to look at these places and think about what is happening
there."

Most of what Dana wanted to look at was sitting in the
driver's seat.

"The Native American peoples who lived in this area regarded this country as holy land, and they had good reason.
Good things happen here. People come here to change their
lives." He gave her a knowing look. "And usually they find
what they seek."

What was she seeking with Kieran? Dana asked herself.
She didn't really know the answer.

First they drove to the mouth of Boynton Canyon and
parked at a well-used trailhead. A resort blocked the very
mouth of the canyon, but beyond the resort Dana could see
a hint of high rock ledges crowded with pine and juniper.

"One of Sedona's famous vortices lives here," Kieran said
with a slight smile.

A vortex, Sedona style, was a hypothetical well of spiritual energy, catalyst for spiritual growth and enlightenment.
Hikers in Boynton Canyon had reported floating above the
ground, all sorts of psychic phenomena, and one woman had
even told of having the bottoms of her feet burned by the
vortex energy when she dangled them over the edge of a rock
ledge.

"I think those hikers may have been drinking something
other than H_2O," was Dana's wry comment.

Kieran merely smiled.

Next they visited the Chapel of the Holy Cross, built in the 1950s as a place for people of all faiths to seek God. Abutting a massive cliff, the simple little chapel with its huge stone cross was a powerful place, Dana had to admit. As they exited the chapel, Kieran told her it was built at the intersection of three of Sedona's vortices. "For whatever reason," he said, "the place has a primal energy. Close your eyes and feel it."

Dana obligingly closed her eyes. As she swayed in her own personal darkness, Kieran's hands landed on her shoulders to steady her. There was energy in the place, all right.

"The energy I feel comes from you," she admitted, and opened her eyes to be caught in the depths of his.

"There's nothing wrong with that," he said with an enigmatic smile. "We are all of us channels for the energy of the universe."

"The universe gets personal, eh?"

"Sometimes very personal."

They drove the short distance to the Village of Oak Creek, a bustling little town that guarded the entrance to red rock country. Bell Rock, another vortex site, hovered over the town.

"The Native Americans call Bell Rock the Home of the Eagle," Kieran told her. "It's a very masculine vortex."

"Does it watch football every Sunday and go out drinking with the boys?"

He laughed. "I like you. I live among too many people who are afraid of irreverence. You're a breath of fresh air, Dana."

"You approve of irreverence?"

"Sometimes. It's as necessary to life as laughter."

"I thought you believed in all this stuff!"

"I believe in some of it. Some of it is pure claptrap."

She had to laugh. "Which part is claptrap?"

"You have to decide that for yourself."

"You're no help!"

He just smiled. "No one knows the whole truth of the universe, but I wanted you to see this beautiful world, Dana, so when you're back in your own world you can draw it from your memory and feel some of the peace that most of us find here."

She felt no urge to scoff. "Kieran, you are . . . you are a very nice, sincere man."

For a moment his eyes seemed to look straight into her soul. Then he broke the spell with a boyish grin. "Aren't I?"

In the Village of Oak Creek they stopped for lunch at the Wild Toucan. The weather was warm enough to eat on the patio that looked out on a golf course where the duffers "braved" the sixty-degree weather to play their eighteen holes.

"The place we're going to see next has been painted at least a thousand times. It is the home of a feminine vortex, nurturing, creative—"

"Shops at Lord and Taylor's and wears three-inch heels."

He grinned. "It's a special place. You'll see."

It was also a very high place. "The Mother of the Red Rocks," this one was called by the peoples native to this land. The white man had named it Cathedral Rock. It towered above Oak Creek in a scene of such spectacular beauty that no camera or painting, Dana mused, would ever capture it. She was a bit less appreciative of the stately landmark, however, when they began to climb. And climb, and climb, and climb. Only determination to appear competent in Kieran's eyes enabled Dana to make it to the end of the trail, where steep hill became sheer, vertical rock. They could go no farther, thank God!

"Sit," Kieran commanded. "Catch your breath, then look around you."

He wasn't even breathing hard, Dana noted resentfully. He could probably climb to the top of the Washington Monument without stopping for a breath.

He sat down close beside her, so close their shoulders touched. A fluttery sense of joy made Dana go soft inside. She liked to think of herself as a hard-boiled woman of the world, an unsentimental sophisticate who wasn't easily fooled or impressed. But right then, with this man beside her and some of Mother Nature's most stunning artwork spread before her, Dana felt positively teary-eyed. She didn't even know what brought on the tears. Uncontrolled emotion boiled up from somewhere inside her, where it had hidden for a long, long time.

She turned her face away, not wanting Kieran to see the tears. But his hand landed comfortingly on the back of her neck and kneaded.

"The Mother of the Red Rocks affects many people this way, Dana. She shows us the splendor of the world, and in comparison, our own lives look very small."

Dana shook her head. "You can't really believe all this nonsense."

He nodded obliquely. "I believe the spirit behind it. I believe the things that feel right to me, and I know that this place is special."

"I love my life. There's nothing wrong with my life. This isn't the real world—sitting on a mountaintop and ohhhhing and ahhhhing over Mother Nature. You have no idea how irrelevant this is to the real world. My world." She suddenly sounded defensive and sullen, even to herself.

His hand kept kneading, stroking, comforting. Working

up a good fit of indignation and scorn was tough with him touching her in such a way.

"I lived most of my life in New York City," Kieran told her. "I was a partner in a very successful law firm. Entertainment law, mostly. Actors, dancers, singers. Lawyering a few multimillion dollar lawsuits for the stars of stage and screen can make an attorney very wealthy."

Dana's mouth nearly fell open. She tried to picture Kieran in a three-piece suit. It didn't work.

He went on, sounding as if he spoke about someone else. "I worked sixteen-hour days, six days a week. Drove a Ferrari. Had a town house with a harbor view." He chuckled. "Dated only the hottest women."

"Part of the jet set." Dana was impressed in spite of herself. "What happened?"

His eyes were dark and serious, lost in the past. "I drank too much, slept with too many women, had a good start on an ulcer, and my blood pressure could have launched the space shuttle. Then I came here on vacation, here to this very spot. And something here told me my life was bogus, that there was something more important for me to do."

"So you gave it all up?"

He laughed. "Oh no. I was troubled, but not stupid. I sold out my partnership and came away with around five million. Then I went on a search for what I was supposed to do."

"And this is it?"

"This is it," he said with certainty. "I studied yoga, meditation, religion, philosophy and everything from the Koran to the Bible. It occurred to me that similar searchers without my resources needed a peaceful place where they could study."

"The Gardens of Oak Creek."

"It's a special place, I hope. I wish I could spend more

time there, but lately I've been making tracks from one end of the country to the other, lecturing, giving classes."

"But you live here."

"Sometimes. I have a house in New England where I spend a lot of time also. I like the sea. But, the point is, sometimes the lives we make for ourselves are not what we need, and even though it can be frightening to take an honest look at ourselves and where we are in life, the result can often bring happiness."

Dana shook her head. "This is like another world to me. Another planet even, nice to visit, but not . . . not me. Yet when I think of going back to Washington and falling into the same old routine—work, clubs, dating . . . yuck. I'm not like you were. I don't drink too much, my blood pressure is perfect and I certainly don't have an ulcer. But everything in my life is shallow, on the surface. My relationships last—well, two weeks is some kind of a record."

"Maybe that's because you don't know yourself and don't truly know what you're looking for."

"I can tell you're leading up to an advertisement for meditation."

"You need to wipe the slate clean, Dana. Go back to the beginning and start new and pure. Present yourself virgin to the universe and then see what fits and what doesn't."

She laughed loud enough for the rocks to laugh with her, an echo of her own rather cynical merriment. "Oh, Kieran— present myself virgin to the universe? Believe me, that ship has sailed! And I don't think it's coming back." In spite of her attempt at insouciance, she blushed.

He didn't laugh with her. "The physical doesn't matter, Dana."

That was news! Dana thought. For most guys, the physical was all.

"A mating without spiritual joining"—he touched a finger to the center of her forehead, and then to her heart—"here, and here, is no mating at all. You must find the spiritual virginity which you probably never lost, then keep yourself pure for a man who is truly the other half of your soul. Then you will be able to recognize the right man when you meet him."

She wanted to joke in the face of his seriousness. She wanted to make a smart crack like "But superficial sex is so much fun!" But she looked into the deep pools of his eyes and kept her mouth shut.

"If a meaningful relationship is what will make your life right, Dana, then that is what you must do. When the right mate comes along, he will touch your spirit, your soul, your heart and body, and beneath his loving hand, you will be touched for the very first time."

Back in her room, Dana tried to be cavalier, tried to pretend that her senses weren't stunned and her body wasn't on fire with longing for something she couldn't have. She groaned as she pulled off her sweater and peeled off her jeans, the very jeans that Kieran had claimed were too tight. Jeans were supposed to be tight, she thought resentfully. They were supposed to show off her long dancer's legs and sleek hips, but apparently he wasn't impressed, with all his stupid talk of spiritual virginity. Virginity, my foot! she scoffed. What world did he live in, anyway?

Maybe a better world than hers, the honest part of her whispered. *Face it. You're disappointed that he didn't put the moves on you. You've fallen for the guy. Head over heels. Positively panting. You are so not smart!*

I could care less, she tried to tell herself.

Are you kidding? You've been drooling like a dog whenever you see the guy. So obvious.

I'll forget him once I get back home, Dana comforted herself. He won't be a blip on my memory.

The agony of taking off her shoes cut short her discussion with herself. Nikes really weren't meant for climbing mountains. And her legs and back weren't taking the activity too well, either. She ached in places she'd never ached before. The hotel spa seemed the logical solution.

Ten minutes later found her lying naked beneath a sheet on a massage table, with a cheerful masseuse kneading her sore legs and lubricating her abused muscles with oil of arnica. Dana felt herself drifting into fantasy, wishing, wishing, wishing . . . Then a deep voice invaded her dream.

"Good evening, Judy. I see my friend Dana was wise enough to seek your healing touch."

"Kieran! My brother in Atlanta says hello. Says your talk there really made him think. Anyone who can make my brother think is a miracle worker. The slave driver CEO of his company heard you, too, and he's even thinking of coming out for a workshop."

"I'm glad. I enjoyed meeting your brother. I will take over here. Why don't you take the rest of the evening off."

"Thanks! Dana, you don't mind if Kieran takes over, do you? He's a certified therapist, and he's great with abused muscles."

Dana mumbled something that must have been assent as she realized Kieran's voice was real, not a dream.

And then his big hands, warm and soft with oil, were upon her.

Chapter 4

$\mathcal{S}$*ometimes a woman's body simply rages out of control,* and for Dana, tonight was one of those times. Not a single muscle listened when she told her sore body to get off that massage table, bid Kieran a chaste good night and march up to her room. He was the wise guy who told her she should reclaim her virginity. He was the one who advised her to reserve herself for that once-in-a-lifetime special man who would be the magical Right One.

Well, a newly born-again virgin definitely shouldn't allow a sexy guru turned masseur to knead her bare body into a rapturous, incoherent collection of muscles and nerves that were far along the road to pure ecstasy. Who would have thought that mere fingers and hands, touching nothing more sensual than her neck and back, could fan such a flame inside her at the same time they turned her to jelly.

She should definitely get up and leave. Very definitely.

But there were problems with getting up. For one thing, she was totally naked beneath the sheet. Not that Dana was a prude about her body. Far from it. But the words Kieran had spoken high up on Cathedral Rock had fallen on fertile ground, making Dana take stock of herself and her future. She wasn't anxious to reveal all her stripes to the man who told her to bridle her inner tigress. Born-again virginity aside, if Kieran took in her charms and showed the least spark of desire, she was going to be all over him like a cat on a heap of catnip. Some things were simply irresistible.

Another problem was that her physical self had firmly separated itself from any high-minded resolve of her mind. Every muscle had been seduced into bliss; her nerves caroled the "Hallelujah" chorus. Even her mind was fast sinking into a state of animal pleasure.

Back in the real world, Dana occasionally indulged in a therapeutic massage to relieve stress, but none had been quite so therapeutic as this one.

Kieran's voice rumbled above her. "Is this doing the job?"

If he only knew.

"Tell me if I hurt you. Sometimes I go too deep."

All Dana could do was sigh in delight as his thumbs blazed a road on either side of her spine and his fingers spread warmly over her ribs. The sheet now barely covered her backside, but she forgot the issue of nakedness, forgot everything but the feel of Kieran's strong, supple hands coaxing the soreness from her back. He traced a line of tenderness down her buttocks, pausing at every tangle of painful nerves, penetrating the pain with gentleness and warmth.

"Breathe into the pain," he advised her softly. "Soon it will be gone."

He promised truly. Everywhere he touched surrendered and relaxed.

Born-again virgin, Dana reminded herself. Her body simply snickered.

Kieran next worked the muscles in her neck, traveling them to the knot at the back of her head where she was always sore and stiff. His touch sent waves of something very like orgasm from her head to her toes.

"Ah! You store all your worries here, Dana? Right here?" He challenged a muscle that screamed only briefly before capitulating in quivering ecstasy. His fingers then worked their magic on her scalp, tangling into her hair, caressing in slow, rhythmic circles that made her want to gasp with pleasure.

"Oh, don't stop," she practically begged when his hands left her.

He chuckled. "We aren't even close to stopping. I want you to turn over."

At that point she would have stood on her head if he'd asked. She didn't even worry about the sheet as she flipped over on her back, but he conscientiously kept her covered. Was the Enlightened One having a bit of trouble respecting her newborn virgin state? Dana wondered. Served him right. Then she stopped thinking when his hands went to work once again—on her scalp, then gently on her face, at pressure points she didn't even know she had. Her arms and hands surrendered next. Each one of her fingers seemed to sigh with delight. Her palms tingled to his touch. When the master turned his attention to her legs, the calf muscles turned to warm putty, and tired thighs yielded their knots one by one. Then there were her poor abused feet. Kieran laved warm, fragrant oil onto his hands before gently kneading her heels, instep, and each individual toe. Dana felt the heat of his attention through her whole body.

"Do you know that almost every system in your body has a reflex point in the foot?"

Dana could well believe it. The particular physical system that was responding most had nothing to do with her feet, but it certainly had a trigger point there. But the slow, lazy burn of desire was muffled in a cocoon of relaxation and well-being. Dana felt as though she were floating on wonderfully warm clouds, limp as a silken doll. Pampered. Coddled. Even loved.

"Let go," was Kieran's soft advice. "Let your body go, Dana. Here you're safe. No troubles can find you."

In her state of half awareness, Dana believed him. Kieran would protect her. Kieran would never hurt her, never let her be hurt.

With his hands still upon her, Dana drifted into sleep.

Reality is stubborn. It can be pushed aside for short periods of time—moments or sometimes days—but it inevitably snaps back into place. For Dana that happened somewhere over Kansas. Or maybe Oklahoma. Wherever it was, the land was very flat. State boundaries were hard to see from thirty thousand feet in the air.

She had awakened that same morning in her hotel room, in spite of her last waking memory being on a massage table with Kieran performing sorcery on her toes. She didn't remember going to her room because she'd fallen so soundly asleep that Kieran had carried her, sheet and all, to her bed. He had knocked on her door at six A.M. with a reminder that she had a three o'clock flight from Phoenix's Sky Harbor Airport. They had eaten breakfast together, but in silence. Dana was overwhelmed by the sense of a new person liberated inside her, and that new person couldn't quite accept that her time with the Great Guru Kieran, aka sexy, funny, gentle and smart Joshua Gellis, could be over so soon. She'd known him only a few days, yet he seemed a necessary part of her. Her life in Washington, DC, along with its fast-track ambitions, priorities and lifestyles had blurred around the edges.

But as her Boeing 747 flew high over the Midwest, all that had happened in Sedona began to take on the fuzziness of a dream. The temptation to dismiss it all and fall back into her old habits was strong. Her resolves for daily meditation, positive attitudes and more attention to her inner needs could easily be left behind with Sedona's sunshine, except that they were part of what now resided at her center. When she ventured to look inside, she saw him there. Kieran, with his smile, his dark, beckoning eyes, and the twist of wryness that sometimes turned up the corner of his mouth. Those resolves were somehow a promise to him. And that other resolve too—Dana reflected with a certain amount of trepidation. To reclaim and preserve her "spiritual virginity." Unfortunately, that meant shutting the door on certain aspects of her social life. She couldn't very well reclaim any kind of virginity while cutting a swath through the male population of DC.

Could she do it? Did she even want to do it? Dana didn't consider herself promiscuous. She was careful. She was smart. But she enjoyed an active, healthy sex life, if one could consider a dozen failed relationships a healthy sex life. Could she reel herself in and make her self behave?

And really, why should she? It's not like she would see Joshua Gellis—Master Kieran—ever again.

Except that she would. Dana knew she would. There was a connection between her and Kieran. Distance could stretch the connection, but she could go halfway around the world without breaking it. Her certainty didn't make sense, but there it was. Kieran knew it also, maybe better than she, because he believed in such silly things as fate and karma and the universe manipulating individual lives.

That morning they hadn't really said goodbye. He had

played bellman again, carrying her luggage to her little sunshine-yellow Beetle. While she literally vibrated with the tension of his nearness and the prospect of leaving him behind, he had merely smiled his relaxed smile and kissed her chastely on the forehead.

"You'll carry all this with you inside." With a sweep of one arm he encompassed the gardens, the magnificent valley and—Dana was sure—himself as well. "Think on the important things, and they will come to pass."

But he hadn't said goodbye. Neither had she.

"Hello," said a masculine voice.

Dana looked up to see a pleasantly attractive man standing beside her row of seats.

"I notice you have a couple of seats empty. Do you mind if I sit down? My seatmate back in row twenty-five is airsick, and I thought I'd give him some privacy." He grinned engagingly. "Actually, it was either leave or join him in his misery."

"Be my guest."

He sat in the aisle seat. Far enough away from Dana's window seat to be polite, but certainly close enough to start a conversation. "Flying has gotten to be quite a chore in the last few years, hasn't it?"

"I suppose so." Dana gave him minus points for an unimaginative opener, though his initial gambit about the airsick seatmate wasn't bad. He was good looking, with sharp blue eyes and just a few strands of distinguished gray in rich brown hair. A nicely tailored sport coat, chinos and a shirt open at the neck gave him just the right look of nicely dressed combined with relaxed casual. His shoes were either Gucci or a very good imitation.

All in all, the guy oozed success, good taste, and availability. Dana's kind of man. At least, it used to be Dana's kind of man.

"Do you live in the DC area?" he asked.

"Adams-Morgan."

He smiled. "Very trendy place, I've heard. I've been looking into places to live. My company is opening an office in
Arlington, so I'm relocating."

"You'll like Washington," Dana assured him. "Great
nightlife, cultural stuff, lot of sports, especially if you like
baseball."

"Oh yes. I'm a fan."

"Then of course there's the everyday entertainment of political scandal and skullduggery. There's no place like DC
for that sort of thing. Never a dull day." She allowed a certain flirty slant to the smile she gave him, and he responded
by leaning closer.

"You work in politics?"

She laughed. "I'm one of the very few in town who don't.
I work for an Internet greeting card company."

"Really? How interesting. I work for a software design
engineering firm. Mostly business applications."

And from the look of him, he did very well for himself.

"What do you do in your spare time?" he asked.

And on it went, the standard cautious get-to-know-you
conversation, feeling each other out for husbands/wives/
children, boyfriends/girlfriends, likes, dislikes, favorite stage
play, favorite music groups. The point was to eliminate phi-
landerers, geeks, vegetarians, teetotalers, guys who liked
Barry Manilow, fans of foreign art films and anyone who had
ever been kidnapped by aliens. Other strangenesses cropped
up from time to time, but those were the most common.
Dating in the modern world was full of pitfalls.

Dana had the technique down pat, and she played along
without even thinking about it. This sort of thing was second nature to a socially active, attractive single. It was an

art, really. Thrust and parry. Advance and retreat. Find out all you can without seeming too interested, reveal as little as possible without seeming uninterested—just in case the guy was worth dating.

And Mister Software Engineer was certainly worthy of a second look, and maybe a third. He was obviously successful, articulate and well-traveled with a nice laugh and good teeth. And he didn't hide his interest in her. This guy was prime territory. Divorced, no children, hot to trot.

So why did the whole process suddenly seem so dull? Dana had always felt a tingle of excitement at the beginning of a new relationship. The ending generally left her in a blue funk, but beginnings had always been fun. But all she felt as she talked with Mister Software Engineer was a weary sense of boredom. Beside Kieran, this guy seemed colorless, bland, ordinary. He didn't have eyes in which a woman could drown. His smile didn't seem as if he knew everything she was thinking. His clothes and hair didn't suggest a casual independence from the tyrannies of fashion and fad.

She caught herself smiling. The smile was from inside her, where she saw Kieran lift a brow at her thoughts. It definitely wasn't for the vanilla-flavored fellow flapping his jaws at her, but he took it as encouragement.

"If you're not too tired when we get in, maybe we could go somewhere and get a bite. You could fill me in on the best places to look for an apartment."

A week ago she probably would have taken him up on the offer and looked forward to another chance at finding Mr. Right. Now she just wanted Mister Software Engineer to go away. Was this change because of that double-damned notion of reclaiming her virginity, or was the change because she had found Mr. Right? Found him and left him behind in Arizona.

"You know? I'm feeling a little tired. Actually, your mentioning airsickness a while back has made me feel a bit queasy myself. It's an awfully rough ride today, isn't it?"

"Uh, yeah, it is. That's too bad. But listen, Dana, I'll call you in a few days, okay? You're at Heartline, did you say?"

"Allheart.com. We're in the book. Georgetown."

"Georgetown. Great area, I've heard. I'll call you."

"I'll look forward to it. Really. But right now, I think I'm going to close my eyes and try not to throw up."

There was no surer way to discourage a man than threatening to toss your cookies all over him. Dana closed her eyes and tried not to smile as Mr. Software Engineer got up and left.

When the right mate comes along, he will touch your spirit, your soul, your heart and body, and beneath his loving hand, you will be touched for the very first time.

Kieran had ruined her for any other man, it seemed. And he had done the job without even getting her into bed. Dana felt cheated.

Dana's life picked up where it had left off. The Valentine's Day cards were the priority, with Easter, Mother's Day, and Father's Day around the corner. These concerns were in addition to updating the sympathy, friendship, birthday and get-well cards, not to mention several different lines of romantic greetings of varying sensual degree.

Yes, indeed, there was plenty to keep Dana, queen of greeting card copy, busier than a bee at the honey farm. She didn't even have time to be cranky.

Not that she really felt like being cranky. When she'd first walked into the Allheart offices the day after flying back, she had laughed at the look on Robyn's face—caution (an unusual restraint for lively Robyn) mixed with curiosity, both overlaid with an unmistakable desire to run for cover.

"Was I that bad?" Dana had asked Robyn.

"Worse."

"Well, don't lock yourself in the closet. I'm better."

Robyn's pert face broke into a grin. "Was it great? Did you sit cross-legged and chant?"

Alix popped out of her office at the sound of Dana's voice. "More likely they danced naked around a huge bonfire under the full moon. Well, Dana, do you have hairy armpits?"

Robyn's jaw dropped, but Dana just laughed. "My Epilady still has a job."

"Were you attacked by any goats?"

"Almost. I did get to milk one."

Robyn's jaw dropped lower. "Goats? You guys are teasing."

Dana laughed. "No, we're not. If you ever go to one of these seminars, Robyn, check the curriculum first."

"At least you're not such a bitch anymore." Robyn was never one to mince words.

"I'm not a bitch," Dana told them, posturing theatrically. "I'm a tumultuous spirit with shining potential. That's what the guru says."

"Well, I hope that potential is ready to get back to work." Elyssa had stepped out of her office to see what the commotion was. "Welcome back, Dana." The boss's eye probed. She was one of the best probers that Dana knew. You couldn't hide much from Elyssa Wentworth. "How was Arizona?"

Words could not describe. Arizona was warmth, sunshine, cactus, mountains, scarlet sunrises. But what descriptors could she find for The Great Kieran? Deep, dark eyes. Beautiful smile. Quirky humor. Shoulders where a woman could hide her face. Words were lame. Sexy was not nearly strong enough. Sensual didn't quite catch it.

"Arizona was nice." *Speaking of lame.*

"That's all?"

"The seminar was cool. I bought the book. You guys are welcome to borrow it next time you feel bitchy." Her smile was a satisfied "gotcha" as she sauntered off to her office.

The office did lunch out that first day in honor of Dana's "recovery," as they insisted upon calling it. They descended upon Cafemyth.com, the very place where Alix had offered Dana her place at Kieran's workshop. So much water had passed under Dana's bridge that it seemed that day had been in another life.

"The land of concrete and smog is my native habitat."

"Perhaps in this life that is true."

The snippet of conversation with Kieran popped into Dana's mind like a flashcard. There he was, spying on her, commenting on her thoughts. Crazy, offbeat Kieran with his meditation and medicine wheels, multiple lifetimes and karma. He lived in a different world, and she should forget him. So why did he make her itch to board a plane headed back to Arizona? "It's really sick that we spend our lunch break at a cyber café," Robyn complained. "As if we aren't glued to computers most of the day as it is."

"Some of us are glued to computers." Elyssa gave Robyn a salty look. "And some of us spent most of the morning with a nose in this month's issue of *Vogue.*"

Robyn grinned unabashedly. "Some of us work so fast that we have extra time on our hands."

"That'll be the day," Alix chortled.

"I just think that the guy who put computers in a restaurant so you can work while you eat should be staked out on an anthill somewhere. Dana, do they have anthills in Arizona?"

"Probably, though I didn't see any. Lots of cactus. Coyotes that sing at night. Rattlesnakes."

"Rattlesnakes would do," Robyn said with a wicked grin.

"Knowing our Dana," Carole said, "I'm surprised she didn't come home with a cowboy on each arm."

"I didn't meet one cowboy. Although the whole state looks something like a set from an old John Wayne movie."

Alix snickered. "Meet anyone who isn't a cowboy?"

"Like who?"

"Like who!" Carole snorted. "Listen to her! She acts so innocent."

Dana scarcely heard. She wondered what Kieran would think of this place, where the yuppies and workaholics of Georgetown could stay plugged into cyberspace or their office network while they sipped cappuccino and ate the chef's special of the day. Would he say it was a crime that people couldn't shrug out of the work harness even at lunchtime? Would he laugh at the coffee and juice bar in front—painted completely in Revlon Silver Glitter nail enamel—and make some wry remark about how many women had sacrificed their nails for the Cafemyth décor? Would his eyes crinkle with humor at the ridiculous thought? Maybe he would reach for her hand, as he had sometimes during their conversations in the gardens, unknowingly sending a scalding wave of helpless desire through her veins while he explained that all the trendy places and with-it clubs of her world were only the surface of life that had no importance to her inner self? Did he know how fast her inner self came to a boil when she was with him?

"Dana?"

Carole's voice jerked Dana out of her reverie. "Huh?" Carole was looking at her strangely. For that matter, so was everyone else.

"Where were you?"

"What do you mean? I'm right here."

"Oh yeah." Alix snickered.

"She did meet someone!" Robyn crowed. "I knew it! Look at her blush! I never thought I'd see Dana Boyle blush! He must be really something! There's nothing like the right guy to get a girl back into her groove!"

"Oh Robyn, you little twerp, be quiet!"

"See!" Robyn laughed with girlish glee. "She wouldn't be so touchy if I hadn't hit right on."

"I am not touchy! I'm hungry. Where are our sandwiches, anyway?"

"Don't try to change the subject." Elyssa took charge. A certain amount of smugness on the boss's face told Dana that Alix wasn't the only one in the office who had known that Kieran wasn't an ancient graybeard with false teeth and wizened lips. In fact, just looking at Kieran's lips was enough to mesmerize a woman. Dana wished she had kissed him goodbye. How would that sculpted mouth feel upon hers? The tongue that was so honeyed delving into a person's soul—how would it taste on a woman's mouth?

"She's gone absent again," Alix noted.

Dana snapped back to the present. "I have not!"

The whole table laughed.

"It's got to be the guru," Alix said smugly.

"A guru." Robyn giggled. "How weird is that?"

"A very hot guru." Carole snickered.

Dana snapped. "Will you guys quit it? You know nothing about it."

"Then tell us," Elyssa commanded.

"Kieran is nationally known," Dana insisted. "Internationally. He's lectured in Great Britain and Germany. His book has gone through three editions and six printings. This guy is not small potatoes."

"Then it *is* the guru," Elyssa concluded smugly.

Dana groaned. She'd been had.

"Okay," Alix advised. "'Fess up, Dana. Just how hot is this guy? What did I miss?"

"You should know, Miss Nosey. You saw his picture."

"Pictures don't tell all," Carole observed.

"Pictures don't tell diddly," Robyn agreed. She sighed blissfully. "There's a man's voice, scent, the shape of his hands, the way his hair curls around his shirt collar, the shine in his eyes when he looks at you, his voice, the way his jeans hug his butt . . ."

"Goodness!" Carole exclaimed. "Does Steve know you have such a dirty mind?"

Robyn smirked. "He knows."

"Back to Dana's guru . . ." Elyssa directed.

"He's not my guru." *Unfortunately.*

"Not even once?" Alix asked wistfully.

"Talk about dirty minds! I'll have you know this was a very high-minded seminar. We discussed meditation, inner peace, philosophy, spirituality—"

"Sensuality?" Alix interjected.

Dana blushed.

Robyn pounced. "A-ha! Look at her!"

"You guys are cheapening this experience," Dana complained. "Kieran is a very nice-looking man. But there's a lot more to him than good looks."

"Like broad shoulders?" Alix suggested slyly.

"Good pecs?" Robyn asked.

"You people," Dana said haughtily, "have no depth. There's more to a person than what's on the outside. Kieran has a unique understanding of what makes a person tick. He has a talent for making you want to be a better, wiser person. He has an understanding of . . . of life, of what's important and what's not."

Elyssa eyed her knowingly. "You're head over heels, aren't you?"

"Of course not!" Dana denied smoothly. *She wasn't, was she?*

"He doesn't make you the tiniest bit warm?" Alix coaxed.

Heat, indeed! Kieran's massage had left scorch marks. She was surprised she didn't come away with blisters. Yet that kind of burning felt so good.

The women around the table looked at her expectantly. Like hens pecking at a sack of corn, they were not going to give up until Dana spilled out what they wanted. She shrugged in what she hoped was a casual manner.

"He's a hunk. I can't deny that."

"Hoooo!" Robyn caroled.

"And he's a very smart, nice man. Just the tiniest bit strange."

"All right!" Carole grinned. "Tell all."

"There's nothing to tell, really." That was the sad truth. Well, almost the truth. "He treated me the same as any other student." That was a lie.

"Oh, come on!" Alix scoffed.

"Well, maybe we did have a few sparks flying, but we didn't so much as kiss."

"Oh, darn!" Robyn groaned.

"You can cover a lot of territory without kissing," Elyssa observed sagely.

Dana flashed her a look, and Elyssa flashed right back.

"He did something to put that glow in your eyes and make your mind float off on clouds every time it gets a chance."

"It would have been very unethical for him to put the moves on a student," Dana said stiffly.

"Then maybe he'll fly out here to put the moves on you when you're not a student," Robyn said hopefully. Since hooking up again with Steve, the girl was an incurable romantic.

"We could start an office pool," Carole suggested. "How long will it take for Dana's guru to fly east and claim his enraptured love?"

"I like that," Alix said. "Enraptured. Very good."

"I think she is enraptured," Robyn agreed. "Look at the way her face glows whenever someone says his name."

"That's embarrassment," Alix informed her.

"If she's embarrassed when someone says his name, then she's enraptured," Robyn said with a sniff.

"You guys are impossible!" Dana told them. "Here come our sandwiches. Stuff those into your mouths and stop giving me a hard time."

They did. But Dana's high color didn't fade when she tucked into her turkey sandwich. Kieran did travel all the time. He'd told her so himself. Had that been a message that he might, just might, drop by her neck of the woods and give her a call? What would she do if he did?

The image that leapt into Dana's imagination almost made her choke. Robyn didn't have the market cornered on a dirty mind.

Dana's Adams-Morgan sublet was tiny—one small bedroom, a galley kitchen, a closet-sized bathroom, and a dinky living room with a dining alcove crowded by her midget dining table. It was too small for her, but she'd taken it because she loved the neighborhood, a trendy, international-flavored district with plenty of clubs, unique cafés and interesting shops.

Yet on this first day back after her ride in Spaceship Sedona, coming home after work was a letdown. A January wind made the evening seem colder than it was, and the on-set of night was simply a darkening of the gray that had reigned the entire day. The streets were empty. Everyone had taken shelter from the cold. The world seemed very lonely for some reason.

That was wrong, Dana decided as she turned on the lights in her own little apartment. The world wasn't lonely. The world was just fine. Dana was the lonely one. It was her own fault. Robyn had invited her to go to Deep Blue, the club where her heartthrob, Steve, was play-ing the piano, but Dana couldn't face an evening of watch-ing Robyn melt all over Steve. Not that she had anything against Steve. Steve Rood was definitely hot, and he was perfect for flighty, good-hearted Robyn. But watching the two of them mushing over each other would have just re-minded Dana that her own love life was in a state of sus-pension. A couple of days away from Kieran and her inner tigress was already straining at the leash. Poor kitty didn't know exactly where she wanted to go, but she did want to go.

Why was she doing this? Dana wondered as she shrugged out of her Chanel coat and shed her dress, a long-sleeved, scoop-necked, calf-length knit. The dress had cost her a week's paycheck, but it was worth every penny. It made her feel sleek and sexy—not that looking sexy did her any good these days. But it was good to be back in a place where women actually dressed to look like women. Clothes had al-ways been an important part of Dana's life.

Her inner eye caught Kieran tilting his head in her di-rection, gentle admonition in his expression.

"Clothes are very important!" she said to the man who wasn't there. "They have a lot to do with how you feel in-side. So there!"

Hard to believe that jeans and sweaters had been almost her entire fashion statement in Sedona. Scary.

During some of the most important moments of your life you aren't wearing clothes at all.

"Who said that?" Dana demanded of the empty bedroom. The voice had sounded like Kieran's. She was going insane. And even worse, she was thinking about sex again. Sex with Kieran. And it was true, she didn't have a stitch of clothing on in that particular fantasy.

Defiantly, she donned a baggy T-shirt and sweatpants—the most sexless outfit she could devise—poured herself a glass of Chardonnay and settled under the covers of her queen-sized bed with Oprah's latest reading recommendation. The book held her attention for about five minutes, when she decided that Oprah was looking for social edification, not entertainment. Dana's eyes kept wandering off the page to another book sitting on her bedside table. Kieran's book. Opening it would be tantamount to inviting the author to come out and play. Wasn't he already plaguing her enough?

Temptation was too great. She closed her novel and tossed it to the foot of the bed. From the back cover of *Finding Strength in Meditation,* Kieran watched her with knowing eyes.

"Quit bugging me," she warned him. "This is ridiculous."

But she opened to the first chapter and read. Within a few minutes she decided that she should have done the reading when Kieran had assigned it. He had something to say, and he said it very well.

She could almost hear the sound of Kieran's voice, deep, mellow, laughing one moment and contemplative the next. She relived the delicious shiver that had traveled from head to toe the first time he had touched her in the garden, one of his hands pushing her back straight and the other on her stomach, urging her to breathe. An innocent encounter? Or had his heart jumped, too, when he laid his hands upon her?

Dana closed her eyes, wanting suddenly to preserve all those feelings and carve them in the stone of her memory. The massage—how could a man be so sensuously wicked at the same time he refused to trespass beyond a single forbidden boundary. Had Kieran known all the while how his touch scorched its way through to her very soul?

In the dark privacy of her own mind, Dana relived every stroke, every caress. If she could have worked up the courage that night, could they have ended up lovers? Could she have taken his warm, oh-so-skillful hands and guided them beneath the sheet, where the ache of her body had nothing to do with the day's overexertion? Would he have denied her? Could he have resisted? And could anything have come of it other than one night's passion?

Dana grimaced and opened her eyes. One night's passion would have been a start, at least.

"Damn!" she muttered to herself, contemplating a cold shower.

Kieran recommended meditation to calm an agitated mind and body, but what did he know? Every time she tried to find her center through meditation, she found him instead, waiting for her with a slow burn in his dark eyes and a welcoming smile on his sensuous mouth.

Just what would Master Kieran prescribe to cure that?

Chapter 5

The January skies stayed gray for the next week, and Dana found herself actually missing the scarlet sunrises of Sedona, even missing Tamara's warbling praise of them at the time of morning when normal people were barely alive. She wondered how Tamara was doing at the commune, wondered if her old roommate had made the acquaintance of Sheila, the goat that she had milked with Kieran so close at her back. She wondered if Tamara got to see Kieran every day, talk to him, bask in his smile, laugh at his sometimes wry observations about the universe and the people in it.

Or had Kieran left on one of his lecture tours? Would he call her if he ever traveled through DC? Did he ever think of her, dream about her, grow distracted at his work from thoughts of her creeping in upon his mind? Was she insane to fixate on the man? She'd known him for only a handful of days. They hadn't so much as kissed, much less anything heavier. Quite the contrary of trying to maneuver her into bed—which was pretty standard male behavior among the single set—he'd advised her to find her lost purity. Crazy notion! The fact that she'd bought it just showed how badly he knocked about her common sense. Perhaps Kieran handed out that advice because he thought she was a slut. Could he think she was a slut? Maybe she should have given him a piece of her mind when she had the chance.

These thoughts and others kept Dana distracted both at work and at home. Despite cold, dreary weather, lack of a love life and periodic calls from her gloatingly engaged sister, her depression didn't return. How could she be depressed when she was so busy being frustrated? Everything reminded her of Kieran. He lounged in her subconscious, waiting for her to sleep so he could torment her with erotic dreams. How often had they lain together beside a musically rippling Oak Creek, her naked body intimately cradling his, the warm sun beating down upon their bare skin? And just as Kieran started to thoroughly prove he was as good a lover as a talker, Dana always woke up, sensuously entangled with nothing more exciting than her pillow.

During the daytime, Dana's creative inspiration blossomed anew. Innovative copy for the upcoming Valentine's Day cards flooded her mind. But her creativity was a weed growing out of control. Her imagination was equally creative in spinning a web of daydreams and fantasies starring guess who? She couldn't step into the shower, go to bed, drink her morning coffee or fry an egg without thinking about Kieran. Her one evening out with her friends had been a disaster. All those couples happily dancing had nearly reduced her to tears, and Robyn's touchy-feely teasing with Steve Rood made her want to get up and walk out, just because it wasn't Dana Boyle larking about with a man who loved her.

Even worse, Joe Monteigne visited the office during their weekly staff meeting. Joe was the drop-dead gorgeous venture capitalist who, along with his partners, was pouring money into Allheart.com. He was also Elyssa's lover. They were always very properly professional when in the office, but nothing could disguise the warm looks, the smiles, the surreptitious touching of hands that marked them as something more than mere business partners. The small exchanges would only be noticed by someone insanely obsessed with romance and sex—Dana, for instance. Watching them, such a wave of envy choked Dana that she had to plead sick and leave the meeting.

That same night Dana faced herself in the mirror and gave herself a good talking-to.

"What are you?" she asked the face that stared back at her. "Are you a thirteen-year-old with a hot crush?"

No, she was a twenty-seven-year-old with a hot crush. Or maybe it was more than a crush.

"No matter, Dana, you twit. You and Kieran are ships that passed sailing opposite directions, and when you met, he didn't even board you. There are plenty of other ships in the same sea, kiddo, and they're sailing a lot closer to shore than Kieran, with all his talk of meditation and an inner self and born-again virginity. Sheesh!"

That was telling herself!

"So will you just pull yourself together and start living your life again? You are a with-it lady, and with-it ladies don't obsess over men who have no real place in their lives. Dating them is one thing. But you don't daydream, nightdream and wet dream yourself into a tizzy. Got it, girl?"

She got it. She believed it. But could she help it? Dana marched away from the mirror with firm resolve but little hope.

Kieran was too much a fixture in Dana's apartment for Dana to begin her new resolve closeted with him there. His book occupied the bedside table, and she couldn't quite work up the determination to move it. Kieran himself seemed to lounge on her bed. He was in her living room and kitchen as well. The man just wouldn't leave her alone—an invisible stalker. So she decided to begin her new resolve by the most distracting activity a woman can engage in—shopping. In truth, she needed a new outfit or two. Her week in Sedona without hamburgers and liquor had left her a half size smaller. Besides, there was absolutely nothing better for boosting a woman's morale than new clothes.

But even in the mall Kieran walked beside her. She found a Moschino dress and three-inch-heeled sandals that made her look like a *Cosmo* model—almost. But the sandals pinched a bit. And the dress was short enough and snug enough that bending over would definitely be a mistake. Dana couldn't help but smile at the memory of Kieran unsnapping her jeans, telling her that comfort was necessary to peace of mind. Fashion, she reminded herself, wasn't supposed to be comfortable. It was supposed to be chic. These shoes weren't meant to walk in; they were meant to show off sexy legs.

But she didn't buy the ensemble.

The day was Thursday. One day after hump day, and the week was winding down, as much as Elyssa ever allowed it to wind down at Allheart's offices. Dana had been in the office a full hour before even Elyssa came in, working on an idea that had occurred to her in between dreams about the Gardens of Oak Creek.

Elyssa glanced into Dana's office on the way to her own. One graceful brow inched upward. "You *are* in early, Dana. I thought you didn't feel well yesterday."

"I'm better. I'm working on a great new idea."

"Excellent. Are you ready to pitch it? Joe is coming in a bit later. I'm sure he'd like to hear about it, too."

"It's an innovation, E. You and Joe are going to have to keep your corporate minds open."

"I think we can manage that," she said dryly. "Just let me redo my hair bun and find a place for my pitchfork."

"I didn't mean you were stodgy." Dana laughed as she grabbed her coffee cup and headed for the pot in the reception area. "But this idea is out there a bit. In a nice way."

"Whoa!" Elyssa whistled. "So is what you're wearing. New?"

"Went shopping last night."

"That's sort of a departure for you, isn't it?"

Robyn walked through the front door, fifteen minutes late. It was earlier than she usually showed up. Sweet satisfaction with Steve hadn't ended her ongoing morning battle with the alarm clock.

"Hey, Dana! Great outfit! New look!"

By now Dana was beginning to feel self-conscious. "It's not that different. I was shopping last night."

"It *is* different." Alix stepped out of her office to join the conversation. "You're usually all sleek and slinky. But I like the flowing trousers and drapey jacket. Very feminine."

"Very now!" Robyn gushed.

"Kieran thinks confining clothes stifle creativity," Dana admitted.

Robyn snickered. "I've heard of tight Jockey shorts stifling a man's creativity."

"Not that kind of creativity, you twit."

"Trust Robyn to bring the conversation back to animal basics." Alix laughed.

Elyssa cleared her throat meaningfully. "I hate to break

up this little fashion confab, but all this talk of creativity reminds me of work. Lovely as it is to huddle around the coffee machine and admire Dana's new look, we do have a
business to run."

Robyn rolled her eyes, but promptly assumed a meek demeanor before Elyssa caught her. Alix filled her tankard-size
cup and headed back to her office, and Elyssa raised a finger
for Dana's attention.

"Carole's going to be in late this morning. She has a
dentist appointment. When she comes in, why don't all of
us get together, along with Joe, and you can pitch this new
idea of yours. Are you ready?"

"I can present the basic concept."

"Good. You might even get with Alix and see if she has
any ideas for graphics that might go along with what you
have. You know these moneymen. When it comes to the
creative stuff, sometimes you have to hit them over the head
with four-color glossy."

"You got it."

Elyssa turned for her office, but over her shoulder she
threw Dana a smile. "And I really do like the new look,
Dana, even if it was a fellow in a guru toga who gave you the
idea."

"Kieran doesn't wear a toga!" Dana said to Elyssa's disap-
pearing back.

Elyssa waggled her hand in a dismissive wave. "Whatever."

Dana pulled a face. She heard the snicker in Elyssa's
voice. The good-hearted razzing would never end. At least
not until something more interesting came along to divert
her friends' attention. They would get a good laugh out of
the new line of cards Dana was going to propose.

As it turned out, the staff did get a good laugh, and Joe

Monteigne's brows shot so high they almost disappeared into his hairline. But Elyssa, always the businesswoman, took a serious look at Dana's proposal after joining the others in a round of chuckles.

"You may have something here, Dana. This New Age stuff may be bunk, but it has caught on in quite a few places. In California it's huge, I understand."

"In California," Carole said, "every crazy thing is huge."

"Not just in California," Dana told them. "I have a friend who lives in the Chicago area, and just down the street from her is a shop that sells crystals, pendulums, incense and books on everything from reincarnation to finding your spirit guide."

"I like this line," Alix joined in. "It's cute. *I'll show you my soul if you'll show me yours.* We were picturing maybe the old-fashioned shot of two kids looking shy but sidling up to each other."

Elyssa tapped her finger on the proposal Dana had handed out. "This is nice. *May the peace of the universe give you comfort in your time of need.* This New Age copy could not only be a separate line, but we could incorporate this orientation as an expansion of some of our other lines."

Joe gave a noncommittal "Hmm."

Elyssa flashed him a look. "Don't be an old stodge, Joe. Whether or not you think the New Age movement is bunk, this is a lively, growing market that we haven't tapped."

"Besides," Carole told him, "plenty of respectable people buy into this. High-profile people, too. And several mainstream churches have recognized the legitimacy of some of the New Age–style philosophies. I think there's a possibility of advertising accounts that would be drawn in by this. In some parts of the country, this is big business."

Robyn laughed. "I can picture a banner across the top of

the screen. *Your personal crystal: Don't leave home without it.*"

Alix was becoming enthusiastic. "I like this one: *The energy of Creation shines forth from your eyes.* So romantic. That's a great one, Dana. I could do some wonderful graphics with that."

"Or how about *Join your spirit with mine and live the rest of our lives together.*" Robyn chortled. "Lives. Get it? Lives, plural."

"Sheesh!" Joe groaned.

"Marketing, Joe! Marketing!" Carole reminded him.

"Oh, this is cute!" Now Elyssa was truly getting into the swing of the idea. "*My planet would like to be in your house.* Clever."

Joe shook his head and laughed, bowing to the inevitable. "I know—marketability. Usually I'm the one pushing the bottom line. Tell the truth, Dana: Did this Kieran fellow brainwash you the week you were in that place?"

If he hadn't been so obviously teasing, Dana might have jumped to Kieran's defense. Instead, she teased right back. "There are some around here who might say my brain needed a good washing, Joe."

Everyone at the table laughed. "Hear, hear!" Alix applauded.

"If you ask me," Robyn snickered, "that Kieran could brainwash me any time he wants. His website just put up a really hot photo of him. A real sizzler."

Dana riveted her attention to Robyn. "Kieran has a website?"

"You didn't know?"

"I told you about it," Alix insisted.

"I guess I didn't think anything of it when you told me," Dana said thoughtfully.

"It's cool. Nice design."

Carole slanted Dana a smile. "Apparently Kieran is a nice design, also."

Elyssa stood. "All right, children. This meeting is deteriorating into a hen party, so let's be about our business. Dana, this is an innovative idea, and I think Joe will agree that we should try to develop something along these lines."

Joe conceded with a wry smile. "Those who stand still in business are generally left behind. We do have to take changing ideas into consideration."

"Dana," Elyssa continued, "get with Alix and put together some firm ideas, both for a distinctive new line and possible additions in this direction to our established lines. Especially the sympathy and romance-oriented cards. New Age seems very appropriate there. And Carole, explore the possibility of bringing on board some advertisers that could take advantage of this approach. Call on Robyn for help if you get in a crunch. She could use the experience."

Robyn rolled her eyes. "Like I don't have enough work?"

"What was that, Robyn?" Elyssa drilled her with eyes that were only half amused.

"Me? What? I said I'd welcome the work."

"Is that what it was?"

"It was!"

The others filed out of the conference room, and Carole whispered to Robyn in passing, "Enjoy living on the edge, do we?"

Robyn looked at her watch and sighed. "All everybody around here thinks about is work. God, is it only eleven-thirty?"

Dana wasn't about to let the subject go too far afield. "What is this about Kieran's website?"

Robyn shot her a smug look. "Interested in that, are you?"

"Don't make me get harsh, Robyn."

Robyn feigned terror. "Ooooh! Touchy, touchy. Come with me, Miss Lovelorn, and I'll show you."

"I am not lovelorn!" Dana denied vehemently. But she followed.

Robyn pulled up the website with a speed that showed she'd been to that particular URL plenty of times before. Dana's knees turned to water when Kieran's photo came up on the screen. He wasn't smiling. The photographer had made him look contemplative, wise, sensitive, farseeing— all the things one expected in a nationally acclaimed instructor in meditation and self-healing. He had glossed over the wry humor, the wicked smile, the mischievous glint that sometimes sparkled in his eyes.

"Tell the truth, Dana. Is Kieran really that hot, or did they do a touch-up job on him?"

Dana sighed. "He's really, actually, positively that hot, Robyn. Hotter."

"Whew! A week with him, and I'd come back with some soul-searing smarm, too."

Dana grabbed a pen and Post-it note and wrote down the url. "Robyn, no drooling over this website. This is mine."

"Hey! No fair. This is a public forum."

"Yes it is. If you want Steve to know about the night you got hammered and told us all about your scoring system for bedroom gymnastics. His in particular."

Robyn's eyes grew wide. "You wouldn't. That's treason!"

"That website is mine."

"It's yours. It's definitely yours."

"Very wise."

Time heals all wounds, makes passion fade and sends even the fondest memories into the back of the mind—

supposedly. For Dana, time wasn't working. Two weeks passed. She labored hard at the office. The new Valentine's Day line was a done deal. Her New Age concepts were well along the way to being a reality, thanks to Alix's enthusiastic input and Elyssa's support. Her social life, at least the duller part of it, resumed. She went to Deep Blue with the girls and managed to hide her envy when Steve sat with them between sets. She and Alix spent a Saturday at the Smithsonian Art Museum, one of Dana's favorite kickback spots. She had a halfway civilized phone conversation with her sister discussing the wedding plans—only halfway civilized, because Dana was only human, after all. And she went to the movies with Carole, whose young senator beau was politicking in his home state of Colorado.

But in spite of her best intentions to return to a normal, obsession-free life, Kieran still shadowed her every move, pushed his way into every thought. His website rose to the top of Dana's "favorites" list. She was almost surprised that her home computer hadn't learned to call up that site the moment she launched her web browser. He still waited for her every night in bed, his slow smile promising passion when she came to him in her dreams.

Just as well, Dana reflected more than once, because in her sleep was the only place she found passion. She asked herself severely why she clung to the stupid idea of reclaiming her "virginity." Just who did she think she was saving herself for? The notion that some Mr. Right, her true spiritual and physical mate, would come along and sweep her into his arms was patently ridiculous. She was depriving herself for nothing. Not that she'd met anyone tempting since returning from Arizona. On the contrary. Every man she saw Dana compared to Kieran, even her friends' men.

Joe Monteigne was truly a hunk, but he was too conventional.

Steve Rood was a very sweet guy, but so brooding at times.

Carole's Mitch Evans was a hottie, but a politician. Even a good politician was still a politician.

Dana's own ex-heartthrob, Paul—cripes! What had she ever seen in Paul?

Her sister Lara's fiancé, Dr. William Ringle, was okay, but very stuck on himself.

Jim Tremaine—the guy her mother tried to fix her up with when she'd suffered through a family "engagement celebration" dinner—had long hair the same color as Kieran's, but Jim's looked as if it came out of an upscale styling salon. The wind wouldn't dare to move a single curl.

It was hopeless, Dana finally concluded. The man she wanted might not be Mr. Right, but he had a stranglehold on her desires. She wondered if Kieran had laughed about winding her heart around his little finger, or if that was something he did so naturally that he didn't even think about it.

Then one early morning her world changed. She walked into her office, took off her overcoat, replaced her snow boots with a pair of stylish—but comfortable—Gucci mules. Who knew that Gucci could design a shoe that was comfortable? If you looked hard enough, you could find anything.

A gulp of hot coffee gave her the energy to turn on her computer, and there waiting for her was e-mail from Kieran@sedona.net. Her heart pounding in double time, she rushed to open it. Her hand trembled so on the mouse that she almost opened a note from Elyssa instead.

"Scotch that!" Dana muttered to herself. "Right now, whatever Elyssa wants can wait."

Kieran's note was just like the man who had sent it—open and friendly with an undertone of something deeper. Dana wished she knew exactly what that something deeper was.

I have been thinking about you since you left, he wrote. *I hope the insights you gained here are shedding light on your everyday world.*

Dana smiled. Always the guru.

Remember that happiness comes from what is inside, not from what the world tosses our way from the outside. If you continue to meditate, calming your spirit will become easier with practice. You have too rich a spirit to allow stress to impoverish you.

He thought she had a rich spirit? That was something.

A new workshop started today with eight students, so all the hours of my day belong to others. I need to follow my own advice and reserve time for my own meditation. Physician, heal thyself!

If he needed some comforting strokes, Dana would be only too glad to provide them.

Remember that one of the keys to your happiness is the recapture of the essential innocence that resides within you, Dana. You might be unable to see it. We are frequently blind to qualities in ourselves that others can see very plainly. That is simply the way Nature made us. But I can see an untouched purity about you that is still intact. Find it. Preserve it for the one who will appreciate it. It may be that this one is closer than you know. Life has a way of surprising us.

"There you go again," Dana said to the screen with a sigh. "Just as I was about to decide you're nothing but bunk, you reach across cyberspace and give me a tweak."

"Who are you talking to?" Alix asked from the doorway. "I knocked, but you didn't answer. Have you grown deaf?"

Dana hurried to get Kieran's e-mail off the screen. "Uh . . . no. I'm sorry, Alix. I guess the caffeine hasn't kicked in yet. Can I do something for you?"

"Goodness but you're polite this morning?" Alix arched a suspicious brow. "What are you up to?"

"Me? Nothing! I'm just checking my e-mail. Oops! Here's a note from Elyssa. She wants new instructions written for the send-your-own-message cards. She thinks the current ones aren't clear enough."

"Want to do lunch with me and Marc?"

Dana snorted. "Three's a crowd. Thanks for asking, though. I'm going to have lunch with my computer."

"That sounds exciting." Alix grimaced.

Dana merely smiled. If Alix only knew.

Over the next week Kieran e-mailed her every day. He urged her to take time for herself and assured her that daily meditation would lower both her stress levels and listlessness. He also entertained her with profiles of his workshop students. Of course he didn't reveal anything that would be considered confidential, but his reactions to his current crop of disciples did show how well he understood the human spirit. He was particularly taken with an eighty-one-year-old lady who had raised nine children and outlived two husbands. He related her words, "It's about time I looked for myself after too many years of looking for toys under the beds, cookie crumbs in the couch cushions and dirty dishes in every room in the house." Sometimes, Kieran told Dana, the oldest students are the best listeners, both to him and to themselves. As the body ages, the spirit grows richer.

Dana wondered what Kieran would be like when he was eighty. As far as she was concerned, he was remarkable even now, with just thirty-five years of living under his belt. How strange that among all the men she'd dated, not one had prompted her to speculate what he would be like anytime further in the future than a couple of weeks. Of course, a couple of weeks just about maxed out most of her relationships. That probably explained it.

Dana e-mailed Kieran faithfully, once he had started the correspondence. And if she longed to make the computer keyboard sizzle, she did manage to refrain. Instead, she sent him amusing stories about her cohorts at Allheart, insider perspective on the antics in the nation's capital, news of her wonderfully balanced state of mind. Okay, she lied a bit. Her state of mind was balanced only if one considered sexual obsession to be balanced. Not that she was really obsessed, Dana told herself. She was simply into heavy daydreaming. And night dreaming. And didn't every woman think of sex when she sharpened a pencil or ate a hot dog? Of course she was balanced.

Then came the Friday evening that she had nowhere to go. Every one of the Allheart ladies had weekends planned that started Friday night. Dana's mother had invited her to come home for a weekend in Virginia. She had promised to be there Saturday afternoon to attend her sister's bridal shower. Turning that down would have been too small-minded. But no way was Dana going to spend the whole weekend listening to her sister gloat.

So that Friday evening she curled up beneath the covers of her bed with a romance novel. If she couldn't have a love life of her own, at least she could read about someone else's. Her television chattered away at a low volume, just for company. Lately the silences in her small apartment made her feel lonely. She had always enjoyed living alone. Solitude had never been a problem for her—until she had returned from Sedona.

She was absorbed in a very heavy breathing scene in her book when something on the TV caught her attention. She reached for the remote and turned up the volume. A chirpy

reporter for the ten o'clock local news was talking about upcoming events of interest. Dana could have sworn she'd
heard Kieran's name spoken by someone other than her own
inner voice.

"A noted New Age healer and authority on what he calls
the art of meditation, Kieran's workshops have won praise
from mainstream therapists and counselors as well as the
more esoteric."

Yes! She'd been right. Cripes, to hear this woman talk,
Kieran was some kind of a public icon. A photo of Kieran
flashed onto the screen. He was shown against the backdrop
of Sedona's vermilion castles and cathedrals, but as far as
Dana was concerned, the background scenery didn't hold a
candle to those eyes looking out of the screen at her.

"As part of their program on modern philosophies, the
University of Maryland is sponsoring his two-day seminar
entitled 'Relating Ancient Wisdom to Modern Life.' Less
than one year ago, Kieran was the subject of controversy after NBC's *The Bottom Line* took hidden cameras and micro-
phones into his learning center and resort at the Gardens of
Oak Creek."

How did they dare! The jackasses!

"The controversy was settled in Kieran's favor, however,
when the show's producer admitted that they had no real ba-
sis for stating on their show that the Gardens was another
Guyana waiting to happen. Dr. Thomas Myers, a U of M
professor of psychotherapy and private counselor, claims that
if more people practiced the methods preached by Kieran,
half the country's clinical psychologists would be put out of
business.

"Anyone interested in attending the seminar should call
the U of M Department of . . ."

Dana punched the remote to switch off the set. Kieran was coming to the U of M. He would be within an hour's drive. He was going to be here! Right here! In the flesh! And he hadn't told her.

"Aaaaaagh!" She threw her hapless romance novel against the wall. Her pillow followed it.

Dana's pique lasted all through the weekend. Monday morning she stormed into the Allheart offices fifteen minutes late, lightning and thunder brewing in a dark cloud over her head. She mumbled a greeting to Robyn at the front desk and stalked into her office.

"Uh-oh!" Robyn sighed. "Relapse."

But five minutes later, when a wary Alix stuck her head into Dana's office, she found only sweetness and light.

"I got an e-mail from Kieran!" Dana declared.

"Didn't you say that he e-mails you every day?"

Dana grinned. "True. But this e-mail says he's coming to the DC area, and he wants to see me. He'll be here on Friday!" She practically sang the last few words.

"And this is the guy that you're not, positively not, hooked on?"

"I lied." Dana was unabashed as she danced around her office. But after a few pirouettes, she hedged. "Not positively hooked. No." Her mouth twitched upward in the beginning of a wicked smile.

"Not in love?" Alix teased.

"In lust? Does that count?"

"Can you tell the difference?"

She pirouetted to the door, singing, "Of course I can!"

As she danced down the hallway, Elyssa and Carole

stuck heads from their offices to view the commotion.

"What happened?" Elyssa inquired dryly. "Is the war over?"

"I'm in heaaaa-ven!" Dana sang.

"She's flipped her cork," Carole concluded.

"My ridiculous virginity is about to come to an end!" Dana announced to the Allheart crew.

Robyn's snicker was pure disbelief. "You're not a virgin!"

Dana postured. "I have reclaimed my spiritual purity and I am ready to surrender it. You see before you a genuine born-again virgin."

"Call 9-1-1," Carole advised.

"That man is not going to know what hit him," Dana crowed.

"Who?" Robyn asked.

"My guess would be a certain sexy guru from out west," Elyssa said with a smile. "You better be careful, my young friend. These guys are used to this sort of adoration . . ."

"I don't think he's that sort, E. He's so present, so real . . ." Dana's voice trailed off blissfully.

"Oooh! He's coming here." Robyn squealed like an excited teenager. "You will bring him here, won't you, Dana? I'm going to wear my new bustier." Her eyes twinkled.

Dana laughed. "I'll beg the Master to grace us with his presence. But . . ." She paused for effect and swept them all with a stern look. "Keep your greedy hands off the man, you guys. My inner tigress is on the prowl, and I'd hate to see any of you get clawed."

Chapter 6

$\mathcal{K}$*ieran called Dana from the airport at 11:30 Friday* morning. He suggested lunch. When Dana's heartbeat slowed enough for her to speak, she offered to pick him up.

"I have a rental car," he told her.

"You do?" she asked stupidly. Her hormones were on overload, and her brain wasn't operating.

He laughed. "There are some of us out west who do know how to drive horseless carriages."

"Oh . . . cripes! I meant . . . I don't know what I meant." She could almost feel his smile through the phone lines. It made her feel better.

"Just tell me how to get to your office. I'll pick you up."

She did, and after her last stupid remark, she didn't dare caution him about DC traffic. The man had been out of Arizona a time or two.

Dana tried to be casual when she announced that the mysterious Kieran was on his way to the Allheart.com offices. She knew her nosy coworkers had pricked their ears at every phone call she'd gotten that morning. Naturally, when noon rolled around, no one left for lunch. They hovered in their offices like vultures awaiting fresh meat. Dana hopped from task to task, accomplishing nothing, nervous as a fourteen-year-old awaiting her first date. On one hand, she was looking forward to seeing her friends' reaction to Kieran. On the other hand, she was afraid they might snicker instead of swoon. Her friends were good-hearted almost to a fault, but they were big-city girls, and they didn't suffer fools without a snicker or two. Dana's memory had built a pedestal for Kieran, but was he really as she remembered? Here in the city would he seem just too freaky? Would he stand out like a sore thumb?

Kieran showed up at Allheart an hour after his phone call. From her office, Dana heard the front door open. She closed her eyes and froze. She heard Robyn's intake of breath all the way in her office.

Her intercom buzzed and Robyn's voice, somewhat shaky, queried. "Dana?"

"Yes?"

"You have a visitor."

This was It. It with a capital I.

Dana's first sight of Kieran almost made her melt. His gleaming dark hair was tamed neatly at his nape. His open-collared, button-down shirt, V-neck cashmere sweater, and dark brown corduroy trousers gave him the look of an amiable, extremely hunky college professor. Dana thought he looked good enough to eat, and the hungry look in Robyn's eyes showed that she seconded that opinion.

Kieran's white, perfect teeth flashed in a smile. "Dana. Hi."

She had to breathe in and out a couple of times before finding her voice. "Hi." Breathe. Breathe. "How was the trip?"

"Smooth."

"Great."

The vultures were circling. Alix had drifted out of her office, coffee cup in hand—as if she were really after coffee. Lame. Carole sauntered down the hall toward the copy machine. Equally lame. Even Elyssa's door was opening.

"I should introduce you to everyone," Dana said with false brightness.

Alix closed in for the kill. "Yes, Dana. Do."

"This is Alix Harris, the creative genius behind our graphics. Carole Titus is advertising. If she can't close on a sale, no one can. Robyn"—Robyn looked about ready to melt into her desk—"is my boss's right hand."

Elyssa strolled out of her office and gave Kieran a smile that could have melted half of Sedona's rock towers.

"And this is the boss herself, the CEO-in-chief," Dana continued. "Elyssa Wentworth, meet Kieran of Sedona."

Elyssa extended her hand. "We're all so happy to meet the man who did so much for Dana."

Kieran didn't seem to mind the four pairs of female eyes dissecting him. Five, counting Dana's. "Dana did all the work herself."

"Well, I can see why she says you're a phenomenon."

Dana clenched her teeth. She had to get him out of there.

"She's got all of us wanting to attend your workshop," Alix purred.

"It would be a pleasure to have each and every one of you."

"The pleasure would be all ours." Carole nearly panted.

"We've got to go!" Dana said desperately. "Or . . . or we won't have time for lunch!" She panicked, suddenly realizing that the circling she-wolves might take that for an invitation. "Uh . . ." Once again, she lost her gift for words. What could she say to keep them at bay?

The Allheart crew took pity on her. Elyssa's smile looked almost sympathetic. "Go to lunch, you two, and have fun. Dana, you've been working awfully hard lately. Why don't you take the afternoon off and show Kieran the local sights. Have you been to DC before, Kieran?"

"Several times, but I've never had my own personal tour guide."

"Then take her," she said breezily, grinning in private mischief at Dana.

Take me! Dana urged him silently. *And I don't mean take me on a tour.*

They lunched, but Dana didn't notice where. They buttoned up their overcoats and walked the canal path not far from the office. It certainly wasn't a spot of tourist interest, but it was a wonderful place for a private talk on a sunny January afternoon.

"This must be quite a change from Sedona," Dana said. *Lame, lame, lame.*

But he bought into it. "It is a change. I get spoiled with warm Sedona days. But change is good every once in a while. Otherwise we stagnate."

"Well, I do occasionally feel the pond scum growing on my brain."

He laughed. "Dana, you are a treasure."

"Am I?"

"You are. You don't really want to drag me around this tourist city, do you?"

"Well . . . no."

"Have you ever been to Nantucket?"

"No."

"Shame on you, living so close to such a beautiful place and never going there. My seminar doesn't begin until Monday, and I planned to spend the weekend at my house on Nantucket. I was hoping you would go with me."

Dana's heart leapt. She would have Kieran all to herself in a beautiful place by the sea. If she couldn't work that to her advantage then she didn't have the right to call herself a real woman. "I'd love to see Nantucket," she said brightly.

After she'd thrown some warm clothes in a suitcase and Kieran had suitably admired the eclectic décor of her tiny apartment, they hopped in Kieran's rental car and drove north.

"I wouldn't have taken you for an antiquer," Kieran told her.

"I wouldn't have taken you for someone who would rent a Mercedes SL 600."

He grinned. "I like the ride, and for a sports car it has a lot of room."

"And I like chintz and polished oak."

"Perhaps there is quite a bit we don't know about each other."

"And here I thought in Sedona that you read minds. Everybody seemed to think that you could."

He laughed, but he didn't deny it.

They drove to the airport, where they easily found passage to Providence, Rhode Island. There they rented a car and drove to Hyannis where they loaded themselves onto the ferry to Nantucket Island. It was the last boat of the evening, and when they arrived on the island it was quite late. A cold fog made ghosts of the wharf and its buildings, and the town itself appeared only in glimpses through the shifting mist, here a shop, there a hotel, here a house that seemed to be plucked from the eighteenth century. In just a few minutes of driving, the town fell behind. The few lights they passed cast mysterious circles of white-shrouded illumination that revealed nothing but the all-enveloping fog.

"Is your house far?" Dana asked.

"Nothing on Nantucket is far. My house is close enough to walk into town, if the spirit moves you, but far enough away for privacy if you want to do nothing but wrap yourself in solitude with the sea."

"Not much sea-watching tonight."

"Even when you can't see it, you can feel it."

That was true. The sea made itself known as a damp, salty tang in the air and a rhythmic surge that was felt more than heard. When they pulled into a long, graveled driveway and stopped, Dana felt the sea very close by. The car's headlights shone on a white garage door surrounded by a gray clapboard garage.

"We're here," Kieran announced.

"So we are." Dana's stomach was doing flip-flops. What now? She felt like a teenager.

Kieran had called ahead to a neighbor, who had turned on the heat in the house and left a light on by the back door. Kieran preceded her through the house, turning on lights as he went. Dana drew a breath in wonder, then smiled in satisfaction. Early American, from the beautifully crafted dining room table to hand-made oak rocking chair in the living room. The floor was hardwood warmed by thick area rugs. One whole side of the living room and dining room was nothing but glass. She ventured a guess that out there lay the sea, even though right then the view was nothing but fog.

Kieran's smile warmed as he noted her appreciation. How she loved his smile, when his eyes crinkled and something deep within him seemed to glow. Deep inside her, a bell chimed. Something that had been simmering in Dana had finally reached a boil. She couldn't afford to let this minute pass.

To hell with born-again virginity.

"Kieran."

"Dana."

"I have a question."

"Do you?" The warmth in his eyes bore witness that something was cooking inside Kieran as well.

"About this reclaimed virginity you advised me to protect . . ."

Was it her imagination that his smile took on a wicked slant?

"Just how do I know the right one who will come along and make it all worthwhile?"

"The soul recognizes its mate," Kieran said gravely.

"You really believe that?"

"Yes."

He had moved forward, and for some reason Dana didn't understand, she stepped back, maintaining the distance between them. But the living room wall brought her up short. Kieran was close enough for Dana to see the gleam in his eye. Her heart pounded, and curiously enough, she found herself just a little bit afraid.

"You really do . . . believe that?"

"I do."

She gathered all her courage. "Do . . . do you recognize me yet?"

He stepped closer still. In the blink of an eye Dana was caged, with a sinewy masculine arm on each side of her. "I recognized you, Dana Boyle, the moment you parked your little yellow Beetle in front of my hotel."

She could scarcely breathe. His face hovered above hers, and she had run out of words. Desire burned hot in the pit of her very being, anticipation thrilled along every nerve and a strangely delicious trepidation added spice to the mix.

"I didn't recognize you then." She heard herself speak as if from a distance, someone else saying the words, not her. "But I do now."

Kieran's mouth lowered to a mere breath from hers. "It's about time you knew me."

"Yes." She breathed him in and took his mouth onto hers. For a moment he barely touched her, lingering to savor that first, sweet contact. Then he gathered her to him and deepened the kiss. She responded, until finally they devoured each other, bodies straining with hunger long left unsatisfied. The sweet ache that had plagued Dana since she had first seen Kieran sharpened and focused into an incandescent need deep inside her. And something else, more powerful still, crystallized in her heart. She wanted to crawl inside the man and never leave, dissolve so that they were truly one. That desire was a steady pressure behind the edginess of passion, a warm background against which burned the white-hot brand of craving.

"Would you like to see my bedroom?" he murmured against her mouth.

Dana laughed at the politely phrased invitation. "Is this the grand tour?"

"We can make it very grand."

In spite of Kieran's light tones, his erection was unmistakable against the soft pliancy of her stomach. "Yes, then, I'm dying to see your bedroom."

Without further ado Kieran picked her up, like a romantic hero of old, and carried her up the stairs. She didn't have time to take in the dark details of his room—just the fact that the bed upon which he laid her was soft and big. Outside the window, the moon played hide-and-seek in the fog, yielding just enough milky light to paint Kieran's strong features in an otherworldly glow. His eyes burned darker than coal, and there was something almost wicked in the intensity of his expression.

He reached down and touched her cheek with one finger. The gentleness of the gesture surprised Dana, because it was at odds with the current of sensual tension crackling between them.

"This is not a fling." His voice was a low whisper.

"No."

With one knee on the mattress, he lowered his mouth to hers, breathing fire into the deepest recess of her being. Urgency gripped her quite suddenly. "Hurry," she begged as they both gasped for breath. "Please hurry."

"Patience," he advised. But he wasn't patient. Straddling her hips, he deftly pulled her sweater over her head and unhooked the front clasp on her silk demi-bra. But he didn't rush to uncover her. Instead, he drank in the moonglow on her curves. Slowly, almost worshipfully he slipped his big hands under the loosened cups until the bra gave way and his warm, hard palms covered her breasts.

Such a current of desire shot through Dana that she bucked beneath his hips.

"Patience," he said again, shaking his head and giving her his perfect, mesmerizing smile. "This first time is very important."

"Please," she hissed through clenched teeth.

He leaned forward and began to nibble her breasts. She bucked again, helpless in the grip of her need.

"Be easy, my love."

Dana thought she was being very easy. That was the point. But by the time he gave each of her breasts his full attention, she was past the point of thought at all. When he unhooked the waist of her slacks and slipped one hand between her legs, she thought she would die of the pure rapture. He fingered her through the silk of her panties, and her world exploded right then and there. She heard a scream without realizing the sound came from her own throat.

Kieran didn't pause in his attention. Before Dana's heart could slow to a normal pace, he planted kisses in a line from between her damp breasts to her navel, then lower. Bit by bit he eased her trousers from her hips and down her legs, until only the silk of her bikini panties stood between them. He kissed her through the silk, then warmed her with his tongue. Dana's heart jumped into her throat. She had to grab the edge of the mattress to keep from floating off the bed. Tantalizing her, he snaked a finger beneath the silk and slipped inside her. She groaned and spread her legs wider as he delved deeper.

"You are perfect, do you know that?" he whispered in her ear.

Once again her world came unglued. When she could once again see straight, an eternity later, he was smiling down at her.

"You are very bad." She sighed.

"Am I?"

"In a very good sort of way."

His teeth flashed in a moonlit grin.

"If you expect me to just lie here and take this, you don't know me as well as you think you do." She pulled him down to her. Laughing, they wrestled, and Dana almost lost herself again from the feel of his fully clothed body entangled with her nakedness. But she held on. No man made Dana Boyle cry uncle without getting some of his own back. Finally, she got him where she wanted him—with a bit of cooperation from her victim. He lay on his back and looked up at her as she straddled his hips with her long, lithe legs spread wide. His eyes surveyed her with obvious appreciation, and she raised a brow at him. "I believe one of us has on too much clothing."

"That wouldn't be you, would it?"

She laughed and reached for his sweater. "Off!" she ordered.

Obligingly, he helped her get rid of first the sweater, then the shirt. His naked chest gleamed, drawing her hands to stroke him, teasing, her fingers playing with his nipples. Beneath her, his erection blossomed.

"Turnabout's fair play." She grinned wickedly.

"You're going to get cheated if you keep that up."

"You want the main event?"

He breathed deeply, struggling for control.

"Maybe you should meditate on it," Dana purred. She raised herself up just enough to unfasten his trousers and allow him to slide free of them. Graceful as a cat, she dismounted him and caught his hand in the act of pushing off his shorts. "Ah-ah! Not yet. As I said, turnabout is—"

"Fair play," he said with a pained sigh. The sigh turned to a groan when she peeled them down slowly, ending with a gentle swipe of her hand.

"Enough!" The laughter in his voice didn't hide the fact that he was dead serious as he took advantage of his vastly superior strength and flipped her on her back.

"Oh no, you cheater!" Dana sprang up and managed to pin him down again, trying to ignore the breathtaking sight of Kieran naked. He looked like a Michelangelo sculpture without so much as a fig leaf to hide his masculine glory. Her effect upon him was truly gratifying. Dizzying, in fact. She wanted him inside her so much she could scarcely breathe.

"Much as I would enjoy torturing you," she groaned, "I just don't think I can deprive myself much longer."

"Thank the universe." As if by magic he produced the necessary packet and allowed her to do the honors. He pulled her down and kissed her, devouring her mouth at the same time he positioned himself to take her. Slowly, languorously, she lowered herself onto his eager erection until her self-control dissolved at the feel of him sliding inside her, stretching her, pushing a scream from the throat. He thrust upward, entering her fully. For a single moment of bliss, they were still, drunk with the sense of two halves finally coming together to make a whole. Then his big hands grasped her hips. He lifted her, then thrust again while forcing her down upon him. She cried out, "Don't stop!"

"Not a chance," he murmured.

Almost without a break in rhythm he turned her so that she was on the mattress and he rode between her legs. Again and again he thrust, his face intense as he tried to prolong their rapture. Finally he gripped her hips firmly, sealed her to him, and as she felt the pulse of his climax, Dana let herself go. Her own release joined with his to spiral them upward to a place that Dana had never before attained. As she drifted close to the clouds, Dana reflected with utter contentment that Kieran had been right. The right man had come at last, touching her spirit, her soul, her heart and body. Beneath his loving and sensuous hand, she had been truly touched for the very first time.

Dana woke to the first gray light of morning and the warmth of Kieran's face on her breast. When she made a little sound of contentment, he looked up and smiled at her.

"Good morning." He shifted so that his erection rested against the place that was already warm and wet for him.

"Good morning." She sighed happily, still half asleep but completely aroused.

She smiled lazily and wound her legs about his hips.

When they had sated themselves, she kept him in the embrace of her long legs. He seemed content to stay there as she drifted happily and warmly back to the comfort of sleep.

When she next woke, pale sunlight was streaming through the bedroom windows, proving that the island did have some sunlit days even in the winter. Kieran was gone. The bed was cold where he had lain. On the foot of the bed lay a fleece robe—extra large, Dana discovered when she wrapped it around her. She hugged it to her, inhaling the faint masculine scent of its owner.

The day was indeed glorious. From the big bedroom window Dana could see Nantucket Sound glistening in the winter sun. In the far distance stood a picturesque lighthouse. It looked like a scene transported straight from the days of whalers and whalebone corsets. Strange, Dana thought, how every time she was with Kieran, the real world seemed to fade away, replaced by something that was far out of the realm of the everyday.

The master of the house was not in the kitchen, where Dana expected to find him. She located him in a downstairs room fitted out with exercise equipment. He was sitting on an exercise pad facing a huge window overlooking the sound. Cross-legged in a yoga position, eyes closed, he was obviously deep in meditation. Yet he smiled when Dana peeked into the room.

"Dana." On Kieran's lips the name was almost a caress.

"Hi." Dana forced a smile. Finding him communing with whomever gurus communed with made her uneasy for some reason.

He opened his eyes, taking in the robe and bare feet with an appreciative chuckle. "I'll bet you're hungry."

"I'm okay."

"Give me fifteen minutes. I'll be up. Raid the fridge if you want."

"Okay."

As she backed out of the room, he sank once again into his semi-trance. Dana thought she heard him softly utter a mantra of some sort.

"Weird," Dana muttered to herself. Why couldn't Kieran be just plain Joshua Gellis? A businessman, maybe. A salesman, a teacher or the lawyer he once was.

Because that's not who he is, her better sense answered. *Don't do this, Dana. You always do this when you find a guy you could get serious about. Don't shoot yourself in the foot.*

Dana found the coffeemaker. She desperately needed caffeine. Sooner than the allotted fifteen minutes, Kieran joined her. He came to where she sat at the kitchen table and massaged her shoulders through the plush robe.

"Good morning, again." The greeting was a caress of his voice. Something inside Dana melted, while something else panicked. The intensity of this man's effect was scary.

"Good morning, yourself." She tried for brightness. "Coffee's ready."

"I can smell it. I think you make better coffee than I do." He poured himself a cup. "But I'll bet I make better eggs Benedict than you do."

"That's a given. I don't make eggs Benedict at all."

"Then you're in for a treat."

It didn't take long for Kieran to sense Dana's uneasiness. Most men would have tried to smooth over any awkwardness by inane chatter or making plans to gad about the island. But Kieran wasn't like other men.

"You're uncomfortable," he commented halfway through breakfast, which was undoubtedly the best eggs Benedict that Dana had ever tasted. His words were not an accusation, nor did they hint at hurt feelings. But they closed the door to escape.

Still, Dana tried to escape. She was the world's leading lady of confrontation avoidance. "I'm not uncomfortable," she lied.

"Dana?"

"What?"

"You and I belong together. We shouldn't spar. There should be no games between us."

"I'm not playing games!" *Don't do this!* a voice inside her whispered. *You are blowing the best thing that's ever come your way.*

He reached across the table and clasped her hand. The physical connection between them strengthened the bond that was already there. Perhaps it was the sheer intensity of their togetherness that panicked her. It had begun in Kieran's Sedona gardens and become irrevocable the night before, when he had indeed touched a part of her that no one else had ever reached. But what about her independence? What about her lifestyle? What about belonging to herself and no one else?

Idiot! the voice inside her warned. *Don't do this!*

"Dana," Kieran said softly. "This was not a light thing we did together. It came from the soul."

Sedona blarney, the devil in Dana urged her to say. She bit back the rude words before they left her mouth.

"You're afraid, Dana. It doesn't take a mind reader to see that in you this morning. But I tell you, love, we are two halves of a whole."

He was just making things worse. Two halves of a whole implied some serious commitment.

"Kieran." Dana took a calming breath. "Joshua." She hoped his non-guru name would rob him of some of the sensual force that still made her want to fall into his arms. It didn't. "Uh . . . last night was fantastic, but you're making too much of it. Really. This two halves of a whole thing isn't something that happens just like that. In fact, in the modern world, the old-fashioned true love thing is like a dinosaur. No one believes in that kind of commitment anymore. Really."

Insane! You're totally insane! What is wrong with you?!?

"You're a wonderful guy," she prattled on. "A wonderful person. A great cook, too. But we're really different. Really, really different people. But, you know, we've only known each other for a couple of weeks."

Lame. Very lame. Why don't you just shoot yourself and get it over with?

"You don't have to be afraid of me, Dana." Gently he brushed back a long tendril of red hair that had fallen in front of her eyes. "You and I have known each other for a very long time," he told her softly. "You can't run from the connection between us. If you try to leave me out of your life, I will still be there."

Dana bit her lower lip. Now this was getting really scary. "You know, Kieran, this has been great. Absolutely great. But I have to be back in the city before this evening. I forgot that I have this really important . . . thing. My sister is getting married, you know. It's . . . that sort of thing."

Bang! Bullet straight to the brain.

"But I know you were planning to spend the weekend here at your house. If you could just take me down to the ferry, I can catch a flight from Hyannis. No trouble. I don't want to spoil your weekend." She smiled weakly. Very weakly. And he gave her a look that was all sympathy and no anger. If he would just be mad at her stupidity, Dana would actually feel better.

"Whatever you like. There are things between us that won't die, Dana, and there are words still left to be said. But we have time. We have all the time in the world." Abruptly he leaned over and touched his mouth to hers. Dana tried to ignore the lightning that shot through her veins. It was just one more reason to withdraw while she could, before she got absolutely too involved with a guy from a truly alternate universe. She was simply doing what she had to do. She was.

Liar! Coward! You're a lifetime member of the Lonely Hearts Club while your younger sister is joining the couples crowd. It's no wonder!

Dana stuffed her carping common sense to the back of her mind, where she couldn't hear its griping. She'd had enough bizarre misery for one day, and the day had scarcely begun.

When Alix and Carole returned to the office from their lunch break the following Monday, they were greeted by a warning from Robyn. "You'd better tiptoe through the hallway, ladies. The Grinch is back."

"What?" Carole asked.

"Ssssh!" Robyn cautioned. "Don't let her hear you. Dana might come out and lop off all our heads."

Alix looked puzzled. "Dana? I thought she was out today with a cold."

"Don't I wish!" Robyn grumbled. "She decided to come in and make our lives miserable this afternoon. Take my word for it. Don't even try to talk to her."

"I thought this problem was solved," Carole complained.

"And I thought she'd be walking on clouds after a

weekend with the studly swami." Alix snickered. "Unless he turned out to be not so studly."

Just then Dana walked out of her office, coffee cup in hand. She gave them a jaundiced look. "You're talking about me, aren't you?"

"Don't you have a cold?" Carole asked.

"I decided to martyr myself and come to work."

"And give the cold to us," Alix said as Dana poured herself a cup of coffee.

"If you don't want my cold, then just stay away from me."

Carole shivered dramatically. "Brrr. I can feel the chill from here. I take it the weekend in Nantucket didn't go too well."

Dana made a rude sound.

Carole regarded her through narrowed eyes. "Was Mr. Perfect a jerk, or did you have your customary panic attack?"

Dana glared at her.

"A panic attack, then. I sense a pattern here, my friend." Carole took Dana's arm and steered her back toward her office. "Alix, we need to have a little talk with our girl, here. Robyn, warn us when Elyssa gets back from lunch."

Robyn pouted. "I want to be in on the talk!"

"You're too young." Carole winked at Robyn as she closed the door.

Dana felt as though she'd traveled back in time to the weeks before Christmas that had been such misery. Now she felt even worse, because for a while she'd been so happy, so complete. Her self-accusations didn't help the situation. They varied with her mood—whether she was in a self-pitying woe-is-me mood or a take-no-prisoners, make-the-world-as-miserable-as-I-am mood. The woe-is-me mantra went something like: *It's all his fault, he pushed me too fast and who would be stupid enough to make that kind of commitment after one night together?* The take-no-prisoners castigation included things like: *It's all my fault, I never should have gone to Nantucket, I never should have slept with him, hell, I never should have even seen him because the real thing could never live up to the fantasies.*

The trouble was, though, that the real thing had exceeded all expectations. Dana had never known sex could be so overwhelming. They had actually made love. Love, not sex. Sex had certainly been an interesting part of it, but what they had done was Make Love, capital M, capital L. And the experience had scared her right out of her wits.

That was the gist of what Carole and Alix had confronted her with her first day back at work. Dana all but threw them from her office, but their words slowly sank in.

About midweek, though, Dana admitted the truth. She'd been scared, and that was the whole problem. Not Kieran's fault. Dana had been stupid. Lusting after Kieran the great master guru was all very well and good when he was pretty much out of reach, but then he'd shown up, big as life and wanting something from her that she was just too much of a scaredy-cat to give.

"Do you want to live like this?" Robyn said to her on a sunshiney Wednesday as she and Dana took a lunchtime walk along the canal path.

"Like what?" Dana snapped.

"Miserable. Afraid. Cranky as my old great-aunt."

"I'm not afraid of anything! Or cranky."

Robyn the serial risk-taker was sometimes much wiser than she seemed. "Yeah. Right. What's wrong with taking a chance? Kieran's not that weird. Lots of perfectly normal people are very into spirituality and all that New Age stuff. From what I could see, Kieran actually seemed pretty normal. And smart." She snickered. "Not to mention a hunk. Take a chance, Dana. You couldn't be any worse off than you are now."

"Oh, thanks!"

"Besides, you're a real pain to have moping around the office."

Not until Friday morning did Dana decide that Robyn was actually right. She didn't want to live her life wondering what might have been if she'd been just a tad braver. The longing to see and touch Kieran was deep in her bones. He was right. She could try to push him out of her life, but he was still there. So she asked Elyssa for the afternoon off.

Elyssa raised a brow. "Is work interfering with your personal life, Dana?"

Dana smiled. "Yes. At the moment."

"And what do you propose to do with a Friday afternoon off?"

"Go to Sedona."

Both of Elyssa's brows shot up. "Do what you need to do. With my blessing."

Dana suspected the staff had a party to celebrate her leaving.

Nothing quite matches Arizona in the depths of night, when the Milky Way sweeps across the sky in a bright swath and glistening stars fill every corner of the dark. It was such a night, moonless but bright with stars, when Dana turned her rented Beetle into the driveway at the Gardens of Oak Creek. Up the hill, the dormitories were dark.

Only a dim light in the empty hotel lobby greeted her as she parked the car.

The night silence was almost absolute when she stepped out of the car. The quiet ripple of Oak Creek and the mournful howl of a distant coyote only made the quiet seem deeper.

Stupid, Dana told herself. *You should have gotten a room in town and driven out in the morning. Did you expect Kieran to be hanging out at midnight, maybe mooning over you? He doesn't even know you're coming.*

Because you were too cowardly to call, she reminded herself.

Then a shadow moved in the garden. Dana started, remembering suddenly that in this part of the world skunks and javelinas often made night raids into people territory. But the shadow was too big to be either of those creatures. In fact, it was a creature about Kieran's size. It emerged from the garden wearing Kieran's face and Kieran's smile, not to mention Kieran's guru tunic.

Words choked in Dana's throat.

"Do you need help with your baggage?" He didn't seem a bit surprised to see her.

Her mind flew back to the first time she'd seen him, and she almost laughed. Only the laugh might have come out sounding hysterical. "I . . . I don't have a reservation."

Kieran smiled. His smile was the warmest thing Dana had ever seen. "You don't need a reservation. You're signed up permanently." He tapped the area of his heart. "Here."

"Oh, Kieran!"

He opened his arms, and she fell into them. Falling, falling, falling, past where she could ever again pick herself up.

"I was so stupid! No, I was scared."

"You are here now. No fears." His mouth came down

upon hers, gently at first, then branding her with a passion that burned all trace of weariness from her bones.

"Can we make this work?" she asked. "With what you do, and what I do, and you traveling so much, and my job in DC, and . . ."

His finger on her lips shushed her. "Nothing in the universe is impossible. The more difficult something is, the more rewards it brings."

She laughed. "I should have known you would say something like a . . . well, like a guru."

He grinned. "Are you in the mood for a reward?" With his hips pressed against hers, his offer was unmistakable.

"Maybe you should meditate on that," she suggested impishly.

"I can do better than that," he whispered into her hair.

And in a secluded nook in the garden, beneath the Sedona stars, he did.

Nothing Between Them

VIVIAN LEIBER

Chapter 1

"It's because you're a fabulous saleswoman," Elyssa said, smiling at Carole over the big stack of papers on her desk. "And, incidentally, because we have a wonderful product."

"But we don't have the right product for Private Bank," Carole whined, knowing she was whining and knowing she shouldn't be whining. She should be happy, should be pleased, should be thrilled to sign the contract on behalf of Allheart.com. Should be looking forward to popping open the champagne bottle cooling in the lunchroom fridge. Should even be a little self-congratulatory on the eve of the biggest sale of her career. Still . . . "I don't see how a secretary from New York sending an e-mail birthday card to her mother-in-law is going to say, 'Gee, I need a reinsurance consultant for my billion-dollar transfer to an offshore bank. I'll use Private Bank, since it's advertising on Allheart's—'"

"We don't know what new products Private Bank is developing," Elyssa interrupted.

"Elyssa, they work exclusively with the international

banking community. They make sure your cash or your bullion doesn't get stolen on its way to the sweetdeal banks in Switzerland, Liechtenstein or the Caymans. They don't *need* to advertise on an Internet greeting-card site!"

"Just sign the contract. You can't save them from bad business decisions. They're a big business, well regarded, competitive. What do you want?"

Carole stood up, pacing back and forth. She paused at the window overlooking the parking lot. Two black stretch limousines huddled at the entrance. The snow was gray and the clouds were gray and maybe—hell, probably—she was just suffering from Seasonal Affective Disorder. January was a horrible stretch of gray—maybe it was affecting her judgment. She should be happy closing this deal.

"I don't know," she admitted wearily. "I don't know. I stayed up all last night thinking there's something wrong with this company contacting me and asking me if we could sell them ad space. It's almost like they've been selling to me and not the other way around."

"Oh, I understand now. I never buy stuff from telemarketers who call me. Lawn treatment, home security, refinancing a mortgage. If they were really successful and good at what they do, they wouldn't have time to call me because they had so much work to do and, furthermore, they wouldn't have to call me because, again, they're so busy their bottom line's doing just fine without me."

Carole stared at her.

"It's like men," Elyssa continued, warming to her topic. "If a man makes it clear that he's interested in something long-term, that he's available and that he's all yours, you lose interest. Which reminds me, I saw you and Mitch in the Lifestyles section of the *Washingtonian*. You were going into a party to promote forest fires."

"It wasn't to promote forest fires," Carole said. "It was to raise money for a scholarship program for western state fire-fighters."

Elyssa waved a manicured hand.

"Whatever. The *Washingtonian* declared you a fashion '*do.*' But you shouldn't wear a dress twice if you're going to be photographed. You wore that thing to the fund-raiser for that guy from Minnesota. Don't be mad. I'm just trying to be helpful. By the way, are you two going to end up at the altar?"

"What?!"

"Judging by your expression, this is the first you've heard of it. The caption read 'There are bells a ringing.' And you've just proved my point. Mitch is available, he's interested in something long-term and . . ."

"We haven't talked about marriage," Carole said, when what she meant was "Mitch talks about marriage but I change the subject."

"Aren't you glad that freedom of the press means freedom of the press to get it wrong?"

"What else did the *Washingtonian* say?"

"It had an article about the Senate debate on the trade bill. In a different section, of course. Could you tell Mitch that I am all for a global economy but that trade agreement will do more to hurt . . ."

"Okay, okay, I have to run," Carole said, and as she opened Elyssa's office door, Robyn stuck her head in.

"Mr. Avers is here to see you," she said.

Elyssa whistled.

"The president of Private Bank?"

"Himself," Carole said.

"That's impressive. I would have thought he'd just send a flunky."

"There are a few of those, too," Robyn said. "I stuck them

in the conference room. You want the champagne in twenty minutes, right?"

"Yes," Elyssa said. "Twenty minutes. I'll stop in for a glass. Carole, you can't stop a company from making a decision you wouldn't necessarily make. It's their decision, not yours. And just remember, you work for Allheart. This contract is going to bring us a lot of money. And if these upgrade proposals are any indication, we could use it."

She splayed her hand across the stack of proposals for technical upgrades to the Allheart systems. The customers were coming—Allheart.com was gaining market share since one of its competitors had gone belly-up—but to service the customers the company needed better, faster, flashier product. The dot-com marketplace was changing rapidly. Company presidents weren't using their calculators to figure out how rich they were. The new calculation on the street was total capitalization divided by daily burn rate, a ratio that revealed the exact date a troubled company would go out of business. Luckily, that wasn't what Elyssa did with her TI-187—so long as Carole did her job.

"Okay, I'll shut up," Carole conceded. "Just let me work through a couple of details with them. T-minus twenty minutes on celebrating."

Elyssa gave her a thumbs-up.

"Carole?" Robyn said when Carole was halfway down the hall.

Carole turned.

"Yeah?"

"Don't wear that dress again."

Carole looked down at the nubby tweed pencil skirt that she had paired up with a featherweight pink chiffon blouse. The matching full-length tweed coat was just now hanging on the back of her desk chair.

"No, no, this is fine. I'm talking about the one in the *Skyline*. It's a great dress, but we've already seen it. I look at that section of the paper to see what the stars are wearing and it's boring to see the same thing twice."

"I'm not a star, Robyn. I wear what's in my closet."

"Maybe you need some kind of clothing allowance for being his girlfriend."

"You mean, from the government?"

Robyn bit her upper lip. And for one terrible moment, Carole thought she might seriously be considering the notion.

"That's a great idea," Robyn said with just the right amount of sarcasm. "It wouldn't be any crazier than some of the government programs I hear about. You might talk to Mitch about it."

"I'll have him sponsor a bill."

As she entered the conference room, John Avers jumped to his feet, nearly upending his chair. He was thinner than the pictures in *BusinessWeek* and *Forbes* suggested and the same article had suggested he was possessed of a certain feline impatience that could have been coke, neurosis or a double-shot espresso venti. He had brought with him three suits—sales wizard Sam Kinnear, an outside counsel, and an assistant. Sam had been in on the negotiations from the initial phone call from Private Bank to the last-minute details pencilled into the contract yesterday afternoon.

"Carole, a pleasure, finally meeting," John said. They shook hands and the other men nodded their hellos. Then John reached behind his briefcase, open on the conference table, and presented her with an abundant bouquet of white roses wrapped in key lime–colored tissue paper. "I can't send a greeting card to thank you for bringing our companies together. Although some of the stuff Sam's been showing me looks great. You do good work. Thanks for bringing this deal to us."

"Thank you, John, they're lovely," Carole said. "But it isn't me who brought us together. It was Sam who made the initial contact."

Sam Kinnear shrugged. "I got a brain wave after reading the article about you in the *Washington Post*," he said.

"You mean the one about cookie recipes?"

He nodded sheepishly. "Yours was the best recipe."

"All those cookie recipes must have raised a lot of money," John said. He rubbed his hands together. "Good cause, good cause. Now, shall we?"

Robyn had slipped into the office to give her three green folders. She took the flowers and Carole said she should make it ten minutes.

"Now, gentlemen, let's turn to page three," she said, sitting down.

The men took their places. John took one folder and flipped it open to the first page of the Allheart.com contract. He pulled out his pen and initialed the margin of the first page.

"We probably should discuss the reinsurance provision," Carole cautioned. "Sam had some concerns about this yesterday."

John shook his head. He had finished initialing each page of the contract and was poised to put his signature on the final page.

"I don't have a problem with it," he said.

"But Sam said the term was unacceptable to your company."

"We've talked it over," Sam said. "We're okay with it."

Carole had been prepared to make concessions, although of course not without a little tussle. At least for show. Now she had the distinct impression she could have asked for John's firstborn and it would be fine. She believed in her product, but Allheart.com was not that valuable to a banking concern. She watched John riffling through the second folder, jotting his initials on every page's margins. The table vibrated—his kneecap banging incessantly against the underside of its surface. John Avers was living proof of that study about fidgeters losing weight much better than calm people—but who'd want to be vibrating like John just to maintain a size 6?

"Must be difficult," he said. "So many demands. Time. Money. No rest in Washington. Need to get away occasionally. Good-looking couple. Camelot all over again. Last gentleman on the floor of the Senate. Wife'd like to meet you and Mitch."

She had trouble following his train of thought, but she felt an uncomfortable shiver as he slapped the second folder shut and issued his invitation.

"This weekend. Our jet will pick you up. Cayman Islands. Little place; we own the island. Our friends from Washington come out. Mitch'll know everyone. Treat our people well."

"Um, are you inviting Mitch and me for the weekend?"

"Absolutely. Last gentleman of the Senate. That's what he's called. Only member of Congress who is liked by both parties. And these days." He glanced at his suits who made the proper Ain't Washington Awful? clucks. "Glad to have him come down. Got a future, he does."

"I don't mix my business with his."

The knee stopped moving. The table stopped vibrating. John's eyes were lizardlike, unblinking and cold.

"In Washington, Ms. Titus, everyone mixes their business."

"I'm from New York," Carole said.

Sam coughed.

"Carole, all John's doing is inviting you and Mitch to his home in the Cayman Islands for the weekend. It's a social invitation. Nothing more. And in the middle of January everyone welcomes a little sunshine. December was rough."

"Yes, but . . ." And then she understood. "Sam, when you made my cookies, weren't you surprised about the ingredients?"

"Uh . . ."

"Most people don't put potato chips in their cookie dough, do they?" Carole asked. "And yet, it's the salt and the starch in the potato chips that really give the cookies their texture. Don't you think?"

"Uh . . ."

"So you read the lifestyle section every week?"

"Uh . . ."

"You've never made cookies in your life, have you, Sam?"

His face turned red.

"Actually, no, but I did read the article that went with it."

"And that's when you got the bright idea of bringing our two companies together."

Five seconds of dead air.

"Yeah," Sam said. "That's it. I read the article. And then decided that, uh, Allheart looked really good for us."

"Lightbulb," John said, the knee bouncing against the bottom of the table. "Like a lightbulb."

She rolled her chair back on its caster balls and punched Mitch's number on the speakerphone.

"What now?" John asked.

"Inviting. Mitch. Cayman," she said.

Two rings and she had Mabel on the line. Mabel pretended

she didn't know who Carole was, but Mabel always did that. Mabel had worked for the Evans family for years and when Mitch brought her out to Washington so she could spend more time with her grandchildren living in Baltimore, Carole wondered if Mitch's mom had warned her to keep Mitch away from wicked older women who weren't good at politics.

Except what she was about to do was phenomenal politics.

And terrible business.

"And your last name again?"

"Mabel. Get him. On the phone. Now," Carole said, annoyed at herself for talking like John Avers. She just hoped his body tics weren't contagious. "Mabel, it's important."

A silence, either of being put on hold, or else one of Mabel's own dead silences.

"Hey, honey, what's up?" Mitch's voice crackled.

"Do you know Private Bank?"

"Yeah. I do. But why?"

"I have the president of the company in my office."

"Hello, Senator," John said.

"Uh, hello," Mitch said. "Carole, why don't you take me off the speaker? I'm having a little trouble hearing you two."

She picked up the receiver.

"Carole, what's going on?"

"He wants to invite us to the Cayman Islands, darling. He'll send his jet to pick us up."

"Absolutely not. That company is in front of my committee fighting legislation that would cut into their onshore business."

"I thought so, honey."

"They have been trying to get face time with me ever

since I got sworn in and frankly, I don't want even want to meet the guy in the elevator. That guy wants to buy me."

"I know, sweetie. I know."

"Carole, he's listening to you, isn't he?"

"Of course."

"Get him out of your office. He's using you to get to me."

"I just figured that out."

"Oh, and Carole, one last thing."

"What?"

"Are you wearing underwear?"

Carole giggled.

"I'll see you tonight."

She hung up the phone. Pushed her chair back to the table, picked up the green folders and ripped one in half just as John howled. Then she ripped up the other one while he sputtered at Sam.

"What the hell?" he screamed, as she finished off the last one.

Sam opened his mouth and closed it as if he were an alarmed fish. His assistant stood up and then crawled under the table to retrieve the pieces of the folder.

"Did you just call me a bitch? Out!" Carole said. She rose up on her heels, standing toe to toe with John. "Out of this office."

"I'll call you a helluva lot worse than bitch! We're talking about a major contract that's going to give you . . ." Funny how he could only string a sentence together when he was furious.

"Out."

She felt Sam's assistant crawling around on the floor at her feet, trying to put together the pages of the contracts.

"All I'm asking . . ."

"Out."

". . . is a simple favor. A meeting. With the senator. And I'm willing to pay big time for it."

"Get out."

The door of the conference room opened.

"Let's celebrate!" Elyssa exclaimed, holding up a bottle of Taittinger's finest. Robyn edged around from behind her with a tray of Marie Antoinette champagne glasses. They both stared.

"Out," Carole said.

"You know what I can't stand?" John demanded. "A sonofabitch who won't play by the rules."

"Funny thing. I can't either."

For one instant they understood each other. As enemies. John looked as if he might hit her, smash the table, pull out his hair, spit on the floor—a hundred ways to express his rage were possible. And then he simply shook his head, as if to rue her stupidity. His only violence was to shoulder Robyn aside as he left the room. Sam picked up his suitcase and, bobbing his head with an ill-conceived apology, trotted after his boss, the lawyer hot on his heels. The assistant who had gathered up the last pieces of the contracts now understood he had been abandoned. He threw down the pieces and ran after his tribe. They left behind an umbrella and plenty of hard feelings.

"What the hell was that all about?" Elyssa asked, eyes huge.

Chapter 2

The black sedan with the senatorial license plates was parked in front of Mitch's town house on a narrow street in the Georgetown neighborhood of the District. Carole pulled up right behind the car and waved to the driver. He replied with a friendly tip of his fur-trimmed hat.

"Evenin', Miss Titus." When he spoke, pale tufts of steam danced around his face.

"Good evening, Sam. And it's Carole."

"You keep saying that."

"So why the *Miss*?"

"Because that way, I get to keep calling Mitch Mr. Senator. And that makes me laugh every time I say it. Imagine—that's the boy I taught how to ride, how to groom, how to birth a foal. Just yesterday, he was growing so fast his shirt-sleeves couldn't reach his wrists. And now—yes, sir, Mr. Senator. Very majestic, don't you think?"

"Absolutely."

"Hey! Did you see my picture in the *Post* today?"

Sam kept an album of newspaper photographs under his seat. They were all of Mitch, and most of them featured Sam somewhere in the background. The sixty-something ranch hand was certainly enjoying his time in Washington.

"Show it to me later," Carole said.

"Surely."

There were no photographers, no reporters, no weird protesters or groupies on the sidewalk. Like every other member of Congress, Mitch faxed his daily schedule to the papers (actually it was Todd, his chief of staff, who did the faxing). Since Mitch and Carole were going to the gala opening of the Smithsonian election history exhibit, a stakeout of his home was not necessary. Even the press liked a little downtime after a long day.

Carole let herself in with her key. The two-story foyer was papered with butter-yellow silk and tiled in white marble. The staircase led to a second story apartment, which Mitch kept for visiting family and friends. Mitch's mom used to send suitable young ladies who needed a place to stay until they found appropriate living arrangements. The guest apartment had been idle for some time. But not because Mrs. Evans, Sr., had stopped trying.

Carole dumped her briefcase beside the stack of mail on the mahogany console. A dry-cleaner bag hung on a coatrack containing a pale pink silk sheath, ready for wear. It was a beautiful dress that Mitch himself had purchased for her in New York and she had planned to wear it—not for the first time—tonight. But she had taken Robyn's little criticism to heart and had picked up another dress, a three-hundred-dollar extravagance she didn't need, especially after such a horrible day. She and Elyssa had spent a good hour behind Elyssa's closed office door after the Private Bank execs made their retreat.

"We lost a good contract!" Elyssa had wailed.

"It was never ours to begin with," Carole pointed out. "It was about Mitch. They couldn't get to him any other way."

"How often is this going to happen?"

"I don't know!"

"Okay, okay, I'm sorry," Elyssa said. "It's just . . . I wanted that contract. Come on, we've got to stop thinking about it."

"We can't stop. It's all my fault. I knew something was wrong with the way Private Bank was coming on to us, but I couldn't figure it out. Oh, God, I hate this."

"Don't obsess."

"I can't help it."

"I have an idea of a way to distract us."

"It won't work."

It worked. In fact, it worked great. At least for a while. How can a gal keep up a viable suicidal depression when she's shopping with her best friend?

Carole used a second key to open the carved oak door to the left of the staircase. On the floor were several dribbles of melting snow.

"We're in the dining room, Carole."

Mitch's apartment had never been professionally decorated and yet, it had that marvelously muted elegance Mario Buatta and other chi-chi decorators spent careers perfecting. The living room was painted a hunter green, which provided a dramatic backdrop for Mitch's collection of early twentieth-century black-and-white photographs of the Colorado landscape and Native American children. Two Texas lounging sofas idled on a plush Aubusson rug. Nothing went together and, precisely for that reason, everything looked perfect.

She dropped her shopping bag and coat on a brown

leather club chair and kicked off her pumps. Her toes were freezing.

"What a day," she declared. But any launching of her tale of woe was cut short.

Mitch was a tall, impressive figure of a man. When he rose from his chair at the double-length dining room table, he gave the impression of someone who had been uncomfortably making do in doll furniture. He wore his hand-tailored suit well, perhaps because he carried neither an extra ounce of fat nor a too-bulky gathering of muscle. He was undeniably handsome, but saved from a life as a Calvin Klein model by a small scar on his chin. He had dark, shiny hair that always looked just a week beyond needing a cut and just moments before having an eager companion run her fingers through it.

When he took her into his arms, Carole completely forgot about Private Bank. In fact, that was the problem with Mitch. He was such a great kisser—oh, now, when he put his lips on hers!—she could have given up her house, her job, her very name to be part of his life. Forever. And the other things he could do, would do, made the very sensible part of her go weak.

A discreet clearing of throat.

"Oh, hi, Todd," Carole said, pulling out of Mitch's arms.

"Good evening, Miss Titus," Mitch's chief of staff said, bobbing his head. She might tell Sam that he should call her Carole, but it was fun to work this dweeby prep school boy. "I was just leaving."

"Good," Mitch said.

Todd shoveled his papers, pencils, calculator, Day Planner and thirty-five other essentials into the briefcase that he couldn't quite close. He stood up, knocking his head on one of twelve crystal-laden arms of the chandelier. Embarrassed,

Todd's face turned beet-red, a color that clashed badly with his freckles and Irish setter hair.

"I'll just be . . . you know, going, I mean . . . out," he said. He backed out of the dining room. When he slammed the door to the foyer, Carole sighed. A heartbeat later, they heard a grunt, a clattering of a hundred objects on the foyer's marble floor and an expletive.

"He has such a crush on you," Mitch observed.

"Is that why he's such a klutz?"

"Absolutely. You make him nervous. Have you always had this effect on men?"

"Always," Carole said firmly, with an exaggerated roll of her eyes.

"How 'bout if I try to make you nervous?"

He pulled her to him and seemed ready to kiss her again, but then abruptly unclasped the hook on her skirt and let it drop to the floor.

"Tweed is not conducive to my juvenile desire to cop a feel," he observed. "No panty hose?"

"Panty hose is so out," Carole said.

"That works for me. I like when your legs are bare. Because you have the best damn legs in Washington. Smooth as silk and perfectly shaped. A national treasure."

"Flatterer."

He kissed her.

"You're feeling a little better now?"

"This afternoon I was very upset."

"Now you move on."

Since taking office, Mitch had learned that holding a grudge, hanging onto a heartache, mulling over a setback—these were not viable options.

"No, wait," Carole said.

"Oh, boy, I shoulda kept my mouth shut."

She pulled out of his embrace and led him to the living room. He paused at the pocket doors to watch her—after all, it isn't every day that a man gets permission to ogle a woman wearing a nothing of a chiffon blouse and a Cosabella silk tap pant. He shrugged off his jacket as Carole turned to face him.

"This Senate stuff is driving me up the wall," she said. She sat on one of the loungers, glancing back to the bay window facing the street to be sure the voile sheers were closed. "Even aside from the issue of your running with a disreputable crowd."

"Senators, representatives, Cabinet members . . ."

"And lobbyists. Don't forget lobbyists."

"They have their own section of hell reserved for them."

"And reporters."

He sat down beside her. He ran his fingers through his hair, a gesture that normally reduced her to gawking.

"I'm hoping to be part of a new trend—Okay Guys in Washington," he said.

"Not a bad slogan. Take your hand off my thigh, I'm try-ing to have a serious conversation with you."

He held his hands up as if she were a bandit and he her helpless victim.

"Mitch, are you going to run in the upcoming election?"

All the playfulness went out of his face.

"My seat opens in just a year and a half. I might have to."

"Have to?"

"When you called me this afternoon, I was in a meeting about this with the chairman of the party. The Very Rev-erend Jesse Carver is planning to oppose me for the nomi-nation."

"He can't get elected. He's a right-wing loony. Did you know he wants to pass laws requiring people to carry handguns? Says that it'll stop crime if old ladies learn to shoot."

Mitch nodded. He tugged at his tie.

"He might be crazy, but he has a tremendously loyal following. And he's got money."

"NRA money. Right-to-life money. Religious right money."

"Money's money. And he could win."

"You're more popular," she said, before remembering that this conversation was supposed to be about *not* running. "I mean, anybody's more popular."

He didn't hear the second part.

"Among Republicans, Democrats, and Independents combined. In the primary, I'd be running only for Republican votes."

"So, fine, the Republicans nominate Carver. The Democrats nominate a middle-of-the-road kind of guy and the state would be better off in the end. You're just upset because there'd be a Democrat in the seat."

With a fifty-fifty split in the Senate, every seat counted.

"I wouldn't mind. I get along great with our other senator and he's a Democrat. And Breaux likes me."

"Louisiana Breaux?"

"Yeah. His position, and mine, is that with the two extreme sides of each party nearly equal in influence, it's the moderates in the middle who must form bonds. I told him at the meeting today that I supported him on that."

"Why would the chairman of the Republican party and the Democratic senator from Louisiana consent to being in the same room?"

Relations in Washington were as frosty as the steam rising

up off the Potomac. All that talk of working together in a bipartisan manner—*Puh-leeeeeze!*, that was just for the network news and the *New York Times*.

"They both are pledging their support. They both want me to run."

"The chairman I can understand. But you'd get the support of a Democrat?"

"His endorsement. Because the only name on the Democratic ballot is going to be Maurice Smith."

"He's an ecoterrorist. Nobody takes him seriously."

"Except the Justice Department. Torching suburban homes outside Denver is ecoterrorism, Mitch."

"You're right, you're right. He's so far to the left, I can't tell if he's more or less dangerous than Carver."

"Oh. But you're not going to run just because two very deranged people are. Or are you?"

He didn't answer.

"Mitch, I'm beginning to think you like politics."

"I like public service."

"Oh, get out, politics is politics."

"I don't like the campaigning, it's true. Seems to me it's beauty contests for people who aren't pretty enough for beauty contests."

He stood up, pacing across the soft rug.

"I went into this because of a favor to a friend," he said. Mitch had worked as Senator Snyder's senior aide. He got a big promotion by the governor of Colorado when Senator Snyder's wife developed pancreatic cancer and brought that popular senator's career to a close. Mitch was appointed senator to fill the vacancy. "It started off as a favor to a friend, but now it's something more. It's about service. It's about the public good. It's about something a lot bigger than ego. Even mine."

The average thirty-seven-year-old woman has heard, as a matter of scientific certainty, a gazillion politicians yakking away on a gazillion newscasts, campaign ads, talk shows, debates, town hall meetings. The words *public* and *service* are peppered throughout these yakfests. But when Mitch said it, boy, Carole actually believed him. It was the eyes, Carole thought—so pure, so innocent, so clear, so intense. She didn't want to lose him, didn't want to waste their time in conflict. And besides, who can have a rational discussion wearing just a nothing blouse and silk scanties?

"Let's talk about this later," she said, tugging at his sleeve. She wasn't going to change his mind tonight so another course of action suggested itself.

He grumbled.

"Please?" she purred, trying very hard to recapture the good mood that ordinarily existed between them. "We'll talk later, if you want. But not now."

He looked at her. Tried to maintain a suitably stern and remote expression.

"I thought women were the ones who wanted to talk about things."

"Not this one. I've got other things on my mind. And they don't require much conversation. Come here."

He sat down. Leaned back. Spread his arms out. Growled contentedly when she straddled him and pulled off his tie.

"Are all men as easy to wrangle?"

"Absolutely."

She kissed him.

"I'm yours, baby, I'm yours," he said.

When Carole was younger, getting excited—nipples-aching, leg-shaking, heartbreaking excited—only happened after a long bout of kissing and caressing. One difference in her sexuality—or maybe it was just in having a relationship with a bona fide hotboy—was that she could go from zero to sixty in one kiss.

"Do you have your 'device'?" she asked. Referring to a condom as a birth control "device" had appealed to their strange sense of humor. Using a condom wasn't Carole's idea—she would have happily gone back on the pill. But Mitch was convinced that soon, very soon, they would want to try to make a baby—and then, he argued, they wouldn't want to wait months to conceive.

"I thought you might be interested," he said, pulling a plastic packet out of his shirt pocket.

"Such a Boy Scout," she quipped. She undid the buttons on his shirt and yanked the tails out. When she pushed up his T-shirt, she thrilled at his smooth, muscular chest. Even though it was January, and Washington besides, his skin was like toasted caramel.

She unbuckled his belt. He sighed sharply and pushed her blouse up so that he could unclasp her bra.

"Oh, God, I could do this forever," he groaned a few minutes later when she guided him into herself. "Forget being a senator. Just keep me as your love slave."

"Mitch, please, look at me."

He stared at her with an expression both vulnerable and confident. She liked his eyes, brown like cappuccino, and could measure his excitement, as it goaded her own, by the way his eyes met hers, turned wide and then seemed almost—but not quite—to fill with tears.

And then she felt the urgent rhythm of her orgasm, brought on by his gaze. As a moan escaped her lips, he bucked sharply. For what seemed like a place beyond time, but was really just the ordinary tick-tock of a minute . . .

Then they were quiet and Carole leaned forward, resting her head on his shoulder.

They startled when the doorbell rang.

"Shit," Carole said. "That's gotta be Todd."

"Mr. Senator!" the aide called from the front porch. "Mr. Senator, we need to get you there by seven-thirty."

"Does he always call you Mr. Senator?" Carole asked.

"He picked it up from Sam. I keep telling Todd to call me Mitch or Mr. Evans, if that makes him happy. But he insists. And Sam's having the time of his life being a senator's chauffeur. Which is good because he's getting too old to do much at the ranch."

The doorbell again. Todd's muffled voice.

"Mr. Senator, I radioed ahead and the traffic is heavy on K Street, so if you would, I'd like to . . ."

"Cover your ears," Mitch said, putting his palm over Carole's hands and guiding both to her ears. "Todd! I'll! Be! Just! A! Moment!"

"Where'd you learn to shout like that?"

"The Army. Right along with opening C rations with a Bic pen and keeping warm with a bicycle tire."

"I don't even want to know what you can do with a tire," Carole said. She stood up and stretched a kink out of her knees. "I call dibs on the shower first."

"Why don't we share?"

"Because I have to shave my legs."

"I'm a very experienced shaver. I do it every day, and sometimes, if I don't want to look like Nixon, I do it twice."

In ten minutes flat, Carole and Mitch stepped out of the town house. Carole wore her new dress, a knockoff of the Prada yellow poppies gown with ruffles cascading down the neckline, with a matching cashmere shawl. Unlike the original, this dress had a cotton lining, more appropriate for Washington. Sam whistled.

"Mighty nice," he said, helping Carole into the car. "But I hope you're going to be warm enough."

"We're getting in and getting out of a car. Forget the weather."

Todd stammered a bit and jumped into the shotgun seat.

"Mr. Senator, I wanted to brief you on a few of the guests you'll be seeing tonight. Secretary of the Interior . . ."

The black tinted privacy screen rolled up.

"Poor Todd," Carole said.

*W*ashington women had never given up their pastel suits for black and now that the editors of *Vogue* and *W* were coming around to color, the women in the Mayflower Hotel ballroom looked absolutely *au courante.* Lilac Dupioni suits with portrait collars. Kittenish pink structured numbers with matching jackets. Belted patterned wrap dresses by von Furstenberg. Never red, as that is the stump color, and after election day, women are more than happy to put it in the back of the closet.

Men were easy—gray, black or navy blue suits being the norm—but the last presidential election had provoked a fad for solid red ties with white shirts. And cowboy boots were back—ugh. The occasional dress uniform glittered with an array of medals over the officer's heart.

Carole had attended enough of these events that she was able to match names and faces even when the people in question weren't regulars on Sunday's *Meet the Press.*

"What can I get you?" Mitch asked.

"White wine," Carole said. "No, make it a club soda."

He did a double take and then shrugged. Carole had been finding out what every woman knows—a relationship with a man puts five pounds on a woman. There weren't many Lean Cuisine nights with Mitch and who could resist a bite—make that two—when your man orders a sinfully tempting dessert? On her frame—five seven and a tad muscular—it wasn't yet noticeable. But if she didn't watch herself and all those empty calories . . .

"I'm so glad you could make it!"

Carole startled.

"Oh, Pepper, good to see you."

The voice was familiar to Americans as the NBC White House correspondent and a Washington insider. Pepper January was a robustly proportioned woman with a brash, easygoing style, which proved that not every television viewer wanted a blonde, made-up, stick-thin woman delivering the news.

"Kiss, kiss," Pepper said.

"Kiss, kiss."

"You've been a busy girl," Pepper teased. "All over town with Mitch. When do you get some time alone?"

"Not as often as I'd like."

"Well, I'm happy that you gave up a Friday night for the Wildlife Foundation. I've been on the board forever. And Mitch, as usual, made a substantial contribution but refused to be listed in the program. He said all his best friends call him Anonymous."

"Is his contribution substantial enough that I can make him leave before the afterdinner speeches?"

"Honey, he gave enough you could go home right now and I'd send you off with a doggie bag and a thank-you note. Now let's talk about you—you look wonderful."

"Thanks, I—"

"—and now that the personal stuff is out of the way, let's move on to the market. What the hell's going on? Nasdaq unloaded another couple of percentage points today. The Dow's looking dangerous. And the earnings reports are enough to make me throw my Gateway out the window."

"I know," Carole said. "Everybody's getting hurt. The money's dried up, profits are not living up to expectations and some people are bailing out. I have a friend who was a multimillionaire up until a week ago. On paper. And now the paper's worthless."

"Is your company publicly traded?"

"No, so we're insulated from the market a little, but when some of our investors lose money we feel it. I just have to do my job more and better—selling Allheart.com to advertisers. We have to make our money the old-fashioned way."

Pepper laughed.

"Carole, you could succeed anywhere you found yourself."

"I'm a good saleswoman," Carole admitted. She was old enough, and experienced enough, that she didn't have to be falsely modest. Likewise, she didn't have to brag or boast. "But I like what I do now. Except . . ." She glanced toward the bar where men gathered to get drinks for themselves and their women.

"Except you're finding out that you don't have much time."

"Oh, I'm used to being busy."

"No, I'm not talking about that. I'm talking about you and Mitch. You can't take your time about making a commitment. If he had stayed a senator's aide, it wouldn't be as much of a problem."

"Possibly. It's also my age."

"Thirty-five?"

"Thirty-seven."

"We like to keep our options open."

"Oh, yes."

"But we can't. Nobody can. Carole, you need to think about what you and Mitch want. Ultimately. Because time moves a lot faster than you think."

"It seems so unfair."

"It's that way for all of us."

Carole looked thoughtfully at Pepper. Really looked at Pepper. Not in the way we glance at people at cocktail parties while we juggle a drink and hors d'oeuvres and notice the women's dresses and think about our aching feet. She looked at Pepper, the same woman that ten million Americans invited into their homes at six-thirty Eastern Standard Time.

"Pepper, you've lost some weight," she said.

"A little. But not enough to get me into a Brazilian bikini."

Pepper tugged at her dress to show off the soft folds of chiffon and satin. But her face didn't have that glee Carole would feel at finding herself a few pounds lighter.

"Pepper, are you okay?"

A woman with a very tall, very stiff hairdo shrieked at Pepper's shoulder and the two women hugged. Pepper introduced her co-chair for the event just as Mitch presented her with a glass of club soda with a dainty slice of lime.

Whatever Pepper January had on her mind would have to be saved for another occasion. Carole made a mental note to call her the next day.

Chapter 3

Mitch was full of energy as they left the party.

"I talked to the new interior secretary," he said. "We're setting up a meeting next week to talk about the wildfires."

"Where are there wildfires in December?"

"There aren't any right now. But we've got to start planning now."

Sam tipped his hat as they approached the curb. Since becoming a senator, Mitch never drove and his little sports car gathered dust in the alley garage behind his town house. A couple miles over the speed limit, a whiff of alcohol on his breath, a make-a-name-for-himself police officer—with that combination, Mitch could be the next poster boy for political bad behavior.

"Todd went on home," Sam said. "But he said to tell you that he'll catch you after the Pentagon briefing. We gotta be on the road by six-thirty. Five-thirty if you're going out to Miss Titus's house."

Carole made a quick calculation.

"Sam, I'll drive him to the Pentagon tomorrow morning."

"You'd have to pick up Todd."

Carole muttered an unladylike oath.

"Why don't we stay at my place?" Mitch asked.

"Because I've got a conference call with some European prospects tomorrow morning. They're six hours ahead of us, Mitch. I need some sleep."

"Oh."

Said with all the enthusiasm and empathy of a man who thrived on less than four a night.

"Why don't I pick up my car at your house?" Carole asked.

His jaw tensed. Carole resisted a smile. Men were so transparent, especially Mitch as he had not yet learned the distinctly Washington, utterly political talent of hiding feelings and pretending sentiment.

"Sure. Sam, let's get back to my house. Carole will drive herself home."

"I can follow Miss Titus's car so she gets home safe."

"Please don't," Carole said. "Last time you did that, Mitch went with you to make sure you were kept company. I get home just fine on my own. I don't need a parade."

Sam looked slightly wounded. Then he shrugged, opened the back passenger door for them and held out a uselessly so-licitous hand to Carole as she slid into her seat.

"You're sure this is okay?" Mitch said, as Sam slid the car away from the curb.

"Mitch, it would be nice if one of us had a little more flexibility about work. But it can't be you—and it won't be me."

"Mad at me?"

"Not a bit," she said, but there was a niggling feeling—

not exactly anger—but you might call it resentment. But against whom she couldn't have said.

He leaned back in the plush leather seat and pulled her to him. She loved this driving in the mellow hours, the rhythmic pulse of the streetlights as they passed each corner, the feel of his strong chest against her cheek. She closed her eyes. He talked about coordination of firefighting efforts, FEMA and ATF and the National Parks and half a dozen other names and initials that she had never heard of. He wanted so much to help the people in his state that he sometimes forgot he was in Washington, and because he was so passionate, he was able to make the car feel like a pup tent in the middle of a pine forest. The air so crisp and cool. The crunch of pine needles beneath a crepe-soled boot. The owl's insistent questions. All of that replaced the sirens and the horns honking and the swipe of tires on day-old puddles.

When she woke up, he had stopped talking. They were parked in front of his house. Sam had left for his garden apartment tucked away out back behind the yard.

"Can't believe I'm such a scintillating speaker."

Carole stretched and groaned deep in the back of her throat.

"Sorry."

"Not a problem. Are you okay to drive?"

"Absolutely. Just give me a diet Coke for the road."

She followed him into the kitchen and he handed her a can. Mitch didn't drink the stuff, but all kinds of things had been showing up in the refrigerator and medicine cabinet since he had met Carole. She drank a long, satisfyingly bubbly gulp.

Mitch leaned across the island counter and gave her a lingering kiss.

"Sure you don't want to stay?"

"Europeans are the next big market."

He walked her out to her car. When she drove away, she looked in the rearview mirror. He stood on the curb watching her until she turned the corner.

The drive was longer than she remembered, even though traffic was light. If nothing else, having a man in her life was causing a lot of late nights. She pulled into the single-car garage of her quaint little Alexandria cottage just after one o'clock. Whiskers snarled his displeasure with her night out by refusing to come when she laid out a can of tuna.

Her mailbox had two days' worth of bills and catalogues and solicitation letters from worthy (and not-so-worthy) charities. She put all of the bills on the dining room table with the others from the week. Most of the solicitation letters she put in the recycling bin without even opening. She lingered over the catalogues. Before Mitch had vacuumed every available free minute out of her day, she had sometimes enjoyed reading catalogues and putting Post-it notes on items she would seldom get around to buying.

Tiffany's and Nieman's were fun for fantasy. Pottery Barn and Restoration Hardware had stuff that was interesting but which she could just as easily pick up at a Saturday morning estate sale. Williams-Sonoma she used to plan out dinner parties that she never quite brought to fruition.

She made herself a cup of hot chocolate, changed into her chenille bathrobe, told Whiskers again how sorry she was about her neglect and plunked down in the comfy chair-and-a-half in the living room with a half a dozen catalogues under her arm.

When she awoke with a start some time later, she was surprised to see it was 3:30 A.M.—so much for getting some quality sleep for her conference call. She was also surprised to see a Hanna Andersson catalogue open on her lap, with three or four pages of sweet little baby outfits dog-eared. *Now who was I thinking about when I marked those pages?* Carole wondered, as she dragged herself upstairs to bed. *My nieces are in grade school, for heaven's sake.*

The next morning's meeting at Allheart.com was opened with Carole's announcement that the Europeans seemed somewhat interested in advertising on the Allheart page.

"They're a small upscale cosmetics firm, mostly selling in England and the Northern Continent," Carole explained. "But if they advertise on our page, we not only get the revenue but we increase our visibility."

"We need to explore every new market," Elyssa said. "Sounds great. And you talked to them this morning?"

"I got up at six, because they wanted our call to coincide with a meeting of their marketing execs."

"Great work," Elyssa said. "I was getting a little worried yesterday."

Dana stopped doodling in her idea notebook. Robyn and Alix were all ears. Carole had only to glance at each woman to know that the Private Bank fiasco was Topic One yesterday afternoon.

"I'm going to be more careful in the future," she said carefully. "It was never something I anticipated."

"Honey, I told you before it's okay."

"It won't happen again."

"Don't tell me you're breaking up!" Robyn cried.

"No, not at all. I'm just saying I'm going to investigate our potential clients *before* we get to the table."

"Phew. Because it is so cool actually knowing somebody who's going out with somebody who's in *People* magazine. It makes me a sort of celebrity by association. If you get married to him, I'll be really happy. Except for the fact that he's such a dreamboat you'll be getting hate mail from fifteen-year-old girls who were hoping he'd wait for them to grow up."

"We're not getting married." Carole answered more emphatically than she meant to.

"Hey, don't," Alix warned. "Some other woman might come up and snatch him out from under you."

"Well, thank you, Miss Sunshine. Look, I've got plenty of time to think about going down that road again. Or at least, I feel like I do. I'm sure I look and feel much younger than my mother did at this age. And she was always flying to Switzerland to get Gerovital treatments."

"Gerovital?" Alix asked.

"It's not available in this country," Elyssa pointed out. "It's a lamb placenta treatment."

"Gross."

"They inject it in your butt every day for a week," Carole added. "Then you come back to the clinic every three months and . . ."

"Enough!" Alix cried.

"Point is, I don't feel my age. I hate my age."

"Why are we suddenly talking about age as a problem?" Robyn asked. "*This* is new territory."

"For you, maybe. But I've been thinking about it more and more. Because in a few years I have to have a kid or put it aside forever. I'm not going to be one of those women in their fifties and sixties doing fertility treatments."

"Didn't I just hear you say you weren't getting married? Is this all biological clock ticktock talk?" Robyn threw up her hands in exasperation.

"It's just that time has a funny way of moving along faster than we expect," Alix said. "And no time is the right time for love. If it was as convenient as it was in high school, we'd all go steady for a month. And then pick out another flavor."

"Would you guys stop talking so fast?" Dana exclaimed. "You're creating a whole line of cards just with this conversation and I can't keep up. We can call them Timecards. Get it? Timecards."

"You and your inspirations." Alix sighed and then added, "But yes, Robyn, you're right. Carole is making a point about women facing biological choices on a different timetable from men."

"I think Mitch is facing his own clock—he's thinking he needs to prove himself in a . . ."

Elyssa sighed.

"Could we maybe, just maybe, have a little business discussion thrown in here? Enough to give me justification for paying for the Krispy Kremes and the Starbucks pushpot?"

As conversation turned to the relative merits of some new hires, Carole's thoughts drifted back to the summer, when she had first met Mitch. She had been cautious, of course, because the memory of her painful separation from Hal was still fresh. Hal had been a musician, with emotional flaws sized to fit his enormous talent. Womanizing, drugs, drinking and all-around immaturity. Not the best qualities in a husband, but Carole hung in there for thirteen years. Because she loved him—or at least *had* loved him. Because her vows meant something. And because she had said 'til death do us part. It wasn't over until she realized that she was killing herself with anxiety and preventing Hal from hitting the rock bottom that might make him turn his life around. When he checked out after eight days of a thirty-day rehab program and landed on their marital bed with the groupie who had driven him home, Carole said *finito*—giving him his walking papers and virtually every dollar they had accumulated.

After the divorce, she dated. And had a series of forgettable one-night stands that left her drained. Then she entered her weird celibacy phase. Any man who wanted to be part of her life had to understand he came third—behind work at Allheart and the refurbishing of her refuge in Alexandria.

Since most men come complete with an outsized ego, she had never had to compromise.

Mitch was different, and not because he was accommodating. He wasn't, particularly. He was tough, he was a workaholic, he was proud of his accomplishments—but not so much that he needed to brag or boast. He had crashed her solitary party. And the trip to his home state of Colorado had been key. They had both thought it would be a little romp, concluding with a leisurely rafting expedition. Instead, the boat lost its moorings, her cell phone ended up in the drink, she got a painful ankle sprain—and Mitch had proven himself her hero when he managed to get them both to safety.

But that was the same weekend Mitch was offered the Senate seat when Senator Snyder's wife was diagnosed with pancreatic cancer. There was no cure, no care except to provide comfort and minimize pain. And Snyder wanted every minute with his wife. A public servant in the real sense, he couldn't resign unless he left his seat in the hands of someone he trusted—the governor and he chose Mitch.

Mitch had been sworn in less than a week after their Colorado trip. They had not had a weekend away together in the four months since he had become the youngest working senator, since he had been crowned "the last gentleman of the Congress." Trips together? Carole didn't think the overnight trip to New York in September to attend an important senator's funeral counted. After all, there was a huge contingent of senators and their spouses staying at the same hotel—and while Todd was put up at his parents' apartment four blocks away, he played barnacle every waking minute.

"Carole, wake up! Yoo-hoo!"

Carole startled.

"What? You were talking about personnel."

"No, I wasn't," Elyssa said. "I was asking about upcoming trips. Do you have a trip scheduled that we should know about?"

"A trip? Lemme think . . ."

A little later in the afternoon, Mitch asked the same thing.

"A trip? Where?"

"I was thinking Quebec City."

"Okay." A cautious okay.

"It's a foreign country, which means you won't be recognized. Or, at least, you won't be bothered. And it's close—we can be there in three hours. Europe is a good ten or twelve hours."

"But why not go back to my ranch?"

"Your parents."

"Oh, yeah, right."

Saying parents were the problem with visiting the Colorado Evans ranch was shorthand for the general atmosphere—a weekend "alone" would turn into a family reunion.

"And Mitch, we need some time together."

"You're right about that."

"Can't you ditch Todd for a weekend?"

"It would be my pleasure. Could you hold on a minute? Todd, I'm scheduling a trip to Duluth," and then when

Carole cried out, "*Duluth!*," he added, "Shhh. Honey. Todd, could you get us tickets? Say, Friday afternoon. I'd need you to advance there a few hours before me."

Carole heard Todd's voice in the background.

"What have we got going in Duluth?"

"Constituent outreach."

"Duluth is in Minnesota."

"I know. I'll give you all the details later. It's a need-to-know thing. Now clear out of my office and get those tickets. Put it all on my personal account—not the office budget."

"Yes, sir."

Carole giggled.

"Are you really going to send him to Duluth?"

"I could be cruel and send him to International Falls."

"Well, I plan to have you in a hotel room all to myself. There will be no meetings with any Canadians of any kind, unless you count room service."

She hung up the phone feeling quite pleased with herself.

Friday afternoon, she found herself in the international terminal of Ronald Reagan National airport on the phone with Mabel.

"I could transfer you to Todd, but oddly enough, he's on his way to Duluth," she said. "You wouldn't happen to know why he has to . . ."

"Mabel, I don't need Todd. I need Mitch."

"He got called to the White House. Haven't you been paying attention?"

"To what?"

"The Middle East. There's been new violence on the West Bank and . . ."

"There's always violence in the Middle East!" Carole shouted. The middle-aged suit sitting next to her stared. "Sorry. Mabel, our plane boards in fifteen minutes. Is Mitch on his way?"

"Can you hold for just a minute?" A click.

Carole picked up her black nylon weekender and headed for the Air Canada gate. Just before she got to the security check, Mabel popped back on the line.

"Miz Titus?"

"Mabel, it's Carole."

"Miz Titus, the senator is being briefed on the situation in the Middle East. When you get called to the White House, you go."

"The president is only doing this to score points with the media."

A long pause.

"And what part of this surprises you?"

The two women shared an unexpectedly companionable laugh.

"Mabel, do I get on this plane or not?"

"Get on the plane. After all, the president will shoo everybody out the door just as the evening news starts. Mitch'll do that talking heads thing on the drive and be on the next flight. And Carole? Were you the one who got Todd sent to Duluth?"

"Only indirectly."

"Bless you, doll. It's been a very peaceful afternoon."

"Anytime, Mabel."

She hung up. Miffed. Really miffed. Not that there hadn't been dates she had canceled or been late for because of business. Not that the president was somebody to whom you said, "Hey, sorry, can't make it, got a date tonight." Not that she'd want Mitch to bail out if there was a crisis in the Middle East. She didn't mean to be insensitive, but there would be a crisis in the Middle East tomorrow and the next day and the next day after that.

Jeez Lou-eez, how could a woman consider herself in a relationship with a man if a romantic weekend away started off like . . .

"Champagne or orange juice?" the flight attendant asked. She presented a tray of short glasses and flutes.

A glass of champagne was exactly what she shouldn't have right now. Precisely because it sounded so good.

"Orange juice," Carole said sullenly. And it was good champagne. "Sorry, bad day."

"We get that all the time. If you'd like me to hang up your jacket . . .?"

Business class Air Canada was very nice. Soothing, really. Canadians have such a competent, civilized air. Like the British, but less judgmental. Like the French, but not so high-strung. Carole sat down in an unexpectedly comfortable window seat and pulled out her cell phone for a last check. One message from Mitch: Sorry.

Gggrrrrr!

And then another from Pepper January. Sorry she hadn't returned Carole's phone calls. Busy. Very busy.

Carole didn't think of herself as a phobic flyer. She flew two or three times a month for business and a phobia would just get in the way. But she didn't like flying.

And she missed Mitch. Mitch held her hand when the engines roared and the plane careened over the bumps on the runway, at the first stomach-bobbing lurch into the air.

She sipped her orange juice and waited for the preflight instructions. She had never felt this kind of lonely. Not even when her father left home. Not even when she gave Hal the keys to the car and told his new chippie to drive him . . . anywhere. Not ever this lonely before.

Chapter 4

Quebec City was dark when the plane touched down. Carole retrieved her jacket and bag from the flight attendant and headed out of the somewhat bleak, industrial terminal. There was black snow on the curb and a damp, coal-infused scent on the air. She hailed a cab and used her careful high school French to ask to be taken to Rue des Carrieres en de Vieux-Quebec.

"Sure, have you there in a jiffy," the cabbie said, flipping on his meter.

"I thought . . ."

"Everyone does. Don't worry—people speak English here. French, too. Well, I mean the Quebecquois. Most of the people in my building speak Thai."

"You're not from . . .?"

"Thailand? Nah, I'm from Brooklyn. So, whatcha doing here?"

"Romantic weekend."

He glanced back at her.

"Some romance."

"Yeah, well."

In forty-five minutes, after following a tortuously convoluted path through the Basse-Ville, the industrial and port section of the city, they entered the walls surrounding the Haute-Ville. Carole felt transported a hundred years, maybe more, back in time and across the Atlantic to a Paris that no longer existed—to a France of the Old Regime. The cab stopped in front of the Hotel D'Accord, the oldest continuously operating hotel on the continent. Not nearly as elegant as its cousin across the street—Le Château Frontenac— but every bit as charming in its own way.

Carole paid the cabbie, who wished her luck and suggested a restaurant around the corner. Carole checked in at the desk and followed the narrowest of hallways to her room. It was a cozy, dark wood–paneled room with a large leaded pane window overlooking the square. A fire was blazing, with logs stacked beside the iron acanthus-leafed screen. On the dresser was an arrangement of roses and eucalyptus in a vase. The attached card was from Mitch and reiterated his earlier apology.

An apology that felt hollow as she unpacked her things and changed into a comfortable gray fleece skirt and matching turtleneck. She put on warm boots and picked up her bright red pashmina. It might be out of fashion according to the best and brightest of New York style editors, but it was warm and easy to pack. As a thin layer between her tweedy jacket and the cold—in a word, heavenly.

The streets were crowded in a friendly way. Horses' hooves clip-clopped on packed snow and cobblestone. A folk band played violin-heavy holiday favorites beneath the softly glowing streetlamp. The church bells pealed in celebration of the end of five o'clock mass. The air was heavy with the scent of pine, bakery goods and the coal from the shipping concerns on the St. Lawrence River.

Carole stopped at a newspaper kiosk to pick up the *Wall Street Journal*—an acquaintance from college had just gone bust-up and his story was the top story in the left column. She thought she'd have a problem paying in American money, but the kiosk owner didn't seem to mind the Washingtons. Moving on, she stopped only to watch a dozen children pulling sleds with their younger siblings urging faster and faster. She passed couples who were so entranced with each other they barely heard her *excusez-moi*'s. She stopped at the restaurant the cabbie had recommended, negotiated a table by the fireplace and made a point of opening the paper. She looked up only briefly to order a glass of white wine and not at all to order an appetizer of escargots en croutes. She lost herself in the story of the roller-coaster ride of her college contemporary.

"Perhaps you would be so kind . . .?"

Carole looked up. Fortyish, handsome, a certain Gallic charm. Since a Russian beaver hat and a well-lined trench coat aren't de rigeur for a maitre d', she guessed him to be another diner.

"Yes?"

"Perhaps I could sit down."

She glanced around the dining room, which had filled up. But not completely so. A few tables near the kitchen . . .

"The maitre d' suggested that if I shared a table with you, he could seat a few more . . ."

He bowed fleetingly so that she could see behind him the podium where the maitre d' was lodged between two couples, a ringing telephone and a white reservation book covered with scribbles. Carole had a mild pang of guilt—she had been quite firm that she wanted the table-for-four so she could spread out with her paper. That wasn't an issue when the restaurant was empty but now . . .

"Sure, no problem," Carole said. She picked up the discarded sections of the *Journal*. "I'm from New York and we take up a lot of room when we read a paper."

"But of course."

He took off his hat, revealing thick, mink-colored curls. As he shrugged off his coat, a waiter rushed to take it. Her new dining partner wore an impeccably tailored charcoal gray suit and an ecru silk shirt that was a welcome continental relief from the preppy oxford button-down cottons of Washington. She noted the barely-there scent of a sophisticated men's cologne—she guessed Ferragamo.

He hadn't brought any reading material, which was mildly awkward. She didn't have any obligation and yet, it felt rude to jump back into the paper. It had reached a low point, anyhow, as she had finished the True Hollywood Story article about her classmate and was now reading about monetary policies in Kenya.

"No, no, please, feel free to go back to reading. I am the one who has imposed. In fact, if you're finished with this section . . .?"

"Absolutely."

Just as they opened their respective sections, the waiter appeared.

"The maitre d' wishes to offer you this champagne with his deepest thanks," he said to Carole.

"Veuve Clicquot," her table partner said. "The beautiful war widow Clicquot. I believe we should accept."

Aw, hell, it was very difficult to feel sorry for one's self— or at least, put on a good pity party—in the face of good champagne. Good *free* champagne.

"Only if we share it," she said.

"It will be my pleasure."

That French accent! Lord, a woman could fall in love, she thought, with just the faintest sense of guilt. Mitch was only missing that one thing to make him the perfect man.

The waiter quickly undid the foil wrap and popped the cork. Carole tasted and approved the sip of wine. The waiter filled her flute to the top and produced another one for the gentleman.

"Jacques Chancet," her table partner said, holding his hand across the white damask expanse.

"Carole Titus," she said, watching his dark brown eyes for a flicker of recognition. None, thank goodness.

Instead, just the slightest smile of pleasure.

"To your kindness," he said.

The champagne tickled her throat and left just the faintest taste of grape in her mouth.

"First time in Quebec City?"

"I came here on a high school field trip once. A long time ago. I remember the Citadelle and having to write a report on the French-British conflicts."

"But now you are here for business," Jacques guessed. He tapped the first section of the *Wall Street Journal*.

"I should be—I do a lot of business travel. But no, this is supposed to be a romantic getaway."

Being a gentleman, his face betrayed only the slightest puzzlement.

"My boyfriend didn't make the flight," Carole explained. "Not that he didn't want to. He got tied up."

"Will he be joining you later?"

"Much later. He's catching a plane that will get in around midnight."

He smiled, but the faint lines around his eyes betrayed

the slightest disappointment that Carole found intriguing.

"Then we should construct an itinerary—so that when he arrives, you waste not a moment deciding on the best places to go."

At last. Jacques had found a safe, comfortable topic that two strangers could discuss over dinner. She appreciated his discretion in never asking more than the bare minimum of personal questions. Yet, he exuded such warmth and charm that she felt a chat with her dearest friend—Elyssa, or her sister, maybe—could have been no more intimate. Europeans are very much like this, she thought, remembering her too few trips to the continent. Americans rush to free confessions while Europeans wait in sly, sophisticated reserve. And enjoy themselves.

She shared the escargot en croutes as an appetizer and he returned the favor by enticing her with a pâté. He declared that she must revisit the Citadelle, but there was also the Terrasse Dufferin for shopping, the Rue de Tresor where the artisans sold their wares and the Cathedrale Catholique Notre-Dames' light show. He didn't seem to think the light show held in a church was totally appropriate and advised, instead, that she consider Eglise Notre-Dame-des-Victoires and its relics.

"Saint's nightgowns, fingernail clippings and locks of martyr's hair," he said. "It's all very amazing. I was raised in the Catholic Church, and I don't tell my parents that I've never been to St. Patrick's although it's just around the corner from my flat."

She could not resist investigating the personal reference.

"You live in New York?"

He nodded. The waiter offered him a wine menu.

"On Park Avenue—when I first moved in, I lived next to

a Ladies Who Lunch restaurant. Now it's where yuppies buy 'restoration' supplies for ten times what they'd pay in a regular hardware store."

She giggled.

"I grew up in New York," she said.

"Really?"

"I went to St. James the Lesser. The Episcopal school."

"On Sullivan Street."

"My mother got a tuition break because the headmistress watched *The Beautiful and the Damned*. My mother was a recurring character."

"*The Beautiful and the Damned*—you mean the F. Scott Fitzgerald novel?"

"It's a soap opera. No relation. My mother's been in it for nearly twenty years."

"And so you are an actress?"

"Absolutely not. Unless you count *acting* like I'm reading the *Wall Street Journal* over dinner in a lovely restaurant in a lovely city like Quebec . . ."

"Ah, then put your newspaper away. Could I interest you in sharing the Chateauneuf-du-Pape? They have a Domaine Du Vieux Telegraphe."

"I really shouldn't."

"Some people object to that year because of the July temperatures the vines endured," he said mildly. "I could suggest an alternative . . ."

"No, I don't have any quibble with the weather, it's that I'm getting a little tipsy."

"Telegraphe does run high in alcohol. Perhaps we shouldn't."

"No, let's try it. You seem to know your stuff."

"I am French. That's what we like. I couldn't order a decent beer if my life depended on it."

He ordered a bottle and returned the menu.

"You live in New York now?"

"Washington," she said.

He did not give way to a flicker of recognition. This was interesting. And great. Now she knew why she wanted to get out of DC so badly.

"It's a terrible atmosphere right now," she said. "Republicans and Democrats won't speak to each other even though they all say *bipartisan* and *civility* as if they mean it. It's a crazy town."

"I am not a citizen, so I have no right to an opinion. But still, this last election made me think your Founding Fathers should have given an American monarchy a little more thought."

"But the British monarchy's no great shakes either."

"That's because the British are so pompous," he said, with just enough of a twinkle in his eyes to let her know he was joking.

"My boyfriend is a senator." She didn't know why she blurted that out, just when she was enjoying a little anonymity.

"I hope I did not suggest that elected officials are the problem."

"Oh, he's never been elected. He was appointed just a few months ago."

Jacques's puzzlement gave way to intrigue.

"From Colorado, yes?"

She nodded. The waiter poured their wine and retreated.

"You are so very young."

"I'm not much younger than you. He is the one who is young."

"And he has been given a difficult job."

"That's part of our problem. His work, his ambition, the whole Washington scene. It's very difficult." Now she'd gone from being happily anonymous to spilling all the beans on her feelings about being with Mitch. *Blabbermouth,* she thought with a tsk.

"Be gentle with him. He has a lot to prove. All men do, even if it is only to establish that they are the best butcher in town or the bravest fireman. It is not something women feel to the very core of their being. Because they define themselves by who they are and men define themselves by what they do."

She bristled at the inherent sexism and yet, she had to admit that he was not too far off the mark. As ambitious as she was, she could still walk away. Maybe. But Mitch walk away? Never.

"What have you had to prove?"

"That I was the best jeweler of Baie-Comeau. And when I became the jeweler who sold the wealthiest merchant his wife's anniversary ring, I was free to really be myself. Now I am a jewelry designer in New York. Not the best, not the worst. But I enjoy myself because I have already proved everything I needed to prove."

"So you think if Mitch believes he's shown he's the best senator from Colorado, he can kick back, relax and be himself?"

Jacques shrugged.

"We have grown too serious," he declared. "And since I do not know the man and he is not here . . ."

As if his words were a signal to the waiter, their plates were put in front of them. Carole, never having ascribed to the lettuce leaf and diet Coke mode of life, was impressed with the tender filet mignon with coarse pepper and mushroom sauce.

She was grateful as Jacques effortlessly steered talk back to "safe" topics and she found herself laughing at his charming stories of growing up in a poor, rural village in French-speaking Canada.

". . . And then the priest told him that he was forgiven of his sins but to never, ever bring a pig in church again. Especially one wearing a hat."

"I can't believe that."

"Oh, true, true," Jacques protested, with overdrawn indignation. He crossed his heart. "Carole, this has been a wonderful evening. Just as wonderful as this dessert—can you imagine the amount of chocolate that went into making this soufflé?"

She looked around. The dining room was empty, save for a couple smooching in a booth by the kitchen and a waiter laying out napkins for the next day's customers. A glance at her watch confirmed that it was nearly midnight. Mitch would be coming in soon. . . .

"Oh, my gosh. I'd better go," she said. She lifted up her hand. "Check, please."

"Non, non, Cinderella. The bill's been taken care of. Let's get your coat. I'll walk you back to your hotel. The Quarter is very safe, but I have developed such New York habits."

"Let me pay my half of the bill."

"Oh, no," he said firmly. "You have done me the most delightful favor. Your company saved this lonely man from a Friday evening all by himself."

"But I'm not . . . I'm not . . ."

He sensed her trouble at putting thoughts into words.

"The evening's pleasure is not diminished because it ends now or because it will not be repeated. Flowers are beautiful in their vase almost precisely because they are so briefly with us."

Carole sensed it was time to gracefully accede.

"Thank you," she said. "It's been truly magical."

They said good night to the maitre d', who was taking his coffee at the bar. The air was crisp, cold and infused with the mingled scents of pine, cinnamon and freshwater from the St. Lawrence. The streetlights were aided by shopkeepers' Christmas lights in creating an almost angelic atmosphere. A distant police siren competed for their attention with the clip-clop of tourist-friendly horse-drawn carriages with their sleigh bells and squeaking wheels.

At the door of the hotel, Jacques kissed her cold, pink hand.

"Good luck with your fine senator," he said and bowed so slightly that she might almost have imagined he was making the courtly gesture.

And then he disappeared around the corner.

As she passed the front desk, the captain stopped her.

"There's a message for you, Miss Titus," he said and leaned over the oak counter to pass her two small pink slips.

"Thank you."

She waited until she was in her room before opening the messages that she dreaded. The first one, at eight-thirty, was from Mitch: He had missed the flight but would catch one in the morning. The second—at ten-thirty—that she could call him at home anytime, no matter when she got in.

"Shit," she hissed. "Shit, shit, shit, shit."

That having been got out of the way, she dialed out of the hotel. Mitch picked up on the third ring.

"Honey, I'm sorry," he said by way of hello. "Usually he has the attention span of a three-year-old."

"Some would say that's an ability to delegate."

"Still, I'm very sorry."

"I know you are."

"I couldn't get out. I mean, how do you tell the leader of the free world that you need to leave early?"

"You say, 'Half the country thinks you're a buffoon, and by the way, it's Friday.'"

She said this with just the barest margin of humor.

"I'll remember that the next time I'm invited to the White House. But Carole, I'm probably the only Republican who is still speaking to Democrats. I had to be here tonight, if only to keep the tone civil. The president counts on me for that."

"I understand," she said wearily. And she did understand, even more so after dining with Jacques Chancet. "When is your flight coming in?"

"I'll be there before you wake up."

"And I'll believe it when I see you."

They hung up and Carole changed into yellow fleece jammies. The room was cold—the thermostat was at an arctic 65 degrees—and the down comforter seemed too thin for a gal who was conditioned to temperate Potomac winters.

It took her a long time to get to sleep.

She thought she smelled the scent of Ferragamo in her room. *Jacques Chancet. What an interesting name.*

Chapter 5

He's not here, she thought. I'm stuck in the most romantic city in North America and he's not here. He promised me he'd be here before I woke up. I'm awake, it's already nine-thirty—she opened her eyes long enough to check her watch—and he's not here.

The phone rang.

"If you've missed another flight, don't bother," she grumbled into the phone.

"Miss?" An unfamiliar voice.

"Oops, sorry. What is it?"

"A gentleman here to see you. Shall I let him up?"

For the scantest second, she thought of Jacques Chancet. He was handsome, he was secure in himself, he was a New Yorker—well, by way of Quebec City—and he was charming.

"What's his name?"

"Mitch Evans."

She sat up. And with a pang of guilt that she had even thought of another man, she let out a shriek.

"Sure, sure, send him up."

She slammed down the phone. Threw off the covers and ran to the bathroom. Great, what a time to discover the effects of not getting every smidgen of mascara off the night before. She squeezed a little toothpaste onto . . . *Where, oh, where was the toothbrush? Oh, hellwithit,* she squeezed the toothpaste onto her index finger and vigorously rubbed her teeth. Swiped a wet washcloth under her eyes, taking away some of that raccoon look. At least she didn't have the morning-after champagne puffiness. She spat out the toothpaste, spritzed Angel perfume in her hair, slapped her cheeks for color and dashed to the bed before remembering he wouldn't have a key. She jumped back up, unlocked the door and dove under the covers.

Oh, sure, the most *soigné* effect would be achieved by allowing him to caress her into wakefulness. Think what mischief they could make as she drowsily welcomed him! But Carole's brief indulgence gave way to enthusiasm. So what if he knew just how excited she was to see him?

She scarcely noticed the slippers she stepped on and over, the robe laying forlorn on the arm of the upholstered club chair and the housekeeper in the hallway just beginning her morning rounds.

She clobbered him on the landing. Her arms around his neck, he lifted her long legs to straddle his waist. Their kiss was long, hard and sharply focused.

"God, it's good to see you!" he said.

She made to stand but he stopped her.

"I like this," he said.

He carried her back to her room, past the housekeeper who tried not to stare.

"Sir, you forgot your bag," the housekeeper noted as Mitch nudged the door open with his shoe.

"I'll get it in a minute," he said. "Or in two minutes," he added as he strode to the bed. "Or maybe I'll just leave that thing in the hall until it gets stolen. Because, baby, I'm not leaving this bed for a long, long time."

"But the door," Carole warned.

He stood up, regarding her languid pose with a familiar glint in his eye. Then he walked over to the door, throwing off his suit jacket and pulling his tie free from the collar of his shirt. A shirt which, by the way, soon fluttered to the floor.

Lord, it was wonderful to have a man who was such a delectable treat to watch! His skin was lightly tanned, as if the sun just licked him. His muscles swelled at all the right places and what little body hair there was gave the appearance of gold dust.

There were advantages to a younger man, Carole sighed to herself.

He swiped his belt out from his pants and regarded her lazily.

"Those p.j.s are cute. But you don't need them."

"Shouldn't we take our time?"

"Honey, there's no time to take our time. I've missed you."

She rolled over, pretending indifference. A rough tug at her pant legs, and her bottom was bare. An instant later, he was on top of her, his naked flesh pressing against her, his elbows on either side of her, supporting his weight.

He might be smart—hell, he *was* smart. He could digest a government agency budget for breakfast, make a five-minute speech that would clarify a hundred pages of a State Department policy briefing, talk with an R & D genius with the same ease as with a disgruntled voter. But this genius seemed lightweight when compared to his true expertise— her body. He knew every secret place, every neuron that begged to be kissed and stroked, each pleasure zone that needed his attentions. And just when a kiss or caress would, by repetition, lose its power, he explored new territory.

She had never known a man so interested in making her beg for more. Oh, those groupies and staffers and agency wonks who wanted him so badly—if they only knew that on top of being handsome and charming and smart and funny, he was . . . well, his apartment would be besieged with women.

He leaned to one side to caress her hip and while he seemed to focus his attention on telling a funny anecdote about the vice president's bumbling attempts to charm the attendees of the previous days' meetings, his true self was devoted to only one cause.

"And then he said, 'Let me quote you some statistics I uncovered in the Government Accounting Office's latest report on the matter' and that's when the senator from South Carolina told him to go to hell."

Carole laughed.

"Come here," she said, shifting her body to face him. "No offense, but I don't give a damn about government."

"Funny, I don't either."

The first time, she was still wearing her pajama top, and he hadn't even gotten his shoes off. The second time, they had managed to remove all their clothes but only because they thought they were going to take a shower. And the third time, they made it as far as the shower.

"We missed breakfast, you know." Carole was supremely content, but her stomach was starting to growl.

"What kind of place doesn't have room service?" Mitch complained. "Could you get my garment bag? I don't think I should go out there in my towel."

Ten minutes later, they were dressed for sightseeing. Carole realized with a start that it had been several months since she had seen Mitch in jeans—suits, with the occasional tuxedo, were now his everyday uniform. With his blue plaid flannel shirt, the barest sliver of a red T-shirt peeking out from the collar, he looked like a handsome version of any American tourist.

"We can see the fort," Carole said, putting just the slightest coat of mascara on her lashes. She was vain about her lashes and her legs, her two best qualities as far as she was concerned. She didn't need blush today, and her lipstick—Estée Lauder's Nightlife—seemed a little too harsh in the morning light. Instead she slicked on a little sheer gloss. "Next, we could go to the Musée de la Citadelle. It was built by the—"

"Can we not have an agenda?" Mitch asked. "How 'bout if we just walk out the door and be surprised?"

She looked at herself in the mirror. Lord, when was the last time they hadn't had a schedule?

"You're right," she called out. "Good idea. But breakfast. I've got to have breakfast."

They walked out onto the street, newly fallen snow powdering the cobblestones. The church bells chimed twelve times as they followed the crowd into the Rue de Tresor, where the market was teaming with crafts, from stained-glass animals to watercolor vistas and beaded jewelry.

"I think we're talking about lunch," Mitch said. He guided her into a café, where they ordered baguette sandwiches of thick bacon and soft brie. The Saturday newspapers were displayed near the door and Mitch began to ask for the *New York Times* and then abruptly changed his mind.

"No papers *au jour d'hui*," he said to the owner, who made a face at Mitch's savaging of his language.

After lunch, they walked through the Quarter, and decided to stop and attend a mass at a church too quaint and inviting to resist—though neither Mitch not Carole were Catholic. The church was nearly empty, but the priest offered mass with the passion and enthusiasm one would expect if he were facing a full house. Carole and Mitch sat huddled in the pew, listening intently to the sermon and the readings, watching as the few parishioners made their way to the front of the church to take communion. On their way out, Carole and Mitch stopped to thank the priest, who welcomed them warmly. Before they knew it, he was guiding them to a spot behind the sacristy, where they were shown the relics of long-dead saints.

"And here are the registries of every parishioner since our founding," the gray-haired priest said, and he pointed with pride to the two gold-leaf and leather-bound tomes that listed every baptism, marriage and death of his flock.

"You know, I was never baptized." Carole realized too late that she was thinking out loud and glanced apologetically at the priest, as if he were of a mind to disapprove. "My mother wasn't anything, really. I used to think that was so cool, so smart. Not being bound by anybody else's ideas of what God is like."

The priest discreetly appeared to be interested in wiping some dust off the protective glass case.

"And now?" Mitch asked.

"Now I don't know how parents teach their kids right from wrong without a little help," Carole said.

"I think we'll do a good job."

She glanced at him sharply.

The priest coughed self-consciously.

"I must prepare for the next hour's mass," he said.

"Thank you, Father," Mitch said.

When they stepped out onto the square outside the church, Mitch put his arm around her.

"You said we *will*," Carole said. Her words came out in puffs of fluffy white vapor.

"Will what?"

"That we *will* do a good job."

"Well, we will. Carole, we're going to be great parents. You'll be a natural mother. I know you think your mother wasn't a good role model but . . . oh, boy, I blew it. I can tell. Your muscles are tightening. What'd I do now?"

"I'm not so sure about kids."

He took her hand and while she had the instinctive urge to deny him this, she couldn't.

"I want kids, honey," he said. "I've always said that. I hope you do, too. I'm pretty certain you do—even if you don't consciously think about it."

"Mitch, let's not talk about this."

She slipped out from under his arm with apparent nonchalance.

"I overreacted, I know," she said. "Just a little jumpy. That book kind of scared me."

"Now I look at a book like that and I see a beautiful thing. It's life, Carole—births and deaths and marriages. It's the thread of life that makes up the past and future. I'm not scared, Carole. I want to marry, be a father, become part of a book like that. I want to be part of that book with you."

Oh, my God, she thought. It was said. It was out in the open. The lifetime commitment words. And she had two choices: respond seriously or brush it off.

Luckily, Mitch was good at guessing what she'd prefer.

"In fact, we can go back to the hotel and start a family right now."

"Too sore," she said, affecting a light tone.

He looked disappointed, but quickly recovered.

"Hey, we never got down that street, did we?"

They walked on the cobblestone sidewalk, pausing at a

chocolaterie window rich with an intricate display, an entire town made of chocolate.

Mitch pointed across the street. "Hey, a jewelry store. Let's go in. You can help me shop for a very special woman."

"Who?"

"Some dame who's got a birthday coming up."

The twinkle in his eye gave him away.

"Mitch, my birthday's not until February."

"Can't start too early. I was thinking earrings."

Earrings. Safe relationship jewelry.

"And a matching necklace."

Still safe.

They entered a cozy little shop with a display counter lined with black velvet. Diamonds, some loose and others set in gold and platinum, glistened alluringly. Lengths of pearls—pinks, whites, South Seas blacks, freshwater grays—tumbled this way and that. Carole studiously avoided the cabinet in which single diamond rings were housed and instead, made an appreciative murmur over the colored gems.

"Pearls," Mitch said. "Ah, sir, could we see this one right here?"

An elfin-sized man with a face like a dried apple had appeared from a back room.

"Certainly, monsieur."

Carole was presented with a long, lustrous strand of white pearls.

"Too beautiful," she cried.

"Try them on," Mitch urged. He tugged off her jacket so that her slim turtleneck was exposed.

She worked the clasp and put the pearls around her neck. The shopkeeper adjusted the counter mirror so that she could see her reflection. She couldn't stop smiling—what woman could resist feeling like a princess in pearls?

Her eye caught Mitch's mischievous grin.

"Beautiful," a softly seductive voice said.

Carole startled, looked at the back room door, and met the eyes of Jacques Chancet.

"Oh, dear," she said.

"What a pleasure to meet again," Jacques said, stepping forward from the back room door. He wore an impeccably tailored black suit and an ivory turtleneck. She thought he might give her a kiss on both cheeks, but he confined himself to a pleasant handshake. "And monsieur, you must be Senator Evans."

Mitch was too much of a gentleman, or perhaps too secure about himself, to display a nanosecond's hesitation. He held his hand out to Jacques, smiled and told Jacques that he wasn't sure they had met before.

"We haven't," Jacques said. "Mademoiselle Titus was so kind as to take pity on me last night when I couldn't find an empty table at the restaurant. We shared a meal and she told me how she looked forward to your arrival. You seem to be two very busy people who are right to avail yourselves of our Quebec hospitality. If we could only persuade more Americans to do the same . . ."

Mitch nodded with a pleasant smile. "Absolutely."

"But I forget myself. My name is Jacques Chancet. I'm a jewelry designer. I work out of New York. Some of my creations are even sold by this gentleman, who has taught me so much. Monsieur DeLaCroix."

The elf beamed.

"Would you like to see Monsieur Chancet's latest pieces?" he asked.

"We'd love to," Mitch responded eagerly.

Carole slipped the pearls off and handed them back to Mr. DeLaCroix. Couldn't Mitch feel her tension? And yet, what did she have to feel tense about? She hadn't done anything wrong, anything untoward. She had had dinner with a gentleman. But for some reason, she didn't like being near him just now and it was with a vaguely sickened feeling that she allowed herself to be ushered into the back room, an office with a desk on which was strewn a staggering array of jewels.

You're being silly, Carole. This isn't high school.

"This is such an honor," Mitch said. "Thank you so much for showing us all this. Her birthday's coming up in February. Do you have anything special you'd like to show us?"

"It's all special," Mr. DeLaCroix said.

"Mitch, I don't feel like . . ."

"Honey, this is beautiful. Check out these earrings. They're perfect. What kind of stone is this?"

"It's a pink sapphire," Jacques said, sitting at the desk. Mr. DeLaCroix brought in another chair for himself and used the faintest gesture to urge Carole and Mitch into a buttery leather love seat. "Pink sapphires really make a woman's face glow. They're wonderful for evening. But don't forget to look at these canary diamonds. The yellow will set up a beautiful contrast with your dark eyes, mademoiselle."

"Mitch, I don't think I want—"

"Mr. Chancet, you do extraordinary work. I've never seen jewelry like this."

"Thank you," Jacques said.

"Mitch, I don't really wear a lot of—"

"The real question is do you have anything we can afford?" Mitch said and slipped a folded piece of paper across the desk.

Jacques opened the paper, glanced at a pencilled figure and put the paper in his suit jacket pocket.

"Not a problem," he said. He pulled a worn leather case from under the desk and opened it to bring out several velvet boxes. "You missed a most delightful meal last evening, Monsieur Evans. I understand you were delayed by business?"

"Politics," Mitch corrected him.

"But of course."

Carole stood up.

"I can't do this."

"What?

Three simultaneously, hopelessly, tiresomely clueless men.

"Mitch, I'm very sorry. I'm just not in the . . ."

Mitch's expression was painful to her—he was so bewildered. And frankly, so was she. Why would the presence—or absence—of Jacques Chancet make any difference at all as to how she felt as she sat there with Mitch?

"I've got to go," she said abruptly. Adding, as she backed out of the office, "Thank you, Mr. DeLaCroix, Mr. Chancet. Mitch, I'm getting one of those headaches. I think I need to get back to the room."

The next thing she knew she was on the sidewalk, puffing crisp clouds of steam. Mitch followed a few moments later, a cheery bell announcing his exit through the jewelry store door.

"What was that all about?" Mitch asked as he sidled up to her.

"Nothing. I have a headache."

"It was something. You *like* to shop. Maybe as much as you like to—"

"Mitch, nothing happened."

"Are you talking about last night? Having dinner with that guy?"

"I didn't 'have dinner' with 'that guy.' He just happened to have been sitting across from me. There weren't enough tables in the restaurant."

"And that made you so jumpy you had to leave just now?"

"Are you suggesting that there was anything more to it?"

"Oh, boy, this is one of those relationship fights. Men are from Mars. Women are from wherever they're from. No, I didn't think there was anything more than dinner involved. But I don't understand how a simple dinner can turn into this weird little scene," he said with a bewildered shrug.

"You're right. You don't understand."

For a moment, they were at odds. Then Carole softened.

"I don't understand either, Mitch. He just made me feel funny."

"We don't have to see him again."

"Good," she said more forcefully than necessary, and more than she felt.

"So what do we do now?"

"We get out of here. I'm hungry."

"Me, too."

He put his arms around her and she leaned against him as they walked back in the direction of the hotel. Once, just once, she looked back—under the guise of checking to make sure her purse was closed—and she saw Jacques standing on the sidewalk outside the jewelry store watching them.

While she changed into a smoky gray cashmere tank dress and black heels, Mitch returned phone calls. The manager behind the front desk had confided that he had never known a guest to receive so many phone calls in one afternoon. She came out of the bathroom where a swipe of mascara and a spritz of Thierry Mugler's Angel Innocence had worked wonders—Mitch was finishing up a rather contentious conversation.

Carole brushed her hair and pinned it up with two black enamel combs.

"Todd's stuck in Helena, Montana, now," Mitch said when he hung up.

"How'd he end up there?"

"His flight got rerouted."

"Poor Todd."

He put aside the pile of pink slips.

"He'll survive. *I'm* the one who's hungry."

Later, after a dinner at the Bar Maritime overlooking the river, they made love. Slowly, very slowly, and she caught herself only once thinking of Jacques. Every choice, she thought, meant giving up the opportunity of something else. Being with Mitch meant giving up everything but him. Not so much a case of so many men, so little time. More a matter of so many choices, so much a woman has to give up to enjoy any one thing.

She drifted into a shallow sleep and felt him inch away from her and slip from the covers to the desk where he opened up the small handheld Jornada that served as his link to the Capitol. When she woke up at two A.M., he was still working.

The desk clerk called at ten o'clock the next morning.

"*Bon matin,* mademoiselle," he said cheerily. "Your flight is in two hours."

"Umm," Carole murmured. She hung up. "Mitch, it's time to wake up."

Mitch pulled the covers over his ears.

"But, Mom, vacation can't be over!"

"Mitch."

"I hate school!"

"You do not."

He shoved aside the blanket, revealing his long, lean muscles.

"You're right, I suppose. But I do think we need a vacation—a *real* vacation."

"Longer than a day?"

"Hey, we used to get three months in the summer, right?"

Mitch threw on a pair of jeans so he could go down to the lobby. He brought back a tray of café au lait and croissants and assorted jams. Carole dressed in jeans and a sweater and shoved everything else in her bag. Mitch showered, shaved and packed in less than half an hour. The desk clerk called for a cab, which was unaccountably prompt.

"A bientot," the clerk called out. "And have a safe flight."

The cab pulled out of the old city and followed the downward slope of the hills to the flat, unforgivingly gray industrial sections of Quebec City. The airport was even more depressing than usual because not a single passenger in the terminal looked as if they wanted to leave. Even the people waiting for the incoming flight from Montreal looked forlorn.

There seemed to be something not quite finished about their time together. But they were herded onto the 727 and shown to their seats. First class, of course, since Air Canada, like any other airline, automatically upgraded congressmen, Cabinet members and assorted celebrities. Carole and Mitch had met on a flight from Chicago to Washington when Mitch was still a senior Senate staffer. He hadn't been entitled to an upgrade but on that particular flight from hell—delayed, noisy, chaotic—Mitch had shown his Capitol I.D. and the flight attendant had shown him past the curtain to first class. And he had had the gallantry to get his seatmate Carole upgraded as well.

Carole and Mitch settled into their seats, accepting a pre-flight glass of orange juice and steaming-hot hand towels to freshen up. Outside, snowflakes tumbled from puffy gray clouds.

"Bonjour," the pilot announced.

"Give me your hand," Mitch said.

When they took off, his fingers entwined with hers, Carole remembered again why she loved him. Why she needed him. Why she could never leave him. She could endure anything, even the plane crashes she rehearsed and reviewed in her head every time she flew—if he were with her. If plane crashes were truly as rare as statisticians claimed, it was hardly enough to base a relationship on. But being with Mitch was more than that—he made her feel that she could live every part of her life in happiness and courage. And Lord knew that every day was just a little like hugging your shoulders against a seatback, your face tilted up to the heavens, your mind rattling off terrible scenarios—and the only way to get through it was with someone holding your hand.

"Carole, I know it's not the most romantic moment to ask . . ."

"Don't ask me anything." She stopped him with a touch of her finger to his bottom lip. "Things are perfect just the way they are."

Chapter 6

Carole needed java bad. She hadn't visited the pushpot since she got into the office at six. Already it was ten and the phone calls and e-mails had been flying. It was time for a little mental downtime. A small crowd was huddled around Dana, who was seated at the table in the lunchroom.

"Check this out," Dana murmured.

"What is it?" Carole asked brightly, breezing over to the coffeepot.

Alix, Elyssa and Robyn jumped as if they had been caught shoplifting or something. Dana slid a folded copy of what looked like the *Washington Post* onto her lap.

"Nothing," she said.

"Nothing," Alix agreed.

"Nothing at all," Elyssa said.

"Did you get the ring?" Robyn asked.

"ROBYN!" her tablemates screamed.

"What are you talking about?" Carole said. She filled her cup at the pushpot and sat down across from Dana.

"Noth—"

"Don't give me that nothing crap."

"Okay," Dana said. "But I didn't think it was a good idea to spoil the surprise."

"If she reads a newspaper she's going to see it," Robyn said indignantly. "So I didn't spoil anything."

"We'll see about that," Elyssa said.

Dana pushed the newspaper across the table to Carole, pointing to a page. It was Mitch standing on the sidewalk outside Tiffany's. The caption read "Sen. Mitch Evans (R-Col.) was spotted at Tiffany's buying a two-carat princess-cut diamond ring. Sources close to the senator say he's planning to pop the question to Internet exec Carole Titus in just a few short days. I'll be wearing black and not just because it takes off a few pounds—I'll be in mourning when this hunk is taken out of circulation."

"Oh, Lord." Carole sighed.

Robyn squealed.

"Aren't you excited!?!"

"Congratulations," Elyssa said. She patted Carole's hand. "I'm thrilled for you."

"You say congratulations to the groom," Dana corrected. "That is to suggest that he's accomplished something of great importance in persuading the woman to marry him. Best wishes are offered to the bride-to-be because congratulations suggest she had to work to capture the man."

"So why do you say best wishes?" Robyn asked.

"Maybe because all brides need them?" Dana offered.

"When did you become the etiquette expert?" Elyssa demanded.

"I think of it as part of my job," Dana said. "We have to set the right tone with every one of our cards. And the ones that celebrate marriage and engagement are the trickiest."

"I'll just give you a high-five," Alix said. "And I don't mean anything by it. Congratulations or best wishes—whatever."

"I hate to disappoint you, but this is just gossip," Carole said shaking her head, but staring at the photo. Mitch wore his usual impeccable suit, white shirt, dark tie, but he looked somewhat vulnerable as he stood alone on the sidewalk. Was he really going to ask her to marry him? Newspapers got so much wrong so much of the time and this gossip columnist was one of the worst purveyors of speculation. "I haven't heard a word about any of this."

"Well, of course, you didn't know about this," Robyn said impatiently. "That's why they call it 'popping the question,'—because it's supposed to be a big surprise."

"Not if it's up to you," Carole snapped. She was instantly sorry for snarling at Robyn, whose enthusiasm and *joie de vivre* were her most endearing features.

She put her arm around the young woman and gave her a squeeze. "Look. All I'm saying is this is all news to me. If and when Mitch Evans asks me to marry him—and if I have an answer for him—you'll be the first to know."

"Girlfriend, if he asks you, say yes or some other gal will snap him up like that!" Alix snapped her fingers.

Carole felt a headache coming on.

"Ladies, I am just not in a frame of mind for marriage right now. If anything I think we'll live together for a while."

"Right," Elyssa said. "With a senator from a conservative western state. That would do wonders for his career."

Carole stood up. Her headache was now promising to be a big one. "Okay, girls, enough."

She strode out of the lunchroom, hearing Robyn's wounded "What's got into her?" just as the door slammed shut.

Shouldn't the prospect of marriage to Mitch make her happy? she thought as she sat down at her desk. Her keyboard—and every other available inch of space—was covered with paper printouts, message slips, letters and contracts. She cleared away enough space to put a coaster down. Her coffee was steaming.

Marriage. The word felt like a brick on her brain. This would have to be the last time. Women who divorced once had simply made a mistake. Twice, they were flighty. Three times, clearly not able to manage their lives. And four? Certifiable! Unless they were in a soap opera, and Carole shook her head, remembering that her mother's character in *The Beautiful and the Damned* had been married seven times, twice to the same man and once to a bigamist with amnesia. If she listened to her mother—or her mother's character— she would say, "Go ahead, get married, next season you can get a divorce. Hal was just a practice husband."

If she were younger, it would be easier to just go with her emotions. She loved Mitch. She wanted to be with him. She wanted to laugh at his jokes and have late-night conversations. She wanted to live in the same home and share the same bed. She wanted, even, maybe to have children together. Someday.

But her first marriage was a big issue for Carole. Hal had been a musician, talented and fiercely ambitious. Carole had felt honored to be sharing his life. And that was the point— it was always about *his* life. His group, his gigs, his problems, his creative blocks, his groupies and ultimately his struggle with drugs. Her life? Well, did Carole exist if Hal wasn't there to need her? That was the koan of her marriage!

When she had left him, Hal had accused her of being too uptight. Too conventional for him. Too, well, boring. At the time, she had been terrifically wounded.

How would Hal have known whether I was boring? she thought now with a scowl.

If in every relationship there is the beloved and the lover, Carole had been the lover to Hal's beloved.

Could Mitch be just the same—albeit with a better job and no musical talent whatsoever? Did women always end up being Mom to their man?

Screw this, she thought. *I'm not solving anything here.*

She picked up the phone and made some calls. Within minutes, she had her itinerary, which she handed to a temp in her office named Lisa.

"Okay, I have an appointment in Dallas on the fourteenth and I can stay overnight there or take a late afternoon flight to Phoenix. Either way, I have to be in Phoenix by noon. Make reservations under my name at a good restaurant in the downtown area."

"Anything else?"

"Yes. Does your mother know you have all those piercings?"

"Yeah. She's cool with it."

"What do guys think?"

"I don't care. I'm a lesbian."

Now that's a solution, Carole thought.

"I'll have your shuttle tickets for New York on your desk by noon," Lisa said. "And if you ever decide guys are not worth the hassle . . ."

"Thanks. I'll keep it in mind."

She called Pepper on her cell phone and was mildly surprised she got through. The two had been exchanging messages for a week.

"When we ran into each other at the party, I thought it'd be fun to do lunch one day," Carole said, not adding that she was just a tad worried about her.

"I'd love to, but I should warn you my schedule's a little up in the air right now."

"Oh, because of the mess at the White House?"

"No, I'm actually taking a leave of absence."

"Why?" Carole was surprised. There wasn't anyone more devoted to the Washington news scene than Pepper.

"Carole, I'll tell you because Mitch and the rest of the Hill crowd will find out soon enough. I've been diagnosed."

"Oh, God, with what?"

"Ovarian cancer."

Carole couldn't help the cold, hellish tingle up her spine.

"I'm so sorry." Stupid phrase. Impotent. Weak. But what else can be said?

"I am, too. I was trying to have a baby and took a lot of hormone shots. And I guess there were consequences."

"Pepper, what can I do?"

"Take me to lunch. Funny thing, I spent all these years hoping I'd lose some weight, and now, between chemo and radiation, I've got to keep as many pounds on this frame as possible. So let's eat something fattening."

"Pizza."

"And ice cream. And Carole?"

"Yeah?"

"If you've got friends up there somewhere, talk to them about me."

"You'll be in my prayers. How does week after next sound? I'm looking at Thursday. One-ish?"

She told Mitch immediately, but asked him to not say a word to anybody. He promised, though he'd already heard rumors that she was taking some time off.

"Why don't we invite her and her husband over to my house tomorrow for dinner?" Mitch offered.

"I can't. I'm taking an early shuttle to New York."

Mitch had brought dinner to her house—Dean & DeLuca caviar, fresh salmon grilled with soy and sesame, baby veggies and a box of dark chocolate truffles. He also brought a bottle of champagne, which he only opened after he established that he had an invitation to spend the night and could send Sam home with the car.

Carole told him about New York while they ate the caviar on thin, toasted bread. Mitch had a strict no condiments policy—no hard-boiled egg, no sour cream, no onion. He liked to say that condiments were only for those occasions when bad caviar happened to good people.

"What time do you leave?"

He reached down to slip a few precious beads of caviar onto Whisker's tongue. Carole tsked enough to show both of them she disapproved.

"I'm going to catch the seven-thirty. So don't let me drink too much of this, okay?"

He loosened his tie and slid farther down on the soft sofa cushions.

"When do you get back?"

"Maybe Friday. But then it may be easier for me to go directly to Dallas. The mechanics union is threatening another slowdown, so I want to be in Dallas before their contract deadline."

Mitch reached over to the chair on which his suit jacket was draped and began searching his pockets.

"Hmmm. You sound like you're not going to be around much. I guess I'll just have to ask you . . . ."

She cut him off. "Mitch, I've been thinking about our relationship."

"Oh, good, then this is relationship talk."

"I'm being serious."

Mitch continued patting down the pockets of his jacket, where no doubt rested a velvet-lined box. She pulled his hand to her before he could retrieve the box.

"I'm just as serious," he said. "Honey, I think we both know we love each other and we're mature enough to make decisions to—"

"Absolutely," she interrupted. "And so, we both know that there are times when our careers take priority. That time is now."

His eyebrows came together.

"I don't think that's incompatible with what I want," he said in his very best *Meet the Press* voice.

"It might be, if you want what I think you want."

"And what do I want?"

"Mitch, look, just trust me. We need to take things slow. Focus on where we're going. Find out if this relationship can work before jumping into things. You know, you have a lot on your plate these days and—"

"Oh, damn, Carole. What you really should be saying is that you're nervous. You're nervous about the *M* word."

"I don't think it would be a good idea for us to get married," Carole said.

He tugged his hand out from her fingers, but didn't reach again for the pocket inside his jacket. Instead he put his plate on the coffee table and straightened up. She felt his bristling displeasure.

"We could live together," she offered. "Maybe a few months from now. If things are going well. I could look into renting out this place. Or we could keep both. Then, if things don't work out it's not all messy."

"It's always messy when it doesn't work out."

"But if we're living together at least lawyers don't get involved."

"Living together is not an option for me. I don't want to be in a position where I have to defend a lifestyle many of my constituents don't care for."

"You're allowed to have a private life."

"I am. But I also have a duty to live in a morally responsible fashion. That may not be for everyone in Washington, but it's just the way it is for me."

"I don't see what's wrong with living together. It's a perfectly moral choice. And for the small-minded people who think it's not—"

"Those small-minded people put their trust in me. In fact," he added, "I *am* one of those small-minded people."

Silence. And then . . .

"When did you start talking like Elmer Gantry?"

"Oh, get out, Carole."

"No, really, I don't think two adults should take one giant leap when they could avoid a whole lot of heartache by taking one very small step at a time."

"And I *believe* in marriage. Which happens to be a giant step."

"Exactly my point. And it's not necessarily a giant step I want to repeat."

Sometimes when he looked at her, she had the sneaking suspicion that he was much older than her, in all the ways that mattered. He was wiser than he let on, he gave everyone (including her) a lot of room to have contrary opinions and to make mistakes. And he was as sure-footed and as purposeful as a man twice his age.

"Do you remember when I asked you out the first time?" Mitch asked.

"Of course I do."

"Remember you told me there were only two things that could happen and both of them were bad?"

"I did say that. Either a one-night stand that made me feel uncomfortable or a long affair that ended with one of us hurt."

"Yeah, well. I think we're there now."

The shuttle was nasty and brutish, but mercifully short. When she stepped out into the drizzly walkway to take the last cab from the taxi stand, a squat suit elbowed her aside for it.

Ah, Home Sweet Home, Carole thought, watching the purloined cab slither out from the pile of black snow at the curb.

Thankful when another cab pulled up just minutes later, she directed it to East 64th Street and Park Avenue. The driver flipped the meter and turned up the radio.

Carole flipped open her cell phone and called her mother at the studio. Her mother's character had been revived— recovering her memory after the amnesia brought on when her lover threw her out of his private plane over the Atlantic Ocean. *Soap Opera Digest* had done two showcase interviews about her. And a *Soap Opera Daily* columnist had been slipping little tidbits about Honoria Titus in her latest columns.

"I'm getting my arms waxed," her mother said. "I have a nude scene coming up."

Carole cringed.

"You'll have a sheet, right?"

"Of course, although Jaime is a little better about showing off my pets now that I've had them redone."

A mother who called her breasts "pets"? Carole shuddered.

"I'll be staying at the Lotos Club," Carole said.

"What's that?"

"A private club just off Central Park. It's a block away from the Athletic Club. I've got a meeting with Cartier. They have a membership and got me a room. There isn't an available hotel room in all of Manhattan."

"Ouch! Son of a bitch! Do you have to pull so— Ouch! Crimmeee, the things I do for my career. Why don't you stay with me?"

"Because I don't do dishes on business trips. I'll call you later, Mother. Maybe we can have dinner."

"Okay, honey. Call me then? *Ouch!*"

When Carole put her phone back in her bag, she noticed a stack of business cards held together with a rubber band. She undid the rubber band and flipped through the cards, discarding most and paper-clipping a select few in her Filofax for later. Near the bottom of the stack was one for Jacques Chancet, Personal Jeweler, an elegant card in raised gold leaf lettering.

She fingered the card. *What if? Why not? No way.* She should most definitely not be seeing another man if she and Mitch . . . what?

What exactly were they doing now?

He had spent the night, but it had had all the joy of a funeral. When Sam brought the car around, Mitch kissed her goodbye as if it were forever—and maybe it was.

She had left for the airport from home, checking in with Elyssa before going.

"It's not really an official breakup," Elyssa concluded.

"We're not in high school. I don't have to return a varsity jacket. But he did take his toothbrush and his shaver."

"Carole, I thought you loved him."

"I do."

"Why does marriage spook you so much?"

"Why shouldn't it? And why does he have to move so fast?"

"You've been going together for six months. Carole, his timing's a little swifter than yours. He has his work to consider. And children. I always thought you wanted children, too."

"Yeah, but not yet."

"There's not much yet left, if you don't mind my saying so."

She ripped up Jacques's card and pushed its pieces deep into the bag.

The Lotos Club was a six-story Federalist brick with white trim, squeezed in between the Wharton Museum and a minor Vanderbilt cousin's mansion that had been broken up into twelve minor millionaire flats. As the cab pulled to the curb, two young men in exquisitely plain black suits stepped forward to greet her. One man opened her door and welcomed her to the Lotos. The other negotiated her carry-on out of the trunk.

"Miss Titus, right this way."

The club had a cozy foyer scented slightly with orange, bergamot and a freshly drawn fire. On the wall opposite the door was a six-foot-high portrait of the author Tom Wolfe in his trademark white suit.

"The author himself donated this portrait to the club," the man with her luggage explained. "Our members are mostly associated with the arts and patrons of the arts."

"Ah." Carole now understood Cartier's Lotos connection.

"Right this way."

He led her into a small study with floor-to-ceiling windows overlooking the street. She took a seat on a burgundy leather sofa near the crackling fire. A capable young man rose from his perch behind a mahogany desk, welcomed her to the club and offered her tea or coffee from a silver service on a Chinese red hutch.

"Coffee, please. Black."

Coffee was presented in an eggshell-thin china cup and a heavy damask napkin. He gave her a leather-bound register to sign and took the letter of introduction that Cartier had mailed to her.

"Their car will be here at two o'clock," he said. "Now, may I show you your room?"

"My bag?"

"It's already upstairs, ma'am."

He escorted her along a carpeted princess staircase to the second floor and presented her with her key outside her door.

"Enjoy your stay."

The room was enormous. Bigger than the apartment in which she and her sisters were raised. And the ceiling? She estimated it was twenty feet high, with an ornate scagliormo medallion anchoring a crystal chandelier. A uniformed maid was hanging her suits in an oak armoire.

"Shall I press this one for you, miss?" She seemed to be suppressing her disapproval of Carole's packing system. Which is to say, no packing at all, just shoving in as many things as possible until the zipper doesn't work.

"No, that's all right. Well, actually, sure."

"I'll have it back within the hour."

Carole freshened up and went over her notes for her meeting. When the maid returned with her suit, she slipped it on, reapplied her lipstick and made it downstairs just as a black Lincoln Town Car pulled up to the curb.

The five-story Cartier building was done up with red bunting that tied into a pretty bow overlooking the corner of Fifth Avenue and East 52nd Street. Gay swags of fir draped across the second-floor balconies and a battalion of seven-foot nutcrackers guarded the entrance. The driver pulled up to the curb and jumped out to open her door.

I've made it, Carole thought, and she wasn't talking geography. Carole used to oooh and aaahh at the city's window displays on her way home from school every day. Once, she had seen Stevie Nicks alight from a limousine on the very same curb from which she had just got out of her borrowed car.

Oh, life was easy then. Those days, Carole would have been happy with long blond hair and black lace-up boots with a perfect heel.

Funny, thirty-seven was just old enough that what was perfect then seemed perfect once again.

Chapter 7

The meeting went long but did not seem particularly successful. She felt like she was slogging through mud and sand. Every concern was met and then another problem would pop up in its place. But Carole gamely made arrangements to come back the following day. She told the driver she didn't need a ride, and he couldn't hide his relief—rush-hour traffic wasn't pretty. She knew she'd have to pick up a cab eventually, but she enjoyed walking with the anonymous throng. The street smelled cold and greasy. The cabs honked more frequently than they did in Washington and the drivers were more creative in their denunciations of those who blocked their path. It was something of a homecoming, even a relief, to get annoyed at the music blasting from a passing car.

She walked for nearly a half hour, stopping to look in the occasional shop window, until she found herself in front of a slender Georgian building with white Doric columns. It was squeezed in between a sporting goods megastore and a brightly lit Restoration Hardware. The two-story brick looked like it was being squeezed from its granite base to its white portico. The eagle weather vane at its peak looked desperately brave. And only the very smallest of gold-plated signs screwed on top of the door knocker let on that this was a serious jewelry establishment for serious lovers of gems.

You can't, she thought.

Why bother? she asked herself. *You'd only be doing this because you're feeling blue about Mitch. I mean, yes, you had a wonderful time with this man, but it was just one night and it was in circumstances that would make any man look good because he showed up and Mitch didn't. One would think you can't spend two minutes without a man, which is absolutely not true because right after you divorced Hal you had a wonderful period of quiet solitude, to say nothing of celibacy, which could serve as a model for women everywhere.*

Persuaded by the unbearable logic of it all, she turned from the door and stepped down the first marble step into . . .

"Madam," he said.

. . . his arms. The firm sweep of cashmere coat and gloved hands ensured that she didn't stumble.

"Mademoiselle Titus!"

Carole looked up into Jacques's face.

"What a pleasure to see you, Carole."

"I was out for a walk," she said and then lied, "How surprised I am to find myself here."

"It is my surprise. Would you care to come in and warm yourself? A new client's insurance company absolutely insists that when I carry this bag I cannot stay in one place." He gestured to a tall, broad-shouldered black man wearing a pale camel overcoat. The man nodded at Carole but retained his cautious, vaguely hostile expression.

"That's an insurance company?"

"Mr. Smith has been sent to guard some gems that I've been asked to reset. And if we stand out here on the sidewalk for a moment longer he will become quite agitated."

"If I come inside, will he kill me?"

Jacques laughed easily and took her arm.

"Let's not find out. Mr. Smith, meet a friend of mine, Carole Titus."

Mr. Smith shook hands and made an appropriately courteous comment about the weather in an accent that suggested the finest British education.

"I cannot ask Mademoiselle Titus in for a drink?"

"Regretfully—under the terms of your contract—no."

Carole squirmed. "It's quite all right, really. I just happen to be here on a business trip and I . . ." *Liar, liar, pants on fire—why don't you tell the truth? I scheduled a business trip because I'm a relationship coward and . . .*

"Then take my keys, Mr. Smith, and make yourself at home. I'll step out with Mademoiselle Titus for just a bit."

"Jacques, I just . . ."

"Non, non, I need a break. These Saudi clients are very demanding."

He transferred a titanium briefcase to Mr. Smith and gave him the keys to his building.

"I am allowed to leave, am I not?" Jacques inquired.

"Of course," Mr. Smith said. "As long as I keep the bag. A pleasure to meet you, miss."

Jacques put her arm through his own. He smelled good and given that New York was a constant assault on the senses, that was saying a lot.

"Take pity on a man who has worked too hard today. Have dinner with me without an argument. How are we to disagree with the fate that has brought you here?"

He guided her along the crowded sidewalk. He talked about the job he was doing for a Saudi princess. Her Royal Highness wanted a collection of very large emeralds and diamonds to be set in a single necklace.

"I had to talk sternly with her. No woman should be outdazzled by her jewelry. So I refused the work."

"But you still have Mr. Smith."

"Yes, I refused. She pleaded. I refused again. She pleaded. I refused once more and then she acceded. The jewels will be set the way I want. But the gems are insured for over eight million dollars and so I have Mr. Smith."

"But why were the gems out of your office?"

"This is New York! Emeralds and diamonds like to take in the sights like any other tourist," he said. They both laughed. "Actually, I needed to confirm for myself that they have not been heat-treated—a very common problem for emeralds. I do not have the laboratory equipment for that."

He took her to Petrossian, where caviar, salmon and other delicacies of Russia were sold. A small dining room was laid out on the second floor and Jacques was welcomed in the way old friends are. The maitre d', chatting with Jacques in French and Russian, showed them a table overlooking the street. It was laid out in glowing red damask, which glowed as brightly as the tapered candles in crystal holders. Only one other couple was seated and several staff members dined quietly at a table near the kitchen.

"Luc, we put ourselves in your hands," Jacques said. "Would that be all right?"

Carole nodded.

They were very quickly given two flutes of crisp, clear Taittinger champagne.

"So you are in New York for business?"

"Cartier. They are thinking of advertising on our website."

"That would be a very wise move for them," he said. "Who are you dealing with?"

She told him. He related an anecdote that perfectly captured the head of their negotiating team's personality. She was acutely aware of Jacques's vibrant intelligence, a kind of laser-sharp interest in people.

They chatted about the other people at her afternoon meeting; Jacques knew most of them. They were presented with eggshells filled with pale, fluffy spoonfuls of scrambled egg and topped with the lightest garnish of Beluga pearls. Toast triangles were laid on the rim of the plates. It was clear Jacques knew how to live well and the waiters who served them took pride in gaining his approval.

It was while they ate a second course of salmon that Jacques graciously asked after Mitch.

"Nearly all the news out of Washington sounds ghastly. And yet, I've never heard anyone say a word against the senator from Colorado. How does he manage?"

"He's the only man in Washington who doesn't hold a grudge."

"That's a remarkable gift. Possessed by a remarkable man."

Carole put down her fork.

"We're breaking up," she said abruptly. "Or, at least, we seem to be in that process. He wants marriage."

"He's asked you?"

"Not officially, exactly, I never let him get it out of his mouth."

"A man should just ask. No hints, no long talks, just ask. The element of surprise is important. Makes success more likely."

She wondered briefly about how many times this had come up in his life.

"His picture was taken outside Tiffany's. It was in the *Washington Post*. So I knew."

"Poor man."

"I told him we should live together. Try it out for a while. I don't want things to end badly."

"You are the sort who likes to take off a bandage slowly."

"I suppose I am."

The waiter took her plate and topped off her champagne. She waited until he was out of earshot.

"He is very old-fashioned."

Jacques shrugged.

"Most of the world is."

"I don't know why I'm telling you any of this."

"Because we are very much alike. And while opposites attract, you harbor the suspicion that such alliances shouldn't succeed."

This would be the best time for a waiter to interrupt them. For Carole to say something. For the candles, half drawn down, to fall out of their holders and provoke a table fire. But none of this occurred and she was required to answer.

"If anything happened here, between us, wouldn't it just be a rebound thing?" she asked limply.

"Not the worst thing."

"But not the best thing."

"Perhaps you are right. And in any event, nothing will happen tonight. I have Mr. Smith and I feel compelled to issue him pajamas and a midnight snack."

"And I'm at the Lotos Club."

He chuckled.

"The staff are notorious gossips. Comes from being the favorite club for actors and writers. The maids are always leaking information to Liz Smith."

"So we're agreed."

"Nothing happens," he said, touching his flute to hers. "We're utterly safe."

She felt a scarcely realized anxiety leave her. This was not an affair. This was not the start of anything new. This was simply two people having dinner—punctuated by the most natural form of flirting Carole had ever encountered. It was so *direct*.

The waiter presented them both with their entrées— braised lamb chops with chopped mint leaves and buttery baby vegetables that made clear the establishment was not in favor of healthy eating.

"Shall I bring the soufflés when they are ready?"

"Yes, of course," Jacques said.

The mention of soufflés nearly killed all appetite for lamb and vegetables. They waited for their dessert and Carole let the champagne, the warm glow of the dining room, the fullness of her stomach conspire to make their magic. She enjoyed herself even more fully than she had in Quebec City. When the very last morsel of soufflé was swallowed, she regretfully put an end to the evening.

"Cartier wants to continue its discussions tomorrow," she said.

"Then let's get you to your club."

He got up and immediately the maitre d' brought their coats.

"The check?" Carole asked as they went downstairs.

"House charge," Jacques explained.

He walked her back to the club and on the sidewalk out- side its doors, kissed her on both cheeks in the continental fashion.

"When you see those nice people at Cartier tomorrow, give them my warmest regards."

* * *

The regards from Jacques had the most unexpected result.

"I think they thought if they didn't conclude the deal immediately, *you* would advertise on our website," Carole told Jacques when she called him from the car. "I was out of there in ten minutes flat with the best terms possible. I thought I was going to be there all day and into the next. And I was assuming failure."

"So your business in New York is complete?"

"Yeah, but my flight into Dallas isn't scheduled until day after tomorrow. And unfortunately I have a nonrefundable ticket so I guess I'll just have to bite the bullet and spend a little time with my mother. She wants me to come down to her set and so I'm headed there now." She glanced out the window. "If we ever get out of midtown, that is."

"The set of *The Beautiful and the Damned*," he said, sighing dramatically. "Its actors and actresses are so very talented, the story line so compelling. I wish I could meet the very talented people involved."

She laughed.

"I'm sure. It's a soap opera and it's hideous. You can't possibly want to come with me."

"Oh, no. You've seen through my very ungraceful ploy. I want to see you again and I don't know how else to ask."

Actually, his ploy worked very well indeed. She felt flattered and, well, what the hell? She was a free woman.

"How about we get together after I visit my mom? It looks like we're going to be having a serious mother-daughter talk." Carole bit her tongue against saying that it was very often unclear which one of them was really the mother. "I'll take her to lunch and then I'll be free."

"Wonderful. By then, my back will be aching and my eyes sore and red from hunching over this worktable."

"The Saudi princess's necklace?"

"I'm nearly finished."

"I'll drop by around two o'clock."

"Mr. Smith will let you in. On his way out to take the princess her jewels."

*W*hen *Carole arrived at the set, her mother was pouty.* Not miserable-pouty, just the kind of pouty that was the unfortunate result of the enthusiasm with which her doctor had injected collagen into her lips.

"I think it looks fab-oo," Carole's mother said. "Very Esther Canadas."

La Grenouille was never particularly well-lit, but today, with snow threatening and gray clouds suspended over the skyline, it was especially difficult to assess the damage. One thing was clear—her mother didn't look remotely like an exotic young runway model.

"Can't you get some of that stuff sucked out? And did you leave any for Steven Tyler?"

Her mother looked puzzled.

"Aerosmith."

"I don't have as much in here as he does."

"Bullshit. You've co-opted the nation's reserves."

"Don't be so critical. And no, you can't just take it out. It goes down on its own. It is reabsorbed back into your tissue."

"Mother! *Eeeuuuuwww!* Won't that cause cancer or something?"

"You sound like Jaime!" Jaime was the director of the show. "He's demanding that my story line be cut for a month because he says viewers will think I've been attacked by killer bees."

"I don't blame him. Your lips were fine before."

"You don't feel the pressure of age."

"Oh, yes, I do. More than you'd imagine."

Her mother picked up her water glass.

"Then here's to us. Living as fast as we can."

Her mother ordered scrambled egg whites—no oil, no butter, no salt—and a salad—no dressing, no croutons, just a lemon wedge, thank you.

"Do you think, by the way, that Mitch would be willing to do a guest appearance? Elizabeth Taylor did *General Hospital* and . . ."

"Absolutely not! He's a senator, for cripe's sake."

"So?"

"He's supposed to be serious and dignified."

"Right. Like any of those clowns in Washington are."

"And besides, Mother, this is why I needed to talk to you. We're . . ."

A photographer appeared at the booth. Carole leaned back in her seat and turned her head away so that the photographer would have an unobstructed shot of her mother.

"No, doll, don't do that. What kind of mother doesn't want her beautiful daughter photographed with her? Especially when her engagement is about to be announced . . ."

"Mother, we're not . . ."

"Of course, they're being hush-hush about it. But we know it's coming, don't we?" She winked at the photographer. "Now, darling, make sure the caption mentions the show. *N'est-ce pas?*" Her mother fluttered her lashes at the photographer.

"Mother, we're not getting married! We broke up last week."

A full-on shot of her mother would have been perfect, especially with those killer bee-stung lips wide open to display a very good porcelain veneer job. Instead, the photographer captured Carole full-on, with flushed cheeks and a double-dare-you tilt of her chin.

"Hand it over," her mother whispered sharply at the photographer. She held her hand palm up, the Mandarin red nails curling ever so slightly heavenward.

The photographer raised his shoulders.

"No way. This is real news."

"Hand it over."

"Fuhgeddaboutit."

"I know about the chippies you keep all over town."

"So what?"

"And the *real* story about your coverage of the debutantes last month. And the panties that disappeared out of the dressing room at the cotillion dance. I must say I find you morally repugnant."

"Bitch."

He opened the camera, pulled out a long length of film and left it curling on the floor as he stomped out of the restaurant. Carole's mother waved over a busboy and asked him to take care of the mess. For a striking moment, Carole was aware that as flawed as the quality of her maternal love, it was still vibrant and strong. Then her mother spoke.

"Did you do this just to hurt me?"

"Breaking up with Mitch or telling you about it?"

"Both."

"Absolutely. I would destroy my own happiness if it would hurt you."

"Is that a joke?"

* * *

"*One good reason never to have kids is that I won't turn* out like my mother."

Jacques considered this as he watched the skaters outside at Rockefeller Plaza.

"You mean selfish, really. Because that seems to be your major objection to her."

"Selfish. Self-involved. Self-centered. It *is* always about her. It's always her. And she has never been able to see outside of herself. To see what others need. Well, maybe when she told the photographer to hand over the film. I think she did that to protect me. At least a little bit."

"That won't be how you'll be a mother. In fact, I predict you'll be just the opposite. Your problem will be to remember that you are a person, too. But with the right man, you'll find the balance because he will provide all the love you need."

"Maybe I don't want kids."

He clicked his tongue in a distinctly Gallic display of contempt.

"You are meant to be a mother. It is what you were born for."

"That's a little sexist."

"No, no, it's the way you look at children on the street, the way you pause at the windows of baby clothes shops, the obvious mothering love in your heart that's waiting for a child to give to."

Carole was a fighter, an arguer, a debater. And she was ready to jump in and disagree with him then and there. But she considered his words. They had spent the afternoon strolling down Fifth Avenue. There had been the woman with triplets—triplets!—wheeling her darlings through the halls of MoMA in a triple carriage. Carole had asked her how she managed. The young mother allowed as how a good mother-in-law and an occasional glass of wine before dinner worked well for her. There was the Oilily baby store on West 57th Street with its display of overalls and onesies—she had felt downright peeved that she didn't know anyone with a newborn she could spoil. And then there had been the couple standing outside St. Thomas, the Episcopal church three blocks from St. Patrick's Cathedral. They were twentysomething—he with a backpack and scarce beard and she with a belly that looked like a basketball that she had slipped into her jeans just before leaving the house. They had stood on the curb trying for a cab. When the yellow stopped, the woman tried to climb over the snow mountain left by the plows. Failing, she looked like a beached whale in a nature show, until her man picked her up with amazing virility and grace. He deposited her at the cab's door and they were soon on their way. The whole drama lasted not more than ten seconds. Jacques hadn't seen her watching them, had he?

"Okay, so let's say I concede the point. How do I know I've met the right man to have a child with?"

As soon as she said it, she realized it was an extraordinarily provocative question. One that a woman didn't ask a man she'd only recently begun seeing. If she could call whatever this was "seeing" Jacques.

But she hadn't been thinking of Jacques, really. She was thinking of Mitch.

"You don't know," Jacques said. "Do you think anybody does? It's a gamble. Just like the lottery game. Even with the odds so much against us, we still play."

"Do you play the game?"

"Me? I've never played the lottery. I think of it as a tax on people who aren't good at math."

"I was talking about . . ."

"I know what you were talking about."

Interestingly, he didn't answer the question. Rather, he motioned for the waitress, paid for their hot chocolates and asked Carole if she would like time to dress for dinner.

"I have a friend who has a little restaurant here in town. I made reservations, but they're not until nine. There's a new singer at the Algonquin tonight. We could stop in, listen for a while and then eat."

"Sounds wonderful. Is it fancy?"

He shrugged.

"My friend will want to seat you by the window even if you wear blue jeans . . ."

"I'll dress."

Chapter 8

He *put her into a cab and said he'd pick her up in an* hour. And an hour was just about enough time to shower, pin her hair into a twist, paint her nails dark as night and throw on a white sequined gown that grazed her ankles while a side slit showed off bare legs and gold *peau de soie* T-straps. Jacques, dressed in a midnight blue suit and an elegant shirt, met her in the club sitting room. He rose from the club chair when she entered the room and he didn't need a word of flattery to convey his approval.

"I hope you don't mind," he said, reaching into his inside jacket pocket. He found the white velvet pouch with his name embroidered on it in gold thread. "I think this will do."

She opened the pouch to find a set of earrings. Long, pale ellipses of carved white jade dangling from platinum wire with the very tiniest of diamonds to give it sparkle.

"I just made them yesterday. They are to be called Paper Whites. Because if you notice, the jade seems to glow from within like a newly blooming narcissus."

"Oh, my gosh, I can't take these."

"Please do. I have already written up the plans and some-day soon this design will be made available to the public. But for now, take them and wear them. I made them for you. You were the inspiration."

She put them on, and the deceptively simple earrings made her outfit.

"Beautiful," Jacques said.

"They truly are."

"I wasn't talking about the earrings."

They took a cab to the Algonquin Hotel, famous for its history and guests—writers and other intellectuals from the twenties and thirties had made its bar and lobby their salon. These days there was a certain shabbiness to the place, the rich burgundy carpet just a little frayed, the cushions on the club chairs done in, the occasional floorboard creaking with age. They were seated on a leather love seat tucked behind a maple folding screen with two palmettos guarding their privacy. The singer was a tall black woman who could have made millions as a supermodel. Her backup consisted of a drummer, a bass and a piano player who kept his eyes closed the entire set. Jacques ordered them martinis, very cold and dry.

She felt wonderful and didn't mind at all when he put his arm around her shoulder. He was perfect in every way. Smart. Funny. Established in his business so that he didn't need her reassurances. Old enough to have done what he needed to do and not so old as to have lost interest in doing more. If they were together . . .

A fantasy as common as first dates and chance meetings. Starting when she wrote out her first wedding invitation in her math notebook when she was in eighth grade. If she married Gordon Terrace, the captain of the lacrosse team, did she have to include her father's name in the invitation? And then in freshman year of college, imagining what kind of life she'd have if she married Cowboy Kennedy. Cowboy (his real name was Bob) majored in business administration so he could run his family's grocery store chain. They once had an argument because on a Saturday morning he wanted to watch cartoons and she wanted to watch a news program. The argument and a little fast-forward fantasizing about life as a grocery story magnate's wife was enough to put that relationship out to pasture.

An if-we-were-together fantasy while the singer crooned an old Cole Porter favorite was reassuring. She imagined not so much marriage and living together as a bunch of reassuringly sweet weekends in New York. Friday night dinners out, Saturdays spent in museums and Broadway matinees, Sundays reading the *New York Times* in bed. Jacques would come to Washington, and he'd fit in but never so well that he could be mistaken for a native. She'd take him to private gallery openings, barbecues with her friends, they'd do brunch at home (wasn't this relationship what Williams-Sonoma waffle irons are for?).

But what about Mitch? She imagined campaigns—hotel suites, bad food in ballrooms, watching the evening news, grimacing over columnists who thought they knew you. Todd—and a series of replacements—trailing their every move. Speeches, nice ladies' suits, smiling in public all the time.

But then there was the good stuff . . . being in his arms for one thing.

She clapped enthusiastically as the singer finished her last song.

Dinner was at the new Daniel Boulud restaurant and Carole was stunned when Monsieur Boulud greeted Jacques as if they were brothers. They were shown to a very nice table and Carole was frankly relieved that the menu she was given did not show prices. She was sure she would have a fit or be compelled to order a cup of tea and soda crackers.

Instead, she put down her menu and asked Jacques to order for her, telling him only that she didn't like game dishes and felt too sorry for veal to ever eat it. The waiter returned with an appetizer that was sent by Daniel—small potato and apple pancakes with créme fraîche and a sliver of salmon topped with beads of Beluga caviar.

"I'm going to gain ten pounds," Carole said.

"I wouldn't worry. You look like the sort who doesn't eat for days at a time."

"Nerves. It sometimes happens."

"So eat now and enjoy it. Tomorrow you won't eat a thing."

"I'll be in Texas. You're right. This client worries me, so I'll forget to eat."

"See? Now, if you don't mind my asking, when will you return to New York?"

"For business or pleasure?"

"If it's pleasure, make it very soon."

There. His cards were on the table.

They chatted a bit about their schedules. She had some weekend meetings that couldn't be switched around. He thought he might have some clients who would be in Washington soon. He might like to host a small cocktail party— would she be available as his companion and hostess? All very civilized and very adult. And while they didn't agree on which weekend or even which city, they knew they would be together. Very soon, very often, very clear.

The check was paid—Carole thought it was a little over-the-top the way the waiter presented a box of Mont Blanc pens from which Jacques could select to sign his credit card slip. A second waiter brought her wrap, a little brocade opera coat she had found at a Georgetown estate sale. Outside, Jacques hailed a cab and asked the driver to take them to his building.

"What about Mr. Smith?"

"The emeralds are done," Jacques said. "The princess is very happy."

And Carole wasn't unhappy.

When he opened the door to his apartment, they entered a marble foyer. He switched on the painted crystal chandelier and unlocked a door to the right.

"My office," he said and turned on an overhead light. In the bath of moody golden light, she saw a rich tiger maple desk, a bendable arm lamp and a few exquisitely upholstered chairs scattered about in conversational settings. A display case in lacquered wood with velvet shelves contained a spectacular collection of loose stones and set pieces.

"Here, so you can see," Jacques murmured and put on the halogen lights.

"It's like seeing stars," Carole cried.

Tucked inside the glass doors was a thin red light beam that indicated that the apparent fragility of the case was not to be believed.

"And here is my workroom."

He opened a *trompe l'oeil* bookcase into a cool, dark room that was every bit as utilitarian as the office had been luxurious. They didn't linger, though Carole was fascinated by the trays of uncut jewels. Diamonds were pieces of black rock as charismatic as charcoal. He led her back into the front foyer and up a princess staircase to a second-floor apartment. The living room alone was the size of the first floor of her house. A fire had been laid, and he explained

that he had a houseman who generally left around ten
o'clock. It was clear he had an interest in art, and he admitted with a *soupçon* of pride that the Matisse was an original
but, he added modestly, not a very significant one. Still,
Carole recognized the painting from her many art history
classes.

She paced the room admiring his artwork, but also working through some anxiety. She had never "hopped" into bed
with a man with so little forethought, except for a couple of
very stupid incidents right after her divorce. Well, with
Mitch, it hadn't been long after they met, but then again,
they had somehow committed themselves before their first
kiss.

Am I turning into a tramp? Carole wondered.

*Heavens, no. Thirty-seven-year-old professional women didn't
have enough time or energy to be tramps. This was maturity, going
to bed with a man who was mature.*

He came up behind her as she was studying a canvas of
horses done in a very primitive style.

"Franz Marc," he explained, kissing the back of her neck.
"Finished just days before he left for the war."

"And he died at Verdun. I look at him and Matisse,"
Carole said, gesturing to the frothy floral still life on the
other side of the wall, "and I think of all Marc could have
accomplished had he lived as long as Matisse."

"Are you thinking about that now?"

"Well, not really."

He turned her around and kissed her lightly on the lips.
His mouth was warm and Carole felt the instant message to
her brain—he was very good in bed. Practiced and unhur-
ried.

But why suddenly couldn't she stop thinking about
Mitch's kisses? About Mitch's ardor?

"Um, I need to tell you something," she said.

He stepped away from her.

"No, you don't need to do that," she said. "But I just re-membered something. I don't have any . . . protection."

"That isn't a problem here."

"What do you mean?"

He stepped away and went to a console table where a crystal bottle of cognac and two glasses had been laid. He poured two drinks.

"I can't have children," he said, and offered her a drink. He gestured to the love seat in front of the fireplace. They sat down. "I had measles when I was fifteen. My parents hadn't been able to afford the vaccine. It was a bad case. The side effect—I am sterile." He shrugged slightly.

"No kids?"

"Ever."

He studied her face, which she struggled to keep as blank as possible.

"I'm sorry."

"I used to be. But the blessing is that I don't have to gamble. My life will continue exactly as this. Fine art. Good food. Creative work. It's a good life. But it's not what you want, is it?"

She startled. She thought back to her fantasy at the Algon-quin.

"No," she admitted. "No, no, I guess it's not. At least, it's not *all* I want."

He took her glass.

"Carole, you should think very carefully about all you want."

She sighed.

"It's all right, Carole. I am not the one in pain right now. I've had a wonderful meal. I've had the most beautiful woman on my arm. I've enjoyed the conversation. What more does a man need?"

She knew what Mitch would say. Or at least his tone of voice. He'd talk about wanting to change things in Washington. Do something for veterans. Clean up corruption. Make a difference in the world. Oh, Mitch could go off on a tangent about what a man needs. And then, he'd have one last thing on his mind. Making a family. Loving a woman. Devoting himself to a wife and children.

"It's late," Jacques said softly. "Should I get you a cab?"

She nodded guiltily. When she began to take off the beautiful earrings, he touched her arm.

"You inspired a piece of jewelry that I will turn into a complete line," he said. "The muse has to take the tribute offered to her."

"Thank you."

"My pleasure. And let me give you one more thing."

He took her downstairs to his office and extracted a white velvet box from the drawer beneath the case.

"It's a little strange," Carole said, admiring its contents. "To accept this . . ."

"You don't like it?"

"No, I love it. And he will, too. But as a gift . . .?"

"I understand. Please pay me the full price."

"And that is?"

"One dollar. Each. And I know you're good for it."

"How did you know what I'm thinking of doing?"

"I'm a jeweler. It is my most important function to read the hearts of lovers and carve them into stone so that intentions are remembered and promises are kept. Now, let's send you back to the club. You have a plane to catch tomorrow."

"By the way, I'm very s—"

"Non, non."

He found her opera coat and walked her downstairs. They found a cab on Sixth Avenue.

"Will I have the pleasure of reading about the beautiful earrings you wear at your wedding?" Jacques asked as he put her in the cab.

"I hope so. Oh, Lord, I hope so."

Two days later, she returned to Washington with a contract from a Texas cowboy boot and rib joint that would FedEx both items anywhere in the country. Dana, in creative, would tie in a line of "Howdy Pardner" cards. Elyssa was thrilled and told her that the Cartier people had already e-mailed a set of ads to be featured on the Allheart.com pages.

"Are you coming in directly from the airport?" she asked. "Because we've got work piled up a mile high . . ."

"Sorry, I've got some stuff that can't wait."

"Does that 'stuff' include a certain U.S. senator?"

"Maybe."

Elyssa laughed and said she'd see Carole whenever.

As the cabbie groused about the traffic, Carole dialed Mitch's office.

"Is he in?" she asked Mabel.

"Carole? Here, I'll put him on."

"No, don't. Just tell me whether he'll be there in . . ." She looked out the window to the traffic. "Twenty minutes."

"If you want him to be here, I'll keep him. Do you want me to tell him you're coming?"

"Let me surprise him."

And I will certainly do that, she thought.

She thanked Mabel and put her phone back in her purse.

And then she extracted the white velvet box. Inside were two matching bands of gold, each encrusted with diamonds—on the inside of the band so that only the wearer and the wearer's partner would know the special value and eternal quality of their promises.

"Oh, God, what if he says no?"

The cabbie let her off in front of the Capitol building. Just as she stepped out onto the sidewalk, the junior senator from New York hurried past, trailed by a retinue of Secret Service agents. Carole dashed up the steps and followed a tortuous trail of stairs and elevators and narrow hallways to Mitch's office. Mabel, with her phone stuck to her ear, waved her on in. Carole knocked on the inner office door and stepped in as she heard Mitch's welcome.

He was seated behind a mountain of paperwork. His reading glasses were propped on the end of his nose. He looked surprised and, at first, wary.

For the first time since she had left Jacques's building, filled with forceful purpose, she felt nervous. Gone were all the pretty words she had practiced.

"Would you answer yes to a question I'm going to ask if I told you that I needed you to but was scared of asking you?"

Well that certainly was incoherent, Carole thought miserably.

He paused only an instant.

"Yes, I would," he said. "And yes, I will."

She leaned over his desk and kissed him long and full.

"Just for the record, what's the question?"

"Only the most important one I've ever asked. Will you marry me?"

"Yes," he said and came around the desk, pulling her into a big, wide embrace. "Yes and yes and yes and yes."

They kissed. His kisses always set her on fire. His hands reached up under her sweater. Carole had missed this, very much missed this.

There was a knock on the door.

"Uh, Mr. Senator."

Mitch pulled away.

"What is it, Todd?"

"You have a four-thirty committee meeting that the briefing papers—"

Mitch pulled away from Carole. She tried to pat her hair back in place. Mitch opened the door just a crack.

"Todd, I don't want to be disturbed. Right, Mabel?"

"We're closing up right now," she said. "Come along, Todd, you can help me get these boxes to my car."

"But, I . . ."

Mitch kicked the door shut.

"I'm going to try very hard to keep my priorities straight," he said. "And you remind me if I forget."

And then he kissed her again. She felt his hardness against her and she reached down to touch him.

"Here?" he asked. "But I don't have anything with me."

"You don't need anything. I'm ready," she said. "I'm really ready."

And after Mabel had locked up the outer office, Carole and Mitch celebrated their new life together with nothing between them.

Taking Care of Business

KATHRYN SHAY

Chapter 1

"I don't think you should jump into anything too fast."
Joe Monteigne chose his words carefully, attempting not to incite the lovely woman seated across from him, her teak desk between them like a shield. "I'd rather give a second interview to the other designers, in addition to Quest."

Elyssa Wentworth arched a sculpted dark brow. "Oh, really. Why?" The condescending tone drove him wild. Of course, Elyssa herself drove him wild, both in the bedroom and the boardroom.

"I don't like Parker Quest."

"That's it? You just don't like him?" Her tone was incredulous, like a professor addressing a particularly obtuse student.

"Gut instinct, I guess." Which was true. He just had a feeling . . .

"Joe, he's the premier designer for ancillary products in DC. He's worked with McDonald's on Happy Meal toys, and Hallmark's store gift promotion. Among many others."

Joe shrugged, a gesture that was usually enough to quell anybody who questioned him.

Instead of being intimidated, she shook back her long, black hair and raised her chin defiantly. "Is there something specific you don't like about Quest?"

His reputation as a ladies' man . . . that country-boy appearance . . . how he looks at you as if you're tonight's dessert.

Of course, Joe couldn't admit to any of that out loud. Madame CEO of Allheart.com, the biggest and best online greeting card company, would throw that pretty Baccarat paperweight he gave her for her thirty-seventh birthday right at his head. In truth, he himself couldn't believe he had the objection to begin with.

So he hedged. Tugging at the cuffs of his starched white shirt, visible under his new Armani navy pinstripe, he said, "Actually, I'm not exactly sure why I don't like him."

Elyssa got a suspicious gleam in her eye. After being together only eight months, she knew him so well, and often had a sixth sense about what he was feeling. She rummaged for the three folders on the other candidates in the running for her business expansion and examined one, then each of the others. After a moment, she peered over at him. "The other firms are all run by women." The Ice Queen was back.

Sometimes it turned him on, dealing with that veneer at work, then later, when they were just Joe and Elyssa, it excited him to make it melt. Today, her cool irked him. Like a lot of things had lately. He tried to shrug her comment off. "So, they'll fit in better at Allheart."

"You've got to be kidding me." She pushed back her chair and stood. The rust cashmere dress covered her from neck to wrists to knees but revealed every lovely curve. Its color accented the flush of pique that had risen to her cheeks. He watched her pace in the three-inch high Manolo

Blahnik slingbacks. "Let me get this straight. You don't want me to hire a man, even if he's best for the job?"

"I never said I don't want him because he's a man."

Well, I hadn't actually said *it,* he thought sheepishly.

"I just don't happen to think he's the right choice," Joe hedged again. "At least not any better than Carrie Sandal or Tory Samson." Now *that* was true.

"You're letting our personal relationship interfere with business. I can't believe it."

Because he couldn't believe it either, because he didn't like it one bit, he snapped at her. "This has nothing to do with our personal relationship. You're reading things into my objection because you're overly sensitive about this whole issue of our personal versus professional life."

The last eight months had been, to quote Dickens, the best and worst of times. After his venture capital firm, Highwire Industries, financed Elyssa's company to reach and stay at the top of the web greeting card market, Joe had fallen fast and furious for the woman in charge. They'd tried like hell to resist their attraction to each other—it could easily be seen as a breach of business ethics—but eventually they'd given in to their feelings.

But they had taken grief from the industry because of their relationship, and it bothered Elyssa the most. So she'd drawn the lines around their separation of personal and professional lives in bold red marker.

When she said no more, he asked, "Elyssa, did you hear me?" She gazed out the window now, staring down at the canal. She loved the outdoors, and December in DC had not yet turned too cold to make her yearn for some fresh air.

Circling around, all business, she crossed her arms over her chest. "I heard you. But since part of the agreement Allheart has with Highwire is that I get final say on who I hire to work directly for me, this is really a moot point."

That got his back up. Rising, he mirrored her folded-arm position. "I wouldn't say that hiring a firm to research and design ancillary products is *having someone work for you*. It's a whole new facet of the business. It requires Highwire's approval."

"No, it doesn't."

He tried a different tact. "I just don't see why we can't agree on someone else."

"I want Parker Quest."

He wished she'd chosen some other phrase. He was being unreasonable, blurring the lines, which was her hot button, but he couldn't help it. Angry at himself, he straightened and stared at her. "Interview the others again," he said calmly, turned, and walked out—feeling like an absolute idiot.

"He's an absolute idiot!" Elyssa told Elliot as she hung the last of the Christmas ornaments on the six-foot-tall tree in his brownstone on the Upper East Side of Manhattan. Her brother had moved from DC to New York six months earlier and had already made a name for himself at the *Times*.

Elliot sighed and handed her a cup of eggnog. "Sit. Over there by the fire." He smiled, big brother amused by little sister. "You're not seeing things clearly."

Dressed in red sweats in deference to the holiday, Elyssa dropped down on the floor and sipped her eggnog. December in New York was freezing, and she appreciated the warmth of the fire, which snapped and spit and blazed hotly. The comforting, smoky scent surrounded them. Elliot joined her, their backs against the couch. "You're too sensitive about all this, Lyss."

She shook her head. "You haven't heard the gossip,

Elliot. Everyone from Dupont Circle to Georgetown thinks I slept my way into Highwire Industries financing Allheart."

"You know you didn't. Joe knows you didn't. That's all that matters."

She shivered remembering the first time she overheard this particular rumor. She'd been the guest of honor at a Women in Business luncheon and had been in a stall in the restroom . . .

"Elyssa Wentworth's a terrific speaker don't you think?" one of the women out by the mirror said.

"Yeah. But she omitted a critical ingredient to her success. Sleeping with the boss."

"Yeah, well, have you seen Joe Monteigne?"

"No."

"He makes you wet with a glance. I'd sleep with him for nothing."

"Well, our illustrious guest got him *and* his millions." The women had left then, still dishing and dissing her.

"It's an unfair situation, Elliot. I worked hard to get where I am. I didn't earn my career on any casting couch."

"Honey, you can't let people's gossip bother you. Or affect your relationship with Joe." Elliot reached over, slid his arms around her shoulders and hugged her close. "I've never seen you more . . . content than you've been with him."

Elliot was right, and he had a way of cutting to the quick. "I miss you." She smiled. "But I'm glad you're happy in New York."

A boyish grin lit his face. "Happier than you know. I met someone, sis."

"Really?"

"Uh-huh." He sipped his eggnog but his warm hazel eyes sparkled with a gleam that hadn't been there since his wife died a decade ago.

"Why didn't you tell me?"

"I'm not sure. I didn't want to jinx it, I guess."

"Who is she?"

"A second-grade teacher. She brought her class on a tour of the *Times* and I literally bumped into her."

"It's serious." Elyssa could tell.

"Yes. Her name is Mary and—" The phone rang, cutting Elliot off. "That's probably her. She said she'd call tonight from her parents' house." He grinned again. "I'll be a few minutes."

"Take your time, lover boy. I'll just watch the fire. I'm not going anywhere."

As soon as Elliot left the room, her own words echoed back at her. . . .

"I wish you weren't going anywhere for Christmas, Lyss." She and Joe had been in his bed last night after lovemaking that took her breath away just thinking about it. "We should be spending the holiday together."

"I want to see Elliot." She cuddled into Joe's chest, inhaling his scent—woodsy usually, a little musky tonight. Truth be told, the thought of being separated from him on Christmas made her sad. Too sad. Which was one reason she definitely was going to New York.

He'd grown still. "I know you want to be with your brother."

"And you should be with your family."

He hadn't said anything more. Instead, he'd extricated himself from her, slid out of bed, donned flannel pajama bottoms and loped downstairs. She found him in his study, smoking a cigar. Usually she teased him about the macho habit he indulged in once in a while. But that night she hadn't. What they'd gotten into upstairs was an old argument that needed to be handled gingerly.

She dropped down onto the Aubusson rug, wearing the pretty ice blue robe he bought her to keep at his place. At his feet, resting her hands on his knees, she looked up at him. "I didn't ask you to come to New York with me because you said you always spend Christmas with your family."

"Don't lie to me, Elyssa." He glanced up in the direction of his bedroom. "Especially not after that."

They were so close in bed. Maybe too close.

"I'm not lying. I do want to see Elliot." She tried to quell the note of impatience in her voice but didn't succeed. "I've spent every free minute of the last six months with you, Joe."

"And you've seen Elliot every few weeks." He sighed and took a thoughtful puff on his cigar. "I don't begrudge that, or even you going to New York alone. It's the *reason* you're going alone that bothers me."

She'd stiffened. She hated it when he played psychologist with her but still, she tried to be placating. "It's not what you think."

As if she hadn't spoken, he said, "You're going alone to maintain that distance between us that you insist on keeping."

"There wasn't any distance between us a few minutes ago," she snapped. "Or was I alone in that bed?"

"No, there never is in bed. It's outside of bed that you turn into the Ice Queen."

That stung. "Hey, we both agreed on distance, right from the start."

"Professional distance, yes. Look, I know the rumors bother you. I didn't like defending myself to my partners either." Highwire bigwigs had been understandably concerned when Joe told them about his personal relationship with her. But he'd withstood their doubt and skepticism, and fought to keep her in his life, regardless. "The gossip is a reality. But we can certainly rise above it."

"I know." She grasped his hand. "That's why I want to keep as much professional distance as possible."

"This particular distance has nothing to do with people talking. It has to do with your overblown fear of blurring the roles."

"Because *you* keep blurring the roles. Like today about Parker Quest."

Brushing her aside, he stood and stubbed out the cigar in an ashtray his father brought him from China. He crossed to the window and stared out into the night. "Maybe you should leave now. Let's table all this until you get back from New York. Some time away from each other might do us good."

She'd risen and gone to him. From behind she circled her arms around his waist. "I'm not going to leave like this. Tonight or for New York." She lay her cheek on his naked back, absorbing the heat of his skin. "Come back to bed with me."

He didn't move.

"Joe, please. Let's not fight . . ."

He'd gone back to bed with her, and their lovemaking had been so poignant, so close that it . . . scared the hell out of her, actually. She hadn't come clean with him. She *was* afraid of their relationship, of how much she'd come to care for him. Of the control her feelings gave him over her. For a woman who'd depended only on herself for thirty-seven years, she couldn't seem to get over that particular hump. Joe was asking too much of her. Which was why she didn't relent and invite him to come with her to New York.

Elliot drifted back into the room smiling broadly.

"I'm done." He dropped down beside her. "I need to ask you something."

"Anything."

"I know you came here to spend Christmas with me. But is it all right if Mary comes back tomorrow night to have dinner with us?"

"Of course. I'd love to meet her."

Elliot shook his head. "We're such saps. We can't even stay away from each other for one night. Her parents had a fit when she told them she wanted to get back to see me."

"Sounds like true love."

He waited a minute, his mind almost audibly clicking. "You could call Joe. I'll bet he'd fly up here in a flash. We could make it a foursome on Christmas night."

"There wouldn't be any flights available tomorrow, Elliot."

"If you asked Joe to come, he'd crawl on his hands and knees to get here."

She shook her head. "No, it's not a good idea."

Elliot grasped her hand. "He only wants what any guy wants from his girl, Lyss. And he's not going to stand for this push-pull indefinitely."

Staring at the fire, Elyssa was afraid her brother was right. But she was also afraid, deathly afraid, to lose herself in the boy wonder of Highwire Industries. Already her personal and professional lives were colliding. If she let herself really love Joe Monteigne, let herself go with him, would she ever find herself again?

I thought I'd find you here.

Joe stood at the windows of his father's study, staring out at the Virginia landscape. Christmas had brought a light dusting of snow that made Joe nostalgic for winters at Harvard. "You did?" He sipped the smooth Merlot his mother had served with their beef dinner.

"Hmm." J. Lance Monteigne settled into a big leather chair and put his feet up on the matching ottoman. "You used to sneak into this room all through high school and college when you had girl trouble."

"I used to sneak in here to escape *the girls*," he said, nodding to the family room where his three sisters, all with daughters of their own, visited noisily with his mother.

"Oh, come on. They took it easy on you today."

"Yeah." He stared back out at the crisp night. "My mood must show."

"Do you want to talk about it?"

The red wine was tart on his tongue and warmed him almost as much as his father's concern. "Not much to say, Dad. Elyssa wouldn't come here with me and didn't invite me to New York."

"Why?"

Sighing heavily, he crossed to the couch opposite his dad and sank down. "It has something to do with setting boundaries, I think."

"Ah, an area where you've always had trouble."

Joe chuckled. "You should know." Again he grew serious. "She keeps me in a compartment and I don't like it."

"Why does she do that?"

"I think she's afraid."

"Of what?"

"I'd guess her feelings for me."

Joe's father didn't comment.

Finally, Joe said, "I'm not afraid of mine for her, Dad."

"Are you sure?"

"What do you mean?"

"Joe, she's endured a lot of negative speculation since it's become public that you two are a couple. I know you asked her to go to Highwire's New Year's Eve party with you. That's just the kind of blending of business and pleasure that seems to make her uncomfortable."

"I want her with me, damn it. It's New Year's Eve."

Lance just shrugged.

"Okay, okay, I see what you're saying. But this Christmas thing was all personal."

"Maybe she balks at the personal stuff because you push the other too much. If you laid off a bit, she might let you get closer."

Or maybe she'd keep drifting further away. The thought that he used their professional relationship to keep her tied to him was more than unpleasant.

His father watched him. "Are you in love with her, son?"

It was a question he wouldn't let himself answer. Love was a word both he and Elyssa steered clear of. "I can't afford to be in love with her."

Lance chuckled. "Never worked that way for me. When I met your mother—"

"Sorry to interrupt." Janice, Joe's mother, stood in the doorway. She was a lovely woman of grace and style, with snow-white hair and a still-slender form. Joe had her eyes. "But did I hear my name?"

Lance chuckled. "I was just reminiscing, dear."

She smiled at her husband then turned to her son. "You have a call, Joe, on this." She handed him the cell phone he'd left in his jacket pocket. "It's Elyssa."

Elyssa had met and spent time with the Monteignes and gotten along well with both of them. She shared a love of the outdoors with his mother and a keen insight into politics with his father. They'd had some pleasant evenings together.

Lance rose. "I'll leave you alone." As he walked by his son, he squeezed Joe's arm. "Remember what we discussed. Be patient and understanding."

His dad left, with his mother cuddled close, and Joe spoke into the phone. "Hi."

"Hi. Merry Christmas."

"To you, too." Though it stuck in his craw, he asked, "Are you having a nice visit?"

"Yes. Elliot's on cloud nine. He's in love, Joe."

"Really? Tell me." She filled him in on the second-grade teacher. "Do you like her?" he asked casually.

Her hesitation alerted him. "Yes, she's lovely. Perfect for Elliot."

"When did you meet her?"

A very long pause this time.

"Elyssa? I asked when you met her."

"Today."

Ah, he got it. "So she spent Christmas Day with you and Elliot?"

"Um, just tonight. She came back from her parents' house in Brooklyn to meet me. Because I'm coming home tomorrow."

Her cavalierness *toward* him, *about* their relationship, knifed him in the gut. "I see."

"So," she said brightly, "how's your family?"

"Fine."

"I spoke with your mother. She said you had a nice day. All together."

"We did."

There was a long, cold silence.

"Well, I'll let you get back to them."

"Fine. You get back to Elliot. And Mary."

"Joe, I—"

"Listen, I won't be able to pick you up at the airport tomorrow. Something's come up."

"Oh." Another hesitation. "I'll just get a cab."

Nothing.

"When will I see you?"

"I'll call you. Merry Christmas." And he clicked off.

His father's words came back to him. *Remember what we discussed. Be patient and understanding.*

Slamming his fist against the desktop, he cursed under his breath. No man in his right mind would be patient and understanding about this.

Certainly not Joe Monteigne.

Elyssa drew together the lapels of her leather jacket out of nerves as opposed to the cold. Actually, DC weather was mild for eleven o'clock at night the last week of December. She rang Joe's doorbell with trepidation.

Was he home? Was he with someone?

Stupid. He isn't that mad. No, he's hurt.

So hurt, he refused to pick her up at the airport when she came back from New York, and hadn't called her for two days. Nor had he returned her calls. She was both afraid of and angry at his reaction, but she wasn't going to ignore it, that was for sure.

She pressed the bell again. This time she heard shuffling inside. In a few moments, the door opened. He stood before her in button-fly jeans and a Harvard sweatshirt. His hair was disheveled—beautifully so—and he wore his glasses, which told her he'd probably been working. She was stunned at her visceral response to simply seeing him. However, when *he* saw *her*, his gaze turned from curious to cold. She'd forgotten those sky blue eyes could cut and sliver in seconds. The last time she'd seen that reaction was when he presented Highwire's initial proposal to her, and they'd fought bitterly over it.

"Hi," she said simply.

"Elyssa."

She stuck her hands in her pockets. "Want to go for a walk?"

"A walk? At nearly midnight?"

"Hmm." She peered up at the star-studded sky. "It's crisp but not cold." Tilting her head, she coaxed, "Come with me."

He stared at her hard. Finally, he said, "All right." Reaching into a foyer closet, he pulled on his battered bomber jacket, tossed his glasses on a table and grabbed his keys.

In minutes they were strolling around Dumbarton Oaks, a breathtaking sight in the summer with its colorful and fragrant gardens of flowers. Even in December, the area was impressive.

He said nothing. Clearly this was her show.

"I'm not going to let you dismiss me from your life, Joe, if that's what you're planning to do."

"No, Madame CEO would never allow that kind of major decision to be made without her professional input."

She struggled to tamp down her temper. He often needled her exactly in the right place. "I know why you're angry."

"Do you?"

"We should have spent Christmas together."

"Bingo!"

"I'm sorry."

That deflated him somewhat. "It's not just that."

His conciliatory tone encouraged her to sidle closer.

When he didn't pull away—moved into her, too—she linked her arm with his. "Then tell me."

"It's all your distancing gestures, Lyss."

"If you're talking about work, it's important to me not to blur the lines."

"The lines blurred the minute you slept with me."

His words were cold water in her face. "Well, that's the painful, naked truth."

"It is the truth. I'm sorry about it. I wish I could change it. But it's true. I know you've taken more grief over it than I have. And I know it's hard for you."

"It's embarrassing and unfair and I detest the gossip."

"I guess the question is, is it worth it?"

She stopped abruptly.

He got a few steps ahead of her, then stopped, too, and turned. "Is it worth it, Elyssa, to put up with a few cheap shots to have me in your life?"

"Do you think there's any doubt in my mind about that?"

"Honestly, sometimes I do."

Slowly, she walked toward him. She raised her hand and caressed his cheek. His skin was cool and stubbly. "Of course withstanding the gossip's worth having you in my life. Don't you know how much I care about you?"

He jammed his hands in his jacket pockets and stared at her. "I know I sound like a high school boy needing reassurance." He rolled his eyes, clearly disgusted with himself. "But it's how I feel. I want to know where you are with this relationship. And I need some proof of your feelings for me."

Damn, he always had to spoil it. Always had to put parameters on things. First by getting her to stay overnight on workdays, when they'd agreed to sleep separately during the week. Then meeting his parents, which she'd avoided initially. Finally he insisted they go out in public—no, be an obvious couple in public. She *had* compromised, damn it.

"All right," she said as calmly as she could, but couldn't completely erase the pique in her voice. "How can I prove it this time?"

From the streetlight above, quick anger changed the frigid blue of his eyes to sparking flame. "Don't do me any favors." He moved to walk away.

Her hand shot out to grab his arm. "Wait. What is going *on* with you? Why are you so prickly about this?"

"Look, either you want me in your life, or you don't. Either you're willing to commit, or not."

She knew her face paled, was grateful to the nighttime shadows, which would conceal her reaction. Never once had either of them talked about commitment. "Commit to what?"

"To working on this relationship and dealing with those blurred lines you keep getting all upset about."

"I have been working on it."

"No, you haven't."

"Is this about my wanting to hire Parker Quest?"

"No, it's about you and me and how we deal with things."

Suddenly she was very tired. She hadn't slept well since she left DC for Christmas. And Elliot's words came back to her. *He only wants what any guy wants from his girl, Lyss.* "All right, how can I prove it?" When he hesitated, she added, "I *want* to prove it."

"Go to Highwire's New Year's Eve party."

"Of course I'm going."

"With me."

Her shoulders slumped. She'd wanted to avoid flaunting

her and Joe's relationship in his partners' faces by attending separately. And all the movers and shakers would be there. It would be a huge statement if she went with him.

She thought about Elliot's happiness. She thought about Joe's parents, who'd made sacrifices to be together. But mostly she thought about losing the man before her because of her fears.

So she stepped closer, looped her arms around his neck, and aligned her body with his. "I'll go with you."

She was shocked to see his eyes close with relief.

Not knowing how to handle the vulnerable gesture, she stood on tiptoes and whispered, "Just wait till you see me in the new dress I bought."

Ignoring the sexy quip, he clasped her to him. Hugged her tightly. Softly, so softly it nearly broke her heart, he whispered, "I missed you. Come home with me."

Without waiting for her answer, he drew back, grasped her hand and led her down the street.

Elyssa was right about the dress, Joe thought, staring at her from across the room. She was stunning in it. Black, tight and strapless, the gown was more than appropriate for Highwire Industries' annual New Year's Eve party. As usual, the soirée was being held at the downstairs ballroom of the Willard InterContinental—where every and any figure of historical importance in the life of the country had made a notable appearance. Its ornate chandeliers, Persian rugs and old, fine-aged wood shouted wealth and power. Right now Elyssa was in deep discussion with his parents, who seemed to like her more every time they were with her.

Join the club, Joe thought.

"Joe, darling. Hello."

He turned to see the perfect face and body of his ex-wife, Bethany. Five-foot-seven, model thin, and epitomizing the word *chic*, she leaned over and kissed his cheek.

"Beth, hi. I didn't see you come in."

"I came with Daddy." Her father was on the board of directors of Highwire.

Joe glanced over her shoulder. "Where's Jonathan?"

She pouted prettily made-up lips. "Haven't you heard?"

"Heard?"

"Jonathan and I are getting a divorce."

Shocked, he stared at her. "No, I hadn't heard. I'm sorry."

"Thanks."

"How's Melanie taking it?"

"Hard."

"That kind of thing is tough on kids."

"It's going to get even tougher."

"Why?"

"I'm going back to work." Bethany had been a top interior designer before she and Joe had married. She was good at her work, and very creative. When she quit her job to be just his wife, Joe got bored with her—hell, they got bored with each other.

"Good for you."

She grasped his arm. "I was going to ask you to help me get back into the field."

"Oh." He was surprised. She moved uncomfortably close. He glanced up to see Elyssa peek over at him and do a double take. She frowned, then turned to his father to ask a question. It didn't take Einstein to figure out what she was saying.

Who's the blonde falling all over Joe?

Oh, that's his ex-wife.

Geez.

As quickly as he could, and with a promise to meet with her next week, he extricated himself from Bethany and threaded his way across the ballroom. He breathed a sigh of relief when Elyssa gave him an *I'm gonna bust your balls* look.

"It's a little early for 'Auld Lang Syne,' isn't it?" she asked sweetly. Too sweetly.

He slid his arm around her waist before he remembered that he was going to be discreet tonight, that her coming with him, letting everybody know she was his date, was compromise enough. Giving her a brief hug, he drew back and quipped, "I have no idea what you're talking about."

"How's Bethany, dear?" Joe's mother asked.

Joe cleared his throat. "Beth's getting a divorce."

"Oh, I'm sorry to hear that."

"Me, too," Elyssa said dryly.

With the tact required of the ambassador he'd once been, Lance drew Janice away to visit with a couple behind them. Joe sipped his champagne and said, "Sorry. She—"

"—came on to you."

"Actually, she wants me to help her jump-start her business."

Elyssa raised a brow. "She wants you for more than that, Monteigne."

"Jealous? Hmm, I like that."

"Jealousy is highly overrated." Something beyond his shoulder caught her eye and she frowned. "Joe, what's Parker Quest doing at Highwire's party?"

Pivoting, Joe saw Quest in the doorway. Damn. He studied the man. Dark blond hair to his collar. Big eyes. Long nose. Pronounced chin. Rough-hewn build. Joe knew the guy had just turned thirty. He was almost a decade younger than Joe.

One of Highwire's partners, Martin Sloan, approached

Quest, clapped him on the back and smiled warmly. Quest played best buddy and gave Sloan a bear hug.

Joe turned back to Elyssa. Her face was full of questions.

"Quest is one of Martin's recruits."

"Recruits?"

"We financed his company."

"Highwire *financed* Parker Quest's business?"

"Yes. It was Martin's project."

She didn't say anything. Just glanced from Quest to Joe and back again.

"How much did you invest?"

"Excuse me?"

"How much did Highwire *trust* him, *believe in* him, to invest?"

"That's private information, Elyssa."

"How much?"

"What we invested in you."

She sighed and shook her head. "I can't believe this. Your firm invested millions in Parker Quest's company, and you discouraged me from hiring him?"

Again, a stony silence.

"What the *hell* is going on, Joe?"

Chapter 2

$\mathcal{W}$*aiting for Parker Quest to arrive for lunch, Elyssa* studied The Executive Room, an exclusive business club where, in order to obtain a membership, a person had to have connections in high places. Joe, of course, had facilitated her access into the club. Not that she wasn't rich or successful enough to warrant belonging. But it was who you knew that got you entrance.

Tucked away in a building on Massachusetts Avenue, the place screamed Men's Club—mahogany paneling; heavy, dark furniture; book-filled walls. But it was an ideal place to do business—private, quiet and Elyssa liked it. So she'd suggested the elite spot to meet with Quest when she called him yesterday and accepted his proposal to head up her ancillary products.

Sipping Perrier, she pondered what had really led her to hire Quest's firm. . . .

On New Year's Eve, Joe had suggested they shelve their discussion of the man in question until later when they were alone. About two A.M., at his place, she'd broached the issue.

Calmly, she thought, and maturely. "I don't understand this, Joe. You say it's not personal and I hate to think it's because he's an attractive man, that you don't want me to work with him. But Highwire backed him. You must have thought he was a solid businessman."

Having removed his black tuxedo jacket and tie, Joe had prowled his living room in his shirtsleeves, sipping Courvoisier. "To be perfectly honest, I had some reservations about giving Quest Highwire's money. But Martin was adamant, and he's been proven right. Quest has done very well."

"Then what was your objection all about?"

He'd faced her, guilt and something else in those mesmerizing eyes of his. "You were right all along. Quest's a notorious ladies' man and I don't like how he looks at you."

At first she'd been shocked into silence. Then a piercing pain flooded her. It hurt so much, she could hardly contain it. "You're something of a notorious ladies' man, too, Joe. Is that the connection? You think because I slept with you, I might sleep with Parker?"

Never in the eight months she'd known him had she seen Joe so explosively angry. He'd hurled the brandy glass across the room, shattering it against the fireplace. Then he strode over to her, grabbed her by the wrist and spat out, "Don't you ever imply anything like that again."

His loss of control silenced her, but also made her sane. They squared off like boxers in a ring, staring at each other for a long moment. She finally said, "I guess that was out of line."

"You're damn right it was."

"But so is your reasoning, Joe. It's crazy. You can't keep men away from me."

His anger defused, like snowflakes in the spring. He ran a hand through his hair and she could see it was shaking.

"I know. And I hate myself for this . . . jealousy. It's so un-like me."

They'd made up—as usual in bed, which was beginning to bother her. They promised to be less defensive, to trust each other more. Their lovemaking that night had been different; Joe had been ravenous the first time and she wasn't much more in control. But the second time had been so tender it had brought tears to her eyes.

"We'll be okay, Lyss. I promise. . . ."

"Elyssa?"

She peered up into the smiling face and mile-wide shoulders of Parker Quest. His dark blond hair was like a lion's mane around his face, and he stared out at her from huge, tawny eyes. She rose. "Parker, hello."

He held her hand in a gentle, friendly clasp. "Sit." When she did, he took a chair. His smile was so genuine, it relaxed her. "Did I tell you how happy I was to get your call?"

"Yes, you did." He'd been refreshingly honest on the telephone.

"I'm thrilled to be working with Allheart. You've got the number one rep in the business."

"And so we picked the number one product designer." She smiled as the waiter approached their table. "Would you like a drink?"

He nodded to her Perrier. "I'll have the same as you. I don't mix business and cocktails." Neither, of course, did she. Glancing around, he gave an ingenuous grin. "This place is great."

"Have you been here before?"

"Yeah. Once or twice." He shrugged and tugged at the neck of the fine cotton T-shirt he wore with pressed slacks and a tan wool sports coat that accented his golden eyes. "Not bad for a boy from the wrong side of the tracks."

"Pardon me?"

"I grew up dirt-poor—which always puts this kind of place in perspective." He gestured at the elegant room.

"Where do you come from?"

"Upstate New York."

"Really? So do I."

"I know, I saw a bio on you somewhere."

"Where are you from exactly?"

"A small town south of Syracuse called McGraw. It's so tiny there isn't even a stoplight there."

"Lockport's not exactly a booming metropolis."

Again the Huck Finn grin. "I don't know about you but I don't mind having humble roots."

"No?"

"Nah, it keeps you honest in this business."

"Speaking of which, shall we talk about how we're going to infuse ancillary products into my company?"

"Fine by me."

They ordered first—both chose quiche Lorraine and a vinaigrette salad—and then they got to work.

For all his down-home boyishness and his youth, he wasn't shy. And he had a quick, incisive mind. "You said what made you pick my firm was the prospect of a creative correlation of products with the kind of cards you have."

"Hmm. We have a few companion products already but are looking for a unique line of ancillary products that could go with all our cards. I especially liked your suggestion of the herbal tea basket idea for the You Can Cope cards and the mother's pampering basket for the New Baby cards."

"Both were my sister's ideas," he said with affection.

"Really?"

"Yes, she's my creative consultant. She's a gem." He smiled. "You have a brother, don't you?"

"I do."

"We have a lot in common." Again, his grin was ingratiating.

They talked through their lunch and got down to particulars over coffee. "I prefer to work on-site. Is that going to be a problem?"

"No, of course not. I'll have Robyn ready some space for you. Allheart's offices can handle you easily."

"Good, I—"

"Well, hello."

Elyssa looked up to find Joe standing at their table. He wore a severely cut navy suit and starched light blue shirt, which turned his eyes the color of a midnight sky.

Hanging on his arm was a gorgeous blonde. His ex-wife.

"Joe, hello." It took effort to smile. "Parker, you remember my business associate, Joe Monteigne."

Ever the gentleman, Parker stood. "Yes, of course. How are you, Joe?"

"Just fine." He introduced them both to Bethany, who sidled in closer to Joe.

Elyssa couldn't help herself and asked, "Was I mistaken? I thought you were out of town until tomorrow." He'd flown to New York on business. Had seen Elliot, there, as a matter of fact. They'd taken in a Knicks game.

"No, you weren't mistaken. I concluded my meetings earlier than I expected and took the first plane out this morning." He transferred his gaze to Parker. "By the way, welcome aboard."

Parker smiled. "Thanks. I'm thrilled to be on Elyssa's team."

"Joe, our table's ready." Bethany's breast grazed Joe's arm; the flash of intimate contact made Elyssa's stomach lurch.

"Well, nice to see you again, Parker," Joe said easily. "I'm sure we'll be meeting soon." He nodded to her. "Elyssa."

"Enjoy your lunch." She spoke with more equanimity than she felt.

She didn't watch the couple walk away. She didn't check to see where they were seated. But she couldn't help the backward glance when she left the club.

The scene was cozy and close. Joe, sitting across from Bethany as she daintily dabbed her eyes with what Elyssa would bet was Joe's monogrammed handkerchief. His hand extended across the table—to cover hers. And there was complete absorption on his face.

It broke her heart to watch him with another woman.

Joe spent the rest of the day trying to track Elyssa down. By the time he finished lunch with Bethany and called Elyssa's office, she'd left for a meeting with Carole and a potential advertiser for Allheart. Robyn informed him the boss had an appointment at the gym at six.

He found her in the sparring room, pounding the daylights out of a punching bag. From across the way, he watched her. Dressed in black nylon shorts and a tank top that left nothing to the imagination, she'd donned padded gloves and foot protection necessary in the ring. White headgear and other gloves lay off to the side. The black bag she fought with was almost as big as she was.

Frowning at her *opponent,* she didn't see him until he was upon her.

"Good form," he said, unable to hide the amusement in his voice. "Keep your chin up, though."

Jab, jab. "Thanks."

"How long have you been beating on him?"

"Her."

"Excuse me?"

"It's a *her*." She darted a quick look at him.

"I see."

"Good."

A harder punch. A quick uppercut.

He drew in a breath. Not able to remember when he'd *ever* condescended to explain himself, he forced his tone to be neutral. "On New Year's Eve, Bethany asked if I'd meet her this week to discuss her business. She called my cell phone when I was in New York and said it was urgent that she see me as soon as I got back."

Elyssa's only reaction was a double punch. She wiped her brow on her arm.

"I tried to call you last night and again this morning to tell you I'd be back earlier than I expected, but I couldn't reach you."

"As far as I know, my voice mail is working."

"I didn't leave a message."

"Why not? Just checking up on me?"

His insides knotted. "Is there something to check up on?"

Jab, jab, jab. Her opponent would be sprawled on the floor by now. He grabbed the bag and steadied it. "Stop a minute." She took several more punches, which jarred him. She'd be a strong contender. Then she drew back and looked up at him. "Care to join me?" She nodded to the equipment at her feet. "I was supposed to spar with my trainer but he got busy."

"Not on your life." He was afraid she'd deck him. "Lyss, I didn't leave a message because I knew it would sound bad about Beth, and I wanted to explain in person."

"Well, it looked bad, too."

"Not much different from you and Quest," he said tightly.

She leaned down and got a towel, wiped her face and shook back her hair. "Is that what this is all about?"

"No, of course not."

"Parker and I met on business. If it was something more, I'd hardly go to The Executive Room."

"Beth and I were talking shop."

"Ah, the business she suddenly needs your help with."

He grabbed her by the arm to force her to face him. "Yes. I'm making a plan for her to get her interior design firm going again." For a minute he felt guilty. "And you might as well know now, she's going to do my office as her first job."

A brow arched. "At home or at work?"

"Actually, both."

Elyssa shook her head. "You were holding her hand, Joe. You were absorbed in her."

"She was telling me about the divorce. About her daughter."

"*Your* divorce from her must have been amicable."

"Yes, it was. I initiated it, so I worked hard to hurt her as little as possible."

"Why did you get divorced?"

He glanced around the gym. "This isn't the place to discuss it."

She faced the bag again, said, "Fine by me,"and took two savage punches.

Frustrated, he jammed his hands into his pockets. "I got bored. She quit work as soon as we married and turned into a socialite. It was . . . tedious."

"And now she's morphed back into a businesswoman. Just your type."

When she stopped punching for a second, he stepped between her and the bag. "You're my type, sweetheart."

She eyed him up and down, then landed a couple of mild punches on his chest.

"I know you know that, Lyss."

Another two punches, a little harder.

"I can't believe you'd question my feelings."

Her eyes were wide when she looked up at him. Despite the color exercise brought to her cheeks, he could see the fatigue etched in her face. "I don't know why when you doubt mine."

That was different. Because *she* doubted her own feelings for him, so did he. Or at least she didn't trust her feelings and was afraid of committing to him. He knew it as sure as he knew the contents of his stock portfolio. But he didn't want to fight tonight. Lately, it seemed like that's all they did. "I'm sorry if I upset you today."

Her shoulders sagged and she reached a gloved hand to his face. Not for a punch, but for a clumsy caress.

"Let's go home," he said softly.

"Seems like we always settle things in bed." Her tone was weary.

"Well, not this time. Come to my house. You can take a bubble bath while I cook you supper." He leaned over and whispered, "Then I'll give you a long, lazy backrub."

She rested her forehead on his chest, and his hand came up to grasp her neck. "You don't have bubble bath at your house," she whispered.

"Yes, I do. I brought you some from that fancy soap shop on Madison Avenue that you like."

She grinned against his suit.

"I've got champagne . . ." He continued to ply her.

"Maybe." Her voice told him she was weakening.

Soberly, he said, "I want more than sex from you tonight,

Lyss. I want to be close." Which of course was part of her problem.

Burrowing her cheek into him, she asked, "Will you give me a foot massage, too?"

I'll give you anything you want, he thought, then panicked at the truth to that. But he quelled his unease, drew her away from him and began to unlace her gloves.

The frothy bubbles tickled Elyssa's chin as she sank back into the almost-too-hot water of Joe's huge tub. A blissful sigh escaped her as every single one of her muscles eased. "This is sinful."

From where he leaned against the vanity, Joe chuckled and picked up a jar. "Actually, it's called Sinful Delights."

Closing her eyes she let the heat and scent encompass her. Firm lips grazed her forehead and a deep voice filtered through the haze. "I'm going to start dinner. Relax."

She did. Much to her surprise, she was able to blank her mind of Allheart and jealousy and a thousand other things she might have been tempted to think about and had sunk into a semiconscious state by the time Joe returned.

The scrape of a chair. A masculine shifting. "Here, love."

With a smile, she opened her eyes, sat up a bit, and accepted the champagne. They clicked glasses. "To us," he said simply.

Grateful, she smiled at him. "Hmm. This is wonderful."

"It's your favorite." He dipped a long finger in the soap and streaked her shoulder with some bubbles. Despite the heat, his touch raised goose bumps.

Without thinking about it, she grasped his hand and kissed his knuckles. "*You're* my favorite."

Pure pleasure lit his face. "I like hearing that."

She liked looking at him. He was so . . . male in old jeans and a cotton sports shirt, untucked and half unbuttoned. Enticing glimpses of skin peeked out.

Indulging herself in the view, she lay back in the tub and sipped her drink. Life didn't get any better than this. An incredibly sexy man waiting on you hand and foot. Bubble baths and champagne. She was in heaven. "Tell me about New York."

He filled her in on his work there, and what he'd done with Elliot. She loved listening to the low masculine cadence of his voice, his pithy comments about her brother and his wry sense of humor about the city. He left once, to work on supper. When he returned, she was ready to get out of the tub.

"Not yet." He fished in a bag he'd left on the counter and drew out an oversized natural sponge.

"Oh, I love those," she said.

"I know. You told me once. I got it when I picked up the bubble bath." With utter masculine grace, he whipped off his shirt, revealing a road map of muscles and curling black hair all strategically placed. "Sit up and lean forward."

Giving him her glass, she obeyed, bending her knees, resting her head on them, and clasping her hands together on her shins.

With mathematical precision, he started at her shoulders and worked his way down her back. He repeated the process until he'd done her entire back. She could eke out no more than an inaudible murmur in response.

After a while, he kissed her neck, exposed from piling her hair on top of her head. "Now, lie back again . . . that's it . . . lift your leg and rest it on the edge of the tub." He took his time. First her left leg, then her right. He covered every inch of each arm.

Her bones were jelly by the time he finished. "Done."

She moaned.

In her ear he whispered, "You know, you're a hedonist at heart."

"I didn't know that before I met you."

Again the chuckle. He rose. "Now, up." He assisted her to stand then half-supported her as she climbed out of the three-foot-high tub. She leaned into him. He held her close. "Ah, Lyss." Kissed her hair, then swathed her in a towel.

It was warm. "Oh, God, Joe."

"I put it in the dryer."

"You spoil me," she said into his neck.

"Remember that, sweetheart."

She sat on his lap as he dried her, as she draped all over him like a rag doll. He took his time, whisking the warm terrycloth over her breasts several times, down each leg, between them. When he was done, he wrapped her up in the blue robe and led her downstairs.

The table was set by the fireplace, which was lit now and blazing brightly. "This is lovely." She sniffed. "What do I smell?"

"Frittata. I had the sausage, peppers and potatoes, but it'll be sans onions."

Sinking onto a chair, she stared at the fire and sipped her wine as he left for the kitchen and returned with their meals and thick, crusty bread.

"You do like to cook, don't you?"

"When I have someone as appreciative as you to share it with." He grinned and topped off their champagne. "Even if it is because you're hopeless in the kitchen."

"I have my assets."

"Yes, you do," he said dryly as he sat down. "And if you want to keep this evening platonic, you'd better cover up some of those assets right now." He nodded to her chest.

She glanced down. The robe gaped. She closed it with a chuckle. "The evening doesn't have to stay platonic." Her voice was husky. "I'm feeling pretty mellow." Actually she was half-aroused. The bath. His hands on her. The champagne.

"Too bad. I'm a man of my word. We aren't settling our tiff in bed."

"Then how are we settling it?" She bit into the spicy sausage that reminded her of summer barbecues at home.

"By just being together and enjoying each other's company."

She smiled and continued to eat.

"Tell me about the latest with the Allheart girls. Last I heard Carole and Mitch were getting serious. I don't know what's going on with Dana or Alix. Robyn's an open book, though," he said affectionately.

Through the entire meal, around mouthfuls of hot bread, tart peppers and the succulent meat, she filled him in on the escapades of her friends and coworkers. As she talked about Mitch and Carole, and Alix and Dana, she noticed how Joe's blue eyes were intently focused on her, how his comments were insightful, how his sense of humor so matched her own.

"Done?" he asked when she set down her fork.

"Mmm. It was five-star. If you ever lose your shirt investing, you could certainly be a chef."

"I'll keep that in mind."

She started to stand. "Let me clean up."

"It's all done but these plates. We'll take them to the sink on our way upstairs."

Following him out to the kitchen, they disposed of their dishes and he took something out of the microwave, which he wouldn't let her see. Holding her hand tenderly, he led her down the hall and upstairs.

In his bedroom, he said, "All right, strip down, lady. It's backrub time."

"How can I resist?" She dropped the robe and Joe stilled, his eyes flaring. She noticed the bulge in his jeans. "Joe, we can—"

"No, we can't. Lay flat out, Elyssa."

Well, she'd see if they *couldn't*. After the backrub. She stretched out on the bed.

It was the most decadent twenty minutes of her life. His hands were magic on her body, kneading, loosening, stretching muscles. He used oil that he'd warmed and brought upstairs with him. When his fingers inched up to the top inside of her thighs, she moaned, and struggled to get closer to his hand.

"Hmm." His knuckles brushed between her legs. She startled. He leaned over her. "Want something else?" he asked sexily.

"You know I do," she mumbled into the pillow.

Another chuckle full of smug male satisfaction. "All right. Scoot up a little."

Her arms gripping the pillow, she lifted her hips.

His clever hand slid beneath her and touched her intimately. She gasped.

The climax hit her in seconds—it was long and loud and eminently satisfying.

Afterward, she was unable to move; she felt kisses on her spine. "I love seeing you like this," he whispered into her skin.

Finally, she stirred. Lifting herself onto her elbows, she looked over her shoulder. He was sprawled behind her on the big bed, arm bent, head resting on his palm, watching her.

"Your turn," she said hoarsely.

But instead of reaching for her, he went for the lamp and flicked it off. "Uh-uh," he said into the darkness; gently, he pressed her face back into the pillow.

She could feel him full against her bottom. "Joe, I—"

He began kneading her shoulders again. "Shh, relax. This night is just for you, honey."

She had no choice but to do as he said. She felt her eyes close and her breathing even out. The last thing she remembered was the feel of his clever hands on her.

It was a wonderful five days. In the elevator on their way up to Allheart's offices, Elyssa moved close to Joe and slid her arms around his neck.

His hands gripped her denim-clad bottom. His own jeaned thighs thrust forward. "Hmmm. Kiss me."

She did. Long. Trustingly.

Their escape together to his parents' cabin in the Blue Ridge Mountains had gone a long way to bridge the rift between them. They'd forsaken all cell phones, beepers and work-related materials and holed up in the wilderness to concentrate on each other. It had been a glorious time. She smiled thinking of how she'd paid him back for his night of spoiling her a week ago—and had done a lot more.

Just before the elevator doors opened, Joe released her. She strode to her offices, her mind a muddle. They'd come back at the end of today so she could check her messages and schedule for the rest of the week, but right now she wished they'd stayed cuddled in the big bed with the Indian blanket.

Allheart's offices were buzzing this afternoon.

"Omigod, E's here," Robyn practically shouted when Elyssa strolled through the door.

"Calm down, Robyn. It can't be that bad."

"Where have you *been*?"

Joe came up behind her and put his hand on her neck. "You know we went to the mountains, Robyn."

"I know, but you were supposed to be back yesterday."

"No, today." Elyssa picked up her pink phone slips. As she rooted through them, she asked, "What's going on?"

"You had meetings all morning. And you've got another one at four."

"That's impossible. I told you I'd be out until Wednesday."

"You said you'd be back Tuesday. I scheduled appointments."

"Let's not bicker now, ladies." Joe leaned over the desk. "What did Elyssa miss?"

A bit miffed at his highhandedness, Elyssa listened to Robyn explain the appointments that had been canceled.

"That doesn't sound too bad." Joe smiled charmingly. "And she's here for her four o'clock."

"Not dressed like this, I'm not."

"You look perfectly charming, darling."

She glanced down at her boots, denims, light suede jacket and silk blouse. "No way."

Joe dragged her into her office. "She'll be here," he called to Robyn over his shoulder. He eased her inside and backed her up against the wall. There, he kissed her senseless.

"What are you doing?" she asked, when she was able to pull away.

"Come on, Lyss. So you got your wires crossed. No big deal. Let's not ruin the mood of the weekend."

She arched a brow, then leaned into him a minute. Drawing away, she crossed to her desk and booted up her computer.

She sank to the chair and called up her calendar. Scanning it, she sighed. "Damn, I've got the wrong dates on here. Robyn was right."

"Well, confess, will you, while I use the bathroom?"

Giving him a withering look, Elyssa buzzed for Robyn.

After accepting her explanation, and apology, Robyn said, "Your four o'clock's here. I'll send him in."

"Who is it?" Robyn clicked off and the door opened simultaneously.

Parker Quest strolled in.

He was dressed similarly to her in jeans, boots and a black leather jacket. "Hello, Elyssa." He came toward the desk and she stood. Graciously he took her hand. "Did I catch you at a bad time?"

"No, an error in my scheduling." She smiled and glanced down. "Sorry about the duds."

"I like you like this." He didn't let go of her hand. His light brown eyes sparkled. "Makes you less intimidating."

Walking back into the room, Joe said dryly, "I wouldn't be taken in by the clothes, Quest, if I were you. Underneath she's still the tiger she's always been."

Parker dropped her hand and faced Joe. "Nice to see you, Joe. And don't worry, the last thing I'd do is underestimate Elyssa Wentworth."

Joe's look was glacial. It said Parker Quest would do a lot less than that, if Joe had his way.

"Mind if I sit in on this meeting?" Joe asked innocently. He moved closer to Elyssa and touched her back possessively. "We just got back from the mountains and I'd like to catch up on our business, too."

"Don't mind a bit." Parker's down-home inflection thickened.

"Good." Joe spared her a glance. "You, Elyssa?"

She shook her head. She didn't trust her voice to answer him. Through gritted teeth she said, "Sit down, Parker."

For two hours, Joe watched the young designer charm the pants off Elyssa, figuratively, of course. He'd do it literally, if he had his way, but Joe wasn't about to let that happen. Nor was he going to let the guy influence Allheart the way it was clear he was trying to do.

As Elyssa appeared to be letting him do.

"We don't have seasonal cards, Parker." Elyssa concentrated on the packet Quest had prepared and didn't look up as she spoke. Her delicate brows knitted in earnest thought.

Joe scanned page eleven. "Should have done your homework, Quest. This last section is useless to us."

Stretching out his long legs, Parker smiled at Elyssa and ignored Joe. He'd been treating Joe like the Invisible Man for most of the afternoon.

And devouring Elyssa with his eyes.

"Well, the way I figure it, implementing seasonal cards, and combining the Halloween and Thanksgiving lines under the umbrella of fall, the Christmas ones under winter, et cetera, would accommodate my plan."

Tapping her pencil on the folder, Elyssa studied his suggestions.

"Why not stick with gifts to accompany the holidays?" Joe asked. He phrased his question carefully, as Elyssa had been throwing visual daggers at him all afternoon. He'd been too negative, she'd eloquently told him with narrowed eyes and a tight mouth.

He wanted to kiss the annoyance off that mouth, but then, that was part of the problem. Damn.

Parker faced Joe, exasperation and a trace of annoyance

clouding his young face. "Seems to me Allheart shouldn't stick with the traditional holiday cards because every other greeting card company does the same thing. Allheart should go in a different direction; separate from the pack, so to speak. Elyssa's been doing that all along and it's what brought her to the top."

"That and our money." Joe winced inwardly. He didn't mean to say that. It would tick her off royally. He didn't look at her. "In any case, you weren't hired to design new cards."

Sighing dramatically, Parker faced Elyssa. "I don't want to design the cards. Dana and Alix do that. But going in a new direction has become synonymous with Allheart. I think you should at least explore the possibility."

Elyssa reached for the phone and pressed a button. "Carole, could you come in here a minute? And get Alix and Dana. I know it's late but something's come up and we need some input."

Twenty minutes later, the four women were cooing over Parker Quest like hens over a rooster. "It's brilliant," Dana said, shrugging her shoulders. "I love the summer basket idea."

"Maybe in the graphic design of the cards, we can indicate an item included in the basket," Alix suggested. "A daffodil on the card representing the daffodils in the spring basket. Apples pictured like the ones in the fall basket."

"A cup of steaming tea from the winter basket on those cards." This from Dana.

The brainstorming went on.

Joe finally said, "If you really include all your suggestions the cost of making the baskets will be prohibitive. We'll lose money."

Parker's look was smug. "Not if we charge enough for the baskets."

"But then you run into only a small margin of people willing to pay that much for them."

"Elyssa's image is first class. Anything but Godiva chocolate, exotic teas, RayBans, or Longaberger baskets will diminish the high quality that heralds this outfit, that distinguishes it from Hallmark and their ilk."

Looking exasperated at the byplay, Elyssa finally spoke up, "Let's test market it. Spring's just around the corner. Can you get the spring basket ready if we have the cards in place by then?"

"The cards can't possibly be in place by then." Even to his own ears Joe sounded like a broken record.

"Of course they can," Dana said. "I'll work on the drawings this week. Alix, can you get a sample ready?"

"Sure."

"Mitch is in Idaho, so I can work over the weekend on this," said Carole, who'd been silent during much of the back-and-forthing. "We could get this up in as early as a few weeks." She smiled fondly at Elyssa. "Remember when you had that brainstorm for the sexy card line? We threw it together in ten days and advertisers were clamoring to be part of it. By the end of the quarter we'd brought in hundreds of thousands of dollars."

Dana stood. "It's seven o'clock. I have a date."

"Oh, Lord," Alix said following suit. "I was supposed to meet Marc. Can we leave, E?"

Elyssa smiled but Joe could tell she was peeved. At him. "Sure. Wouldn't want to keep you away from your *honeys*."

Parker stood. "I'll be going, too."

"You got a honey waiting for you too, Parker?" Carole teased, gathering her things.

It was just a glance. The quickest, surreptitious stolen look at Elyssa. But Joe caught it. "Nah, no honey in the picture." He gave them his Huck Finn grin. "But I'm workin' on it."

In minutes they were alone. Joe stretched out his legs and closed his eyes, leaning his head against the chair. "All right, give it to me with both barrels."

Elyssa didn't speak, so he opened his eyes. She was quietly angry, which was eons worse than throwing things or yelling. Arching a brow, she said, "First, don't ever again bring up our personal relationship, with a word or gesture, like that again."

He felt his own onslaught of coldness. "It's no secret with your staff."

"I mean in front of people like Parker. Even a monkey could spot the possessiveness. . . . *We just got back from the mountains,* for God's sake."

His heart, so full of her and her professed devotion over the last few days, clutched in his chest. "I see. Anything else?"

"Yes. Parker's ideas were great. You shot down every one of them."

"I liked his Valentine's Day suggestion."

"The seasonal cards and The Great Big Gift Baskets were a stroke of genius. They'll set us apart from all the other companies. You know damn well it's good business. He's brilliant."

Joe remembered a conversation . . . from long ago . . .

You surround yourself with brilliant people.

It's why I chose you. . . .

"Ah, that's right, you're attracted to brilliant people."

Her shoulders relaxed, losing the stiffness of anger. "Joe, I thought we were past this."

Well, he'd blown it. He stared at her, noting the soft flush the outdoors had given her over the long five days together. "Joe?"

"We *are* past it," he lied. "I didn't like the ideas."

She folded her hands together under her chin and said nothing.

"You don't believe that." His tone was clipped.

"No, I don't."

He stood abruptly. He'd promised himself there would be no more fights over this guy. "Let's drop it. You made your executive decision, overruling me, in front of three members of your staff, I might add." He dug his hands into his jeans. "I'm hungry. We haven't eaten since breakfast. Let's stop at J. Paul's before we go home." He didn't know what he'd do if she refused to go home with him. If this turned into another full-blown argument.

He was grateful when she stood, picked up her purse, slid into her jacket, circled the desk and linked her arm with his. "All right, let's go home."

As they left her office, Joe silently pledged he'd be better. He'd be more objective. He wouldn't let his feelings for her interfere with the business.

When he caught sight of the flowers on a table in the outer office, he stopped dead. He could just make out her name and the note, "Welcome back," on the tag attached to the big yellow bow around a cut crystal vase.

She stopped, too. A smile split her face.

His hands fisted.

She was grinning like a schoolgirl as she approached the wild mess of bright yellow daisies—her favorite because they were wildflowers. "Oh, Joe, they're lovely. When did you do this?"

Fury bubbling inside him, he snapped, "I didn't."

Chapter 3

*E*lyssa was exhausted as she dragged herself into her office Monday morning. She'd been exhausted for two months, ever since they'd hired Parker Quest and launched the ancillary products program at Allheart. The seasonal cards and The Great Big Gift Baskets had been more successful than anyone dreamed, and business was taking off like a rocket. Allheart was solidly at the top of its game, thanks in many ways to Parker.

No other employees had arrived for work yet and she welcomed the quiet. Mornings used to be like this, when she first founded the company, and before they moved into their new digs. In some ways, she missed that time: the excitement of new beginnings, the awe at first successes. Maybe it was time for a change.

That's what life's all about, kiddo. Elliot had made the comment when he'd told her that he and Mary were getting married in June. Elyssa had felt like everything was shifting

under her feet, an emotional earthquake of sorts, and Elliot
had seen right through her.

It's time for you to move on, too, Lyss.

Maybe professionally. There'd been hints at a buyout,
and a couple of companies had even approached her about
selling her baby. In a few weeks, they were meeting with
Highwire to discuss the possibility.

But personally, things weren't good with Joe—who'd
turned into a veritable Othello. He erupted over things
Parker did, like sending the welcome-back flowers, or the
business dinners between just her and Parker that went
late, or the fact that Parker always seemed to be around the
office. Damn! Joe's jealousy was wearing thin and the strain
on their relationship had become unbearable. They were
spinning their wheels most of the time, backpedaling the
rest. They definitely weren't going forward, as Elliot
suggested.

With a malaise she couldn't shake, she booted up her
computer and stared at the screen as all her new e-mail
queued up in front of her. Lord, the number couldn't possibly be right. One hundred messages?

*That's success for you, Lyss. And it's what you wanted, isn't
it?*

Among the dozens of pieces of e-mail she noticed there
was an Allheart greeting card.

She smiled. Only one person ever sent her own company's
cards to her. Joe. Immediately she opened the mail. This one
was from their anniversary collection. Elyssa herself had suggested the idea for this line. Not your typical schmaltzy anniversary greetings for a wedding, opening of a business, et
cetera. The line targeted unique anniversaries: congratulations for a kid on the anniversary of his taking his first step; a
card for a teacher, remembering her first day on the job; all of

the others had the same unusual theme. Red Door, their major competitor, had copied the idea right away.

The card Joe sent her was a couples card. The front pictured a sun, peeking over the horizon, its sky pink and purple and utterly lovely. Inside the simple text read, "A new day dawned when I met you and my whole life changed. Happy anniversary, love. Joe."

She closed her eyes and rested her head in her hands. They'd met a year ago today, when he'd strutted into her office full of masculine grace and cocky arrogance. March fifteenth.

She'd totally forgotten.

Maybe he's right. Maybe you are neglecting him. Maybe you're spending too much time at work. Or with Parker.

Hmm. Parker. Who grew more amenable as Joe got more and more surly. Who grew more understanding as Joe dug his heels in deeper. Who grew more patient as her time with Joe became less frequent and he complained loudly. She had to admit Parker was easier and more fun to be around lately than Joe. *Had* she been spending too much time with him?

Shaking off the thought, she checked the clock. Seven A.M. She and Joe hadn't spent the night together because she had to come in for a breakfast meeting.

You didn't spend the night together because you couldn't handle the tension and it seemed like he didn't care, either.

The whole situation with Joe made her sad so she picked up the phone and dialed his number. If he was in bed . . . she smiled as she pictured him sleep-rumpled, unshaven and totally sexy. He'd love some naughty talk on the phone, even this early.

It rang six times and Elyssa was about to hang up. Then a soft slurred feminine alto answered, "Hello?"

When she got her voice back, Elyssa said, "I'm sorry, I must have the wrong number. I was looking for 965-2422."

"This is that number. Just a second. I'll get Joe."

Stunned, Elyssa clasped the phone tightly. Her mind reeled with possibilities. There was a *woman* at Joe's apartment at seven A.M.? A woman who'd obviously been asleep?

In a few minutes—too long—Joe came on. "Hello." He sounded sleepy and a little annoyed.

"Joe?"

"Lyss?" Immediately, his voice warmed. "Hi, sweetheart."

She said nothing.

"How are you?" he asked.

"Just peachy. Doesn't it even bother you I caught you shacking up with another woman?"

"Shacking up? Oh, you mean with Beth?"

Ah, the beautiful Bethany.

There was a pause. "Just a second." He partially covered the mouthpiece. She heard his voice. And another. "Hmm. Thanks." It sounded like he was sipping something.

Elyssa's heart turned over, the horrible picture of Joe's ex-wife serving him coffee in bed flashing through her mind; she placed her hand on her chest to alleviate some of the pressure. As far as she knew, there'd been no one else for either of them since they met. A year ago today.

"Isn't the anniversary card—I don't know—ridiculous?" she asked when he came back on the line.

"Lyss, you—"

"Never mind. I don't want to hear your excuses. Goodbye, Joe."

Dropping the phone in its cradle, Elyssa stood, walked across her office to the window and stared out. She wouldn't cry. She never cried. And she certainly wouldn't shed a tear over a man who cheated on her. Looking out at the canal, she thought about a year ago today. . . .

Highwire Industries allows people to fulfill their dreams. We give them the necessary capital, business experience and direction to do that. . . . We'll work with you on your vision and business plan . . . it'll take about two weeks of your time . . . What do you have to lose, Ms. Wentworth?

Little did she know what she had to lose. Emotion crowded her throat, as she realized what she'd let happen. Why had she given her heart to him? Why had she let him become so important to her? Somewhere inside she'd known intuitively not to trust him so much. Why hadn't she listened to her fears?

She heard a buzz outside in the foyer. Her first meeting today was early, with a catered breakfast. In the last two months, Allheart had taken off and to keep the five employees motivated and employed here—they'd almost lost Alix to a competitor—nonvoting stocks in the company had been made available to Carole, Robyn, Alix and Dana. If there was a buyout, the women would be well rewarded for their efforts and their loyalty. Her company was healthier, more successful than she could ever have imagined.

But not her personal life. She'd had clues that something was wrong, mainly Joe's irrational behavior over Parker. But Elyssa had had no idea Joe was sleeping with other women.

"Damn it, Robyn, how could you have forgotten that?" Elyssa snapped at her young assistant who, instead of tossing back a sassy remark, stared at her with wide green eyes. All of her staff had been working countless hours to keep up with the influx of business.

"Elyssa." Carole's quiet voice penetrated her pique. Carole

was often the voice of reason and had been a good friend to Elyssa. She looked like Sela Ward and had the heart of Mother Teresa.

Her gaze swung to Carole. "What?"

"You've been snapping at everybody all morning."

"I have?" She made eye contact with all three women and met Alix's quiet, affirming gaze, Dana's pretty half-smile of agreement. "Oh, God." Burying her head in her hands, she couldn't look at them. "I'm sorry. It's . . . it's . . . it's everything. We're up to our ears here. There's even talk of a buyout; I—"

Carole placed her hand on Elyssa's arm. "Hey, we've had stresses at work before. You never took it out on us then. What's going on?"

At first, she balked at sharing such a personal thing with her employees. But they were more than coworkers. They were friends. They'd all trusted her with their love lives. Maybe it was time to do the same.

"Joe sent me an Allheart card. Today is the one-year anniversary of the day we met. I called him at seven o'clock this morning and a woman answered. She obviously got him up. Pardon the pun." Tears formed in her eyes. She sniffed them back. "Then she had the nerve to bring him coffee while he talked to me on the phone."

A stunned silence. Every woman in this room thought Joe was a prince.

Finally, Robyn said, "I don't believe it."

Elyssa glanced over her shoulder. "You think I'm making this up?"

"No way. But maybe there's some kind of misunderstanding."

Shaking her head, Elyssa stared out the window. "You're young, Robyn. After a certain point there aren't misunderstandings anymore. Just choices people make. And it looks like Joe's chosen to be with someone else."

Dana said, "Things haven't been good for a while, have they, E?"

She shook her head. "Not really."

"Since Parker Quest came on board," Alix added.

Elyssa's shoulders sagged. "Please don't start on me about Parker. I get enough of that from Joe."

Dead silence behind her. She turned. They were all staring at her. Carole finally said, "Elyssa, this thing with Parker? You may not be seeing it clearly. The guy, well, he's a cutie, and we all adore him, but . . ."

"He's got the hots for you, E," Robyn blurted out. "Anybody can tell."

Elyssa thought about the way Parker touched her sometimes, casually and slightly, but somehow suggesting that they were more than business partners. And the way he complimented her about her clothes or her hair. She winced. Had she unconsciously encouraged his familiarity? "Even if that is true, I can't control his feelings." Again the stares. "Look, he's taken the business in a direction it needed to go. I can't fire him and I couldn't have *not* hired him, just because he *might* be attracted to me."

"You spend a lot of time with him. Marc would easily be as jealous as Joe is," Alix observed.

"Why can't you recognize this, Elyssa?" Dana asked. "It's so unlike you."

"Recognize what?"

"That you're putting more distance between you and Joe each day. In case you haven't noticed, he's hardly around anymore."

"Are you spending any time with him outside of here?" Carole asked.

She shook her head. "Not enough." Several nights in the last month they'd not only slept apart, but hadn't spent evenings together, missed their usual dinners. Had she even realized how their relationship was fraying at the edges? She buried her head in her hands again. "Oh, God. No, I didn't see this coming."

Carole rose and came toward her. "It's not too late. Call Joe."

"I tried that, remember? And I got another woman."

"Who you're going to just hand him over to?"

"If he's been screwing her, yes, she can have him."

"I don't believe it's gotten that far. Joe has too much integrity. He'd break it off with you before he went to bed with another woman." Carole was that sure of Joe. They all were.

It was on the tip of Elyssa's tongue to remind them that he'd behaved unethically by sleeping with her, Elyssa, his business partner. But she couldn't bring herself to say that out loud. No matter what he'd done.

"Call him." Carole's voice was gentle but confident.

The tightening in Elyssa's chest from this morning returned. It was accompanied by such a sinking feeling in her stomach she thought she might be ill.

Malcolm stuck his head in the door. "The men from LiteTech are here, ladies."

Grateful for the reprieve, Elyssa turned. "All right, Malcolm, send them in." The women stared at her. "Thanks for listening but we've got business to take care of."

She could tell her staff didn't want to end the conversation, but as far as she was concerned nothing more needed to be said.

Seven hours later, she was still taking care of business. In an effort not to think about Joe—who hadn't called, or e-mailed or come over all day on their anniversary—she threw herself into Allheart.

And now she was exhausted. She should go home, maybe call Elliot. Instead she went back to the window and stared out into the star-speckled night. It was clear and pretty.

She felt lonely as hell.

Joe found her there, at the window, small and solitary in a simple black dress and those gorgeous spiked heels. He shook his head; she might look slight but she possessed the emotional muscles to rip him apart—and was slowly doing a good job of it. He was disgusted at himself. Despite all that, he'd come to her. After a day of willing himself not to call her—she should have come to him, damn it, he'd done nothing wrong—he was here, instead. The spell she'd cast over him didn't sit well, but he was powerless against it. He was also beginning to hate himself for his weakness for her.

At least everybody was gone and he didn't have an audience for the fool he was about to make of himself. "Lyss."

She spun around. His heart leapfrogged. She looked terrible. Her face was pale, her hazel eyes haunted. For a minute, she just stared at him. Then she turned back to the window and clasped her arms around her waist in what seemed a self-protective gesture.

"I hope you didn't come to wish me happy anniversary. I've had enough hypocrisy for one day."

He said nothing. He'd seen her in this mood before. Best to let her get it all out.

"And I hope you didn't come to get laid. Even as a kid, I was never very good at sharing."

Ah, she was so quick with the zingers. He closed the door behind him and locked it for good measure. He hadn't expected vulnerability. A tirade, yes. But this unprotected reaction from her pierced his heart.

"Join the club, Lyss. At least now you know how it feels."

Her eyes were flaming when she faced him. "Is that what this is all about? You're getting back at me because Parker is attracted to me?"

Folding his arms over his chest, he arched a brow. "Now, this is progress. You've been denying that little fact for weeks."

"No, I've been denying there's anything between Parker and me for weeks. It takes two, Joe. But you already know that, don't you?" Her voice rose a notch, and got that little catch it got when she was really hurt.

"Yes, I know it takes two," he said. "But not for the reason you think."

"Please, no more. It took me a while to figure things out, but it's pretty obvious now what's been going on."

"Enlighten me, then." His words were clipped. She was making him mad again. Did she really think so little of him? Of their relationship?

"You've been camouflaging your cheating with your needy *ex* by making accusations about Parker."

"And why exactly would I do that? Why wouldn't I just break it off with you if I wanted to be with Bethany?"

"Maybe you wanted both. A blonde and a brunette in your bed. Sounds perfect."

His temper reached the burning point in seconds and he strode toward her, grabbed her arm, and whirled her around. "It sounds seedy and obscene and I resent your thinking such a thing of me."

"Are you denying it?"

"Of course I am."

"She slept with you last night, didn't she?"

"She slept at my house, Elyssa, yes. But she didn't sleep *with* me."

Elyssa rolled her eyes and started to walk away. He yanked her back. "Do you really expect me to believe that?" she said with a sneer.

"Do you expect me to believe nothing's happened with you and Quest?"

"Well, I haven't been caught with him in a compromising situation."

"The hell you haven't. You two have your cozy little lunches, you're alone with him here after everyone else has left. I'll bet he's been to your apartment, hasn't he?"

"I'm not going to answer that. I'm not going to listen to this."

"Is that why you didn't call me or come to see me today? Because you've been with him, like you think I've been with her?"

"*What?*" she practically shouted. "You expected me to come to you? God, you've got gall."

"No, I've got common sense." He shook her. "I've tried to confront this whole issue with Quest, even though it's demeaning and painful, even though it's driven us apart. But you couldn't be bothered to seek me out today when you suspected the worst of me."

She stared at him.

He shook her again. "I always have to come to you. Do you know how demoralizing that is?"

She didn't answer.

"But I do it."

"Why?"

"Oh, Christ, if you don't know the answer to that by now . . ." He stepped back. Shook his head. Turned to leave. But before he reached the door, he stopped and after a moment, pivoted around. "I love you, damn it." Livid at his weakness in telling her, caught behind the knees because she looked so shocked, and despairing that she had no immediate response, he circled around.

She reached him just as his hand raised to the lock on the door. "Joe."

He stopped. Didn't face her.

"Don't go."

He waited. All day he'd tried to talk himself into ending this whole godforsaken relationship, which had been plagued from the start with doubt and innuendo. He needed to get out of it, free himself from the only situation in his life he couldn't control. *Tell her, now. End it.*

Still, he stared at the door, immobile and in pain.

Elyssa's heart was cartwheeling in her chest over Joe's declaration. She'd gone after him instinctively, like an animal chasing her mate, but her mind whirled with uncertainty.

His back to her, she didn't know what to do. So she pulled on his arm, made him face her. It was worse staring into those tumultuous blue eyes.

At her continued silence, he repeated hoarsely, "I love you. Do you understand what that means?"

Her whole body shuddered. She gripped his shoulders for balance. They were big and wide and so strong.

Grasping her upper arms, he shook her. It hurt. She felt her eyes tear, not at the physical pain but at the vise around her heart. Somewhere she recognized the cosmic significance of this moment.

But it was the hurt etching itself out on his face like a van Gogh portrait that shook her from immobility. It was the look of utter disgust when he pulled back that made her react, without censoring what she'd say or do.

She threw herself at him. "No, no, please don't go."

Rigid and unyielding, he stood there as she grabbed onto him. Intuitively she knew he wouldn't bend on this, wouldn't accept halfway measures. She stood up on tiptoes, twined her arms around his neck like a drowning victim, and said, "I love you, too. I do."

His whole body went slack; she felt him draw in a heavy breath, let it out. It was an eternity before his arms circled around her.

She couldn't speak past the lump in her throat. She was scared of her feelings for him, frightened at the power those words gave him over her, but she knew what she felt. She *had* known for a long time, just wouldn't admit it to herself, or to Joe.

He didn't let go, just held her, buried his face in her hair, sunk deeper into her. The intimacy of the embrace, the tenderness it elicited, overwhelmed her. After a long time, he drew back.

She was absolutely stunned to see his cheeks were wet. "Joe."

"I . . . I didn't think you'd ever say those words to me."

Raising her hands, she scrubbed the moisture from his cheeks, whispered over and over, "I love you . . . I love you . . ."

Very fast, the mood changed. His eyes cleared, then burned. The arms around her tightened like steel bands. He was hard, instantly, against her. "Show me."

So like him; the comment was so like him she smiled. She reached for the silk tie. Never releasing his gaze, she loosened it, tugged it off, threw it into a navy and red heap on the floor. Her hands trembled at the buttons of his light blue silk shirt, and when she opened it to the black mat of hair, she leaned forward and brushed her nose back and forth. He started violently. He smelled faintly of starch, mostly of the sexy expensive cologne he wore. It sent goose bumps all over her skin; a rush of arousal coursed through her.

She moaned, slid off both his gray suit jacket and shirt. His hands reached for her shoulders, held her there. Hers went for his belt. Its heavy weight, and the fact that she was trembling, made her clumsy, but he didn't assist her. He let her disrobe him, except to kick off his shoes and remove his socks.

Then he kissed her. His big naked body dwarfed hers, absorbed hers as their lips met. He took her mouth in full possession. It went on a long time.

"Too many clothes," he finally murmured as he began to release the buttons on the front of her dress, ripped off the red satiny bra and panties she wore, slid stockings, everything, from her body.

In seconds she was as naked as he. On his knees, he gently bit the inside of her thigh and she groaned, grasped his shoulders. "Joe."

Kissing his way up her body—stopping at strategic places—he finally stood. The world tilted and she felt herself lifted, cradled against his chest and carried to the couch. Once again the tenderness overpowered her. Something had shifted in their relationship with the words they'd uttered. Something deepened and transcended every other time they'd touched. She banished the fear this realization brought to her consciousness.

He laid her down on the sofa. Its leather was cool on her naked back and on her legs, but Joe's weight soon covered her and her body flushed with an inferno of need inside her. He didn't start kissing her, though. Instead he peered into her eyes, his blue gaze so intense, so profound it stopped her heart. He framed her face with his hands. "Say it again."

"I love you, Joe. I have for a long time."

"I'm never letting you go now. You know that, don't you?"

Her heart kick-started. She knew her face betrayed the shock she felt. The terror.

"Don't be afraid of it."

"I am."

"I know. That's really what this has all been about." Reaching down, he parted her legs and slipped easily inside her; the fullness, the rightness of him made her close her eyes. "I love you so much," he whispered and began to move.

She let herself go, let herself get lost in the sensation of his hard muscles crushing her, his big hand feathering over her skin, his mouth everywhere. She came three times before he climaxed. He spilled into her with a great force and the entire cataclysmic mating left her stunned.

She just held on to him, happier, and more frightened, than she'd ever been in her life.

Within the week, Joe took advantage of her confession. Though saying she loved him seemed to calm his fears about Parker—Joe hardly mentioned him lately—another side of Joseph Lance Monteigne II surfaced from their recent conflict. And this new side of him simultaneously thrilled her and scared her to death.

She experienced both emotions as she lay on his bed— blindfolded. The velvet cloth made the entire room dark as sin. Facedown, her cheek flat against the mattress, her naked body on top of the covers, she said, "But I can't see."

He chuckled. "That's the point, love. Just feel." His hands stroked her, and felt bigger and stronger than ever. Right now they kneaded the base of her spine. She remembered the backrub several weeks ago, after their first big run-in about Bethany and Parker, when he'd handled her with unending tenderness. Tonight was different. Exciting, with a hint of menace. And there was none of that selfless giving. Intuitively, she knew he was going to take, plain and simple. She felt him shift down her body; his hands traced the backs of her knees and softly brushed over her ankles.

"In another culture, you'd wear harem bracelets on your wrists and ankles," he murmured.

"Really," Elyssa answered, not sure she liked wondering where this sexual play was headed. "And what would these bracelets do for me?"

"It's not what they'd do for you. It's what they'd do for me," he answered with a low laugh. "They'd mark you as mine."

The words had made her shudder, but also aroused her so much she almost couldn't stand it.

"Water's done," he said, turning her over. She reached for the blindfold. He grasped her wrist. "No way, sweetheart. Just feel."

His arms came around her back and under her knees. His muscles bunched beneath her bottom when he picked her up. His subtle aftershave teased her nose as she rubbed her face against his rough beard while he carried her to the bathroom.

The water in the huge tub prickled her skin as he lowered her into it. She was reminded again of that night he'd tended to her, the last bath she'd taken here, and his gentle ministrations; again this time, she knew it was different.

Rougher. More erotic. The water level rose as Joe got in; she could tell from the direction of his voice that he sat at the other end of the tub, facing her. She heard a rustle then smelled a faintly exotic scent. It somehow suggested dim bedrooms and heated sex. He began to rub something cold on her legs.

"Hmm, what is it?"

"Scented gel. Smells like a harem to me. And I've got my own little harem girl right here." Then he added huskily, "Whom I can do anything I want with."

Again, Elyssa felt faintly uncomfortable. But acutely aroused. He coated her feet and legs with the fragrant soap, slowly, inch by inch.

She was trembling by the time he finished. Finally he pulled her to her knees and she swayed forward, landing dizzily in his arms. He grasped her waist and turned her around. His chest was rock hard against her back and the scented soap filled her nostrils. He had more gel on his hands, and began to wash her, everywhere—each arm, her breasts, between her legs. Lightly he stroked her. "Being behind you is erotic to me, darling. It's how I want to take you tonight."

Consumed with need, she didn't respond. Just moaned.

"Say it's all right. Say you want me that way."

She barely got the words out.

"But first I want you to come." He increased the pressure of his fingers. Soon, very soon, she climaxed into his strong hand with his big body closing around her.

Later, he fulfilled all of his fantasies, making her moan, even beg for him.

It wasn't until they were cuddled up in bed, ready for sleep, that the unease she felt earlier returned. Now that the playing was over for the evening, the whole harem theme made her cringe. Then when she was in that half-conscious state between sleep and wakefulness, she realized how *masterful* he'd been. Liking it, and fearing it, she banished the thought and fell into a deep slumber.

But she dreamed that night that she was indeed a harem girl—his—and he had total control over her existence. She woke up sweating.

Chapter 4

Sweat dripping in her eyes, Elyssa said to her trainer, Spade, "So, can I increase the weights?"

"Yeah." The trainer checked his watch. "Give me five minutes to finish with this other guy then we'll see where we should go from here. Take a break."

Lying flat out on the bench, she nodded and relaxed. Her energy level was back, she was all caught up at work and the business was booming.

Now, if only her personal life wasn't scaring the daylights out of her most of the time. Sex with Joe had gotten so intense, so intimate, she could barely think about it. But she *had* to think about it because she suspected this escalating intimacy was one of the ways Joe was pushing her to be closer to him. He was also pressuring her to spend more time with his family; they were going to Virginia for the weekend to celebrate his parents' fortieth wedding anniversary. She could feel him inextricably weaving her into his life, even if she didn't want to be part of the fabric. Or did she?

"Gathering wool, lady?"

She looked up into the smiling face of Parker Quest. Dressed in plain blue gym shorts and a white T-shirt, he towered over her. She sat up and smiled. "Yeah. I'm waiting for Spade to get back."

About a month ago, Parker's gym had closed, and since then he'd been scouting out a new place. Once, when they'd been pressed for time, he'd met her here, and turned out he knew Spade, from another gym, so he decided to join Elyssa's club. She hadn't dared tell Joe about this development.

"What do you need from Spade?" He grinned that boyish grin, the one that made her think Joe and her staff were misinterpreting his motives. She kept insisting he was just young and extroverted, a confident, happy guy. "I worked in a gym all through college."

"Really?" Her gaze dropped to his biceps, which testified to his fitness. "I want to up my weights."

"Hmm." He picked up her chart, which was lying on the floor next to the bench. "You could probably add ten easy on the bench press." He leaned over and squeezed her biceps playfully. "Maybe twenty."

She was flustered by his solid grip. "Oh, okay."

"I'll spot you." Hands on her shoulders, he pressed her down to the bench, took two ten-pound weights and added one to each end of the bar then picked up the barbell. "Here. Go slow . . . that's it." He smiled affectionately as he watched her. "Just five reps."

He knew what he was doing. When Spade returned, the trainer laughingly offered Parker a job.

Spade glanced at the clock. "Okay, twenty-five on the treadmill, Elyssa."

Parker scowled as the trainer left.

"You don't do cardio?" she asked, wiping her face with a towel.

"Treadmills bore me." He glanced to the back of the gym. "I think I'll see if anybody's looking for a racquetball partner."

"Racquetball?"

"Yeah, you play?"

Elyssa thought of Joe, and how he'd asked her to play that night more than a year ago, thinking she knew nothing about the game. It was the first time he'd kissed her and she hadn't been able to walk onto a court without remembering the sensuality of the moment. She shivered.

Strong fingers closed over her arm. "Elyssa, are you all right?"

She nodded and made a split-second decision, ignoring the ridiculous voice inside her head that was trying to suggest she would be sharing something of Joe's with Parker. "Yeah, I play racquetball. But don't be surprised if I beat the pants off you."

He laughed aloud. "Well, now there's an image to distract me. Come on, lady, let's see what you can do." Because he held out his hand, she had no choice but to let him help her up.

Shushing the negative thoughts, she followed him to the courts.

Joe guided her around the dance floor, his hand splayed possessively on her naked back. Her dress was, in a word, stunning; made of a midnight blue silk jersey, it rose chastely to her neck in front, plunged breathtakingly low in back, and featured a slit that rose to kingdom come up the front of the skirt. His sisters had fawned over the dress and his father had said she was lovely. Joe himself had wanted to wrap her up in his suit coat to shield her from the preying eyes of other men; but he'd only smiled and told her she looked gorgeous.

As he inhaled her perfume, felt her hair tickle his cheek, he admitted to himself he'd been doing a lot of that lately—smiling to hide his increasingly possessive feelings. Instead of telling her how he really felt, though, he'd found himself pushing an intimacy between them in other, more enjoyable ways, believing somehow that would bring them so close there'd be nowhere else to go. He knew there was a deviousness to his thinking, and this pricked his conscience, but she loved him, damn it, and as he'd warned her when she admitted her feelings, he was never going to let her go.

Since she seemed willing to go along with whatever he instigated lately, he figured the least he could do was curb his jealousy. He had no idea what was going on with Quest. It drove him nuts not knowing how much she saw him, what she did with the guy, but he never asked. And she never volunteered any information. To give her credit, she refrained from queries about Beth, too, which was just as well, because his ex was putting the moves on him in an obvious way. And he had to do something about that.

"What's the scowl for, big guy?" Her hand flitted up to his nape; her eyes drank him in approvingly, making his heart swell.

"I was thinking about my parents getting old." He lied, again, to shield her from his thoughts. "Forty years of marriage—I can't believe it."

They both glanced over to the happy couple, surrounded tonight by friends and family. His father was strikingly handsome in his dark suit and distinguished gray hair. His mother was tall, slender and lovely in a floor-length white crepe dress that left her shoulders bare.

"They both look so content," Elyssa said.

"That's what a good marriage will do for you." He felt her stiffen in his arms, but said anyway, "They love you, Lyss. So do my sisters."

He felt her tense even further, and though it angered him, he quelled his pique.

"Joe, you're frowning again."

"You mistake my look." He leaned down, breathed into her ear. "I can't wait to get you into bed."

"Why? You can't possibly find anything to do to me there that you haven't already done these last few weeks."

He stilled. "You said you liked all that."

"I do. But you have to admit it's gotten a bit . . . unorthodox."

"Is there something about it that doesn't sit well?"

"Joe, let's not get into that tonight."

She'd been honest about the sexual play up to a point. He suspected it was the intimacy that scared her, an intimacy that he craved and intentionally seduced her into. Pulling her close, he shook his head at his own sly machinations. Never in his life had he behaved this way. *So why was he doing it now?*

He glanced over at his mother and father and the answer hit him with the force of a hammer blow. He wanted what they had. With the woman in his arms. Oh, God, what would she do if he mentioned the *M* word?

"I'd like to propose a toast to my lovely daughter." Mary Jenkins's father, a welder from Brooklyn, stood and lifted his glass. The older man sported a slight paunch under his

brand-new suit, but he beamed a million-dollar smile at the happy couple.

Mary's family had wanted to pay for their daughter's engagement party, but Elliot had gently insisted he should foot the bill since the Jenkinses were paying for the wedding. He'd told Elyssa that he and Mary had quietly agreed for financial reasons on a very, very small reception.

Of course, Mary and Elliot agreed on everything. They couldn't be happier about being so deeply in each other's thrall. Why, she wondered as she sipped her champagne in a small party room at New York's Tavern on the Green, were she and Elliot so different? Had he gotten all the commitment genes? Why was he able to fall in love so easily, and she was . . . unsettled by her feelings for Joe?

Frankly, she was beginning to feel terrified he was going to ask her to marry him.

"Having a good time, love?" He looked so damn good in a light charcoal pinstriped suit that turned his eyes slate. His hair had been recently cut and was combed off his face.

"Wonderful. You?"

He kissed her nose. "I always have a good time with you, Lyss."

This wasn't exactly true. Talk of a buyout at Allheart had progressed of late and Red Door, their main competitor, had made inquiries about their company. None of it had sat well with Joe. Elyssa had no idea why, since in recent months their success was phenomenal and they all stood to make plenty of money if they sold. But Joe didn't seem to be interested in a takeover. And though there were no more fights about Parker or Bethany—they never broached either subject—she knew Joe worried about her relationship with Quest.

She'd overheard him with one of his sisters the night of his parents' anniversary party.

"What's with you, buddy?" Susan had asked when she found Joe alone on the patio.

Elyssa had been to the ladies' room and returned unseen. She stood in the shadows and listened.

"Nothing." He slid his arm around his sister and tugged her close. "Just melancholy about Mom and Dad."

"Elyssa looks like she's having a good time."

"She seems to be."

"And you're unhappy?"

"No, no, I'm not."

Susan drew back and gave him a disbelieving, sideways glance. "Tell me. Is she trying to corner you?"

Joe laughed, but it was sad and self-effacing.

"Well, that's the story of your life, big brother," Susan added. "They get too close, you bolt."

"It's just the opposite this time, Suz."

"Really?"

"Oh, how the mighty have fallen. No, I want more, much more, from Elyssa than she is willing to give. I'm not sure she'll ever be able to give it."

"Well, she must not be as smart as I thought if she lets you get away . . ."

"Honey, Elliot asked you a question." Joe's voice penetrated her recollection.

Elliot stood over their table with Mary; they were holding hands, smiling broadly.

"Oh, I'm sorry. What did you say, Elliot?"

"Where were you?"

"Nowhere." She pasted on a phony smile. "You guys look happy."

Elliot moved away from Mary and touched Elyssa's shoulder. "Let's get a drink, Lyss." He left Mary chatting brightly with Joe.

In minutes Elyssa and Elliot were at the bar, sipping more champagne.

"Honey, Joe's not blind. He's got to be aware of the tension coming off you from all directions."

"I'm not ready for marriage—or anything remotely like it." She frowned into her very good bubbly. "Why is that so wrong?"

Sipping his wine, he watched her solemnly. "Do you think *he* is ready for it?"

"I don't know. I just feel him pressing closer and closer, and I find myself worrying all the time now that he's going to bring up marriage. Oh, Elliot, I'm not ready for that kind of commitment."

He stared hard at her. "You should talk this out with Joe."

"No, I don't want to bring up marriage. That would be letting the genie out of the bottle for sure."

"Well, I hope you don't lose him."

"I won't." She frowned. "Damn it, though, why can't he just be satisfied with the small steps we're taking?"

"Joe's a leaps and bounds kind of guy, honey." Elliot hesitated, then asked, "And what's up with Parker Quest?"

"Not much."

"I can't help but think you're playing with fire, Lyss." He scowled. "Unless you're attracted to Quest. Is that what this is all about? And it's making you unsure of how much you care about Joe?"

"Well, Parker is attractive, but no, I'm sure about my feelings for Joe. I love him." She frowned. "That should be enough for now."

"If Joe wants more, Quest is a threat."

Irrational defensiveness surfaced in her. "I don't think there's any harm in spending time with Parker."

Elliot shook his head. "It gives Quest the wrong message and will start World War Three if Joe finds out." He hesitated, then added, "Maybe that's why you're doing it."

"To start World War Three?"

"That would be one way to keep some distance from Joe. To loosen those chains you think he's tying you up with."

She couldn't help thinking of that harem girl remark Joe had made. It made her shudder. "Oh, Elliot, no."

"Think about it. Why else would you spend any time at all with Quest?"

Elyssa, you've got to come with me. Parker smiled at her from her office doorway on Thursday afternoon. Dressed in jeans and a long-sleeved cotton shirt rolled up at the sleeves, his grin was infectious.

She smiled back. "Where?"

"This market opened up in Foggy Bottom. It's different and I think we might get some good ideas." He glanced outside. "Besides, it's a gorgeous day and I like being outside."

"I don't know. I've got a lot to do here."

"Well, how soon could you get away?"

Pretending to check her calendar, she thought of Joe's words on the phone last night . . .

"I miss you, baby. We need to talk when I get back." He'd stayed on in New York for business since the weekend.

"About what?"

"I've been thinking about us. I haven't been completely honest about where my head's at. Just save the weekend for me, okay? I'll be home about six on Friday. Meet me at your place?"

She had agreed to see him, but she still didn't know what she'd do if he asked her to marry him.

"Elyssa?" Parker snapped her out of her reverie.

"I can get away at four. I've got clothes here to change into so we can go right from the office."

"Good." He smiled. "Maybe I can cheer you up."

"I don't need cheering up, Parker."

"Hmm. How about you have dinner with me? Monteigne's out of town, isn't he?"

For some reason, his question irritated her. "Joe's being in or out of town has nothing to do with anything," she snapped.

"Fine. See you at four."

Spring flowers tumbled out of porch boxes and big chunky pots at one of the stalls at the Foggy Bottom outdoor market. The weather was warm enough for just jeans and a shirt, and Elyssa and Parker wended through the new outdoor displays with the gentle April sun beating down on them.

"I wish we could offer flower boxes for spring, like those violets," she said as they paused at a stall teeming with clever flower and plant arrangements. "Doesn't that wildflower look beautiful?"

"Yes. But why can't we offer them?"

"They'd be expensive. It's not like they'd come wholesale."

He grasped her hand and tugged her over to the stall. Fifteen minutes later, he had the vendor's card, a meeting set up for the following week and a bunch of violets in his hand, which he presented to her with a mock bow, like a courtly knight.

"You're a real charmer," she said as she buried her nose in the pretty blossoms, inhaling their sweet scent. "That old woman didn't have a chance."

"Ah, my curse. To be loved by older women." He grinned at her and said flirtatiously, "And how old are you, Elyssa?"

Ignoring the comment, she cocked her head. "Parker, how come there isn't a woman in your life?"

"Haven't met the right combination lately. There was one once . . . I fell hard for her."

They strolled along, stopping at a booth that featured jewelry made of unusual semiprecious stones, their multi-facets glinting in the sun.

"Hmm, an adventurine stone." Parker picked it up and clasped it in his palm as if it had magical qualities. "For good luck."

"You know about this stuff?" She gestured toward the display.

"It's a hobby of mine," he said with a shrug and a warm smile. He studied her for a minute, then picked up a pair of earrings. "Tigereyes. To match yours." And before she could object, he bought them and a chunky necklace of the same stone, which he promptly slid over his head. "Take off your earrings."

"Really, Parker, you shouldn't—"

"It's a done deal." He held up the earrings. "I already bought them. And I stopped wearing one years ago, so they can't be for me."

She laughed. "You have pierced ears?"

"One. I also have a tattoo." He winked. "Maybe I'll show it to you some day."

After she withdrew her earrings, he inserted the tigereyes himself. Her stomach fluttered so she turned away.

As they resumed walking, she asked, "So, it didn't work out with the older woman? I presume the love of your life was one of these older women you're cursed with?"

He smiled sadly. "Yes, she was older and no, it didn't work out."

"Why not?" She knew better than to keep probing but she couldn't help it.

"I'll tell you that if you promise to answer something about you and Monteigne."

She knew she shouldn't. But she liked Parker, and she was enjoying her conversation with him. As the breeze ruffled his tawny hair, and the sun sparkled in his eyes, she agreed.

"Laura was married. I thought she was going to leave him. She didn't. End of story."

"I'm sorry."

He peered at her intently. "Your turn. My big question is how come you put up with that possessive crap Monteigne dishes out? Does the guy live in a different century?"

Parker and Elyssa laughed as they strode up the steps to her apartment building. The night air had turned chilly and they hurried along, but he had entertained her with funny blonde jokes all the way home.

"So, you gonna make me a pie with some of these?" Parker asked, nodding to the bag of cherries he'd picked up at the market.

Elyssa tossed Parker a withering look. "First of all, it's eight o'clock at night. Second, I'm stuffed from that meal we had at New Heights and third, I don't cook, young man."

"You don't bake either?" he asked incredulously as they entered her apartment.

"Nope."

"Hmm. Guess I'll just have to do this myself." Without further comment, he headed for her kitchen. She was surprised to see him make himself at home so easily. She sensed he felt some closeness to her, given all the time they'd spent together in the last few months.

An hour later the house was filled with heavenly scents of baking cherries. Sneakers off, relaxed, she sipped her wine and sat at the kitchen table and sniffed the violets she'd put in a vase. She cast surreptitious gazes at Parker. He was so easy to be with, so unlike Joe, who she had to be careful with these days. "What's with all you guys?" she asked, thinking about Joe. "You actually like to cook?"

He had removed his shirt after it had become covered with flour. His bare shoulders were muscular, but featured a friendly spattering of freckles. Her stomach contracted. "Yeah. What's the world coming to?"

She laughed. He pivoted, revealing a massive chest sprinkled with dark blond hair. A vision of Joe's bare chest came to her, and how she loved to run her hands over it and kiss his pecs.

"Now, *you* have to clean up," Parker said.

She bolted up, to escape both the KP duty and also the sight of Parker in just jeans in her kitchen. Something was wending its way to her consciousness that she didn't want to face. "No way." She plopped down her wine and turned to the doorway. "I've got to check my e-mail."

He caught up to her in the living room. "Whoa, there." She realized then he'd been touching her a lot today. Spinning her around playfully, he was about to speak, but his expression turned sober. "You are *so* lovely," he said softly. He reached up and brushed her hair out of her eyes. "Your hair's so soft." He didn't draw his hand back. Instead, he soothed his knuckles down her heated cheek. "So is this."

"Parker, I—"

"Shh." His thumb swept her lips. "Shh," he repeated.

Grasping her shoulders, he backed her up against the wall and braced his arms on either side of her.

She was speechless at his nearness. He smelled good, like the outdoors. She swallowed hard. His hand went to her throat.

His beautiful tawny eyes darkened. His wide shoulders tensed. His whole body seemed to melt into hers. Without another word he grasped her chin gently, tipped her face up to him.

And then he took her mouth, in a slow sensuous kiss. It was pleasant, warm . . . stirring.

Big hands found her shirt and she felt him release the buttons. Separate the flaps. Slide warm masculine fingers to her rib cage. Drawing back, he breathed sexily, "Elyssa."

The one word stopped her in the act of winding her arms around his neck. She froze with her hands on his shoulders. Joe called her "Lyss." This wasn't Joe.

Oh, my God, she thought, panicking. *What the hell am I doing?*

She placed a hand on Parker's chest in an effort to put the brakes on what was about to happen. "Parker. Wait."

He stilled, and then pulled back fractionally.

"I can't do this." Her voice was sandpapery.

"Why?"

"I love Joe. This isn't right."

His face bore traces of real hurt. He leaned his forehead on hers and sighed.

It was then the door to the living room opened. At the sound of jangling keys, Quest stepped slightly away from Elyssa, giving her a clear view of the doorway.

There stood Joe, a silvery bag in one hand, the keys Elyssa had given him months before in the other.

And an utterly stunned look on his face.

* * *

The images clicked into focus one at a time. Elyssa backed up against the wall. Her shirt open and one of his favorite black lacy bras peeking out. And Parker Quest's hands still lingering on her waist.

"Well, it looks like I was right all along." Joe's face showed fierce, black anger.

Too late, Elyssa and Parker sprang apart like illicit lovers. Now other things came into focus. Both were in socked feet. Quest was shirtless. His hair was disheveled. Frankly, he looked like a man with a good chance of getting laid in the very near future.

And if I hadn't interrupted, the man would have gotten laid by the woman I love, the woman who said she loved me. Joe couldn't contain the ugly thought.

He turned abruptly and strode out the door. At the building exit, he heard Elyssa call to him from above. He didn't stop. He had to get out of here. Flinging open the outer door, he hurried into the night. He halted, disoriented. Where was his car?

She caught up to him then. "Joe, wait."

He didn't respond; instead he wracked his brain to remember where he'd parked. He'd driven in from the airport, but it was after ten o'clock and hard to find a space. He'd had to park far away.

He'd been so anxious to see her, he'd jogged the block quickly.

She grasped his arm. Shaking her off, he started walking, dimly aware she was following him. He increased his pace until he reached his restored Mustang, which was parked at the beginning of the next block.

He still held his key ring clutched in his hand. Using the

remote, he unlocked the car, circled around the back fender and yanked open the driver's side. When he slid in, she opened the passenger side and jumped in, too.

Steeling himself against her, he gripped the wheel, staring straight ahead while the misting rain clouded his windshield. He thought about how he'd rushed home because he couldn't wait to see her. All day long, and on the crowded flight here, he'd had visions of being with Elyssa. But someone else had beat him to it. "Get out," he hissed.

"No. I need to explain."

His teeth gritted. "Nothing you have to say is of any interest to me." He wouldn't look at her. "Get out of my car. And out of my life." He spoke each word distinctly, lest she misunderstand.

"No."

"Fine." He stuck the key in the ignition, started the engine and pulled wildly out into traffic. Horns blared. He ignored them.

By the time he reached his own building, he was just barely able to contain his rage. He swerved too quickly into his driveway and the front bumper of his Mustang hit the garage door with a thud. He didn't care. He was out of the car, at his front door, and had it opened in seconds. She followed him in. He didn't want to look at her. In his mind he kept seeing her pale skin, her black bra and Quest's hands on her. *I wonder if she bothered to button up her shirt?*

He headed straight to the sideboard and poured himself a scotch. He drank it in a gulp, then poured another, which he also downed. As it burned his stomach, he finally turned around.

She looked terrified. And she had reason to be afraid. Crossing his arms over his chest, he watched her, waiting.

She came toward him, tentatively. "Please, listen to me," she said when she reached him. "I love you, I . . ."

He moved like lightning, grasping her arms hard enough to leave bruises. "Don't tell me you love me. Don't you *dare* tell me you love me when minutes ago you let another man touch you. When you touched another man. When you were about to go to bed with him." His voice broke on the last words. He squeezed harder and she winced. He let her go.

"I wasn't going to bed with him," Elyssa answered quickly. "I . . . I . . . I'm sorry about the kiss. I made a mistake."

"A *mistake?* You call this a mistake?" He laughed; it was an ugly sound, even to his own ears. "I'll tell you what's a mistake. You. Me. Us. I made the mistake of thinking there was some meaningful future for us. In fact, this whole ridiculous situation has been *my* mistake." He closed his eyes and shook his head.

"Joe, it's not what you think. I got caught up in the moment. I—"

"I don't want to hear this," he roared. "I don't care how it happened. I just care that it did. And that it would have gone further if I hadn't interrupted."

Unable to bear the sight of her, of what she'd done to him, he turned away. She snagged the sleeve of his suit. "No, Joe, you're wrong. It wouldn't have gone further. Please, give me a chance to convince you. To apologize."

He whirled around. "You don't get it, do you? Nothing you can say could possibly make any difference."

She summoned Elyssa Wentworth, CEO. "I'm not leaving until you talk this through with me."

"No?" He wanted to hit her; he wanted to kiss her; he

wanted to bury himself so deep inside of her and make her tell him what he'd seen wasn't real. But it was real, all too real. "Then I am."

Grabbing his keys from the sideboard, he strode to the door, whipped it open and stalked out. He heard her call his name but he didn't stop. He got in the car and tore out of the driveway. From his rearview mirror, he saw her watching him from his stoop.

Chapter 5

For two weeks, Joe worked like a demon during the day and then at night retreated to his house like a hermit. He talked to people only when necessary, and in no time, everyone was giving him wide berth. He lived in an emotional limbo and preferred it that way. During the third week, he hit the bars and clubs by himself, then escorted Bethany, who happened to be around a lot.

He absolutely refused to see or talk to Elyssa. She phoned several times, but he never returned her calls; he deleted her e-mail messages without reading them. She'd come over to his house twice; he ignored the doorbell the first time and the second, he let Beth answer it, which seemed to get rid of her. She hadn't come to his house again. And of course, she never tried to contact him at the office; separating the personal and professional was paramount to Elyssa Wentworth. Except where Parker Quest was concerned, apparently. Damn it!

Managing to avoid Allheart was tricky since Red Door

had made formal inquiries about a possible buyout; still, he hadn't been to Elyssa's offices once. However, today he was unable to avoid the official Highwire board meeting to decide whether to respond to the bigger company's overtures. She would be there, of course.

Joe was scrutinizing his library, searching for a book on buyouts, when he heard a knock on his open office door. Not much caring who was there, he pivoted around. Parker Quest stood in the entryway.

Suddenly, Joe's rage from that fateful Thursday evening returned. All of the anger and the despair of the last few weeks coalesced in one moment and without thinking about it, he lunged across the room. Catching Quest by surprise, Joe landed a quick upper right on Quest's smug mouth and the younger man slammed back into the wall. He went down, rattling the thousand-dollar pictures that hung there. From the floor, Quest stared up at Joe. "Okay," he said after a minute. "I deserved that."

"Screw you."

Quest sat up, then came to his feet. Working his jaw, he wiped a bit of blood off his lip. The punch had diluted the red haze that had overcome Joe, and he studied the other man. He was a down-home boy, the type Elyssa obviously preferred. Today he was dressed in pressed jeans, a T-shirt and a lightweight sport coat.

The guy kept his distance but cut to the chase. "You're gonna lose her, man."

Joe didn't play coy. There was only one thing he and this jerk had in common. "She was gone the minute she let you touch her." Saying it conjured the images of Quest's hands on Elyssa and it tore at Joe's insides. His father said he was causing himself an ulcer over this. Which was why he refused to think about it.

"You never make a mistake, Monteigne?"

"Not like this one."

"Oh, sure, I believe that."

"What makes you think I give a shit what you believe?"

"She made a *mistake*. We got too close, but when push came to shove, she stopped it. She told me she loved you and to back off."

Joe rolled his eyes.

"You're not gonna budge, are you?"

"Not an inch."

"Then you don't deserve her. Maybe I *will* go after her now."

"Yeah, well, just be careful she doesn't screw the next guy she does business with."

"We didn't screw. I kissed her. She told me she wasn't interested!"

"I don't want to hear this." He enunciated each word carefully.

"You arrogant, self-righteous bastard. You know, anyone else in the world—anyone in their right mind—would forgive her. People get caught up in situations. They make mistakes. *I'd* forgive her and then keep her so happy she wouldn't look at another guy." He straightened. "She's worth it."

Parker Quest strode out the door.

Joe watched him leave then crossed to his desk, picked up the book he'd found and threw it after the guy. It hit the wall with a thud.

He was still in a vile mood from the encounter with Quest when he entered the conference room two hours later. Already his partners were there along with the woman of the hour and her attorney, Patrick O'Hare. Joe knew she'd dated O'Hare before he and Elyssa had gotten together.

Briefly, he wondered if she'd been sleeping with him, too.
God he'd been such a fool. "Sorry I'm late, gentlemen." He
nodded to Elyssa. "Elyssa."

He tried not to notice, but he couldn't help it. She was
wearing a classy moss green linen skirt and a one-button
jacket, but she was noticeably thinner. With grim satisfaction he noted that he never liked skinny women. But it was
her eyes that got to him. They were vacant. So she'd pulled
the emotional robot routine, too. Whatever.

Highwire's board chair, Martin Stanton, began the meeting. "We're here to discuss the desirability of selling Allheart to Red Door. Though Elyssa has the majority voting
stock, our contract doesn't allow her to sell the company
without our approval." He looked to Elyssa.

She gave him her CEO smile. "I wouldn't want to do that
anyway, Martin. I value Highwire's input."

Joe almost snorted. They'd fought like cats and dogs
about control of the company and a myriad of other issues in
running it. Until Quest, Joe had had fun going head-to-
head with her.

"Let's start there, then. Do you want to sell?"

"I'm open to it. Patrick thinks we should investigate it,
in any case. So do my accountants."

The men and one woman around the table smiled. Everybody knew the sale of a hot company like Allheart would
make them all a decent bit of money.

Martin looked at Joe this time. "Joe, since Allheart's your
baby, let's hear from you."

Carefully, he folded his hands and refused to even glance
at Elyssa. "I'm not sure this is the right time to sell. Allheart's record is so good I'm predicting the company will be
worth more in six months. The upshot is, if this was my decision alone, I'd probably wait."

Sam Roncone sat forward. He was a doctor at Georgetown Medical School, on the board of Highwire. "That's unlike you, Joe. You're usually a strike-while-the-iron's-hot man."

"Yeah, well, having been burned a few times"—now that was an understatement—"I'm becoming more conservative." Even to his own ears, his rationale sounded weak. And somewhere in his quick businessman's mind, he knew selling Allheart was definitely a good option. So why was he balking?

"Joe could be right." Martin rarely contradicted his favorite partner. "His instincts usually are."

Not lately.

"But I see no harm in letting Red Door *investigate* a buyout of Allheart." This from O'Hare the lawyer. "As Allheart's chief attorney, I say we give Red Door enough information to let them at least decide if there's interest. If we get it, then we can determine to go forward or not."

The rest of the board agreed. Joe knew in cases like this it was common courtesy to go along for consensus. He stood and picked up his folder. "Fine by me. We can revisit this later." He nodded to the group and strode out the door. Absolute quiet behind him, but he didn't care. He needed to get out of there before he made a complete fool of himself in front of his partners. He'd already hit bottom personally, and he'd be damned if he'd ruin his professional reputation, too.

Martin Stanton followed him to his office. Joe had just sat down at his desk when his friend and colleague came in. "What's going on, Joe?"

"Going on?"

Martin angled his head over his shoulder to the boardroom. "That's the first time I've ever seen you behave capriciously. You can't really think selling Allheart is a bad idea."

"We won't know that until we investigate."

"Exactly. Which is why we should go forward a bit."

"I agreed, Martin."

"Under duress. Why?"

"I have reservations, that's all. It seems too soon to me."

Too soon for what, Monteigne? Too soon to lose all that's left of a connection to Elyssa?

"Joe, does this have anything to do with you and Elyssa?"

"No."

"I hope not. You assured us your personal relationship wouldn't affect business."

"It's not. It hasn't."

Martin stood. "I'll take your word for that." He stared down at Joe. "As your friend, can I say something?"

"Of course."

"You're about as miserable as any man I've ever seen and she doesn't look any happier. I'd try to work it out if I were you."

He didn't deny his mood. Only a moron could miss his surly attitude lately. "Life's complicated, Martin."

"Not unless you let it be." His friend turned and walked out of the office.

Joe sat back in his chair and closed his eyes. God he was tired of this. Of keeping his emotions at bay. Of fending off the well-meaning attention of people like Martin and his father.

Were they right? Was he being foolish? But God, how could he ever trust her with his heart again?

"Joe?" He opened his eyes. And there she stood. Looking so fragile, so sad that he wanted to pull her to him and make the last few weeks go away. He said only, "Come on in, Elyssa. Close the door."

*   *   *

Elyssa heard Joe's cold tone and watched his gaze turn flinty, but it was better than being kicked out, so she took it as a good sign that he invited her into his office. On shaky legs and four-inch heels—she'd changed her outfit several times getting dressed this morning—she strode into his office. She hoped on the outside she looked confident and in control, because on the inside, her stomach was so rife with anxiety that she was afraid she'd be ill.

"Sit down. Before you collapse." He didn't smile.

"Do I look that bad?"

"Yes."

He only looked more handsome to her. The cleft in his chin stood out in stark relief, and though his shoulders were tense, they were big and wide. Wearing a lightweight Italian suit of heather blue, he was still the most attractive man she'd ever met. How *could* she have let Parker kiss her when she had Joe Monteigne?

"Do you want to discuss Allheart and Red Door?" he asked with absolutely no inflection in his voice.

"No, I want to discuss us."

He arched an arrogant brow. "On company hours? Isn't that going to blur the lines for you, Elyssa?"

She tried to ignore the barb. "Are you ever going to talk to me about this thing with Parker?"

"No."

She lifted her chin. "Then I want to know outright. Is it over between us?"

A muscle in his jaw twitched. "To be honest, I don't know."

Well, that was better than three weeks ago when he said he never wanted to see her again.

"Is there anything I can do to make our relationship right?"

He tented his hands as if he was making a corporate decision. "I don't know."

She'd grovel if she had to. After all, she was the one
who'd screwed up. "Can we try?"

"What do you suggest? That we pick up where we left
off?" His icy demeanor was getting to her. And he knew it.
First the rage, now this cold calm.

"I don't know exactly. I didn't have a plan in mind when
I came in here."

He picked up a folder. "I have work to do. When you decide what you want, let me know."

"You."

He looked up.

"I want you. On any terms I can have you."

Sitting back again in his chair, he pondered her, "That's
an interesting proposal." He raised an eyebrow. "*Any* terms?"

Intuitively she knew a show of weakness would be her
downfall. She could barely tolerate this cruelty from him.
But she'd thrown so much away. "On any terms."

He cocked his head. "I'll think about it. Call me later. I'll
let you know."

"Will you take my calls now?"

"Today I will." He nodded to the door. "As I said, I have
work to do."

She stood, her legs wobbly. Clutching her Fendi purse,
she turned and strode to the door.

"Elyssa?"

She turned to face him. "Yes?"

"If I do agree, it won't be like it was before."

"What does that mean?"

"Don't expect too much from me in the way of emotional
investment."

"I see."

"Still interested?"

"Yes."

"All right. Call me later."

Tears formed in her eyes, but she battled them back. It was clear she was going to have to fight for him. And it might not be a pleasant fight. Physically exhausted, emotionally drained, she wondered if she was up to the battle.

That thought resurfaced days later when Bethany answered Joe's front door dressed in one of his shirts, long black leggings and what were likely his socks on her feet. Her smile was candy-sweet, as it had been the last few times Elyssa had seen her here. She was always around, doing God knew what, but Joe had made it clear that Elyssa had no right to ask questions. The day of the board meeting, when she'd called him in the afternoon, he'd made everything very clear. They'd date occasionally. He didn't think he was interested in sex with her right away. She wasn't to question him about other relationships. Or complain about his treatment of her.

"Is Joe here?" Elyssa asked, wanting to wipe that sugary smile right off Bethany's face.

"Yes, he's upstairs. I'll get him."

Elyssa stepped inside, watching Bethany's lithe body bound up the steps toward Joe's bedroom.

Elyssa wandered into the den, and over to the French doors, remembering the first time she came here and how she struggled to suppress her attraction to Joe. She hadn't been able to do it, which had led her to this very untenable place in her life.

"Well, this is a surprise."

She turned, and her heart somersaulted in her chest. He

looked rested, healthy, content. Today, he also looked . . .
satisfied, dressed in jeans and an unbuttoned sports shirt.
She'd suspected he might be sleeping with Bethany, but she
didn't ask. She'd taken the coldness. The broken dates. The
absolute reserve he had with her when they were together.
But this . . .

"I shouldn't have come." She glanced upstairs where
Bethany had gone. "It was a mistake." Straightening, she
crossed the room and brushed past him.

She had reached the door when he came up behind her.
Close. He hadn't touched her once, not even casually, since
he'd agreed to see her on his terms two weeks ago. He
slapped a hand against the door, preventing her from opening it.

"I can't stand to think of you with her, Joe. It's worse
than not having you at all."

"Now you know how it feels."

Resting her forehead on the smooth wood, she asked,
"That's what this is all about? Revenge?" When he didn't
respond, she added, "You know I didn't sleep with Parker."

"You would have."

Shaking her head, she reached for the knob. His hand
came out and covered hers. His felt big and warm and she
wanted him to hold her more than she wanted to take her
next breath.

How pathetic.

Her whole body deflated. As if he knew he pushed her too
far, had hurt her too much, he placed his hands on her shoulders but didn't turn her to him. She let him cradle her back
against his chest. Kiss her hair.

"I can't stand this, Joe. You're being so distant."

She felt him swallow. "I can't let you close, Lyss."

Lyss. The word brought tears to her eyes. "Will you ever?"

He hesitated. "I don't know."

"I see."

His hands stayed on her. Squeezed her gently. She reveled in his touch. "Why are you here?"

"I thought you might want to go for a walk today." She nodded outside. "It's a gorgeous day." She shrugged. "But you're busy. I'll be going."

She prayed he'd ask her to stay. Tell her that nothing was going on with Bethany, that the woman was indeed redecorating his office. But he said neither, and let her go.

She walked out into the beautiful summer afternoon alone.

"In light of the information Allheart released to Red Door, they're prepared to give us a letter of intent to buy, subject to due diligence." O'Hare made his comment with a fat smile on his face and a fond glance at Elyssa.

Joe wanted to jump across the table and stuff that smile down the lawyer's throat. It had been three weeks since he and Elyssa had started seeing each other. And it had been four days since she'd come to his house. If anything, she looked worse than she had at the last board meeting. Of course, the way he was torturing her wouldn't be good for anybody's health.

But this brief moment of self-denigration flew out the proverbial window for Joe when O'Hare reached out and touched Elyssa's arm. In an instant, he was filled with the image of what would have happened if he hadn't arrived to break it up.

"I think the time is right for due diligence." Her voice was firm. Grace under pressure. She was tough, in so many ways.

Still he tried to thwart her. "Do you understand, Elyssa, that once you put this in motion, it's almost impossible to reverse?"

"Not if the price isn't right, Joe. All she has to do is reject an offer based on money," Martin argued.

"You don't think we should do this, do you, Joe?" she asked simply.

He shook his head and picked up a folder. "No. I've done some research on Red Door. They have a track record for eating up smaller companies. They're a huge corporate structure; what makes Allheart special will be absorbed by policies and procedures already in place. Your company will lose its identity completely."

Martin shook his head. "But if the owner and stockholders are remunerated well enough, what does that matter? None of us will be there anyway."

Joe saw the frown on Elyssa's face and went in for the kill. Just like he'd been doing personally for three weeks. He'd taken emotional target practice on her, and damn it, she accepted it all. "Is that what you want, Elyssa? You created this baby. Took it to where it is today. Do you want to see it disappear, as if it never happened?"

She waited a very long time to answer. "I'm not sure. Maybe it's time to move on." She bit her lip. "Some things don't seem as important as they did before."

He knew she didn't just mean Allheart. He didn't blame her, of course, but he was surprised she couldn't weather his mood for even a month.

"What you say is poetic, Joe, but a little too sentimental for my taste." This from his partner, Harold. "Elyssa will walk away from this with more than enough money to go anywhere in the country and start whatever kind of company she wants."

Anywhere in the country.

Away from me.

"Or, she can retire to the Caribbean and drink piña coladas all day if she wants." O'Hare touched her again and Joe felt his fists clench.

Other board members chuckled nervously.

"How many piña coladas can Elyssa drink before she gets bored to tears?" Joe asked nastily.

Martin said, "I don't think that's the issue. Where are you on this, Elyssa?"

Joe could see a thousand thoughts flash through her mind. "I'd like to accept a letter of intent. Let them come in and investigate the company. If the price isn't right, we just won't sell."

"And if it is?" Harold asked.

She shrugged her shoulders, the action making the sleeveless green silk dress ripple across her skin. "Then I'll develop a taste for piña coladas, I guess."

She'd successfully broken the tension Joe created. The board seemed relieved.

Joe felt fury bubble up inside of him. He stood. "Fine. Just don't say I didn't warn you."

And, making a complete and utter ass of himself, he stomped out of the conference room.

Elyssa held the phone away from her ear. She felt battered these days by everybody close to her. "Quit yelling, Elliot. I can hear you just fine. And you haven't said anything I haven't already told myself."

"Then stop this . . . this penance right now. Even Mary thinks you should tell him to go to hell."

"Well, if Mary's pissed off at Joe, we know he's in big trouble."

"Damn right."

Elyssa had had enough of the badgering, so she lied to her brother. "Someone's at the door."

"Don't let Monteigne in."

She snorted. "It's not him. He hasn't come here since that night. He wouldn't stoop that low."

Elliot let out a blistering curse, but she finally got him off the phone with a promise to call him later.

After she set down the receiver, she picked up her wine and wandered around the apartment. Alone—again—this Friday night, she was unable to stop the memories.

She saw her and Joe that first time here, when they'd decided to make love and how he'd taken her standing up against the door. Then she saw him a week ago, when she sat across from him in a restaurant and he flirted outrageously with the young waitress.

Maybe Elliot was right. Maybe she should just end it now. Not only was Joe treating her like dirt, and hurting them both in the process, today he'd made a complete fool out of himself in front of his colleagues. And her staff was walking on eggshells, afraid she'd shatter like delicate Steuben glass if they said something wrong. She and Joe were destroying each other.

She stopped in front of a pretty antique mirror they'd found at a market in Virginia. One night, he'd undressed her in front of it, and his sexy commentary as he took off each piece of clothing was almost enough to make her come.

That was probably the worst of it. Physically, he wouldn't get near her. That one Saturday afternoon when he touched her was an aberration. He'd gone back to his cold, long-distance approach the next time she saw him. And she missed him so much, she was willing to do anything if he'd just make love to her.

The buzzer rang and Elyssa distractedly went to the door. She was shocked to find Joe on the other side of the peephole. She opened the door and greeted him, trying not to seem too surprised or pleased to see him.

He barely resembled himself. His hands were jammed in his pockets. His tie was off, his suit rumpled. His face was stubbled and he looked terrible. "I want to come in," he said brusquely.

"Come in then. You have a key, you could have used it."

He strode through the door and she closed it, her hand trembling on the knob.

"I threw your key away."

"I see."

"Are you alone?"

She swallowed hard. "Yes, Joe, I'm alone."

He prowled the room.

"Can I get you something?"

"A scotch. Make it a double."

She remembered the night she followed him to his house, the night he found her with Parker. He'd downed two scotches. Now he drank the one she gave him fast, too.

"You seem upset."

He faced her, finally. She couldn't decipher the mood he was in. "Wouldn't you be if you'd made an ass out of yourself like I did today?" he spat in answer.

"Joe, I don't understand this. Why are you behaving so negatively about the possible sale of the company?"

He didn't answer. Instead, a look came into his eyes, but it wasn't a pleasant one. Setting the glass down, he came toward her. Reaching up, he pulled the tie out of her hair, which fell around her shoulders. He fisted his hand in the unruly mass. "I remember the first time I saw this."

"At the gym."

"I almost swallowed my tongue."

She smiled.

He pulled on a thick lock. "Does Quest like it?"

Her throat clogged.

"I know he joined your gym."

"Joe, I—"

His fingers slid to her mouth. "Shh. Have you missed me? Missed us?"

"You know I have."

In an abrupt, unexpected move, he yanked her hips to his. He'd played rough before; she shouldn't be afraid, but . . . something was different.

"I've missed us, too," he said without a hint of affection.

She raised her arms to wind them around his neck. He stopped her. Instead, he exerted pressure on her shoulders. "I want you on your knees."

Nothing she hadn't done before. Nothing she hadn't loved doing. But tonight it seemed . . . Banishing the thought, she lowered herself to the floor.

Before she finished, he pulled her up. Backed her to the sofa. Came down on top of her like a man crazed. "I want you to scream for me. To beg." His mouth was everywhere.

Somewhere in the drugged recesses of her mind, she knew she should object. He tore off her clothes, then he pinioned her hands above her head.

During the next half hour, Elyssa screamed. And begged.

He came on a ragged shout. On a blistering curse. When he was done, and sanity returned, he drew back. His face was ravaged as he looked down at her.

Raising his hand, he touched her cheek. "I've never seen you cry. Not once in the fifteen months I've known you."

Tears streaming down her face, she whispered, "I've never had this much to cry about."

As indictments went, it was powerful. "I told you I couldn't let you close."

Swallowing hard, she answered, "Then let me go."

"*What?*"

"I can't take this anymore, Joe. I thought I could. But it hurts too much. And it's wrong."

She watched him shut down. She wished he'd open up, tell her how hurt he was, let her make it up to him. But after what had just happened she knew he wouldn't and she knew she *couldn't* take it anymore.

"Fine." He rolled off her. He was still dressed, and when he rose, he turned his back to her to rearrange his clothes.

She reached for the blanket on the couch and wrapped herself up in it.

He faced her. "I'm going and I won't be back."

"I know."

"Goodbye, Elyssa."

"Goodbye, Joe."

After he left, Elyssa lay there for hours thinking of how far she'd gone for the sake of that man—and how far she had to go back to the woman she had been before.

Chapter 6

"Thank you, ladies. It's been a pleasure working with you." Garson Cummings, the head accountant from Red Door, smiled his slick golden smile, aimed particularly at Carole. He looked like a three-piece-suited Robert Redford. "You've got a shipshape operation here."

Carole smiled back weakly. "We like to think so, Mr. Cummings."

Dana and Alix choked back grins.

"Call me Garson, please." He grabbed his laptop and turned to leave Elyssa's office.

"I'll show you out." Robyn's demure demeanor—aided by the black leather miniskirt and black stretch blouse she was wearing—made them want to laugh all the more.

Avoiding each others' eyes, they let the June breeze waft in from the window while they waited for Robyn to return; when she did and they were sure the Red Door executive was gone, all five Allheart ladies collapsed into gales of laughter.

"Shipshape?" Carole could barely get the word out. "My grandfather used to say that."

"I thought his eyes were going to pop out of their sockets when you leaned over him, Carole." Dana couldn't stop giggling.

Carole grasped the top of the short-sleeved Bill Blass jacket she wore. "I didn't realize I was gaping."

"You look dynamite." Elyssa smiled. "It was minimal gaping, really. All of you look great." Elyssa smiled at Dana and Alix and Robyn. "Monogamy becomes you."

For a change, all of the women were settled and happy with their respective men at the same time and it showed. The four couples had rented a cottage on the Maryland shore for the first week in September; Elyssa and Joe had been planning to join them.

As if they'd all had the same thought, her coworkers quieted.

"All right, lose the sympathy. I'm fine."

Smiling briefly, Carole squeezed her arm. "We know you are."

Thanks in many ways to them. Without Elliot in town, all four Allheart women had pulled Elyssa through the blackest period in her life. Joe had taken to heart what she said that night—and literally dropped out of her life; she'd guessed he was probably as disgusted by his own behavior as she'd been with hers. She hadn't seen him outside Allheart business again. At first she'd cried for a week. Then she channeled everything into working until she dropped. It took intervention by these friends—in the form of late-night girl talk, several bottles of wine and mile-long walks in the warm summer weather—to bring her around. But finally Elyssa was on the mend. And it felt great.

She stood and smoothed down the new daisy yellow

DKNY sundress she'd bought on one of their therapeutic shopping expeditions. The strappy black Ferragamos on her feet complemented the outfit.

"What time are you leaving for Elliot's wedding?" Carole asked.

She checked her watch. "Four."

Robyn smiled. "I hear Mary's brother is dreamy."

Elyssa rolled her eyes. "Cameron Jenkins is a nice man."

"Is he cute?"

"I guess." She gathered up her papers from the meeting with Cummings.

"I think it's so neat you're best man and he's ma—" Robyn scrunched up her pert nose. "What *is* he?"

"We're both called honor attendants." Elyssa was standing up for her brother and Cameron for his sister. Elyssa thought it was neat, too.

"E, it's time to go out again." This from Alix, who wanted everybody else as happy as she was with Marc these days.

Elyssa swallowed hard. "I've had a few dates."

"Patrick Stuffed Shirt O'Hare doesn't count," Dana joined in. The full-court-press approach had worked to get her over Joe.

Smiling at the women she loved dearly, Elyssa nodded. "I know." She winked at Robyn. "Maybe I'll check out Cameron after all."

Taking their cue, the others rose to leave. Robyn gave her an impulsive hug and said, "Have fun, girl."

As Elyssa crossed to her computer to check her mail once more before she flew to New York, she smiled to herself. She *would* have fun. These days Elyssa was taking care of herself. Physically she was working out almost every day. Mentally, she was ready to sell Allheart. Emotionally—well, she hadn't stopped thinking about Joe, but she no longer cried over losing him, and admitted her part in ruining their relationship. Yes, she was doing just fine.

Which was why she considered deleting the Allheart greeting card from her computer when it appeared in her incoming mail. Seeing it was like getting zapped with an electric shock. Only one man ever sent her one of her own candy.

She stared at the screen. She thought long and hard before opening it. Finally she clicked on the familiar icon.

She couldn't help grinning. It was from their successful Change series. Along with the card you could send a big ceramic container—with the quote "Change is good for the soul," painted on it, chocked full of change-related treasures like aspirin, a book of proverbs, a plant symbolizing growth and several other goodies. Parker had outdone himself on that collection.

Elyssa concentrated on the card. Dana's text read, "Embrace the future. Learn from the past. Live. Love. Enjoy."

Alix's design showed an abstract drawing of a woman, or a man if you wanted, on top of a big mountain with a beautiful sunset behind her.

Inside, the sender could leave his own message. Joe had written, "On the last day of due diligence, know that you made the right choice. Good luck in the coming weeks. I'm proud of you, babe."

But it was his signature, his bold masculine scrawl, that almost undid her. Sometimes, she missed him so much she felt physical pain.

But she *had* made the right decision. About him. And about selling Allheart. They expected an offer from Red Door by the end of the month. If it was acceptable, she'd sell. It was time to go on with her life. Though she hadn't told anyone but her brother, she was seriously considering moving to New

York and planned to stay on after Elliot's wedding to examine her options. She knew Carole was checking out other firms, Alix and Marc planned to open their own ad agency, Dana would travel and Robyn, well, that one was always up in the air.

And Joe would continue to wheel and deal for the hottest businesses in DC.

At this point in her life, it seemed like maybe it was best to leave the city where it had all happened. She'd had contact with him during the sale process; they'd both been prepared and were excruciatingly polite to each other. But occasionally she bumped into him in social circumstances and that had been hard—like at the National Gallery reception for Martin, or a chance encounter at the Kennedy Center. She'd scrutinize him and his date—it was never Bethany—when he wasn't looking. And he'd check out her escort—who was never Parker.

For Elyssa, spending time with Parker was too difficult, resurrected too many memories of all the mistakes she'd made.

Reaching out, she traced Joe's name on the screen. It was just so sad. Too late, she realized how much she did love him, how she would have been deliriously happy committed to him, even married to him. But they'd both blown it. And irreparable damage had been done. However, instead of wallowing in what she had lost, she dropped her hand, and hit the delete button.

She grabbed her purse out of the drawer—it was a sleek beaded Judith Leiber number she had treated herself to after deciding to sell Allheart—and headed out of her office.

She didn't look back.

* * *

Joe stood in the back of the St. Mary's Catholic Church in Brooklyn, New York, and stared at the beauty on the altar. The bride was lovely, too, in an old-fashioned cream-colored lace gown and netted veil over her face. But he only had eyes for Elyssa.

Mary had chosen a simple light pink, scoop-neck lacy dress for the female honor attendant. Though it was so unlike anything Elyssa would pick for herself, she looked young and beautiful in it. With her hair tumbling down over her bare shoulders and—he checked carefully—three-inch matching heels, Elyssa Wentworth was utterly gorgeous. And he'd lost that beautiful package because of his stupidity and dumb male pride. His heart lurched in his chest.

It's your fault, you jerk. You deserve to be alone.

Of course he did. In an effort to possess her, he'd behaved abominably that last night in her living room. He could barely think about what he'd done. She'd been right to kick him out. Right to make it clear she was finished with him.

Was there anything worse than watching the woman you loved—the strong, vibrant woman who commanded a multimillion dollar company without losing a wink of sleep—sob in your arms? He'd hurt her unforgivably. And the visit from her brother the next day confirmed it.

Elliot had shown up at Joe's apartment early Saturday. He'd come straight from the airport, hadn't seen his sister yet. But he knew something had happened the night before—apparently he'd talked to her but was unaware of the details—and he'd flown down that morning. Joe had been up all night, alternately berating himself for his behavior, and forcing himself to face facts. By the time her brother arrived, Joe was far down the path of self-flagellation.

"You son of a bitch," Elliot had said when Joe answered

the door. "What the hell is wrong with you?" He'd grabbed Joe's shirt. "I want to know, now."

Though Elliot was as tall as Joe, Joe had bulk and weight on the guy and could easily have shrugged him off. But he'd invited Elliot in.

Over strong coffee, Joe had talked for hours. "It was a culmination of things. She was hiding from commitment to me for months before Quest came into the picture. If she hadn't been so on the fence about us, I might have been able to handle better what happened with Quest."

"Elyssa needed time, Joe. You should have been patient with her. She's always been so self-sufficient. I advised you to tell her you wanted to marry her, but not to badger her with it."

"I blew it. I blew the whole thing."

"You know she didn't sleep with Parker."

"I know she didn't." It took all the strength he had to meet Elliot's eyes. "But I don't really know if she would have if I hadn't interrupted. That's what's driving me crazy."

"She says she wouldn't have. Isn't that enough for you?"

"No. And I couldn't deal with the uncertainty."

"Life's full of uncertainty. You should have believed in her, in your relationship."

"I might have but I let my own insecurity about her get in the way. I was as vulnerable to her as she was to me. She turned my life upside down, too, Elliot. When she talked about selling Allheart, I completely lost it. I knew the sale of the company meant she'd be out of my life for good." He shook his head. "Isn't it ironic how we accomplish exactly what we *don't* want by trying our hardest to avoid it?"

Joe's heart pained him as he watched the priest bless Elliot and Mary. Elyssa looked so calm and serene up there. For a minute, Joe let himself picture Elyssa and him in the place of the bride and groom. He'd been honest in what he said to Elliot. He'd wanted her to belong to him so badly he'd made every mistake in the book, taken every wrong turn in trying to bind her to him.

But he wouldn't make any more mistakes. He wasn't staying for the reception. He knew it would hurt her to see him. And it would kill him to watch her avoid him all day. So he'd leave. Go back to Washington and move on.

Alone.

He sidled out of the pew and headed out of the church.

Though it was difficult returning to his parents' cabin where he'd spent time with Elyssa, Joe knew he needed Lance Monteigne's sober influence in his life. With that in mind, he agreed to spend the week before Labor Day up in the Blue Ridge Mountains with his father. He figured some rest, some fishing and a good dose of his father would improve his mood.

"What are you thinking, son?" Lance asked as they lounged out on the deck watching a hot ball of pink and red settle into the horizon. Crickets chirped noisily and Joe could smell the rich scents of the outdoors.

He cradled a glass of light red wine in his hand. "How I needed this time away with you." He glanced over at the man who'd always been there for him.

"You're exhausted, Joe. And you look . . . pale." His father's brow knitted. "When was your last physical?"

"Hey, it's usually Mom who rags on me about that."

Lance didn't laugh. "When?"

"A little over a year ago."

"Hmm."

"Dad, I'm not sick."

"This has been a tough time for you."

Joe stood and wandered to the porch railing. "I thought we weren't going to talk about this."

"We weren't. But I heard you prowling last night. And you seem worse today than you did on Thursday when we got here. More depressed."

In the shadows, Joe could just make out a little squirrel scampering up a tree. "I dreamed about her last night. This week we were supposed to go to the shore with the Allheart crew." He shook his head.

Lance cleared his throat. Up until now, his father had refrained from asking specific questions about Elyssa. "Did she go anyway?"

"I have no idea. Maybe she brought Quest and kept it an eightsome."

"Do you honestly think so?"

"Honestly, no. I'd guess she's still as raw over our breakup as I am. I can't imagine her with somebody else so soon." He smiled over his shoulder at his dad. "Stupid, isn't it? How I can be so sure of the exact thing that my *not* believing drove us apart."

"Hindsight's always twenty-twenty."

Talk of Elyssa really did pain Joe. He pressed his hand to his chest, where he felt it again. Maybe he *should* schedule another physical. But what would the doctor say? *It's a broken heart, Mr. Monteigne. Give it time to heal.* Maybe when Elyssa left town—Elliot said she was considering a move to New York—he'd be able to make the black hole inside him disappear.

"What is it, Joe?"

"Indigestion, I think. Must be that bass you caught. I knew he looked a little tough."

His father didn't say anything.

"I'd rather not discuss her," Joe said.

They moved on to baseball and politics and stayed outside until it was time to go to bed. Joe dreaded turning in. He fell asleep all right, but more often than not, woke up in the early hours unable to settle back down. His father was right; he was exhausted. Maybe he needed a sleeping pill.

He *knew* he needed a sleeping pill five hours later when he awoke with a start. He'd dreamed someone had shot him through the heart. Sitting up in bed, he clutched the left side of his chest.

It was a few minutes before he realized that the pain in his chest wasn't leaving, that he was short of breath and sweating profusely.

In twenty minutes, he was on his way to Memorial Hospital, his father calm and cool in the driver's seat of Joe's Mercedes.

"I think we're overreacting, Dad."

"Probably." Lance's nonchalant tone didn't fool Joe. His dad was scared. "But you can't ignore chest pains. Just close your eyes and relax."

Doing so, Joe smiled. "You used to say that to me when I was a kid and couldn't get to sleep."

"I know."

Apparently the hospital staff also felt you couldn't mess with chest pains. Joe had never seen medical personnel move so fast. He was settled into a wheelchair in the ER waiting room, his blood pressure taken—it was high—and his father was giving the nurse admittance information when Joe was whisked into a treatment room. Within ten minutes, by the time his dad joined him, Joe had had an EKG and they'd drawn blood to test for the enzyme released during a heart attack.

On the bed, exhausted now, he said to his father, "A heart attack? There wasn't that much pain. And my arm didn't get numb."

"Doesn't need to be either." Lance's voice was strained and his face pale. "But don't jump the gun. Let's see what the tests show."

Joe rolled his eyes when the doctor entered. She looked too young to be in charge of anything. "I'm Dr. Ward. I've just read your EKG. It's . . . odd."

Lance gripped the edge of the bed. "Odd?"

"Yes, the rhythms are highly irregular."

"I have an irregular EKG," Joe said smoothly. "The first time it showed up, the doctors panicked and sent me for a stress test. I passed with flying colors."

She smiled. "Good. What doctor has the baseline results?"

Joe gave the name of his physician.

Making notes on his chart, she said, "It's a holiday weekend so we might not be able to get through to the office."

"It can wait until Tuesday, can't it?"

She shook her head. "No, Mr. Monteigne, it can't." She turned to his father. "We're going to keep him here overnight and draw blood every six hours. The enzyme can appear at any time in the next twenty-four hours. In addition, we'll monitor his heart. I've scheduled an echo stress test tomorrow morning at nine." She described the sophisticated procedure where he would hit the treadmill while a sonogram would take pictures of his heart. "If all that checks out, and the EKG information comes in, he can go home."

"Isn't this extreme?" Joe asked irritably.

When she faced him, she no longer looked young. "No. It's very possible you did indeed have a heart attack."

*   *   *

"You're up early."

Sipping hazelnut coffee, Elyssa turned to find Carole standing behind her on the deck, holding a mug, dressed in silky taupe pajamas and a robe.

"I wanted to catch one last sunrise." Elyssa peered out over the water. "It's beautiful, isn't it?"

"Yes." Carole dropped down into the lounge chair beside her and quietly drank her coffee. Finally she said, "You sure you have to go back to DC tonight?"

Elyssa grinned. "You know very well I don't *have* to. None of us ever *has* to do anything we don't want to again."

The offer from Red Door had come in at an ideal price. Patrick had warned it would be lowered, after the buyer unearthed every conceivable problem with advertisers, suppliers and customers. But her lawyer had confidence that the final price would be more than acceptable.

The only downside of their offer was that they insisted, after this brief vacation, that Elyssa stay on for six months to help with the transition. She wasn't happy about it. She didn't want to watch some other firm take over her baby, and she really wanted to put the whole experience—especially Joe—behind her. But if she wanted to sell, she would have to agree to stay on.

"You're thinking about him, aren't you?"

"Yes."

"It hasn't gotten any easier?"

"In some ways it has." She looked back at the sprawling beach house they'd rented. "Being here, though . . ." She shook her head. "He was supposed to come with us. It's why I only came up for the weekend."

Carole bit her lip, then sipped her coffee again. "Elyssa,

you may hit me for saying this, but I've just got a feeling maybe you should give him another chance."

"Yeah, I ought to hit you." Problem was, Elyssa didn't really agree with that sentiment. Sure, she and Joe couldn't get along. Their personalities were too strong. They demanded too much from each other. But he was a good man. Loving. Kind. Smart. Funny. And so sexy it made her ache just thinking about his snapping blue eyes, wide shoulders and square-cut jaw. They just weren't meant for each other.

Elyssa swallowed hard, missing Joe more than she thought possible. And for the first time, she wondered if maybe she shouldn't try again. If she should rush back to DC, find Joe and demand they give their relationship a second chance.

As the waves of the Atlantic crashed against the shore, the terror of that thought eclipsed the intense pain in her chest. God, she wanted him back in her life.

When Joe's Mercedes pulled into the huge circular driveway, he immediately spied Robyn peering out at him from the picture window.

Joe bit back a smile. Everything seemed so right on this sunny September afternoon. It was good to be alive. So he didn't hedge when she answered the door and demanded to know what he was doing there.

"I came to see Elyssa. To tell her I've been wrong—and some other things that are none of your business." That drew a scowl from Robyn.

"You couldn't make it work before, what makes you think you can now?" She spoke with all the authority of those chatty women's magazines she was always reading.

It took Joe five minutes to convince her. Finally, disgusted with him, and disgusted with herself, she gave up. "She's down at the beach."

The sight he came upon as he approached the beach made him smile. Three women were stretched out on a blanket. Sun glistened off Carole's dark hair, kissed the freckles on Dana's nose and highlighted the beautiful brown of Alix's skin. They were talking and sipping from bottles of water as they pointed toward the ocean.

There Elyssa, like Aphrodite, rose from the sea, headed toward the beach. She emerged from the water by degrees, wearing a hot pink bikini, which barely covered her. He drank in the sight, parched for just a taste of this woman he loved. As she drew closer, he could see her wet hair starting to curl around her face and shoulders as it began to dry in the sun. She'd gained back the weight she had lost and she looked healthy.

For a minute he wavered. Had he done the right thing by coming here? Was the decision he'd made in the early hours of that morning, while he and his father talked about the preciousness of life, the right one for *her*?

He knew as he saw her now the answer was yes.

When Elyssa spotted him, she froze, letting the water lap around her ankles. Carole noticed and followed her gaze to where Joe stood at a distance behind them. Simultaneously the women stood.

Carole spoke first. "Joe." At first he wasn't sure if it was a welcoming "Joe" or a warning "Joe." When he saw the stern, sober faces of the others, he knew it was a warning "Joe."

"Look, I've been a jackass and I love her. I'm not giving up."

"She doesn't want to see you," Dana said staunchly.

"Yes, she does," Carole said quietly.

The women gaped at her. Carole's eyes narrowed. "But I warn you, Joe, if you hurt her again, you'll have to deal with us. And we won't be kind."

"I'm sure that is true. You have my word," Joe said with a slight bow toward the women.

"Ladies, let's excuse ourselves," Carole said. "We'll wait for Elyssa on the deck."

Joe glanced at the house as the women trekked up the beach. So, he'd have an audience when he groveled. Who cared? He'd do this in the middle of Camden Yards baseball field if it would get Elyssa back.

Joe turned his full attention to Elyssa, who'd come out of the water, but stayed close to the shore as if she might have to beat a hasty retreat. As he came near, he saw her skin glowed in the sunlight and her eyes were shining, though he couldn't read the look in them.

Elyssa watched Joe come toward her. She'd bought him those navy shorts and checked sport shirt at a Ralph Lauren Polo sale one day when they shopped. The Docksiders on his feet squished in the sand but the sound was drowned out by her heart pounding in her chest.

When he was no more than a yard from her he stopped and said simply, "Hello, love."

She felt tears threaten. She'd never expected to hear that soft endearment again. But she was more than ready to hear it. She wanted to hear it. Badly. "Hi, Joe."

Hands in his pockets, he looked out to sea. "I've had an interesting weekend."

"You have?"

"Yes, I spent the last thirty-six hours at Memorial Hospital in Maryland."

"Oh, no, it isn't your father, is it?" Elyssa's face filled with alarm.

"No," he said, turning his full gaze on her. "I had chest pains two nights ago at my father's cabin."

Oh, my God. Spontaneously she reached out and grasped his arm. "Are you all right?" She'd never let herself consider something happening to this man. He was always so strong, so indestructible.

"I didn't have a heart attack. They did about a million tests and said I have the heart of an athlete."

She breathed a relieved sigh and dropped her hand. "Thank God." She frowned. He didn't even look tired, let alone sick. "So what caused the pain?"

Shrugging, he cocked his head. "They're not sure. Probably stress. I have to make an appointment with my GP this week."

She tossed her hair back over her shoulders and wrapped her arms around herself. "You need to take it easy, then. For a while. Rest, eat—"

"I can't rest. I can't eat. I keep thinking about how I lost you. How I blew it."

God, she loved him so much. "We both blew it, Joe."

He reached out to her and touched her cheek gently. Ran wonderfully male knuckles down her cheek. "Think there's a chance we can put it back together again? This time do it right?"

Her heart caught in her throat. She managed to say, "Do you want to?"

"More than I want anything in the world." He stepped closer. "I know what's important in my life." He ran his fingertips along her shoulder, making her shiver. "It's you."

She grasped his hand and kissed it. "I've been miserable without you."

"I made you miserable when you were with me, but I won't do it again. I promise."

She scrutinized his face. Up close she could see pure and simple regret in those blue eyes that gave the sky behind him a run for its money. She thought about how hard she'd worked to forget those eyes. And how far she was planning to go to leave the memories of him behind.

"Don't."

"Don't what?" she asked, knowing he was reading her heart and mind.

"Leave me. I want another chance to make you happy. You don't have to sell Allheart to get away from me."

She shook her head. "I want to sell Allheart. I want to start over again without all that baggage separating us."

His shoulders relaxed and he expelled a heavy breath. It wasn't until that moment that she realized he'd feared she was going to reject him. His hand curled around her nape and his forehead met hers. "I'm so sorry for being pigheaded. For hurting you. I love you, Lyss. I'll do this any way you want."

"On any terms?" Though she parroted his taunting words at the office that day, there was a smile in her voice.

"On any terms."

She moved in closer, her barely clad breasts brushing his chest. "Then I want the whole shebang, big guy. A diamond that could eat Brooklyn." She raised her arms and circled his neck. "And a beautiful matching wedding band to go with it." She stood on tiptoes.

His arms vised around her. "You mean it?"

"More than I ever meant anything in my life."

He just held her; they basked in the sun, in the air, in the bright and beautiful future that suddenly loomed before them.

"I want to touch you," he whispered against her ear. "Be inside you. I want us to be whole again." His words were raw. She knew he was thinking of the last time.

"I want that, too."

She glanced over his shoulder and giggled. "But we have an audience. I'm sure they won't take it well if we disappear into a sand dune." She smiled. "They're all mad at you."

"Do you blame them?"

She placed her fingers on his mouth. "Shh. No more of that."

He smiled, the sexiest, most devastating smile he'd ever cast her way. Then he looked out to the water. "Hmm."

"What?"

"I have an idea."

Slowly, never letting his arms drop from around her, he backed her up. The water lapped around her ankles first. "Joe, you're dressed. Shoes, everything."

The waves reached her knees.

He said, "Once we're underwater I won't be."

The cool, salty Atlantic curled around their waists. When her breasts were submerged, he cupped her in his hands. "I never thought I'd be able to touch you like this again."

She sighed and reached down to touch him intimately. "Me, neither."

She looked back at the house and saw that the Allheart crew had disappeared inside. "It looks like we're alone, Monteigne. Waddya say?" She untied the top of her bikini and pulled him to her.

"I say we begin our life together here and now." And he kissed her like she'd never been kissed before, like it was the first kiss and the last kiss, the whole of their past and future coming together in one glorious moment in the sun.

Discover Romance

berkleyjoveauthors.com

See what's coming up next from your favorite romance authors and explore all the latest Berkley, Jove, and Sensation selections.

Fall in love

- See what's new
- Find author appearances
- Win fantastic prizes
- Get reading recommendations
- Chat with authors and other fans
- Read interviews with authors you love

berkleyjoveauthors.com